The Child Thief

ALSO BY BROM

The Plucker

The Devil's Rose

The Child Thief

BROM

An Imprint of HarperCollins*Publishers*

THE CHILD THIEF. Copyright © 2009 by Brom. All rights reserved. Printed in the United States of America. No part of this book may be used or reproduced in any manner whatsoever without written permission except in the case of brief quotations embodied in critical articles and reviews. For information address HarperCollins Publishers, 10 East 53rd Street, New York, NY 10022.

HarperCollins books may be purchased for educational, business, or sales promotional use. For information please write: Special Markets Department, HarperCollins Publishers, 10 East 53rd Street, New York, NY 10022.

FIRST EDITION

Eos is a federally registered trademark of HarperCollins Publishers.

Designed by Paula Russell Szafranski

Library of Congress Cataloging-in-Publication Data has been applied for.

ISBN 978-0-06-167133-3

09 10 11 12 13 OV/RRD 10 9 8 7 6 5 4 3 2 1

This one is for John Fearing

Prologue

It would happen again tonight: the really bad thing. The girl had no doubt. It had started a few months ago, around the time her breasts had begun to develop, and now, with her mother gone, there was no one to stop him.

From her bedroom she could hear him pacing the cluttered living room of the cramped apartment. He was in one of his fits, muttering to himself, cursing the television, his boss, the president, Jesus, but mostly cursing her mother for taking all those pills, cursing her to hell and back, over and over. But her mother was dead and would never have to suffer through another of his tirades, not ever again. The girl wished she were so lucky.

There came the sharp snap of a beer tab, then another, and another. Her hands began to tremble and she clutched them to her chest. She wished she could fall asleep, then she would at least be spared the waiting, the dread. But she knew there'd be no sleep for her tonight.

He was there. The flickering light from the television silhouetted him as he leaned against her door frame. She couldn't see his eyes, but knew they were on her. She twisted the sheet tightly about her neck as though it were some magical talisman to ward away wickedness. Sometimes he stared at her like that for hours, muttering to himself in his two voices: the kind, soft voice, and the harsh, scary voice. Back and forth the voices went, like two men debating their religious convictions. Usually, the soft voice prevailed. But tonight, there was no sign of the soft voice, only a low rasp punctuated with sharp barks of profanity.

He moved into the room, setting his beer on the dresser next to her Betty Boop radio-alarm clock, the one that woke her up for school with its crackling rendition of "Boop Oop a Doop." She'd missed a lot of school lately, partly because she was tired of the looks and whispers from the other students, from the teachers, all so careful around her, as though her mother's suicide was somehow contagious. But mostly she wanted to avoid Mrs. Stewart—the guidance counselor—and all her prying questions. Somehow Mrs. Stewart seemed to know and was determined to get her to talk about it. This scared the girl. There was a two-inch scar on the side of her head where her hair would never grow back in. He'd made that mark with a dinner fork the one time she'd tried to tell her mother. The girl found herself thinking more and more about the pills her mother had swallowed, wondered if those pills could take her to her mother. She thought about that every time the bad thing happened.

His hand was on her—heavy, hot. She could feel his heat even through the sheet. He pulled the cover away then sat next to her, his weight sinking into the small box springs and causing her body to slide against him. He laid a calloused hand on her calf, slid it slowly up along her inner thigh and under her flannel nightgown, his thick fingers squeezing and prodding. His breathing became heavy. He stood. She heard his thick brass belt buckle hit the floor then he was on top of her, the small mattress protesting his bulk.

She clutched her pillow and struggled not to cry out, staring out the window and trying to take herself somewhere else. The stars were particularly bright tonight. She focused on their magical glow, wishing she could fly up among them, fly so far away that the man could never touch her again.

A shadow blocked the stars. Someone was at the window looking in. In the faint glow she could see it was a boy. The boy pulled the window up and slid into the room with a quick, fluid movement.

"What the fu—" the man started, but the boy bounded across the room and hit the man with both feet, knocking him backward and into the hall. The boy moved fast, faster than the girl had ever seen anyone move, and was at the man before he could regain his feet. Both the man and the boy crashed down the hall and out of view.

Someone hit the wall hard enough to shake the girl's bed frame. The man let out a howl and something shattered. There came a single sharp cry from the man, followed by a low "Oh, God" that sounded more like an exhale than a heavy thud. The apartment fell silent.

The girl glanced at the open window and wondered if she should run, but before she could, the boy reappeared, his wiry frame silhouetted in her doorway.

He moved into the room and she drew back. This seemed to trouble the boy and he slipped over to the window, leaped up, and perched on the sill. He had a tangle of auburn, shoulder-length hair, a sprinkle of freckles across his nose and cheeks, and his ears were—*pointy*. He looked up at the stars as though drinking in their magic, then back at her. She noticed the color of his eyes: gold like a lynx.

He cocked his head, then smiled, and when he did, those golden eyes sparkled. There was something wild in them, something exciting and dangerous. He slid a leg out onto the fire escape and nodded for her to come along.

She started to follow, then stopped. What was she thinking? She couldn't just follow this strange boy out into the night. She shook her head.

His smile fell. He glanced back up at the stars, then waved to her as though to say good-bye.

"Wait," she called.

He waited.

And that was as far as she got, unsure what to do next. The only thing she was sure of was that she didn't want this magical boy to leave her. A sparkling star caught her eye. The stars were all so brilliant she found herself wondering if she were in a dream, if maybe this boy had come down from the heavens to take her away.

She blinked, tried to clear her head, needing a minute to think. She wanted to go to the bathroom, but that would've meant going down the hall, and she didn't want to do that, didn't want to see what the golden-eyed boy had done to the man. And she didn't want to let the boy out of her sight, afraid this might break the spell, that when she returned he'd be gone forever and she'd be alone. Her eyes fell on the man's big brass belt buckle sitting atop his wadded-up pants and she began to twist the hem of her nightgown, tighter and tighter, until finally a sob escaped her throat. Tears overtook her and she slid off the bed onto her knees.

The boy came and knelt beside her. While she cried into her hands, he told her of an enchanted island where no grown-ups were allowed. Where there were other kids like her, who loved to laugh and play. Where there were great adventures to be had.

She wiped her eyes and managed to smile as she shook her head at his silly story, but when he invited her to come along, she found herself *believing*. And even though a voice deep within her warned her to stay away from this strange boy, she wanted nothing more at that moment than to follow along after him.

She glanced around the tiny room where the man had stolen so much from her. There was nothing left but painful memories. What else did she have to lose?

This time, when the boy stood to go, she dressed quickly, following him out onto the fire escape, down to the street, and into the night.

If the girl could only have spoken to the other boys and girls, the ones that had followed the golden-eyed boy before her, she would have known that there is always something left to lose.

PART I

Peter

Chapter One

Child Thief

In a small corner of Prospect Park, in the borough of Brooklyn, New York, a thief lay hidden in the trees. This thief wasn't searching for an unattended purse, cell phone, or camera. This thief was looking for a child.

In the dusk of that early-autumn day, the child thief peered out from the shadows and falling leaves to watch the children play. The children scaled the giant green turtle, slid down the bright yellow slide, laughed, yelled, teased, and chased one another round and round. But the child thief wasn't interested in these happy faces. He wasn't looking to steal just any child. He was particular. He was looking for the sad face, the loner . . . a *lost* child. And the older the better, preferably a child of thirteen or fourteen, for older children were stronger, had better stamina, tended to stay alive longer.

The thief knew Mother Luck had smiled on him with the girl. She'd been a good catch, too bad about her father. He smiled, remembering the funny face the man had made as the knife slipped into his chest. But where was Mother Luck now? He'd been hunting for two days. *Nothing.* He'd come close with a boy last night, but close wasn't good enough. Grimacing, the thief reminded himself that he had to take it slow, had to make friends with them first, gain their trust, because you couldn't steal a child without their trust.

Maybe Mother Luck would be with him tonight. The child thief had found city parks to be good hunting grounds. Strays and runaways often camped among the bushes and used the public restrooms to wash, and they were always looking for friends.

As the sun slid slowly behind the cityscape, the shadows crept in—and so did the thief, biding his time, waiting for the falling darkness to sort the children out.

NICK DARTED INTO the warehouse entryway, pressed himself flat against the steel door, his breath coming hard and fast. He leaned his cheek against the cold metal and squeezed his eyes shut. "Fuck," he said. "I'm screwed. So screwed."

At fourteen, Nick was slender and a bit small for his age. Dark, choppy bangs spilled across his narrow face, emphasizing his pallid complexion. He needed a haircut, but of late his hair was the last thing on his mind.

Nick dropped his pack to the ground, pushed his bangs from his eyes, and carefully rolled up one sleeve of his black denim jacket. He glanced at the burns running along the inside of his forearm and winced. The angry red marks crisscrossing his flesh crudely formed the letter N.

He tried to put the nightmare out of his mind, but it came back to him in heated flashes: the men pinning him to the floor—the floor of his own kitchen. The sour, rancid taste of the dish sponge being crammed into his mouth. Marko, big, thick-necked Marko, with his beastly grin, smirking while he heated the coat hanger against the burner. The wire smoking then turning red then . . . the *pain* . . . red-hot searing pain. God, the *smell*, but worse, the sound, he'd never forget the sound of his own flesh sizzling.

Trying to scream, only to gag and choke on that gritty, soggy sponge while they laughed. Marko right in his face, Marko with his long, straggly chin hairs and bulging, bloodshot eyes. "Wanna know what the N stands for?" he'd spat. "Huh, do you fuckhole? It's for *Narc*. You ever say anything to anybody again and I'm gonna burn the whole fucking word into your tongue. You got that you little prick?"

Nick opened his eyes. "Need to keep moving." He snatched up his pack and unzipped the top. Inside the pack were some chips, bread, a jar of peanut butter, a pocket knife, two cans of soda, a blue rabbit's foot on a leather cord, and about thirty thousand dollars' worth of methamphetamines.

He dug through the hundreds of small clear plastic bags until he found the blue rabbit's foot. The rabbit's foot had been a gift from his dad, the only thing Nick had left of him now. He kissed it, then slipped it around his neck. He needed all the luck he could come by today.

He leaned out from the entryway, glancing quickly up and down the busy avenue, keeping an eye out for a beat-up green van. He'd hoped for some congestion to slow the traffic down, help him make it to the subway *alive*, but currently the traffic chugged steadily along. The day waned and soon the van would be just one more pair of gleaming headlights in the night.

Nick slung the pack over his shoulder and ducked out onto the sidewalk, weaving his way between the thin trail of pedestrians as he jogged rapidly up the block. There was a bite to the wind and people had their collars up and their eyes down. Nick pulled up his own collar, skirted around a cluster of elderly men and women lined up in front of an Italian restaurant, and tried to lose himself among the thin stream of returning commuters.

You fucked up Nicky boy, he thought. *Fucked up big.* Yet part of him was glad, would do about anything to see the faces of those sons-of-bitches when they found their stash gone. It would be a long time before Marko was back in business.

A horn blew behind him. Nick jumped and spun—heart in his throat. But there was no green van, just someone double-parked. He caught sight of the trees and felt a flood of relief. Prospect Park was just a block away. He'd be hard to spot in the trees. He could cut across the park and come out at the subway station. Nick took off in a run.

5

THE SHADOWS TWISTED and crowded together, layer upon layer, until darkness claimed the playground. One by one the sodium lamps fizzled on, their shimmering yellow glow casting long, eerie shadows across the park.

The parents were gone now, the playground empty. Garbage cans—overflowing with empty soda bottles and soiled diapers—stood like lone sentinels as the distant sounds of traffic and the steady thumping of someone's pumped-up stereo echoed across the grounds.

The child thief saw the boy sprint into the park, saw him from far across the way, catching glimpses of his face as he dashed through the pools of yellow lamplight. The thief saw the fear, the confusion, and he smiled.

What had led this child here: abuse, neglect, molestation? All of the above perhaps? It really didn't matter to the thief. All that mattered was something had caused the boy to leave his home behind and venture out into the night alone, a *runaway*. And like so many runaways, this boy didn't know where to run away to.

Not to worry, the child thief thought. *I have a place for you. A place where we can play.* And his golden eyes twinkled and his smile broadened.

NICK PASSED A young couple on their way out of the park, giggling and clinging to each other like Siamese twins. He took a wide detour around a man and his dog. The dog—some sort of large poodle—gave Nick a shameful look as it went about its business. The man stared dully at his phone, texting away, seemingly unconcerned that his dog was laying down landmines along the public walkway.

Nick noticed a pack of youths far up the path. They were cutting through the park, shouting and acting up. They looked like trouble and Nick didn't need any more trouble. He veered off the path and drifted into the trees.

Nick pushed through a dense line of bushes and jumped down into a wide ditch. His foot hit a slick chunk of cardboard and he stumbled, landing atop something soft. The something soft moved. "Hey," came a muffled cry beneath him.

The something soft was a sleeping bag, worn and oily, like it'd been dragged through the gutter. The someone was a woman and she didn't look much better—the smear of cherry-red lipstick over layers of caked-on makeup unable to hide the ravages of the street. Nick thought she might've been pretty once, but now her matted hair, hollowed eyes, and sunken cheeks reminded him of a cadaver.

She rolled over and sat up, got a good look at Nick, and smiled.

A bald man with a long, white, grizzly beard poked his head out from a nearby sleeping bag. "Who's that?"

Nick realized there were several sleeping bags scattered among the bushes, along with cardboard boxes, blue plastic tarps, and a shopping cart full of garbage bags.

"It's just a boy," the woman said. "A tender little thing."

Nick rolled off of her, but when he tried to get up, she grabbed him, her hard, bony hands locking around his wrist. Nick let out a cry and tried to pull away.

"Where you going, sweetheart?" the woman asked.

"You looking for something, kid?" the man said, climbing to unsteady feet. Other heads began to poke out from sleeping bags and boxes, dull, bleary eyes all on Nick.

"Of course he's looking for something," the woman said and smiled wickedly. "Ten bucks, sugar, and I'll blow more than your mind. Got ten bucks?"

Nick stared at her, horrified.

The old man snorted and let loose a chuckle. "That's a sweet deal, boy. Trust me. She'll make you holler *hi-de-ho*." Several of the other men nodded and laughed.

Nick shook his head rapidly back and forth, and tried to twist his arm free. But the woman held him tight.

"Five bucks, then," she said. "Five bucks to blow your little rocket. What'd you say?"

Nick caught sight of two men moving around behind him; they looked hard and hungry, eyeing him like a free lunch.

"Let me go," Nick pleaded, trying to peel away her fingers. "Please, lady. *Please* let me go."

"You're missing out," she cooed and let go, causing him to stumble right into one of the men. The man snatched Nick by the hair and spun him around, got a hand on Nick's pack. Nick cried out and twisted away, felt his hair tear loose in the man's grip, but didn't care so long as he still had his pack. The pack was all that mattered, all he had going for him now. He clutched it tightly to his chest, reeled, got his feet under him, and scrambled out of the ravine. He tore through the bushes and sprinted off, with their ghoulish laughter echoing after him. He didn't stop until the ditch was well out of sight. He found a playground, collapsing against a big smiley-faced turtle, trying to catch his breath and get control of his nerves.

In a ditch, he thought. *Is that where I'll be sleeping tonight? And the next night, and the next? With creeps like that around.*

He dropped his pack between his feet, heart still pumping. He searched the shadows, the trees, making sure no one was around or following him, before digging a wad of bills out of his pocket and quickly counting them. *Fifty-six dollars. How far is that gonna get me?* He hefted the pack. *No, that's not all. Just as soon as I find a dealer I'll have all the money I need.* Of course he hadn't quite worked that part of the plan out: how a fourteen-year-old was supposed to go about arranging a major drug sale. *I can handle it,* he reassured himself. *Just have to play it smart. I'll take it down to . . . take it . . . take it where?* "Fuck," he said, then told himself that for now all that mattered was getting to the subway and getting the hell out of here. *Then what? Well?* He glanced at the bushes, realizing he didn't even have a sleeping bag. It made him wonder if maybe his mother had been right. Maybe it would've been better to just stay out of Marko's way. If he had, he'd at least still have a place to sleep, food to eat. He rolled his sleeve back and stared at the burn on his arm, and Marko's hateful grin came back to him, his angry, bloodshot eyes. *No,* Nick thought. *This was her fault. All of it. She's the one that let those bloodsuckers into Grandma's house in the first place. None of this would've happened if she hadn't been so selfish.* He felt tears coming and wiped angrily at his eyes. "Fuck," he said. "Fuck."

A thump came from back in the trees. Nick spun around expecting to see Marko, or maybe the ghoulish woman with the painted lips. But there was nothing there but the trees and the yellow lights. He glanced about. There was no sign of anyone; the park had become eerily quiet.

He caught movement out of the corner of his eye. A boy-sized shadow climbed straight up a tree and disappeared into the branches. "What the hell?" Nick whispered, then decided he really didn't want to know. He turned and sprinted toward the street.

NICK CAME OUT of the park just down from the subway station. He waited for traffic to clear, then started across the street. He made it about three strides, then stopped cold.

"Shit!" he said. Propped against the station stairs was Bennie, one of Marko's boys, one of about a dozen kids that ran his junk for him. A chill slid up Nick's spine. *Does Bennie know what's up?* Bennie had his cell phone pressed up against his ear. *Of course he knows.*

A car horn blew, reminding Nick he was in the street. He spun and leaped back to the curb. He ducked his head down and kept going, heading back toward the park. *Don't run,* he told himself. *He didn't see you. Just keep walking. Keep cool.* He ventured a glance back as he entered the trees. Bennie was gone.

Nick knew if Bennie had seen him he'd call everyone, and then they'd all be looking for him. *God,* Nick thought, *what am I gonna do?* He pushed deeper into the park, keeping a sharp eye out behind him. *Can't stay in the park forever.*

"Yo, cuzz. Whut up?"

Nick let loose a cry as someone came gliding up alongside of him on a tricked-out BMX bike, then wheeled the bike around and blocked Nick's path.

The squinty-eyed boy looked to be a couple years older than Nick. He sported a puffy jacket at least two sizes too big for him and a pair of wide-legged pants with the waistband hanging low on his hips. His blond hair—braided into cornrows—sprouted out from beneath a Mets ball cap like electrified caterpillars.

The kid slouched back on his seat and let a sly smirk drift across his face.

Nick's heart began to drum. *Is he one of Marko's boys? Sure looks like one of those assholes.*

The kid with the caterpillar hair scratched at the pimples along his chin and leaned forward onto the handlebars. "Yo, dawg. Spot me a dollar?"

Nick relaxed a degree. This was just another prick trying to shake him down. Did he really believe every kid in the neighborhood was looking for him?

When Nick didn't reply, caterpillar-head sighed, pulled a wad of gum from his mouth, and stuck it on his handlebars. He gave Nick a dark look, one that said let's get down to business.

Nick dealt with assholes like this every day—a little humiliation, a little physical abuse at the expense of his self-respect—around here the fun never ended. But Nick didn't have time to play the game right now. He needed to get out of here. Nick thought about just forking over the wad of bills, then maybe he'd get away with his backpack at least. But how far could he get without any cash?

"Yo, cuzz, I'm talking to you," the teenager said in a tone clearly indicating that good ole Nicky boy was unduly trying his patience.

Nick wondered if this beaked-nose wannabe was going to work *Yo, cuzz* or *dawg* into every sentence.

"Yo, dawg," the teenager said. "You deaf or sumptin?" He snapped his fingers right in front of Nick's face. Nick flinched and fell back a step.

"Dawg, look at you getting all freaked and shit," the kid said with a snort. "Chill, cuzz. I'm just fucking witchu."

Nick managed a strained smile and forced a chuckle, and immediately hated himself for it. The only thing worse than getting dicked around was having to act like you were in on the joke. In this case, the laugh was the wrong move. Nick wasn't at school. He was alone in the park, and that weak laugh told this kid that Nick wasn't a fighter, that Nick was—*prey.*

The kid's voice dropped, cold and serious. "How much money you got?"

The tone scared Nick; it sounded mean, like this kid just might go over the line and really hurt him.

"I'm here with my big brother," Nick said, trying to sound cool, like he really *did* have a big brother looking out for him.

The kid didn't even bother to glance around. He just sat there with his arms crossed over his chest with a don't-give-me-that-shit look on his face.

"He just ducked in the trees over there," Nick said, pointing into the dark woods. "To take a leak. He'll be back any sec."

There, of course, was no big brother relieving himself in those murky trees, but if either of the boys had looked, they might have seen a shadow with golden eyes inching toward them along the branch of the big oak.

The kid shook his head slowly back and forth. "Fuuuck." Letting the expletive slide out like a long, disappointed sigh, as though asking Nick why he'd lie to a nice guy like him.

"Yo, what's in the pack?"

Nick's fingers tightened on the shoulder straps. He pushed his bangs out of his face and glanced about for a place to run.

"Hey," the kid said. He squinted at Nick. "Don't I know you?"

Nick's blood went cold.

"Sure. You live at Marko's place."

Only it wasn't Marko's place, Nick wanted to shout. It was his grandmother's house. Marko was supposed to be a tenant, but Marko and his pals had taken over and his mother, his goddamn mother, wasn't doing a damn thing about it.

"Yeah," the kid said. "You're that weirdo that lives upstairs with his mommy, the one that never comes out of his room. Marko says you're queer or something."

If by weirdo he meant that Nick didn't play grab-ass with the wannabes on the street corner, didn't yank at his crotch and call girls bitches, didn't wear oversized jerseys and pretend to be a gangsta all day, then yeah, Nick had to agree. But there was more to it and Nick knew it. Even back at Fort Bragg, before the move, he'd had trouble fitting in. But here in Brooklyn, where *weirdo* was a term of endearment compared to what most of the kids called him, he'd begun to feel like a leper, like he came from another planet. As of late, he'd given up on making friends altogether and

The Child Thief

11

probably did spend far too much time in his room reading, drawing, playing video games, and anything else he could come up with to avoid pricks like this jerk-off.

"Hey, you seen Bennie?"

"Who?" Nick said, as he eased back a step.

"What you mean who? *Bennie.* Dawg, he's over yo place all the time. You seen him?"

Nick shook his head and took another step back but the kid rolled his bike forward.

"Look, I gotta go," Nick said. "Umm . . . just a little favor for Marko. Y'know."

"What? Marko? You're running for Marko now? No way."

"Nothing big," Nick added quickly. "Just an errand."

"Oh, yeah." The kid's voice was suddenly cordial, like he hadn't just been about to slap Nick sideways and shake him down. "Bennie put in a word for me. Said Marko might be setting me up soon too." Then, almost as an afterthought, "Dawg, you know I was just fucking witchu, right? We all good, right?"

"Sure," Nick said, and made himself smile, anything to get out of here already. "See ya then." He started away toward the playground.

"Yo," the kid called after him. "When you see Marko, give him a shout-out from his bro Jake."

That's exactly what I will do, Nick thought. *While he's burning my tongue with a hot wire, I'll be sure to let him know his bro Jake said hi.*

Jake's phone came to life. Nick knew it was Bennie, knew it before Jake even answered it. Nick walked faster.

The kid dug out his phone and flipped it open. "Yo. What? Dawg, you said at the park. What—*no way.* He did that? No way. No *fucking* way."

Nick caught the kid cutting his eyes toward him. "I can do you one better than that," the kid said. "No man, I mean I got just what you're looking for."

Nick's heart slammed against his chest.

"Yeah, that's just what I mean. Okay, it's cool. By the turtle. Y'know that fucking green climby thing at the playground." He glanced at Nick again. "Don't worry he's not—"

Nick took off. If he could make it into the trees he might be able to lose himself in the bushes, might have a chance. He was running so hard he didn't even hear the bike bearing down on him. The older boy kicked him as he flew by. Nick lost his footing and slid across the sidewalk, the concrete tearing into his palms. Nick let out a cry and tried to get up, but Jake was right there and kicked him back down.

"You ain't gonna leave without yo big *bro*, are you?" Jake asked, then kicked him again.

Nick heard tennis shoes slapping the sidewalk and two boys came running up. "Yo! Yo! Jake!" one of them yelled. It was Bennie.

"Dawg, you see that kick?" Jake hollered, his voice pumped with excitement. "See that? I'm Steven-*fucking*-Seagal." He tugged his crotch with one hand and made a rapid snapping gesture with his fingers, all while sucking his lower lip and bobbing his head. "You don't want to be messing with Jake-the-Snake. What'd ya say, Bennie?" Jake stuck out a knuckle-fist. "Give it up, bro."

Bennie gave Jake a look close to pity, left Jake's knuckle-fist to hang, and turned cold eyes on Nick, eyes that said he wasn't fucking around like this retard beside him.

Bennie was big. From what Nick had picked up, he'd been a defensive tackle over at Lincoln High before getting expelled for assaulting his math teacher—the word was he'd put the man's eye out with a pencil. Bennie had thick, hard hands like tree roots, the kind of hands that could tear quarters in half, and one long, bushy brow overhanging small, squinty eyes. Those eyes were cold—not mean, just cold—like he didn't feel.

Bennie stared at Nick, letting those empty eyes bore into him. Finally, he said, "Man, if I had to pick one person I'd least wanna be right now, it'd be you."

"True dat!" Jake added, then turned to the third kid, a short, muscular boy with stumpy arms and slumping shoulders. "Yo, Freddie. Check out his shoes. Wouldn't catch my ass dead in pussy shoes like that."

"Fucken' faggot shoes," Freddie ordained, in a Brooklyn accent so thick it sounded like his mouth was full of marbles. He kicked the bottom of Nick's shoe.

They were referring to Nick's leprechaun-green Converse knockoffs.

Nick didn't even hold it against them—no one hated those shoes more than he did. They were the kind of shoes you find in a bin at the discount store, right below the dollar watch display. He'd outgrown his green Vans—best pair of skate-shoes he'd ever owned—shortly after the move. He'd asked his mother for a new pair and she'd come home with these wonders. When Nick asked how he was supposed to skate in those, if she expected him to actually wear them to school, and if she was the biggest cheap-ass in all of fucking New York, she'd called him a spoiled brat and left the room. Of course, his skateboard had disappeared shortly after Marko showed up, so that part didn't really matter, but being ridiculed at school every day certainly hadn't helped him fit in.

Bennie flipped open his cell phone and thumbed redial. He pushed the hood of his Knicks sweatshirt back and rubbed the dark fuzz atop his head. "Hey, Marko, who's the man? That's right. No, I ain't shitting you. Of course I got him. Dumbass headed straight for the subway just like you said. We're in the park. I dunno." Bennie glanced around. "Over near the playground. No, not that one. The one with the stupid turtle. We'll wait. Don't worry, this little bitch ain't going nowhere."

Bennie slapped his phone shut. "Check his bag."

Freddie grabbed the pack. Nick jerked it away and scrambled to his feet, but Freddie nabbed him before he made half a step, wrestling him into a painful armlock.

Bennie yanked the pack out of Nick's hand.

"Wonder what's in here?" he said sarcastically and unzipped the pack. He let loose a whistle and held it out for Jake and Freddie to see. Their eyes got big.

"Fuck! Must be a hundred gees worth," Freddie said.

Jake looked at Nick in amazement. "Cuzz, Marko's gonna cut you up and feed you to the fishies."

Nick jerked an arm free and tried to twist away, started screaming and yelling at the top of his lungs. Bennie hit him. It felt like a flare went off in his head. Nick started to yell again when Bennie drilled him in the stomach, doubling him over. Bennie snatched him up by the hair and leaned right into his face. "You wanna run?" Bennie grinned, then grabbed the sides of Nick's pants, yanking them down to his ankles. "Go on. *Run.*"

Nick coughed and wheezed, trying to suck in a breath.

"Let 'im go," Bennie said.

Freddie let go.

Nick clutched his stomach and almost fell over.

"C'mon pussy," Bennie said. "Whaddaya waiting for? Take off."

Both Jake and Freddie let out a snort.

Bennie shoved Nick. Nick stumbled, did a duck-waddle, but managed to keep his feet despite his pants twisting around his ankles.

Freddie and Jake crowed with laughter.

Then Bennie hit Nick like a linebacker. Nick's feet tangled and he slammed to the ground.

"Check his pants and underwear," Bennie said. "Little queer probably stuffed the stash up his ass."

Freddie patted Nick down. He shoved a hand in Nick's pocket and pulled out the wad of bills. "Pay—*day*!"

"Give me that," Bennie said, taking the bills. "That's Marko's money."

Bennie leaned over to Nick, so close that Nick could see tomato sauce stains on the sides of his mouth. "Marko said he's bringing his toolbox. Said it's gonna be a real horror show. I love horror shows. Do you?"

The limb above them shook and a host of leaves rained down. There followed a soft thump. Nick and Freddie saw *him* first. When Bennie and Jake caught their faces, they both jerked around.

A boy, not much taller than Nick, stood on the pathway. He wore some sort of hand-stitched leather pants with pointy-toed boots sewn right into them. He also had on a raggedy tuxedo jacket, the old style, the kind with tails, with a black hoodie on underneath and a rawhide pack, almost a purse, strung across his chest. The boy pushed the hood back, revealing a tussle of reddish, shoulder-length hair littered with twigs and leaves. A sprinkle of freckles danced across his cheeks and nose. The boy's ears were, well, kinda pointy, just like Spock's, like one of Santa's little helpers, but oddest of all, his eyes were bright gold.

The boy planted his hands on his hips and a broad smile lit his face. "My name's Peter. Can I play too?"

THE CHILD THIEF studied the teenagers, making sure to keep up his smile, making sure to hide his disdain. *Have to be wily,* he thought. *Don't want to spoil the fun.*

He looked at the numbed, perplexed expressions on the three older teens and thought, *They're blind. Blind as a nut in a nutshell. There's magic all around them and they don't see a lick of it.* How could this be possible? Only a few short years ago, possibly only a few months, they were still children, their minds in bodies full of magic, open and alive to all the enchantments swirling around them. *Now look at them, miserable, self-conscious fuckwits, going to spend the rest of their lives trying to find something they never even realized they'd lost.*

I'd be doing them a favor. To gut the three of them. His eyes gleamed at the thought. *Hell, and it'd be fun too. Watching their faces as they juggled their own guts. Much fun indeed.* But he wasn't here to have fun. He was here to make a new friend.

Peter glanced at the boy with his pants around his ankles, the one fighting so hard to hold back his tears. He needed to win this child over, for you couldn't take children into the Mist against their will. The Mist would never allow it. You could, however, *lead* a child into the Mist. So they had to trust you. And you didn't get children to trust you by gutting teenagers right in front of them, not even mean, ugly teenagers. That wasn't the way to make new friends.

Peter found that he enjoyed this part of the game—winning the hearts of children, getting a chance to play for a while. *Games are important. Why, it's playing, is it not, that separates me from the likes of these dull-eyed cocksuckers?*

So the child thief decided he would just play with them.

"CAN I PLAY too?" the boy repeated.

Freddie tensed, his grip tightening. Nick guessed Freddie was as unnerved by this redheaded, golden-eyed boy as he was.

"Who da fuck are you?" Bennie spat.

"Peter."

"What da fuck you want?"

"To play," Peter said, sounding exasperated. "How many times I gotta ask, birdybrain?"

Bennie's unibrow squeezed together. "Birdybrain?" And, for the first time Nick could remember, Bennie looked at a loss. Bennie glanced at Freddie as though unsure if he'd been insulted or not.

"Oh man. Kid, you shouldn't done that," Freddie said. "He's gonna kill you for that one."

But Bennie didn't look like he was going to kill anyone. Because guys like Bennie weren't used to kids giving them shit, and it threw him off balance.

"So, what are the rules?" Peter asked.

"What?" Bennie said, his unibrow forming a confused knot.

"Gee wiz," Peter said, rolling his eyes. "The rules, ball-sack. What are the rules to the pants game?"

"Rules?" Bennie said, no longer sounding confused, but pissed, and regaining some of his equilibrium. Bennie slammed Nick's pack to the ground and jabbed a finger at Peter. "I don't play by *no* fucking rules, asshole!"

"Good," Peter said, and before anyone could blink, he darted forward and yanked Bennie's baggy sweatpants all the way down to his ankles.

"POINT!" Peter called.

There was a frozen moment when Bennie just stood there with his mouth agape, staring down at his own skivvies. As a matter of fact, everyone was staring at Bennie's skivvies, and they weren't the spiffy Calvin Klein kind either. It looked like Bennie had some hand-me-downs, old-school generic white briefs with several generations' worth of stains and holes in them.

Bennie's face went lava-lamp red, and when he looked back up, his squinty little eyes appeared ready to pop out of their squinty little sockets.

"YOU LITTLE PRICK!" Bennie cried, and grabbed for Peter. But the boy was fast, unbelievably fast. Nick couldn't remember seeing anyone move that fast, *ever.* Bennie missed, his feet tangled in his pants, and down

he went, holey underwear and all, hitting the sidewalk like a fat sack of dough.

Bennie's antics were rewarded by an uproariously hearty laugh from the boy with the pointy ears. And all at once Nick found himself smiling. He couldn't help it. Freddie shoved him back and jumped for Peter.

Peter skipped out of the way, effortlessly, stomping right on Bennie's head as he did so, smashing Bennie's face into the sidewalk. Nick heard a crunch that made him cringe, followed by a scream from Bennie. When Bennie looked back up, his nose sat at an odd angle and blood was pouring out of it.

"Holy crap," Nick said.

Freddie dove for Peter, trying to leap over Bennie, who was just standing. Bennie and Freddie collided, landing in a tangle.

Peter leaped high in the air and came down upon Freddie's back with a double knee jam that would've made any professional wrestler proud. Nick heard all the air go out of Freddie in a wounded *uuuff*.

Freddie rolled off Bennie and began flopping around on the grass, gasping, his mouth opening and closing like a feeding guppy. While Freddie struggled to get an ounce of air back in his lungs, Peter darted over, snatched the back of his pants, and yanked them down to his ankles.

"*POINT TWO! That's two for me!*" Peter called. He winked at Nick, then broke into another round of giggles.

Nick wasn't sure if he was thrilled or terrified.

Peter zeroed in on the kid on the bike. He planted his hands on his hips and glowered at Jake, daring him to make a move.

But Jake, good old Wang-fu, Jake-the-Snake, Steven-*fucking*-Seagal himself, was frozen in place and looking like he just might be suffering a seizure to boot.

"*YOU FUCKER!*" Bennie screamed at Peter as he struggled to his feet. He yanked his sweats back up, shoved a hand into a pocket, and tugged out a knife, a big one, and popped it open. "*YOU FUCKING FUCKHEAD, FUCKER FUCK!*"

"Oh, shit," Nick said. Bennie loomed easily twice Peter's height, must have outweighed him four times over. *Get out of here, kid*, Nick thought. *Run while you still can*. But Peter just stood there, hands still on his hips, lips pressed tightly together, his eyes squeezed down to slits.

Bennie's lower lip quivered. He spat blood, screamed, and charged, slashing for Peter's face.

Peter ducked and spun, and again Nick found himself amazed at the boy's speed. The back of Peter's fist caught Bennie full in the face. Nick couldn't see the actual contact from where he sat, but based on the way Bennie's head flew back, based on the horrible cracking sound, he knew Bennie was going down.

Bennie crumbled to his knees, his arms flopping limply by his sides, then he fell over face-first onto the sidewalk.

A chill climbed up Nick's spine. *He's dead. He's dead for sure.* And just for a second, Nick caught a haunted look on Peter's face. Then, as though knowing the boy's eyes were upon him, Peter's quirky smile leaped back into place. But Nick couldn't get that look out of his head. He'd seen something wild, something scary.

Peter ducked over to Bennie, grabbed the back of his sweatpants, and yanked them down to his ankles.

"That counts. That's three for me!" Peter called in a delighted voice. "I win!" He rolled his head back and crowed like a rooster.

Freddie stared on in horror as he tugged his pants up and scrambled to his feet. He took off, bumping into Jake, almost knocking him off the bike. Jake's eyes darted from Nick to the pack.

No! Uh-uh! Nick thought and lunged for the pack, but his legs were still tangled in his pants and he tumbled. Nick yanked savagely to get his pants up. Jake snatched up the pack and pedaled away at full speed. By the time Nick got his pants on, Jake was nowhere in sight.

Peter gave a big wave and laughed, "Later alligators!"

"FUCK!" Nick cried and punched the grass. *"FUCK! FUCK! FUCK!"*

"Hey, kiddo," Peter called. "I did pretty good, huh?"

Nick clasped his head in his hands and clenched at his hair. *What am I going to do now?* he wondered. *What the fuck am I going to do now? Could things get any more fucked up?*

"I did pretty good, huh?" Peter repeated. "Wouldn't you say?"

Nick realized Peter was talking to him. "Huh?" he said, low and unsure.

"Y'know, at the pants game. I won, wouldn't you say?"

Judging by the way Bennie was spread out on the sidewalk with his butt crack peeping out from his underwear, Nick had to agree.

Peter walked over to Nick and extended a hand.

Nick drew back.

"Hey," Peter said. "It's okay. We're on the same team. Remember?"

Nick cautiously extended his hand. Peter shook it, delighted, then pulled Nick to his feet.

"I'm Peter. What's your name?"

"Nick," Nick said distractedly as he scanned the park for Marko and his pals, sure they'd be coming out of the trees at any moment, knowing too well that those guys didn't fuck around, knowing they'd be packing and would have no qualms about shooting either of them.

"Good to meet you, Nick. So Nick, what do you want to do now?"

"What?"

"What do you want to do now?"

"Get out of here," he mumbled and headed into the trees, back toward the subway, then stopped. He dug in his pockets. "Fuck." Bennie had taken every cent. He'd have to find another way out of Brooklyn. Panic began to tighten his chest. Which way should he go? Marko could be anywhere, could be coming from any direction. Nick turned quickly and almost ran into Peter. Nick hadn't even realized the boy had been following him. Peter's eyes were full of mischief. "So, what's the plan?"

"What?" Nick said. "Plan? Look, kid—"

"Peter."

"Peter, you don't understand, there's some bad guys on their way."

Peter looked pleased.

"They've got guns. They're not fucking around either. They'll kill you."

"Nick, I said we're on the same team."

Nick let out a harsh laugh. *God, he thinks this is all some sort of game.*

"Don't you want to kill *them*?" Peter asked. "Could have ourselves a *real* good time."

"What?" Nick said in disbelief, but he could see the boy was serious. "No, I don't want anything to do with them. I need to disappear, *now.*"

"I know a secret way out of here," Peter said, looking left then right. "They'll never see us. Follow me." Peter took off.

He's crazy, Nick thought, but had to fight the compulsion to blindly chase after him anyway. There was just something compelling about the boy, something that made Nick want to follow even against his better judgment. Nick scanned the park again. It was dark. He was alone. It was hard to be alone. He clutched his rabbit's foot, sucked in a deep breath, and took off after the golden-eyed boy.

Chapter Two

Nick

They rested in a small church courtyard. Over the past hour or so Peter had led him along a maze of back streets and alleys, walking, running, scaling walls, and ducking through bushes. Slipping about unseen seemed to come naturally to him.

With the park long behind them, Nick began to breathe easier. He collapsed on a bench and Peter hopped up next to him, perching on his heels, reminding Nick of a gargoyle as he gazed up at the stars.

"Nick, you got someplace to go?"

"Sure," Nick said. "Well, I'm going to . . . heck, over to . . . Well—" He stopped. Where was he going? His money, his pack, everything was gone. He didn't have so much as a nickel, not even a jar of goddamn peanut butter anymore. He felt the sting of tears. He couldn't go home. He thought of the bums in the park. How long before he was one of them? How long before he was dirty, sick, cold, and hungry? How long before he was willing to do almost anything for a handout? That was if he could even get out of Brooklyn alive. The tears came. "I don't know," he blurted out.

While Nick cried big, heavy sobs into his own hands, the golden-eyed boy stayed beside him. He didn't speak, just sat there waiting for Nick to finish.

"I got a place."

Nick wiped at his eyes and looked at him.

"Avalon," Peter said. "I have a fort there."

Nick raised his eyebrows and managed a smirk. "A fort?"

"It's at a secret place. An enchanted island. No grown-ups allowed. It's full of faeries, goblins, and trolls. We stay up as late as we want. No teachers or parents to tell us what to do. We don't have to take baths, brush our teeth, or make our beds. We play with spears and swords, and sometimes," he lowered his voice, "we fight *monsters*."

Nick shook his head and grinned wryly. "Peter, you're a kook."

"Would you like to come with me?"

Nick hesitated, he knew Peter was joking about the secret place, about faeries and all that other nonsense, but you wouldn't guess it by the way he said it. Why, you could almost believe it was true. But true or not, the idea of a fort to sleep in, maybe some other runaways to hang out with, the idea of anything other than being left out here in the dark, *alone*, sounded good.

"You live there?" Nick asked.

"Yup."

"Don't your parents care?"

"I don't have any parents."

"Oh," Nick said. "Me neither. Not anymore."

A long silence hung between them.

"A fort," Nick said. "And faeries and goblins, huh?"

Peter nodded and grinned.

And Nick found himself grinning back.

✦

WHEN ASKED, PETER said his fort lay *thataway*, and pointed in the general direction of the New York Harbor. Nick guessed he must mean down toward the docks.

"Come along," Peter said, pulling up his hood. "You'll see."

So Nick followed Peter as they pushed their way through the dark Brooklyn neighborhoods, still taking care to avoid busy throughways or corners where teenagers were loitering about, but no longer dashing down side streets or hiding behind trees. Nick didn't feel a need to worry about Marko, not this far west, but couldn't help keeping an eye out for the green van. After a while Nick began to relax, felt his step lighten, and realized that he was enjoying simply having someone to walk down the street with.

He snuck several sidelong glances at the pointy-eared boy. There was something captivating about him, something about his strangeness, the wildness in his eyes that Nick found exciting. From his gestures to the odd way he was dressed, even in the way he bopped down the street so light on his toes, like some real cool cat—bold as brass, as though daring anyone to challenge his right to be there. Nothing escaped his attention, not a flittering gum wrapper, a cooing pigeon, or a falling leaf. And he was ever glancing up at the stars, as though making sure they were still there.

He wasn't like other street kids Nick had seen. His clothes might have been worn and dirty, but he wasn't grimy. He was a bit nutty, sure, but he didn't seem strung out on anything and his eyes were clear and sharp—even if they were gold. But though Peter felt like a friend, the best sort of friend, one you could count on to watch your back, Nick had to remind himself that he knew nothing about this weird boy and had to be careful. And there was something else, something below the contagious laugh and impish grins that nagged at Nick, something he couldn't put his finger on, something wicked, something—*dangerous*.

The smell of nectarines filled Nick's nose and his mouth began to water. He realized the smells were coming from the Chinese deli just ahead.

"Hungry?" Peter asked.

Nick realized he was, that he hadn't eaten since breakfast. He also remembered he didn't have any money.

"Hold up," Peter said as he glanced up and down the street. "You be the lookout. Okay?"

"Lookout?" Nick said. "For what?"

But Peter had already entered the grocery.

Nick didn't like where this was going. He tried to peer over the fruit stands to see what Peter was up to, but could only see the top of Peter's head bopping about inside the store. A few minutes later Peter came strolling out with two plastic containers of steaming Kung Pao chicken, fried rice, egg rolls, and three sacks of candy bars, almost more than he could carry.

"Here, help me with this," Peter said, handing Nick the candy bars.

"Wait," Nick said. "You didn't—"

"We should probably skedaddle," Peter interrupted, and headed away at a rapid clip.

A second later a plump, older Chinese man came skidding out of the grocery in his stained apron and yellow rain boots.

The man looked at Nick, then at the sacks of candy bars.

Nick heard the man say something under his breath, and even though it was Chinese, Nick had no trouble recognizing it as profanity. Then the man pointed at Nick and started yelling *TEEF* over and over again.

Nick broke and ran after Peter.

Luckily for Nick, the old man's running was about as good as his English, and Nick put a block or two between them in no time.

Nick found Peter waiting for him along a tree-lined street in front of a shadowy alleyway. Peter ducked into the alley and Nick followed.

Peter fell against some concrete steps and began to laugh, laugh so hard he could barely speak. "Hey, you did pretty good!" he chuckled and patted Nick on the back.

"What the hell was that?" Nick cried. "We could've gotten in all kinds of trouble!" Nick felt his blood boiling. That'd been stupid. The last thing he needed was the cops after him. "It's not funny!"

Peter pursed his lips, trying to stifle his mirth, but his eyes were positively giddy.

"Do you have any idea what they would've done to us if we'd been caught?" Nick snapped.

Peter shook his head.

"Why they'd, they'd—" Nick stopped. Peter was trying so hard not to laugh, trying so hard to look serious, concerned, and sincere. Nick couldn't help but grin and that was a mistake, because when he did, a bellyful of laughter escaped from between Peter's lips.

"Ah, man. You spit all over me!" Nick cried, wiping his face, but by then they were both laughing, big belly laughs. And it was the moment Nick realized that he was having fun. That he was happy, and it'd been a long time since he had been happy.

THEY SAT ON the cold cement steps, eating stolen Kung Pao chicken and watching the clouds roll across a sky full of stars. Nick never remembered anything tasting so good. A sharp wind sent a host of orange leaves and loose paper clattering down the thin alleyway. Late evening dew shimmered off the sooty, graffiti-covered walls. The low hum of an electric transformer sputtered and buzzed incessantly while somewhere in the distance the Staten Island Ferry blew its horn.

Peter sighed. "They're so beautiful."

"What?" Nick asked.

"The stars," Peter answered in a low, reverent tone, staring up at the night sky. "I so miss the stars."

Nick thought this an odd thing to say, but then there were a lot of odd things about Peter.

Peter tore open one of the bags of candy bars, grabbed a couple for himself and handed a few to Nick.

Nick noticed several scars on Peter's arms. There was also a scar above the boy's brow, a smaller one along his cheek, and what looked like a healed puncture on the side of his neck. Nick wondered just what kind of trouble Peter had been in.

"What are you going to do with all that candy?" Nick asked.

"For the gang," Peter said, between chews. "Back at the fort."

"Is there really a fort?"

"Certainly."

"Peter, where are we going exactly?"

Peter started to say something, frowned, started to say something else, and stopped. Then his eyes twinkled. "Hey, what's that?"

"What?"

"By your foot."

Nick didn't see anything. It was too dark.

"Is that a turd?"

Nick instinctively jerked his foot away. "Where?"

Peter reached into the shadow and came up with a lumpy brown clump. He held it up. "Yup, big greasy turd."

It didn't look like a turd to Nick. It looked suspiciously like a Baby Ruth.

Peter chomped down on it. "Scrumptious."

Nick snorted, then burst out laughing. Peter joined in between big, loud smacks. Nick found it easier and easier to laugh. Since his father's death, between moving to the new school and dealing with that fucker Marko, Nick felt he'd forgotten what it was like to be silly, to just be a kid.

"Hey," came a raspy voice from the shadows, followed by a fit of coughing. "Hey what . . . what're you guys up to?"

Nick and Peter looked at one another, then at the pile of boxes beside the Dumpster. One of the boxes fell away and a figure rolled out.

Peter was instantly on his feet.

The shape stumbled into the lamplight and Nick saw it was a teenager, maybe a couple of years older than him. The kid's long blond hair was greasy and matted, and he was wearing just jeans and a ratty T-shirt.

"You . . . you guys spare . . . some change," the kid said, his words slurry and spaced out. "Need . . . to, to make a phone call. Anything will help out. Huh . . . how about it?"

Nick picked up the bags of candy bars and stood up. "Peter," Nick whispered, "let's get out of here."

"Hey, where you going?" The kid tottered forward, put an arm out on the stair rail, blocking their way. Up close, Nick could see cold sores on the boy's lips and how bloodshot his eyes were. The kid was so skinny he had to keep tugging at his jeans. The kid spied the candy bars in Nick's arms. "Hey, how about you give me some of those."

"These aren't for you," Peter said, his tone hard and cold.

The kid looked agitated, started scratching at his arms. Nick could see he had the shakes. The kid looked at them again and actually focused. "What're you guys doing out here?" He took a quick glance around. "You alone?"

Nick didn't like the way his tone changed, and tried to get around him.

The kid made a grab for the chocolates, snagged a bag, yanking it from Nick's arms.

Peter let out a hiss and in a mere blink had a knife in his hand. The damn thing was almost as long as Peter's forearm.

Whoa, where'd that come from?

Peter rolled the blade, letting the street light dance along its razor-sharp edge, making sure the kid saw its wicked promise. "Give 'em back," Peter said.

"Yeah. Yeah, okay," the kid said. "Take 'em." He tossed the bag to Nick, raised his hands, and took several unsteady steps backward until he hit the alley wall. "I ain't got nothing else. Go ahead, shake me down. I ain't got nothing." And then, low, to himself: *"Nothing."* His shoulders drooped and his hands fell. Nick thought he looked worn out, defeated, *alone,* another strung-out junkie with no place to go and no one to care. Nick wondered what had made this kid leave home, wondered how long before he found himself in the same spot—*alone,* with *nothing.*

"Let's go," Peter said, stuffing the knife back in his jacket and heading toward the street.

Nick grimaced. *Growing up can really suck,* he thought. *And bad things sure as shit do happen to good people and for the most part the world just doesn't give a crap.* He reached into the bag of chocolates, pulled out a handful, and left them on the steps. "Here. Those are yours." Then he sprinted off to catch up with Peter.

WITH THE EXCEPTION of a few pubs and late-night restaurants, the shops had all closed up. They passed a bar and Nick stole a quick peek in-side, caught sight of sullen, tired faces, the smell of cigarettes and beer, the clinking of glasses and strained laughter as men and woman went about the business of putting the long, hard workweek behind them.

Next door, in front of Antonio's Camping and Sporting Goods, Nick stopped suddenly and peered into the display window.

Peter came up next to him. "What is it?"

Nick stared at the green-and-black checkered Vans propped against a skateboard.

"The shoes?" Peter asked.

"Nothing," Nick said, but his eyes didn't leave the shoes.

"You want those?"

Nick nodded absently.

Peter disappeared around the side of the building. Nick took a last longing look at the shoes and followed. He turned the corner but Peter wasn't there. Nick glanced across the weedy lot and caught sight of a bearded man leaning against a paunchy woman near the rear entrance of the bar. Her blouse was undone and one of her breasts had escaped her bra, hanging down nearly to her navel. The two of them giggled as the man pawed it like a cat toy. "Jesus," Nick said and watched, mesmerized, until a sharp clank drew his attention. It came from behind the Dumpster next to the sporting goods shop. He peered around the Dumpster—Peter had managed to tug one steel bar from the crumbling masonry of a basement window-well and was using that bar to pry loose a second.

"What the hell are you doing?"

Peter grunted, and the last bar popped off with a loud clang. "Bingo!"

Nick ducked down, peeked back toward the pub. The bearded man still groped the woman, another man had stumbled outside puking, none of them were looking their way.

Peter gave the pane a nudge with his foot and it popped open. The basement was a well of darkness. Peter looked up at Nick. "Well?"

"Well, what?" Nick said.

"Are you going to get those shoes, or not?"

Nick took a quick step back as though from a viper. "Are you kidding me? That's breaking and entering."

A look of deep disappointment crossed Peter's face. Nick was surprised to find this bothered him, that he cared at all what this wild kid thought. "I'm not scared, if that's what you're thinking," Nick said, a bit too quickly. "I'm no thief, that's all. I mean that's—"

"Nick, don't let them win. Don't let them beat you."

"What?"

"Don't let them steal your magic."

"Magic?" What did magic have to do with breaking into someone's store and stealing their stuff?

"Don't you get it?" Peter said. "You're free now. You don't have to live by their rules anymore." Peter pointed into the inky blackness of the basement. "The darkness is calling. A little danger, a little risk. Feel your heart race. Listen to it. That's the sound of being *alive*. It's your time, Nick. Your one chance to have fun before it's all stolen by *them*, the adults, with their cruelty and endless rules, their can't-do-this, and can't-do-that's, their have-tos, and better-dos, their little boxes and cages all designed to break your spirit, to kill your magic."

Nick stared down into the dark basement.

"What are you waiting for?" Peter said, giving him a devilish grin before disappearing through the window.

What am I waiting for? Nick wondered. *What's ahead for me? Even if I could go home, what then? Graduate? Get some crappy job so that I can spend every weekend trying to drink it all away, puking in a parking lot, or playing fiddle-boobs with some skank?* He shook his head. Peter was right: if he didn't live now—right this minute—then when? Too much of his youth had already been stolen. Why should he let *them* take any more? Maybe it *was* time to do a little taking of his own.

Nick took a deep breath and lowered himself through the window. He swung his leg about in the darkness until his foot hit a box, dropped onto the box, and promptly crashed over onto the floor. Something hit the floor and shattered. "Crap," Nick said, and sat there a long moment, heart in his throat, waiting for the alarms and sirens, the lights, the dogs—the *Gestapo*. When nothing happened, he climbed to his feet.

The basement smelled of mildew, dust, and old cardboard. *Where's Peter?* Nick noticed a weak light coming from the top of a narrow staircase. Hands out, he made his way—adrenaline pumping through his every fiber, heart beating louder with each step. "I hear it, Peter," he whispered and grinned. "The sound of being alive."

The streetlights poured in through the display window, dousing the jerseys, bats, balls, and bikes in a soft, bluish glow. No sign of Peter. He crept by the Little League plaques and trophies, going right past the cash register. Nick knew stores didn't keep money in their registers at night, and even if they had, this wasn't about money. He wasn't here to steal, at least not like that. This was different somehow. It was about taking back, about control maybe, the need to be steering his own fate for once—for better or worse.

Nick peered over the racks of jerseys and warm-up suits, searching for Peter's nest of wild hair. He didn't find the golden-eyed boy, but found shoes—a whole wall of them. He passed up the court shoes with their springs, gels, pumps, glitter, and glitz—what the boys at his school liked to refer to as *dunkadelic*—until he zeroed in on a certain green-and-black checked pattern. "Bingo," he said, just like Peter had.

He allowed himself a moment to enjoy the sight, then scanned the boxes for a size nine. He found a ten, several thirteens, a seven, a six, but no nines. His brow tightened. "Oh, be here. Be here, be here, be here." A grin lit his face. There. "Yes!" He snatched up the box but didn't open it, not right away. He just held it, cherishing the moment like a Christmas present you were finally allowed to open. Nick slowly lifted the lid, enjoyed the pungent smell of rubber and glue, then slid the shoes out, holding them up into the light. "S—weeet!" he exhaled, chucking the box and dropping down onto a bench.

He tugged off his bargain-bin specials, stared at the cracked, peeling rubber and frayed stitching. They reminded him of his mother—his *cheap-ass* mother. He slung them against the wall. He had the Vans laced and on his feet in no time and was up bouncing on his toes, checking himself out in the mirror. Nick froze. There, behind him in the mirror, a pale, haunted face watched him from the shadows, watched him like a cat watches a mouse.

SO MUCH JOY over a pair of shoes, Peter thought and felt the sting of jealousy as Nick's simple joy made him aware of all he'd lost. He had to remind himself that soon shoes would be the last thing on Nick's mind.

Nick started and jerked around. "Shit, man. You scared the piss out of me!"

"Killer shoes," Peter said, putting on his best smile.

Nick studied Peter for a moment, then glanced down at his shoes. He licked his finger and touched the laces, making a sizzling noise. "Watch out, man," Nick said, grinning. "I'm lethal in these babies."

Peter laughed.

"Hey, man. Check this out." Nick stepped over to a rack of skateboards, snatched one up, and dropped it on top of his shoe, flipping it onto its wheels with a flick of his foot. "Slick, huh?"

Peter nodded.

"Out of the way," Nick said, hopping on the board, kicking hard, and shooting down the long center aisle. He kicked the tail of the board, catching some air, but when the board landed, the back end slid out on the slick linoleum, sending Nick into a rack of men's sweats, taking the entire rack down right on top of him.

Nick's head popped up between the hangers and sweats, looking disoriented and embarrassed.

Peter let loose a howl of laughter. "Impressive!"

Nick frowned. "Oh, yeah? Let's see what you got."

"Oh, you want me to show you how it's done? Is that it? Why, I'm the skateboard king." Peter snatched up one of the boards. He'd never ridden a skateboard before, but if this kid could do it, he most certainly could. He dropped the board on the floor and set his foot on the deck, shoving off with his other foot, kicking hard like he'd seen Nick do. The board wobbled and he wheeled his arms for balance as he careened straight toward Nick. *"GANG WAY!"* Peter cried, fighting for control.

Nick's face changed from mirth to panic as he scrambled out of the way. Peter tried to swerve, lost control, and landed hard on his butt. The board shot out from under him like a missile, slamming into the leg of a nearby mannequin. The mannequin toppled and the head bounced down the aisle and landed right in Nick's lap, its charming face smiling blissfully at Nick. Nick stared back in astonishment, then up at Peter, and both cracked up.

"Oh, my God," Nick wheezed. "Oh man. That's the craziest thing ever." He got to his feet, holding the head, took aim at a row of basketball hoops, and shot. The head bounced off the backboard, but completely missed the rim and net. Nick raised both fists in the air. "He shoots! He sucks! The crowd pisses their pants!" He did a little foot dance, kicked his skateboard back out into the aisle, hopped on, and raced away. Up and down the aisle he went, doing spins and hops, sliding, skidding, and carving his way around the displays.

Peter got up, rubbing his butt. He gave his skateboard a disdainful look. "That one's defective."

"Yeah, right."

Peter frowned, grabbed another skateboard from the rack, scrutinizing it before setting it on the floor. Nick zipped past, laughing hysterically, almost knocking him over. Peter hopped on his board and raced after him, wobbling and fighting to keep the board from flipping out from under him. Nick cut sharp, wheeled the board around in front of the entrance. Too late to stop, Peter crashed right into Nick, slamming the boy into the door. The impact shook the entire storefront and an alarm began to blare.

"OH, SHIT!" Nick shouted over the noise. *"WE GOTTA GET OUT OF HERE!"* Nick tried to open the door; it was locked. He slapped the door in frustration and tried to yank it open. No luck. *"WE HAVE TO GO BACK THROUGH THE BASEMENT. QUICK!"*

"NO WE DON'T."

Nick looked at Peter, confused. Peter pointed at a swirly pink bowling ball sitting in the display window.

It took Nick a moment to get it. *"OH, NO,"* he called, shaking his head. *"WE CAN'T DO THAT."* Then a spark lit in his eyes. Peter knew the look well. They all got it, once they truly realized they were free.

Nick hefted the ball, locked his eyes on the big display window, his mouth tightened into a hard line. Peter saw the anger, the hostility, and knew this was about more than getting out of the store, more than an act of vandalism, or simple mischief, this went far deeper. Nick needed to strike out—to break out. Nick was like so many of the runaways he'd encountered, too many years of being bullied and mistreated, of being stifled and ignored. They just needed someone to show them how to let it out. And once it was out, once he'd taken them that far, the rest was easy. After that, they'd follow him anywhere.

"GIVE IT TO 'EM, NICK," Peter cried. *"GIVE 'EM THE BIG FUCK-YOU!"*

Nick gritted his teeth, snarled, and hurled the ball like a shot-put. *"FUCK YOU,"* he screamed. *"FUCK ALL OF YOU!"* The ball smashed through the plate glass, shattering it into a thousand glittering shards.

"YEE-HAW!" Nick screamed over the warbling alarm.

The ball bounced onto the sidewalk and rolled into the street, picking up speed as it headed down the sloping avenue.

"AFTER IT!" Nick cried, snatching up his skateboard and leaping heedlessly across the broken glass.

Peter couldn't have grinned any wider. *He's mine.* He snatched up his own board and caught up with Nick in the middle of the street. A host of men and women had come out from the bar to see about all the commotion, some so drunk they could barely stand.

Nick grinned at them savagely, raised both hands in the air, and gave them the double bird. *"FUCK THE WORLD!"* he screamed. *"FUCK THE WORLD!"*

The crowd raised their bottles and returned the salute. *"FUCK THE WORLD!"*

Peter turned his head to the sky and howled, basking in the spreading madness, aware that sometimes even these dull-eyed adults could let loose, could remember.

"The ball went that way," Nick cried, slapping his foot atop his board and kicking off down the hill.

Peter let out one last hoot, hopped on his board, and, fighting for control, chased after Nick. *It's a good night. A very good night. Can't remember a better one in the last hundred years.*

ist

"Where to?" Nick asked Peter.

"To crazy town," Peter howled, and wobbled past.

"TO CRAZY TOWN!" Nick cried, and took off after him. They raced down the street, knocking over garbage cans and setting off car alarms, yowling and laughing, setting the dogs to barking all up and down the street.

The cool fall air filled Nick's lungs, blew the hair from his face. His heart raced, his body flushed with adrenaline, excitement, and the sheer joy of abandonment, of freedom like he'd never known in his life. Thoughts of Marko, his mother, all the bullshit felt a million miles away.

The neighborhoods fell behind, replaced by warehouses and industrial buildings, the steady incline leading them toward the docks. They saw no more headlights, or any other signs of people. Nick felt as though they were the only two souls left in the world, and he wished it would never end.

AS THEY NEARED the harbor, the fog thickened, seemed almost alive the way it swirled and snaked around them. Peter stopped and stuffed the chocolates into his bag. In addition to the knife, Nick noticed a carton of cigarettes and several packs of gum. Peter kicked his skateboard into a ditch.

"Man, what are you doing? That's a killer board."

"Won't need it where we're going."

"What do you mean?" Nick let out a weak laugh.

"The Mist is here," Peter said, and looked Nick in the eye. "This is the point of no return. The Mist will take us to Avalon, a place where you never have to grow up. An island of magic and adventure, but there's danger and . . . *monsters*. Nick, do you go willingly?"

Nick laughed, "Umm, yeah, sure Peter."

"No, you have to say it."

"Say what?"

"Say, 'I go willingly.' "

Nick thought Peter was carrying this whole enchanted island thing a bit too far, but fine, he could play along. "Okay. I go willingly."

Peter looked relieved. "Then we go," he said, and they continued down the street.

As the buildings and streetlights began to disappear behind the foggy veil, so did the sounds of the city—the chug of the tugboats, the occasional long, low horn-blast from the ferries, all faded. Soon he no longer smelled the bay at all. The wind died and the air became stale. It smelled of the earth, of old things. The mist grew perceptually colder and brighter, as though glowing from its own radiance. And Nick finally admitted to himself that maybe things were getting weird, that maybe following a golden-eyed boy with pointed ears to a magical island might not have been the brightest idea.

"Stay close," Peter whispered. "And keep as quiet as you can. We don't want *them* to know we're here."

Nick couldn't imagine who else would be around here this time of night, but kept quiet just the same.

They'd been in the fog for maybe ten minutes when Nick's foot caught on something and he stumbled to the ground. He dropped his skateboard and his hands slid into wet, chalky earth—gray, the same color as the fog. Nick couldn't recall exactly when the pavement had given way to earth. But he wasn't particularly surprised; he'd figured Peter's fort would most likely be hidden in a dump, or an abandoned lot around the shipping yards. But he *was* surprised when the dirt began to evaporate off his hands, drift away in smoking tendrils, as though it, too, were somehow part of the mist. Then he noted what he'd tripped over: a white shape with two large dark holes. Nick squinted, leaned forward, and realized he was staring into the eye sockets of a human skull.

The skull lay half-buried in the dirt, wrapped in the last remnants of worm-riddled flesh, dried and ashen. There was a knot of blond, braided scalp still attached to the top of its head. He also saw what had to be an arm bone, and a few smaller bones scattered about.

"Holy crap!" Nick said, scrambling to his feet.

"Peter," he whispered, fighting to control his fear. Peter had disappeared.

"Peter," he hissed again. *Where'd he go?* He glanced around. No Peter, nothing but the same dull, shifting grayness everywhere. Nick had no clue which direction he'd come from, or was heading to. His breath quickened. He felt the mist was caving in on him, like he would suffocate, like he was being swallowed.

"Peter," he called, a little louder this time, then louder. "Peter." He knew he was losing control, knew he might start screaming at any second.

Peter materialized out of the fog.

"I told you to stay close," Peter said harshly.

"Peter, there're bones. Human bones! What is going—"

Peter snapped a finger to his lips. "Shhhh. *They* will hear us." Peter's eyes were deadly serious and his look sobered Nick up.

"Who are *they*?" Nick mouthed, suddenly very alarmed.

But Peter didn't answer. He only beckoned with quick, sharp gestures for Nick to follow.

Nick had no intention of going another step into this ghostly wasteland. But, as the mist closed in around him, seemed to actually touch him, caressing and slithering along his skin, the touch cold and clammy, as Peter's back began to fade and Nick realized he would be alone again, his resolve evaporated and he sprinted forward to catch up.

Nick stuck as close to Peter as he could and kept a careful watch where he stepped in case there were more bones. And, of course, there were more bones, many more bones, and not *just* bones; he saw helmets, swords, and shields, most looking as though they'd dropped in straight from the Crusades. He almost stepped on a flintlock pistol and noticed the moldering remnants of a three-cornered hat, what Nick thought of as a pirate hat. A bit farther on he saw a skeleton with thin, leathery flesh clinging to its frame; it clutched a canteen in one hand and wore the tattered trappings of a British Redcoat. A few hundred feet away lay the remains of a man in a dusty Civil War uniform. The soldier's rotten hands still dug at his eyes.

Then Nick saw the Nike high-top and his blood went cold. It was just sitting by itself. Nick couldn't take his eyes off it, so was taken by surprise when his foot stumbled on something soft. He halted and found he was standing on a boy's arm, his shoe sinking into the soft, pliable flesh.

Nick staggered back. *Oh, Christ! Oh, good Lord!* Nick put a fist to his mouth and bit hard.

The dead boy looked to be about his age, but it was hard to tell, because his skin was parched and peeling away. The kid's eyes were wide-open, his mouth a big, hollow O. Nick had no problem reading the terrified expression frozen forever on that face. It mirrored his own. *Maybe if I scream,* Nick thought, *maybe then I'll wake up back in my bed, and maybe I'll hear Marko and his asshole friends screwing around downstairs and I won't care, because anything will be better than wandering around out here stepping on dead kids.*

But Nick didn't scream, because he didn't really believe this was a dream—this was real, every bit of it. He knew if he screamed, *they*—whatever *they* were—would hear.

"Peter," he whispered. Peter kept walking. "Peter," he called. "I want to go back." To Nick's alarm, his voice carried, not just echoing but actually rolling across the mist as though the mist itself was carrying it along.

Peter turned, his face horrified.

And that was when Nick heard the voices—soft and far away at first, but quickly moving closer: the light calls of children, sweet chorus of women, and deep baritone of men. Laughing and gay, as though they were all on their way to a summer picnic. But behind these, or maybe within, he heard wailing, a sad, terrible keening. The hair on the back of his neck stood up.

"They've found us," Peter said, his voice dead as stone.

"Found us? *Who's* found us?"

"Nick," Peter said, his words quick and urgent. "No matter what you hear, no matter what you see, ignore them. Avoid their eyes. And whatever you do, don't dare speak to them." Peter glanced into the fog. "If you lose the path, Nick, your bones will never leave the Mist."

Nick's mind was one big *WHAT THE FUCK!* Then he caught movement. The mist had begun to stir.

Shadows, mere shades of gray on gray, began to swim around them, some hulking and sluggish, almost lumbering, others small and fleet as sparrows, most just furtive wisps of indefinable vapor. Their whispers and calls echoed around them, crawled right into Nick's head.

Nick glanced at Peter. Peter kept his eyes directly forward and marched onward at a quick, steady clip.

Nick gritted his teeth, balled his hands into fists, and clamped them tightly to his chest. He tried to slow his breathing. *Don't fall behind. Whatever you do, don't fall behind.* He picked up his pace, keeping tight to Peter's heels.

The mist next to him began to swirl, almost to boil, until the shape of a woman formed, her skin pale and shimmering. She smiled at him demurely, floating along, twirling and rolling. The tendrils of her gown and hair trailed out behind her as though in an underwater ballet.

Nick struggled not to look into her eyes, but felt powerless to do anything but, and when he did, he saw that she was beauty itself. She began to sing to him. He couldn't understand the words, but he recognized the tune. The same lullaby mothers have been singing to their children for thousands of years. It promised to keep him safe and warm. It promised an eternity of maternal love. She stretched her arms, beckoning him to her.

It would be all over if he went to her. Part of him knew this, the part that was screaming somewhere deep inside to stay on the path. The rest of him knew this too, but thought it was okay, because it would be such a sweet death. Cradling him in her loving embrace, she would rock him, soothe him. All his fears, all the bad things would simply drift away forever. Nick found himself wishing for nothing more.

Peter's voice came from somewhere far away, little more than an echo. "Stay with me!" And a face, the terrified face of the boy, the one in the high-tops, flashed in Nick's head. He blinked and forced himself to tear his eyes away from the woman.

Where's Peter?

Nick saw only a vague silhouette in front of him. *Is that him? How'd I fall so far behind?* He noticed sheets of mist drawing together like curtains, as though trying to build a wall between them. Panicked, Nick sprinted forward, stumbling across the soft, undulating surface, almost knocking Peter over when he caught up.

"Hang on," Peter whispered. "You're doing good."

Doing good? Nick wanted to scream. *Doing good at what? What is going on? What the fuck is going on?*

The woman continued to float alongside of him, her face now mournful. Crazily, Nick found himself feeling regretful. Then she raised her arms above her head as though entering a swan dive, arching her back, snaking her body through the smoky tendrils of mist. Suddenly Nick was very aware of how full her breasts were, discovered he could see the shape of her large, dark nipples beneath the thin veil of her gown and the dusky shadow between her legs. A warm, tingling sensation began to grow in his crotch. Nick felt his face flush and glanced away. When he did, he caught sight of something out of the corner of his eye. *A tail?* He blinked. She had a long, scaly tail. She also had scales on her arms, small and delicate, and her fingers were long and clawlike. He squinted. *Oh good God,* he thought, *her hair. Her hair is full of worms!* No, her hair *was* worms, thousands of tiny, squirming worms.

Nick jerked back and almost fell over.

She scowled, dark and angry. Her eyes shrank to mere slits, her nipples stretched into long antennae, her belly opened up into a gaping maw, and Nick saw row after row of jagged little teeth!

Oh, no! Oh no! Oh no!

A sound came out of that mouth, like a thousand angry hornets, and she came for him.

Nick screamed and crumpled to the ground, arms out, watching help-lessly as she fell upon him, watching as her huge mouth, a mouth easily as tall as himself, engulfed him. *So this is how I will die,* he thought. But no jagged teeth tore into his flesh. All he felt was a blast of cold air as she passed through him. It took him a moment to realize that he was still alive.

Peter! Where's Peter? He thought he saw a shape plodding away from him. Was that Peter, or another trick of the fog? *"PETER!"* he screamed and scrambled to his feet. Now there were three different shapes, each heading in a different direction.

"PETER!" he shrieked, then an inner voice, the one from deep inside of him, said, *Stop wasting your breath. Think!* Nick stopped, concentrated, tried to clear his mind. *Footprints. Find his footprints.* They were there, the faintest trace, disappearing as the moist earth rapidly filled them in. Nick gritted his teeth and ran in their direction. And just ahead was Peter, not another illusion but truly Peter.

"PETER!" Nick raced forward and grabbed Peter by the shoul-der. *"WAIT FOR ME!"* he screamed. *"WHY WON'T YOU WAIT FOR ME?"*

"Steady," Peter said, not losing a step. "Have to keep steady or all is lost."

Nick clutched Peter's jacket, twisting his hand in the fabric, wishing he could close his eyes and make them all go away.

They came, dozens, then hundreds, all shapes and sizes, filling the air with their screams, laughter, wails and cries. A swarm of disembodied heads flew past, singing, a host of naked old women with large, saggy breasts skipped merrily around, holding hands and laughing through wide, toothless grins. A throve of tiny children with grasshopper bodies buzzed insistently, all manner of hungry-looking beasts, with sharp teeth and claws, stalked alongside them, and small, shadowy men with protru-sive blank eyes and bird beaks danced wildly.

"What are they?" Nick cried between clenched teeth. *What is going on?* A short time ago he'd been eating Chinese food in the middle of Brooklyn.

How could he now be lost in a fog with these horrors? *Things like this can't really happen!*

He felt their wispy fingers crawling through his hair, his clothes, over his mouth and eyes.

A little girl's face shot up to him, her eyes black holes, her mouth frozen in a scream that made no sound. She just hung there staring at him. He tried to wave her away, but every time his hand went through her, she just giggled, giggled while wearing that horrible scream, giggled until he thought he'd go crazy.

"Oh God," he cried. *I can't do this. Not any longer.* He needed to run, he didn't care where to, he just had to run.

If you run you will die, came the familiar voice. Calm but stern, it was his voice, his inner self, the boy that had been through his share of hard times and had managed to keep it together. And how had he done that? How had he dealt with watching them shovel dirt onto his father's casket? How had he dealt with hearing his mother cry herself to sleep night after night? How had he put up with the bullshit at school—the endless taunts and bullying, and Marko fucking with him every day? He'd simply withdrawn deep within himself, pretended as though all the bad things were happening to someone else and that he was just along for the ride. And this had always got him through. It didn't make it okay. It didn't make the hurt any less painful later, but it got him through. And right now he just needed to get through.

So Nick went there now, to his safe place, and watched the show from afar. And from afar it was clear that the mist was all noise and bluster, merely trying to scare him, confuse him, drive him from the path.

Nick looked through the mist, locked his eyes on Peter's back, kept them there, and plodded onward—steady.

Soon, the voices began to fade. The mist settled down, returned to a state of placid, endless gray. And not long after that he smelled the sea again, felt a breeze, heard the lapping of waves. Finally the mist thinned and Nick could just make out a shadowy bank against a starless night sky.

⁕

NICK STUMBLED TO his knees and planted both hands on the wet beach, clutching the sand to steady himself. He took in a deep gulp of air, like a surfacing swimmer, and tried not to scream, tried not to think about *them*. *What the hell had that been?* He clenched his eyes shut but there was no hiding from what he'd seen. "What was that?" Nick said in a harsh whisper and looked up at Peter.

Peter wore a grin from ear to ear. "You did great!"

Nick glared at Peter. *"WHAT THE HELL WAS THAT?"*

"The Mist," Peter said, as though nothing could be more obvious or natural.

Nick waited for more, but Peter just stood there wearing that stupid grin.

Nick glanced over his shoulder, back into the swirling mist, wondering if it would follow, would come after him. "Those things. What were those things? What were those *fucking* things out there?"

"Mist spirits."

"Mist spirits?"

"Yep, the Sluagh."

Nick realized this was going nowhere. He pushed to his feet and clenched his fist. He wanted to punch the pointy-eared kid, wanted to beat that smug little smile into his face, had never wanted to hit someone more in his life.

Peter took a step back, looking perplexed.

"YOU TRICKED ME!" Nick shouted. "You jerk-ass! You knew about that crap and didn't tell me."

"Not true," Peter stated like a trial lawyer. "I specifically asked if you were ready to enter the Mist. And you said—" Peter mimicked Nick's voice— " 'I go willingly.' "

Nick glared at Peter. "You *know* what I mean. You didn't tell me about all that crap out there. About those *things*!"

"And what, spoil the surprise?"

"Stop being a fucking wiseass!" Nick cried. "I saw a *dead* boy out there. Why are there *dead* people out there?"

Peter's face clouded and he looked away.

"If I'd fallen behind, would I still be out there? Wandering around, screaming your name until I died?"

"Yes."

Nick stared at Peter, stunned, a forgotten word still on his lips. He turned his back on the boy, eyeing the mist, watching it the way you'd watch a dog you know will bite.

"I had to stay the course," Peter said. "I did what I could for you. But if I'd wavered, if I'd hesitated, or strayed from the path . . . all would've been lost.

46

"And Nick, you really did do well. The Mist isn't an easy path to walk."

Nick whirled. *FUCK YOU! FUCK YOU!"*

Peter's jaw tightened. "It's a good idea to keep your voice down or the Flesh-eaters will hear." He peered intently down the shoreline.

Nick followed Peter's gaze. *Flesh-eaters?* He studied the jagged shadows and twisted terrain lining the beach. It didn't look like anyplace he'd ever seen. He shuddered; just why had the pointy-eared boy brought him here? "Peter, where are we? Really?"

Peter's playful smile returned, and his voice fairly danced with mischief. "Oh, there's lots to see. Lots to do. Adventure awaits. Follow me and I'll show you."

Nick shook his head. "No, Peter, I'm not about—"

"Shhh!" Peter jabbed a finger to his lips, his face suddenly hard, squinting into the dark. "The Flesh-eaters, they're coming. Time to go."

Nick crossed his arms. "I'm not going anywhere with you."

Peter shrugged, turned, and headed quickly up the beach toward the woods.

Nick stood alone, staring down the dark shore. "Bullshit," he whispered. "It's all bull—" He caught movement far down the beach, several hunched shapes picking their way toward him. "Oh shit." He glanced at the mist, at its swirling tendrils. "Fuck." He kicked the sand and, to his horror, found himself hustling up the beach after the pointy-eared boy.

✦

PETER PUT A finger to his lips. This time, Nick didn't have to be told twice. He got quiet, dead quiet, barely daring to breathe as they pushed their way up the muddy path and into the trees.

The woods were still and silent, no creaking insects, no croaking frogs, as though the very land was dead. The heavy silence amplified their every step as the mud sucked at their feet. They plodded onward, snaking their way around weedy bogs, sinkholes, and across a few shallow, slow-running creeks. The air was heavy with the smell of stagnant water, mud, mold, and decay. The overcast sky provided only a faint greenish glow to help Nick stumble his way over the roots, rocks, and brambles. He could just make out the tortured shapes of the trees looming above them, their leafless branches—like tormented hands—seemed to be reaching for him as they passed. Nick did his best to avoid touching the trees, as their bark felt soft, yielding, more like flesh than bark.

A low bellow rolled out from the woods ahead of them. Peter ducked down against the twisted trunk of a fallen tree and Nick slipped up next to him. Both boys peered through the tangle of roots searching the shadows ahead. From somewhere behind them came another bellow. *"Barghest,"* Peter whispered and slid out his long knife.

Barghest? Nick thought. *Okay, great. Flesh-eaters, now barghest. What the hell's a barghest?*

In a clearing, not twenty yards up the trail, Nick spotted a pair of orange, glowing eyes. A dark, hunched shape about the size of a wolf crept out of the shadows. It crawled on all fours, stood up on its hind legs, and began to sniff the air. From behind them came the slapping of feet tracking through mud. The sound grew steadily closer. Nick allowed himself to slowly turn his head and saw another set of eyes moving their way. He instinctively pressed himself further into the overhanging roots and ground his teeth as he fought the urge to cut and run. The dark shape moved past them, sliding by so close that Nick could've reached out and touched it, so close that he could actually smell it—a musty smell like an old, wet carpet.

The shape joined with the other in the clearing and a moment later a third arrived. One by one all three of them turned their orange eyes toward Nick. Cold mud oozed between Nick's fingers as he clutched the wet earth, afraid to even blink.

Somewhere far away another howl echoed across the swamp, almost human. All three of the shapes tilted back their heads and answered, and Nick felt the sound in his very bones. He struggled to control his breathing. Every ounce of him wanted to run, wanted to get as far away from that sound as he could. He felt Peter's hand on his shoulder—strong and steady.

Finally the three shapes shuffled away.

Peter waited a long time before he stood up, and they continued down the trail.

PETER HEARD THE gurgling of Goggie Creek and let out a silent sigh of relief. The Flesh-eaters would never dare follow them this far.

He crouched on the bank and put his hands in the fast-moving water. "This water's safe to drink," Peter said, and began slurping down large handfuls. He splashed his face, glad to wash away the residue of the city. He hated the city, hated all the concrete, the noise, the stink of exhaust and garbage, but worse than all that, the city was full of men-kind—men-kind and all their cruelty and brutality.

He glanced at Nick. The kid was holding up pretty good. He'd done well in the Mist. Peter had been sure he'd lost him, and yet the boy had found him on his own. Peter couldn't remember any other child doing that. This boy showed spunk, showed promise. *Just the kind of child the Devils are looking for,* Peter thought. *This one just might live awhile.*

Peter watched the boy drink. It had been a long night and the boy looked worn out, exhausted. *Good,* Peter thought, *a deep sleep will make things easier.*

"Up ahead's a good spot to rest," Peter said.

Nick nodded and they moved on.

✦

THE TWO OF them lay between a cluster of boulders on a makeshift bed of straw. Peter stared up at the overcast night sky. "I miss the stars."

Nick yawned. "Maybe it'll clear up soon."

"No," Peter said. "The Mist is eternal. The Lady protects Avalon, but at the cost of our dear moon and stars."

"Avalon?" Nick said. "I thought that was in Britain somewhere."

"Used to be," Peter said.

"What'd you mean?"

"Oh, you'll see."

"Sure, okay," Nick mumbled and closed his eyes.

Peter watched the boy until he was sure Nick was fast asleep, then rose, slipping silently out from the boulders. There below him a giant tree grew out from the cliff base; a single tendril of gray smoke wove its way through its craggy limbs. A solid round door was set into the trunk, thick iron spikes protruding from its planks; above the door hung a toothless human skull atop a thigh bone.

Peter rapped on the door three times; a moment later, the peephole slid open; one slanted eye peered out at him.

"I bring fresh blood," Peter said and grinned.

PART II

Deviltree

Chapter Four

Goll

✦

It *will all end soon*, the child thief thought as he moved steadily through the forest, back toward the shore, back toward the Mist. *Nick's with the Devils now. His fate is in their hands. What will happen, will happen.* He slid from shadow to shadow, stopping frequently to listen, to watch, trying to keep his mind focused on the danger and away from what he had done, what he had left to do, because thinking about it didn't change it. Thinking about it only led to distraction, and out here, on *their* part of the island, distraction would get you killed.

Peter came to the edge of the thicket and scanned the beach. There, waiting for him, floated the Mist. He could hear it calling, taunting him. Grimacing, he broke cover and started forward when he caught voices. The child thief ducked back and dropped behind a thick knot of roots. Five shadows sat against a chunk of driftwood not thirty paces away—*Flesh-eaters!*

Fool, Peter silently cursed himself. *You almost walked right into them.* He'd allowed the Mist to distract him. *Stupid.* He reached instinctively for his sword and remembered he only carried his knife.

One of them stood, his tattered shirt fluttering in the breeze. "There they be."

Peter followed his gaze; a line of dark figures came marching around the cove, easily forty or fifty of them. He couldn't remember seeing so many out at once, not since the galleons first arrived. *What are they up—* His blood went cold; even in the dark he had no problem recognizing a tall silhouette; there was no missing the wide-brimmed hat with that ratty feather. *The Captain.* Peter clutched his knife.

The faintest glow of dawn touched the low clouds as the Captain tromped his way up to the others.

"Well?"

"Found some tracks, aye, but that be all. Tracks come right out of the mist, they do."

"It's him," the Captain said, scanning the tree line. "The devil boy."

"Think so, do ya?"

"Who else?"

"Ya want we should search the wood?"

The Captain shook his head wistfully. "We've no time this day." He patted his sword. "But mark my word, I shall make a trophy of his head yet."

The line of shadowy figures halted behind the Captain. Peter felt sure every eye was on him. He shuddered and managed to press himself closer to the ground, hoping they couldn't hear the thudding of his heart. Their hunger was insatiable—every day they took more, every day they burned and murdered their way closer to the heart of Avalon. Some boldly wore the bones of the dead around their necks. *How much blood will it take to make them stop? How many more children must die?*

The Captain turned to the line. "Who called a halt?" he shouted. "Move your pockmarked asses. We've much work to do."

The dark figures trudged on; as they passed, Peter caught sight of two large barrels being hauled along. *What's the Captain up to now?* He felt his chest tighten. He glanced back the way he'd come. *I should go back. Should warn them.* He dug his nails into his palm. *No, there's no time. I have to bring more children. Just have to be quick, have to get back before the Captain lays all to waste.*

✦

THE CHILD THIEF slipped from the scrub even before the last Flesh-eater passed. He dashed from one piece of driftwood to the next, broke free from the last bit of cover, and sprinted toward the waves. The Mist rolled up to greet him, seemed to almost dance in anticipation like a dog awaiting a feeding.

Peter's face tightened. *All things come with a price. No one knows that better than I.* He fought to clear his mind, knowing he'd never make it through the Mist otherwise, took a deep breath, and entered the swirling vapor.

The sounds from the beach died in the suffocating silence, even his own thoughts felt muffled. He stood stock-still as he searched for the Path—finding the Path, walking between the worlds, was one of his gifts. "There," he whispered, spotting the tenuous thread of gold sparkles as it drifted across the grayness.

Peter caught up with the Path and followed, moving quickly, and sooner than he would've liked found himself staring at the Nike high-top. He stopped. *Keep moving,* he told himself. *Keep moving or you'll be as dead as the rest of them.* But he heard Nick's words: *"If I'd fallen behind, would I still be out there? Wandering around, screaming your name until I died?"* Peter wondered how long the boy in the high-tops had screamed his name. *The boy?* The child thief laughed at himself, an ugly, contemptuous laugh. The boy had had a *name.* Jonathan. *And Jonathan was among the Sluagh now wasn't he?* Peter thought. "Well what of it?" he whispered bitterly. *Whose fault is that? Am I to blame because he hadn't listened? It's better this way,* he told himself, *better to let the Mist sort them out . . . the weak from the strong.* Peter kicked the high-top. *Everything comes with a price. Everything. Some things just cost more than others.*

Chimes rang from somewhere far away, then muffled laughter and children singing; the Mist began to stir.

55

This got Peter moving, almost running, keeping his eyes forward, keeping to the path.

"It will all end soon," he whispered.

✦

THE SPONGY GROUND gave way to asphalt and the Mist began to thin. The sun could be seen crawling up behind the buildings, and the sounds of the awakening city echoed down the long avenues of South Brooklyn. The Mist slid back into the sea, its swirling, sparkling mass dissipating, leaving Peter standing alone.

The child thief pulled his hood up and headed toward a distant cluster of bleak tenant buildings. A sign, covered in graffiti, proclaimed the complex to be the pride of the Brooklyn City Housing Commission. Peter understood none of the political implications of that sign, but he knew about slums and ghettoes; such squalid, impoverished places had always been fertile hunting grounds. The buildings were larger now, the accents and dress different, but the faces were the same destitute faces of centuries ago: the despair of the forgotten old, and the grim hostility of the futureless young. A breeding ground for troubled youth, sometimes too troubled. But time was short and Avalon needed more children; he would take his chances.

The child thief entered the housing complex through the back alleyways, sticking to the shadows, his keen senses alert for the dispirited and desperate, the abandoned and abused, for the lost child. Because lost children needed someone to trust, needed a friend, and Peter was good at making friends.

He shimmied up a drainpipe and dropped onto a balcony cluttered with garbage bags. He situated himself beneath a rain-sodden sheet of plywood and waited for the boys and girls to come out and play. As he waited, an odor permeated his nostrils, every bit as offensive as the sour rot of the garbage. It was the musky smell of grown-ups: their sweat, their gastric utterances, their dandruff-ridden scalps, greasy pimple-pocked skin, wax-encrusted ears, hemorrhoid-infested rumps. He wrinkled his nose. It hadn't changed since the day he was born—over fourteen hundred years ago.

He could vividly recall that day: the crushing pressure as his watery sanctuary strove to eject him, fighting to remain, a feeling not unlike drowning, sliding from his mother's womb, cold hard hands clamping about his legs and tugging him into the world, the blurry, dazzling brightness, the numbing cold, the shock as someone slapped him across his bottom, the fury and frustration as he wailed at the blurry blob holding him, and their booming laughter.

Then he was wiped down and passed to other hands, gentle, caressing hands that crushed him against warm, milk-swollen bosoms. Someone covered him in a blanket heated by the fireside and he began to suckle. The milk had been sweet, and the woman had begun to hum a soft lullaby. Peter fell into the sweetest sleep he would ever know.

The smells of grown-ups had not been offensive then, not when mixed with the spice of that large, communal roundhouse: the smoky aromas from the great fireplace, salted meats and honey mead, roasted potatoes and boiled cabbage, the musty scent of the two wolfhounds, stale bedding hay, the sharp tang of fresh-cut spruce hanging from the ceiling beams. But what made it all so harmonious to his nostrils was the ever-pervasive smell of his mother, that warm, sweet milk smell that to him would always be the smell of love.

His eyes were amber then, with only the faintest specks of gold, and his ears—though oddly shaped—had yet to develop their pointed tips. Other than a particularly lush head of reddish hair, he looked like any other cupid-faced newborn.

Peter wintered the first several weeks of his life either in his mother's arms or in the great wicker basket by the hearth. His mother's face was lost to him now, but not her grass-green eyes, nor the glow of her bright red hair.

His mother was never far, singing to him while she wove wool and mended tunics with her two golden-haired sisters. He slept away most of his day, dreamily watching his large family go about their daily routines: the two men and oldest boy leaving before dawn to hunt, the younger boys tending the sheep and gathering wood, the old bent man and his old bent wife going about their chores as long as the daylight would allow. At sunset the hunters would return, and with the thick stone walls between them and the winter wind, the family would gather around the rough-hewn oak table for their evening meal.

Day after day, Peter lay there watching and listening. Before long, he could make out words, then whole sentences. When he was three weeks old, he understood most everything said around him.

Each night, before dinner, his mother would nurse him, wrap him in his blanket, and leave him in the large basket near the hearth to sleep while the family ate. But Peter didn't sleep; he watched and listened as they laughed and joked, cursed and argued, encouraged and consoled, as they shared the good and the bad of their days. And when they would laugh, he would smile, and the tiny specks of gold in his eyes would sparkle, for the sound of their mirth was a sweet song to his ears.

One night, on the evening of his seventh week in the world, Peter decided he was done just watching, that he wished to join in. So he kicked his legs free of the blanket, sat up, and climbed over the side of his basket. His legs gave out from under him and he landed on his bare bottom with a solid thump. *What's wrong with my legs,* he wondered; it had never dawned on him that he couldn't yet walk. Everyone else could. He pulled up onto wobbly legs and steadied himself on the rim of the basket. He looked out across the room. Suddenly the table seemed a long way off.

He took a tentative step, fell, pulled himself up and tried again. This time he didn't fall. He took another step, another, then let go of the basket and began to waddle his way across the room. By the sixth and seventh step he was toddling toward the table, his face rapt in concentration.

The old man spotted him first. His jaw hung open in mid-chew and a clump of potato rolled out of his mouth and bounced off the table. The old lady frowned and swatted the old man. He let out a cry and jabbed a bony finger at Peter.

They all turned in time to see the naked infant stroll up to the table.

Peter, delighted to have his family's full attention, put his small, chubby hands on his hips and grinned boldly—the gold flecks in his eyes now positively gleaming. When no one spoke, when no one did more than let out a high-pitched wheeze, Peter asked, "Can I join you?" But this being the first time he'd put words together, it came out more like "an I oin ouu?"

He frowned at the odd sound of his own voice. The words hadn't come out right and the alarmed and astonished looks confronting him confirmed this. His tiny brow furrowed and he tried again. "Can I join you?" he said, much clearer. Then, with confidence, he said, "Can I join you? Can I?"

He looked expectantly from face to face. *Surely that was right?* Yet still they stared at him with those wide, startled eyes. *If anything,* he thought, *they look more alarmed than before—angry even.* His smile faltered and all at once he needed his mother, needed her badly, needed the reassurance that only her soft bosom and warm arms could provide. He put his arms out and took a step toward her. "Mama," he called.

His mother stood up, knocking her chair over, her hands clutched at her mouth.

59

Peter stopped. "Mama?"

Fear—it was on all their faces. But there was more than fear on his mother's face. Her eyes glared at him, as though accusing him of some horrible deed. *What did I do?* Peter wondered. *What did I do?*

The old lady leaped up, brandishing a large wooden spoon. "*CHANGE-LING!*" she cried. "*GET IT OUT OF HERE!*"

"*NO!*" his mother cried. She shook her head. "He's no changeling! It's *HIS* baby. The one from the woods." She looked around at them, her eyes wild and desperate. "Now, do you see? Now do you believe?"

No one was listening to her; all their eyes were on Peter.

"*KEEP IT AWAY FROM THE CHILDREN!*" the old woman cried.

The old man herded the younger children away from the table, pushing them to the back of the room as far away from Peter as he could.

Peter's mother grabbed the old woman's sleeve. "Stop it! Stop it! Peter's no changeling, Mama. I wasn't lying. He took me—the forest spirit." She pointed at Peter. "The forest spirit gave me that child."

The old woman stared at Peter's mother in horror. "No, child, don't speak of it. Never speak of it." She shook her daughter. "It is not yours. Do you understand me? It's a changeling." The old woman glared at Peter. "*ASGER, GET IT OUT OF HERE BEFORE IT HEXES US ALL!*"

One of the men pulled the long meat fork from out of the ham, the oldest boy grabbed the broom, and together they moved toward Peter.

Through a blur of tears Peter saw them coming for him; the man that he'd thought of as *papa* jabbed the fork while the boy circled around him.

Peter took a step back.

"*CATCH IT!*" the old woman howled. "Don't let it get away!"

The broom slapped Peter from behind, knocking him to the gritty dirt floor. The boy pressed the broom onto Peter to hold him, the sharp twigs digging and poking into Peter's soft skin.

"Don't spill its blood in the house!" the old woman yelled. "Or there will be sickness upon us all. Take it into the forest. Leave it for the beasts."

Hard, rough hands held him as the man corded prickly twine about his limbs, the twine bit into his skin, binding his arms to his body and his legs together.

As the man and boy donned boots and furs, the old woman brought Peter's basket and blanket. "Take anything that it has soiled. I will get the grease." She poured warm grease from the ham into a pot and brought it over.

The door was pulled open and a biting winter wind blew in. They took Peter outside into the night. Peter got one last look at his mother. She was on the floor, sobbing, her two sisters kneeling beside her, holding her.

"Mama," Peter cried. She didn't look up. The door shut.

The old woman poured the warm grease all over Peter. It stung his eyes, soaked into the blanket and quickly congealed into a cold paste on his skin. "It will make things go quicker," the old woman told them. "Now take the creature far into the woods and leave it."

The old woman gave the man a wad of wool. "Put this in your ears. No matter what it says, remember, that wicked thing is not of your loins."

Both the man and boy held a torch. They threaded the broom through the handle of the basket and each carried an end. They marched off down the icy trail, the old woman watching them go from the door stoop.

The cold bit at the infant's tiny nose. "Papa," Peter called. "Papa, please. I'll be good. I promise. I'll be good. Papa? Please, Papa. Papa?" But no matter how Peter pleaded, the man wouldn't look at him.

The man and the boy marched steadily, their mouths set tight, neither spoke as they tracked deeper and deeper into the dark, frigid forest.

Peter had no real idea how much time passed, but when they finally stopped, the moon was peeking down at him from high in the cloudy sky. They set him in a clearing surrounded by high shrub and an outcropping of crumbling rocks, then left in a hurry without a single look back.

Peter watched the tree limbs waving to the moon. Thick clouds tumbled in and the shadows wove together. He struggled to free himself, but the bindings were too tight. His fingers and toes grew numb and the cold became unbearable. Peter shook all over. "Mama," he called. "Mama." Over and over he called her name. His mother never came but something else did. Peter heard a loud sniffing and fell quiet.

A large shadow emerged from the bush. Its shape reminded him of the hounds back at the house. The dim moonlight glinted off the beast's black eyes as it sniffed the air. Peter sensed the beast's hunger. He tried not to make any sounds, but couldn't help whimpering as the wolf slowly circled in on him.

The wolf bit one end of the blanket and tugged, tipping the basket over and spilling the infant out onto the frozen ground. Now fully exposed to the winter air, Peter began to wail. The wolf licked away the grease from the blanket, then moved to Peter.

It shoved its snout into his face, licking the grease from his cheeks, neck, and along his belly, then clamped its jaws on Peter's leg and began to drag him into the bush. Peter yowled, but the wolf only clamped down tighter. There came a clatter from the rocks. The wolf let go of Peter and jerked its head up, ears alert.

"A-yuk," came a gruff, gravelly voice.

There, on the flat outcropping of stone, stood a man. Only it wasn't a man, really, as he couldn't have stood much higher than the wolf's shoulder. He was short in the legs, long in the arms, and solid through the chest and shoulders. His head was large, out of proportion, and grew straight from his shoulders. His skin was gray and gritty like the earth itself. He wore a patchwork of mangy animal furs, covered in dirt and alive with moss. His eyes were no more than black specks set deep beneath his protrusive brow. He saw Peter and grinned, exposing black gums and a sharp underbite of twisted teeth.

The wolf's fur bristled, and a mean growl rumbled up from deep within its throat.

The moss man hopped off the rock and into the clearing. *"GO!"* he yelled and clapped his hands together.

The wolf dropped its head, peeled back its lips, displaying an arsenal of long, dangerous teeth, and snarled. The moss man let loose a snarl of his own and before Peter could blink, charged and leaped upon the wolf. He wrestled a hold about the beast's mane, then bit into its ear, snarling and jerking his head side to side until he tore the wolf's ear completely off.

The wolf howled, kicked, and spun.

The moss man let go and sent the animal yelping away into the bushes with a solid kick to the hindquarters. He spat the ear onto the ground and stared at Peter while licking the blood from his lips. "A baby," he said, then picked up a twig and poked Peter. "Make good stew. A-yuk." His speech came out slow and staggered, like words were unnatural for him.

"Please don't eat me," Peter pleaded. "Please. I'll be good."

The moss man's brow rose with surprise then drew together suspiciously. "Baby can talk?" He crouched down, stuck his wide, flat nose into the crook of Peter's neck, and sniffed deeply. Up close Peter could see all manner of bugs and worms crawling around in the man's hair. The moss man looked puzzled. He wiped his finger through the bloody bite marks on Peter's leg and dabbed the blood to the tip of his tongue. The moss man's beady eyes grew round and he spat into the dirt. "Faerie blood!" he sneered. "Faerie blood is bad. Very bad!" His shoulders slumped, his face grew glum. "Can't eat baby."

The moss man bent and picked up the wolf's ear, stuck the bloody end in his mouth, and started away.

For a second, Peter was relieved to see him go, then the bite of the cold reminded him that he was tied up, naked, and there was a hungry wolf nearby. *"WAIT!"* he cried. "Don't leave me here!"

The moss man kept walking.

"PLEASE!" Peter screamed. *"PLEASE STOP! PLEASE!"* Peter's screams turned to sobs. "Please don't go."

The moss man turned around. He looked at Peter and scratched his chin. Finally, after a long minute, he asked, "Can you catch spiders?"

"What?" Peter asked.

"Can you catch spiders? Lot of spiders in cave. Hate spiders. A-yuk."

Peter didn't want to go near any spiders, but he certainly didn't want to be left in the woods either. He nodded. "Yes. I can catch spiders."

The moss man considered while Peter shivered. Finally, he grunted, shuffled back, and untied the infant. "No more crying. Hate crying. You follow. Keep up or wolf get you."

Peter crawled to his feet. He could barely stand, his feet were so numb. The moss man took off at a hearty pace and Peter tried to follow but fell after only a few steps. The frozen ground bit into his knees and hands and he let out a cry. He got up and tried again, but the ice cut into the bottom of his tender feet. After only a dozen steps he fell again. He tried crawling, but the pain was too much. He stopped. He could no longer see the moss man. It was dark, it was cold, he was lost, his knees were bleeding, he was naked and freezing to death, and there was a wolf somewhere nearby. Peter began to cry.

The moss man reappeared, glaring at Peter with his small, dark eyes. His nose wrinkled up in disgust. "No crying. Hate crying."

Peter tried to stop, but couldn't. Instead he began to bawl openly and loudly.

The man put his hands over his ears. "Stop that," he groaned and started away. He made about six strides then stopped. He looked back at Peter, brows drawn together. Finally he let out a great sigh and strolled back to the infant. "Okay. Okay. I not leave. Now stop crying."

Peter continued to wail.

The moss man pointed to the hill behind him. "Goll's hill." He thumbed his chest. "Goll."

Peter wiped his nose with the back of his arm and fought back the tears. "I'm Peter," he said between big, hitching breaths.

Goll hunkered down. "Come, Peter. Climb up."

Peter climbed onto the man's back, got a firm hold on the man's hair, and clung tight as the moss man got to his feet.

Goll handed Peter the wolf's ear. "Here, for you." He wrapped Peter's feet in his large, warm hands and away they went, following the icy trail up the hill while Peter chewed on the wolf's ear.

They came to a dark hollow dug into a ledge; to Peter it looked like little more than a hole. Dirty straw, tuffs of greasy fur, and gnawed bones littered the worn earthen entrance. Shoes hung across the entranceway, sandals and boots, about a dozen all together: small shoes—children's shoes.

Goll set Peter down and grinned. "Goll's home. Very warm. Very nice."

"JUST WHERE THE fuck you been?"

Recalled to the present, the child thief started. He glanced over his shoulder into the apartment. There was a light on now and through the thin, sagging curtain he saw a grotesquely large woman standing in her bra and panties, hands on hips. She was addressing the man leaning against the open front door.

It was raining, a light drizzle that turned the gray public housing to the color of mud.

"I asked you a question," the woman continued, her voice rising. "I said, just where da fuck has your ass been all night?"

The man shrugged. He didn't come in.

"How come your shirt's inside out, Germaine? Huh? How come?"

Germaine looked down at his shirt, then back up at the woman and shrugged again.

"You been with that bitch again. Ain't you?"

The man didn't answer.

"Don't give me that look," she shrieked. "You know who I'm talking about!" The woman snatched a bottle off a TV tray and pointed it at the man.

"Woman," the man said, his speech slurred. "You need to calm down. It ain't like—"

"Goddamn you, Germaine! *GODDAMN YOU!*" She threw the bottle. It exploded against the door right next to the man's head. Then she was slapping him.

The man shoved her away. "You need to back off, bitch! You need to just back—"

She came at him again and this time he punched her hard in the stomach, hard enough to knock her into the living room and onto the floor.

The woman lay there, making a dreadful sound, like someone choking to death.

"*CRAZY BITCH!*" the man shouted. "*CRAZY FUCKING BITCH!*" He slammed the door and was gone.

The woman didn't get up. She just lay there clutching her stomach and bawling.

Peter had had enough. He hopped down from the balcony; keeping his head low, he walked the buildings, his golden eyes peeping out from beneath his hood, scanning the courtyards, the playgrounds. His thoughts kept returning to the Captain, the barrels. Time was running out; he had to find a child today.

Chapter Five

Devils

✦

Light droplets of warm rain sprinkled down onto Nick's face. He could feel the wetness running into his eyes, his mouth, his hair, pulling him out from the depths of sleep. Nick wiped his face, forced himself awake, and blinked up into the faint, misty morning glow.

Three tiny blue people, no bigger than mice, were peeing on him.

"What the fuck," Nick cried. He sat up fast and rammed his head against the top of his cage. *Cage?* He spat repeatedly, trying to rid his mouth of the salty-sour taste. What the hell was he doing in a cage? He shook his head and wiped the pee out of his eyes, then spat some more.

There were at least two dozen of them staring down at him, some no bigger than grasshoppers, others closer to the size of rats—thin, spindly, humanlike creatures with silky insect wings and sharp whip tails. They were nude, their skin a deep sapphire blue, with wild manes of black or blue hair running down their backs.

Peter had said something about faeries, and pixies, and goblins. Of course Peter had said a lot of nutty things. Were these pixies? It really didn't matter to Nick at the moment; he was more concerned with the way these creatures were looking at him, like he'd be good to eat.

"Shoo," he whispered.

They continued to stare at him with their cruel, unblinking eyes.

"Shoo," he said louder, waving his hand at them.

They hissed and bared needle-sharp teeth.

"Skat!" Nick said and swatted at the top of the cage.

They leaped up as one, the air suddenly alive with the humming of wings. Hovering, they shrieked at him like feral cats.

Nick slid as far away from them as he could get. He grabbed a handful of straw from the bottom of his cage and threw it at them. Startled, a small brown mouse darted out from beneath his cage, bounding across the stone floor.

The pixies were at it in a flash. The mouse let out a skin-crawling squeal as they pounced. Fur, flesh, and blood spattered the stones, a dog pile of snarling frenzied blue bodies as they fought viciously over the choicest bits.

"Christ," Nick whispered, clutching his hands to his chest. "I gotta get out of here." He glanced about the gloom and noticed there were at least a dozen kid-sized cages stacked against one wall. Like his, they were built from branches and twine. Many were covered in raggedy tarps looking for all the world like rotting corpses of beasts. A cluster of spears leaned against one another, teepee-style, and in their center—Nick swallowed—a human skull.

A sharp clack came from somewhere behind him.

The pixies stopped fighting and stood up, their faces alert, heads flicking about as they searched the darkness.

A soft thud followed by a long, low growl slid out of the shadows and the pixies zipped up and away, leaving Nick alone. Nick found himself wishing they'd stayed, anything but to be alone in a cage, in the gloom, with whatever had made that noise.

Another creak; this one closer. Pushing his face against the bars, Nick strained to see into the shadows. He made out a twisting pillar of roots that disappeared into the darkness above. Nick noted a shadow hunched next to the roots, and the shadow—it was *moving*! It rocked back and forth then darted away.

"Oh, crap." *What was that?*

The room grew brighter and the fog began to thin. He could now make out objects hanging from the walls. Nick blinked. Knives with wicked curved blades hung in rows. Alongside were spiked clubs and an assortment of jagged-edged hatchets. Instruments designed to rend and maim, and they all looked well used. Hanging above the weapons were three skulls tied together in a pyramid. Their leathery, wormholed flesh stretched across silent screams. A pair of leg bones set in a cross hung below, forming a triptych of Jolly Rogers.

Gotta get out of here now! He pushed on the cage; it didn't open. He noticed the front was tied with leather straps. He frantically tugged at the ties. A low hiss came from Nick's left. He jerked about in time to see *something* skittered by on all fours. Nick gave up on the ties, no longer wanting out, only hoping the bars would keep him safe from whatever was out there.

"God, get me out of here," he whimpered.

The fog continued to lift and he could now see all manner of spears and swords hanging from the walls. He noticed a huge fireplace, easily big enough for three grown men to stand in. Several cooking pots—*kid-size* cooking pots—hung from greasy black chains. Then he saw the *bodies*. He could just make out their limp, lifeless forms hanging on the far side of the chamber. How many were there? Four? Five maybe? They looked to be children.

Oh good God, Nick's mind screamed at him. *Just what kind of place is this?*

Low howls issued from the shadows all around him. Something grunted, like a pig, then snorted, then snickered. Giggles broke out. They sounded like children, strange and wicked. Nick knew he would lose it if they didn't stop.

A clump of shadows crept into the light and all the air left Nick's lungs. They were human, but barely, their bodies gangly and spidery. Child-like in their proportions, but a bit off, as though they'd been stretched. Large, round spots and long streaks of body paint ran along their legs and arms. Their muscles gleamed in the dim light, lean and wiry. Some wore hides, matted and mangy, festooned with bones, tusks and twigs, their ankles and wrists layered in bracelets of leather and twine. Their faces were hidden beneath devilish masks of hide and hair, feathers and antlers.

They closed in on him, dancing about with quick epileptic movements. They surrounded the cage and peered in with wild, crazy golden eyes, eyes just like Peter's. Nick now understood that Peter had indeed played him. The pointy-eared boy had tricked him so that these things could . . .

could *what?* Nick glanced at the long knives, at their hungry eyes.

"WHAT DO YOU WANT?" Nick shouted, his voice quivering.

They answered by rolling their eyes around, like victims of delirium, by grinning wide, toothy grins and clacking their teeth together, clacking and clacking and clacking; the sound was deafening in the silence of the room.

No, no, no, Nick thought. *No more, please.*

Nick withdrew within himself then, just like in the mist. He had no desire to watch his own death, but if he had to, he wanted to be in the very back row with his hands over his eyes.

They untied his cage and dragged him out, strong, cruel fingers pinching into his flesh. Someone put a necklace made of bone and teeth, fingers and ears—*human fingers and ears*—around his neck. They pulled him over to the pillar and began to dance around him in circles, wrapping him in twine, all the while giggling and flicking their tongues at him, rolling their eyes and clacking their teeth. He wanted them to go ahead and kill him, anything to stop that awful clacking.

There came a clang from somewhere far off. The demon spawn, the monster children, or whatever they were, stopped in their tracks. They fell silent.

The mist was all but gone now and morning light filtered in from several angular windows. The extent of the circular chamber gradually materialized out of the gloom. The walls were a mix of rough-hewn stone and natural cave formation. Nick could clearly see a red door surrounded by giant roots, roots as thick as barrels. Nick couldn't imagine what size tree could have roots that big. He tried to see the top but it disappeared into the roof of the chamber.

The demon spawn were all staring at the red door. One of them spoke, his voice hushed. "The Devil Beast comes."

"Comes to break bones and chew marrow," said another.

Several answered in anxious whispers: "We shall all eat soon."

They spread out, forming a wide circle, and began to smack their closed fists into their open palms.

Fear sharpened Nick's senses and he became acutely aware that the air smelled of stale sweat, boiled meat, wet leaves, and beetles. He studied the red door. Could there really be something coming to cook and eat him? He didn't want to believe it. Yet he found his eyes straying to the knives and hatchets, the dark stains saturating the dirt, the child-size pots hanging in the fireplace. He couldn't get the thought of the hanging bodies out of his head. *I don't want to die,* he thought and realized he was crying.

Bells jangled behind the red door, louder and louder. Then it stopped. There came the clack of a bolt being thrown and the door swung slowly inward.

A monster stood in the doorway, a head taller than the other creatures, draped in hides and wearing a mask of bone and fur. A pair of goat horns twisted out from either side of its head and a tangle of coarse hair was captured in a thick braid that ran down the length of its back. And all of it, skin, mask, fur, horns, was covered in cracking red paint. It carried a short club with one long jagged hook protruding from its end.

It locked its eyes on Nick, raised the club, and let loose a loud snort.

"Oh no!" Nick cried. *"No! No! No!"* He jerked wildly at his bindings, tugging and pulling until he freed his arms. He yanked down the twine around his waist and legs, stumbled to the ground as he tore his feet free. Nick rolled to his feet, glanced back, saw the Devil Beast coming for him, and ran. He tried to break out of the ring of creatures, to barrel right through them, but they grabbed him and shoved him back.

The Devil Beast caught Nick across his face with an open palm. Pain exploded in Nick's head and he went sprawling to the stones. He crumpled into a ball and lay there clutching his head. *It's over,* Nick thought. *I'm dead.*

The Devil came for him, driving a hard kick into Nick's upper thigh. Nick screamed, saw a foot coming for his face, and managed to move. The kick caught his shoulder and sent him tumbling.

"STOP IT!" Nick screamed.

71

The Devil tromped after him, raising the club with its wicked hook above his head. Nick sprung out of the way. The club hit the stones, getting knocked loose from the Devil Beast's grasp and bouncing across the floor to the middle of the ring. Nick jumped up, limping away, trying to keep some distance between himself and his tormentor.

The Devil leaped forward, catching Nick by the arm, spun him around, and backhanded him across the face.

Searing pain and white-hot light sent Nick reeling, fighting to keep his feet. And still the Devil came.

Nick tasted blood, touched his lip, and was shocked by the amount of blood on his hand. *"WHAT DO YOU WANT?"* Nick screamed, as though he didn't know, as though he expected anything other than being brutally beaten to death.

The Devil just continued to track him around and around, giving no answers, a predator intent on its prey.

"WHAT?" Nick screamed. *"WHAT?"* Nick spotted the hooked club lying in the center of the ring. His eyes shot back and forth between the hook and the Devil.

The Devil stopped and stared at him.

Nick dove for it, snatching the hook up off the stones. The weight of it surprised him and he almost dropped it. He held it in both hands and pointed the wicked hook at the Devil. *"C'MON!"* Nick cried, blood and spit flying from his lips. *"C'MON YOU MOTHERFUCKER!"*

The Devil just stood there.

"C'MON!" Nick screamed, the club shaking as his arms quivered.

The creatures around him began to chant, "Blood, blood, blood," on and on until Nick thought he would go mad.

"Enough!" He let out a howl and rushed the Devil, bringing the hook around in a wide overhand swing, intent on sinking it deep into the Devil's skull.

At the last possible second, the Devil caught Nick's arm at the wrist and wrung the club away. The weapon bounced off the stones with a loud clank and the chamber fell silent.

"Good," the Devil said and pushed his mask back.

Nick found himself looking not at a beast, but a boy.

The boy smiled at Nick. "You did good." He clasped Nick's hand in his own and raised it up. *"NEW BLOOD FOR DEVILTREE!"* he shouted, then threw his head back and howled.

The creatures joined in, howling and beating the floor; the entire chamber rung with their fervor. They slid off their masks and now Nick could plainly see that beneath the wild hair and body paint, they were just a bunch of stupid-ass kids.

He caught sight of the blue pixies leaping up and down among the rafters, mimicking the boys like little blue monkeys, adding their feral shrieks to the cacophony. The whole chamber rung with hooting, braying, and cackling. The world seemed a spinning kaleidoscope of insanity, and Nick knew that he'd gone stark raving mad.

Chapter Six

Wolf

The child thief sat on a bench near the playground. Buildings loomed over him on all five sides of the large courtyard. As morning pushed into noon, the beehive of apartments began to wake up. He scanned the balconies, alert for any sign of wayward youth, but mostly found himself confronted with the same tired, hungover faces of the adults. They congregated in small clusters, lounging listlessly about the balconies, often with their apartment doors propped open and stereos blasting out into the courtyard. There was laughter here and there, but for the most part it sounded mean. Many of the people just stared blankly, their eyes glazed over, reminding Peter of the dead in the Mist.

A gleeful squeal caught Peter's ear, followed by a burst of spirited laughter that drew him like candy.

A few younger kids had braved the drizzle to slip down the slide and climb the monkey bars. They formed teams and began an energetic game of tag.

The child thief watched them, smiling. Here, among so much drudgery—oblivious to the profane graffiti marring every available surface—these children could find joy. *They can always find joy,* he thought, *because they still have their magic.*

Peter found himself wanting nothing more than to run and play with them, the same deep desire he had when he first came across children all those long years ago. Only things hadn't gone so well then. His smile faded. *No, that had been a day of hard lessons.*

✦

HE WAS SIX years old by then, slipping silently through the woods in his raccoon pelt. It flapped out behind him like a cape, the long striped tail bouncing in rhythm with his stride. He wore the head pulled over his face, like a hood, and his gold-flecked eyes peered out from the raccoon mask, scanning the woods, searching for game. It was spring, so he wore only a loincloth and rawhide boots beneath his coon skin. He carried a spear in each hand and a flint knife tucked into his belt. His body was painted with berry juice and mud to disguise his scent. Goll had taught him that, as well as the importance of always carrying two spears: a light one for game and a stouter one for protection against the larger beasts in the forest.

Peter placed a handful of walnuts in the center of a clearing, then ducked beneath a tall cluster of bushes. When he spied two brown squirrels in a nearby tree, he cupped his hands and mimicked a turkey foraging. Goll had taught him this trick too, that it was better to mimic an animal other than the one you were hunting, because rarely could you fool an animal with its own call, and nothing brought game quicker than the sound of other animals feeding.

Sure enough, both squirrels scurried his way. Peter slowly set the larger spear down and hoisted the light spear to his shoulder. The squirrels saw the nuts, saw each other, and raced for the prize.

Peter stood and threw. The spear hit its mark, leaving one squirrel behind as the other raced away, chattering angrily at Peter.

Peter whooped and leaped up. *No spider soup for me,* he thought. *To-night I get squirrel stew.*

A wolf trotted into the clearing and stood between Peter and his prize. The wolf had only one ear.

Peter froze.

The beast locked its dark eyes on Peter. Its lips peeled back as though it were actually grinning.

Peter snatched up his heavy spear and thrust it out before him. "No," Peter said. "Not this time."

A low growl rumbled from the wolf's throat.

Peter held his ground. The wolf had plagued him relentlessly over the last several months. Every time Peter made a kill, the wolf showed up and stole his meal. Peter was tired of spider soup. Today he would keep his prize.

The wolf's eyes laughed at Peter, taunting the boy, daring him, as though it would like nothing better than to tear his throat open.

Peter swallowed loudly, his mouth suddenly dry. Goll had told him there was only one way to master the wolf: to attack it head-on. "Wolf is hunter," he'd said. "When you hunt wolf, wolf get mixed up. No know what to do. Then you beat wolf. You will see. Show fear," Goll had laughed. "Then wolf will eat you. A-yuk."

Now, Peter told himself. *Rush in. Stab it through the heart.*

The wolf lowered its head and began to slowly circle the boy. Peter knew what the wolf was up to, they'd played out this dance many times. The wolf was trying to cut off his retreat, trying to get between him and the nearest tree. Peter knew if he took his eyes off the wolf, even for a second, it would attack.

The wolf let loose a loud snarl.

Peter glanced toward the tree.

The wolf charged.

Peter yelped, dropped his spear, and ran. Fortunately, even at six, Peter was as fleet and agile as a squirrel. He dashed across the clearing and leaped for the tree, catching a low branch, then swung up. There came a loud clack of teeth and a sharp tug that almost pulled him from the branch. Peter scampered up a few more limbs before daring a glance below.

There, looking up at him, was the wolf, the raccoon tail dangling from its jaws.

The wolf circled the tree a few times, then trotted over to the dead squirrel.

Peter watched from his small, uncomfortable perch as the wolf devoured *his* dinner.

When the wolf was finished, it curled up beneath the tree and went to sleep.

As the long day slowly passed, Peter did his best to keep his legs from falling asleep and himself from falling out of the tree. By dusk, his whole body was numb and he had resigned himself to a miserable night.

"Well, look there," called a gritty voice. "A Peterbird."

Both Peter and the wolf looked up. Goll appeared above them on a short ledge.

Goll glanced at the wolf, what was left of the squirrel, then back up at Peter. He grinned. "You feed old one-ear again? A-yuk."

Peter's face colored and he looked away.

Goll laughed.

Goll leaped down from the stones and strolled through the underbrush toward the clearing. The wolf, knowing the routine, simply gave Goll a disdainful look and loped off.

Peter dropped from the tree, retrieved his spears, and slunk over to Goll.

Goll held up a large rabbit. "Goll will eat good tonight." He nudged the remains of the squirrel with his toe. "Look like Peter get spider soup again. A-yuk."

Peter's shoulders slumped. "Ah, Goll. C'mon."

"You want to eat good. You must hunt good."

Peter kicked at the scraps of squirrel fur and followed Goll glumly back to the cave.

PETER DIPPED HIS spoon into the bowlful of dark, soupy muck. He raised it to eye level and looked from the clot of soggy spider legs over to the half-eaten rabbit in Goll's hand. The aroma of the roasted meat filled the entire cave. Goll licked the grease off his fingers, smacking loudly as he grumbled contentedly.

"Please?" Peter asked.

Goll shook his head.

"Just a few bites?"

"You know rule. You eat what you kill. You want rabbit, you kill own rabbit. A-yuk."

"How am I supposed to do that with that stupid wolf following me?"

"You need kill wolf."

Peter was quiet for a long time. "Goll, will you kill the wolf? Please?"

Goll shook his head. "Not hunting me."

Peter let out a sigh and sat his bowl down. He stood up, walked to the cave entrance, and looked out into the night. He could see the stars twinkling through the spring leaves. He thought of his mother; sometimes he could close his eyes and actually smell her hair. He wondered what they were eating back in the great house, wondered why they'd left him for the beasts. He slapped one of the boots hanging across the entranceway, watched it swing, and wondered what the child had been like who had worn it, if that child had been left in the woods by its family.

"Goll?"

"A-yuk."

"Whose shoes are these?"

"Little boys. Little girls."

"Why do you have their shoes?"

"Must take them off before you can eat them."

"Eat them?" Then he understood. "The *children*?"

"A-yuk."

"You *eat* children?"

"Only when I can catch them."

Peter stared silently at the shoes. "I don't think I would like to eat children."

"You would like. Very tender. Very juicy. Much better than spider soup."

"Where do children come from?"

"From village."

"Where's the village?"

"*NO!* No speak of village. You never go near village. Men are there. Men very bad. *Very* dangerous."

"More dangerous than the wolf?"

"Yes. Very more dangerous."

Peter tapped the shoe again. It would be nice to have another kid around. "Goll, if you catch another one, can I keep it? We could build a cage for it. Okay?"

Goll cocked his head at Peter. "Peter, you very strange. You stay away from village."

Peter came and sat back down next to the fire.

He looked at the hind leg of the rabbit in Goll's bowl, then up at Goll, and smacked his lips.

"No begging. Hate begging."

Peter stuck out his lower lip.

Goll rolled his eyes and frowned. "Here," he grunted. "Take it." Goll slid the bowl over to Peter, watched the boy devour the rabbit leg. After a bit, a smile pricked at the corners of the moss-man's mouth. He shook his head, then crawled beneath his furs and went to sleep.

Peter finished the rabbit, lay back, enjoying the warmth of the meat in his belly. His eyes grew heavy. *Sure would be nice to have another kid to play with,* he thought. *I could teach it to hunt and*— Another thought came to Peter. *Why, together we could kill that mean old wolf.* Peter found he was now wide awake. *I bet I could catch one. Why, I know I could.*

✦

PETER WATCHED THE men through a knot of berry bushes. He'd set off before daybreak in search of the village, venturing far south of Goll's hill, farther than he had ever dared before, and had come across a road, and not long thereafter heard horses. He'd trailed them most of the morning and they now stood drinking at a stream. Four men stretched their legs beside the horses, stout figures with thick braided mustaches and full growths of beard, brass rings in their ears, wearing leather breeches and woolspun tunics. Three of them had great long swords strapped to broad, bronze-studded belts. The fourth man wore hides and carried a double-bladed ax.

After living with Goll so long, he thought these men to be fearsome and giant. Peter understood why Goll was so afraid of them.

There was also a wide-faced, solid woman with flaxen hair that ran down her chest in thick braids. She wore a long dress and, atop her broad hips, a wide belt adorned with swirling brass hoops. But it was the children that captivated Peter. He pushed the hood of his raccoon pelt back to get a better look. There were three of them: two boys about his age and a girl who looked a couple years younger. The boys wore only britches and sandals, the girl a bright red dress. Peter watched mesmerized as they chased each other round and round, leaping over logs and skipping through the stream.

One boy would tag the other and the chase would start anew. The little girl chased both of them, shouting for them to let her play until they finally got after her, their faces twisted up and their hands clutching the air like claws. The girl went screaming to her mother, leaving the two boys falling over themselves with laughter. Peter caught himself laughing along with them, and had to cover his mouth. It looked like fun. *They could play that game at Goll's hill,* Peter thought, and now, more than ever, he wanted to catch one.

He eyed the men, wondering how to grab a child with them so near, decided he needed to be closer, and slipped up from tree to tree.

One of the boys came bounding into the woods, sprang over a bush, ducked around the tree, and came face to face with Peter. Both boys were so surprised that neither knew what to do.

The boy cocked his head to the side and gave Peter a queer look. "Are you a wood elf?"

"No. I'm a Peter."

"Well then I'm *a* Edwin. Want to play?"

Oh, yes indeed, Peter thought, nodded, and gave the boy a broad grin. He started to grab the boy when the girl rounded the tree. She saw Peter's raccoon cape, the red and purple body paint, let out an ear-piercing shriek, and took off.

"Edwin," bellowed one of the men. "Come back here."

Peter heard heavy boots tromping his way and ducked back into the woods.

The man came around the tree and glared at the boy. "I told you to stay close." The man scanned the trees. "There are wild things in these hills. Nasty boogies that live in holes. They steal little boys like you. And do you know what they do with them?"

The boy shook his head.

"They make stew out of their livers and shoes out of their hides. Now come along. We've much ground to cover by dark."

PETER ARRIVED AT the village well after dark. His feet and legs ached, his stomach growled. But he ignored his body's grumblings, there was only one thing on his mind—the *boy*.

He waited in the trees until the men finished putting away the beasts, until there was no one moving in the night but him. There were a dozen roundhouses similar to the one he'd been born in, plus a sprawling stable. These were built around a large square. Pigs grunted, and chickens clucked in a pen somewhere.

Peter slipped silently in among the structures, feeling exposed out among the buildings, sure he was being watched, that the huge, brutish men were waiting for him around every corner. He pulled out his flint knife and ducked from shadow to shadow, sniffing, alert to the slightest sound. He wrinkled his nose; the village stank of beasts, sour sweat, and human waste. Peter wondered why anyone would want to live here instead of in the woods.

He pushed up against the boy's house, sliding his back along the rough stone and sod wall, creeping up to a small, round window. Dogs began barking from inside and Peter's heart drummed in his chest. A deep, gruff voice quieted the dogs. Peter tried to peek in the window, but the heavy shutters were closed and locked tight. He plucked at the mud between the slats with his knife until a thin beam of light appeared. Peter peered in.

The room looked for all the world as his home had when he was an infant: the large hearth, the kettles and pots, the spruce hanging from the rafters. The whole family was seated around the table, passing bowls of potatoes and cabbage, the boys giggling and carrying on.

Peter inhaled, and the rich smell of smoked meat and baked bread brought memories of his own family flooding vividly back to him. An overwhelming longing hit him so hard that his legs gave way and he slid down the wall and sat in the dirt. He hugged his legs as his eyes welled up. He shut them tight and hot tears rolled down his cheeks. "Mama," he whispered. Her laugh, her broad smile, her sweet smell, all of it felt so close, as though he could just walk into this house and she'd be there— would call him to her, would crush him against her warm bosom and sing him lullabies. Peter ground his teeth together and wiped angrily at his tears. He knew very well what would happen if he knocked on this door.

A gale of laughter escaped through the window, not just the boys', but the whole family, all of them laughing together. Peter glared into the night. The laughter continued, pricking at him. He jabbed his knife into the dirt. "Who cares?" he whispered through clenched teeth. "Who wants to be stuck in a stupid stinky house, with mean stupid grown-ups anyhow?"

His stomach growled and he stood up. He made his way toward the stable, seeking out the henhouse. *Maybe I'll burn their house down. Then they'll know how it is to be out in the cold.*

He found the henhouse, silently slid over the latch, and slipped in. A few hens raised their heads, clucked, and eyed him suspiciously. Peter waited for them to settle, then helped himself to all the eggs he could find. He spied several burlap sacks heaped in the corner, picked one up, and measured it against himself. *About right.* He left the coup, prowled the stable until he found some rope and a bludgeon. He held the short, stout piece of wood out, tested its weight. He hoped he wouldn't need it, but brought it along anyway, just in case, because he'd never stolen a child before and thought a good, stout stick might just be in order.

He hid the stash behind a giant oak tree that stood on the edge of a field. He climbed up into the oak to sleep, but sleep didn't come easy. *Tomorrow,* he thought. *Going to catch me a Edwin.*

✦

PETER AWOKE TO the rooster's crow. He sat up, inhaled the brisk morning air, and wondered if the boy was about yet. He hopped down from the tree. The sun was just peeping over the rise, and a fine mist covered the freshly turned earth in the nearby fields. He relieved himself, then crouched next to the oak, watching, waiting. He didn't have a plan, not yet, not beyond getting Edwin to come behind the tree so that he could put him in that sack.

Men, women, and older children came out and began to go about their day. Soon the air was alive with the clank of the smith's hammer, livestock being fed, the calls and grunts of men at field work, but still no sign of the boy.

Peter began to fidget. He didn't like being so close to the village, too aware of the many men about. Finally he heard spirited shouts and caught sight of Edwin and the other boy. Peter watched them head across the square and into the stables. They reappeared a moment later carrying a bucket in each hand, then disappeared into a line of trees at the bottom of a slope. Peter checked for any nearby men, then dashed from haystack to haystack, crossing the field to the trees.

He found them filling their buckets in a small brook. He slid behind a thicket of blackberry bushes. The boys climbed carefully up the slope, watching their step as they lugged the pails of water. Peter waited until they were almost upon him, then leaped out. "Hi!"

The boys screamed, turned to run, and crashed into each other. Both boys, their pails, and the water spilled back down the slope.

Peter fell to his knees, laughing so hard he had to clutch his belly.

The two boys exchanged terrified looks. Then Edwin's face broke into a grin. "Hey, it's him!" he cried.

The other boy looked perplexed.

"It's him," Edwin repeated. "The wood elf! See, Otho. I told you." Edwin punched the other boy on the shoulder. "Now who's the idjit?"

Otho squinted at Peter. "Are you really a wood elf?"

"His name's Peter," Edwin said. "Show him your ears, Peter."

Peter pushed back his raccoon mask.

"See!"

"Well damn," Otho said. "A wood elf. A real wood elf." He reached out and touched Peter, as though making sure he was real. "What are you doing here?"

"Let's play," Peter said.

"Play?" Otho responded. "We can't. We got all sorts of stupid chores to do."

"Not every day you get to play with a wood elf," Edwin said.

"Well, yeah. That's true," Otho agreed. "But if we don't get the hogs watered, Papa will whip us."

"I know lots of wood-elf games," Peter said. "They're a lot more fun than carrying buckets of water about." A sly grin lit up his face. "We could play for a *little* while. Over behind the haystacks, near that big tree. Where no one can see us."

The boys returned Peter's sly grin, because Peter's grin was a most contagious thing.

Edwin nudged Otho. "Wood-elf games. I've never played wood-elf games."

"Well," Otho said. "Maybe for just a *little* while."

"Great!" Peter said. "Follow me. And remember, we can't be seen." He took off in a crouch. The two boys followed him up the path, mimicking his every move.

They reached the haystacks, stopped. Peter peered around, making sure the way was clear.

"Hey, Peter," Edwin called. "Watch this." The boy scrambled to the top of the haystack. Peter started to warn him to get down before someone saw him, when the boy leaped across to another haystack. Edwin poked his head back over the stack. "Bet you can't do that."

Peter frowned. "Bet I can," he said and leaped from one haystack to the next. And for the next hour, they jumped haystacks, raced, played tag and hide-and-seek. Peter forgot about the sack, the rope and bludgeon, even about the men, he was having too much fun. Soon, they'd lost their shirts—Peter only in his loincloth—their torsos glistening in the hot morning sun, covered from head to toe in mud, leaves, straw, and big, fat grins.

They were mighty berserkers now, and a particularly tall haystack behind the stable was a terrible dragon. In a ferocious attack, Peter leaped upon the haystack and tried to climb to its summit. The stack tilted, Peter yelped, and the whole heap toppled over, pinning him beneath a blanket of soggy hay.

The boys ran up and began to dig Peter out. When they uncovered his face, Peter spat out a mouthful of straw, began to cough, then laughed. He choked, spat out more straw, then laughed some more. Soon they were all laughing so hard that they rolled on their backs, helpless.

"Hey," Peter hollered, between bouts of giggling. "Hey . . . get . . . me . . . out of here."

"*THERE YOU ARE!*" came a woman's sharp, angry shout.

The laughter died. Peter's heart leaped into his throat as he suddenly remembered just where he was.

"What nonsense is this? I've been—" She stopped in mid-sentence, her mouth agape. "Who . . . ? What . . . ?" She let out a scream.

Peter twisted around to look at her and she pointed at him with one fat, trembling finger and screamed again. *"GOBLIN! GOBLIN!"*

An older bald man and a wiry pockmarked youth stuck their heads out from the stable. They saw Peter and came in at a run. The youth carried a pitchfork.

Peter yanked his arms out from the hay and dug frantically to free his legs.

The two boys looked from their mother to Peter. "No, Mama," Edwin cried. "He's not a goblin. He's a—"

Peter jerked one leg free and kicked and twisted to free the other.

"GET AWAY FROM IT!" the woman screeched. *"EDWIN! OTHO! HEAR ME, GET AWAY FROM IT NOW!"* When the boys didn't move, she ran up and snatched them back.

The pockmarked youth raced up, raised the pitchfork, and drove it right for Peter's face.

Peter jerked his head away, but not fast enough. One of the prongs sliced down the side of his scalp. He felt a red-hot slash of pain and let out a howl. In a wide-eyed fit of panic, he kicked his remaining leg free and scrambled up. He almost made his feet when someone grabbed his arm and jerked him off the ground. The bald man slammed a huge fist into the side of Peter's face. Peter's head exploded with white light and pain. His legs buckled, but before he could fall the man punched him again, a hard jab in the ribs, sending the boy tumbling backward. Peter hit the ground in a heap and everything went blurry.

"*KILL IT!*" the woman shouted.

Peter tried to suck in a breath but his mouth was full of something wet and warm. He coughed violently, spraying the ground with his own blood. The side of his face had gone numb. Through tears and blood he saw a blurry figure moving toward him.

"*NOW, KILL IT! QUICK!*"

"I got it!" the youth cried.

Peter cleared his eyes in time to see the youth coming at him with the pitchfork. Dizzy, and slow, Peter made it to his feet.

The youth jabbed him. Peter tried to twist out of the way, but the prongs raked across his side, leaving behind three flesh-deep gashes.

The bald man made a grab. Peter ducked and ran, stumbling at first, but once he got his feet under him, ran, ran like the wind into the forest.

Once within the trees, he collapsed to his knees, clutching his side, his face clenched tight with pain. He let out a loud, hitching sob, then spat repeatedly, trying to clear his mouth of blood.

They were yelling and pointing at him from the field. Several more men and women had come around the stable. They weren't following him, just standing and pointing excitedly into the woods. He could see their faces, could see the revulsion, the fear . . . the *hatred*.

Other men came up then. Men with thick, braided beards carrying great, long swords. Peter ran.

✦

PETER'S LUNGS BURNED. He'd been running most of the day and still he dared not stop. He glanced back, eyes wide with terror. He could hear them, their dogs, and the hard clumps of the horses' hooves. They were closing in.

Peter spotted Goll's hill far ahead through a break in the trees, and the horrible realization that there was no safety there, that there was no safety anywhere, hit him. Goll couldn't stop these huge men with their terrible swords and axes. The men would kill Goll. Peter cut down a new path, headed toward the cliffs, leading the men away from Goll's hill, hoping the horses at least wouldn't be able to follow him up the steep ledges.

Peter made the cliffs and stopped, listening for the men as he tried to catch his breath. He didn't hear them. A touch of hope lifted Peter's spirits. Maybe they'd given up. Maybe he wouldn't die today after all. Then he saw the smoke and his chest tightened. *"Goll,"* he whispered.

Peter ran, ignoring the stabbing pain in his side, the throbbing in his head as he sprinted as fast as he could back to Goll's hill. He topped the rise and froze.

Smoke billowed out from Goll's burrow and there, dangling from the great oak, hung Goll. The rope was strapped about his chest, pinning his arms to his side, his feet twitched only inches above the ground. The huge men surrounded him, some on horses, some on foot, all with swords and

axes in hand.

The moss man was charred and smoke drifted from his red, raw skin. He had no less than a dozen arrows in him, and yet still he kicked and spat. The dogs bit at him, tearing open the flesh on his legs as the men brayed with laughter.

Peter's knees gave way and he stumbled against a fallen tree, his fingers digging into the rotting bark as he slid to the ground. He wanted to stop them, do anything to stop them, but couldn't move, couldn't do more than stare on in utter horror.

A huge fellow with a thick black beard and long knife walked up to Goll.

Goll stared at the blade with wide, terrified eyes.

The bearded man grabbed Goll by the hair and jerked his head back. He first cut off Goll's left ear, then the right. As the moss man struggled, the men laughed and the dogs ran around in tight circles, howling.

The man jabbed the blade into the moss man's stomach. Goll screamed and twitched spastically as the man sawed his gullet open. The man slid the blade into a loop of intestine and pulled it partially out of the wound, then whistled to the dogs. The dogs snatched the loop and pulled Goll's intestines out onto the dirt in wet, rolling coils, tugging and fighting over them as the moss man wailed.

Peter watched, stone-faced, unable to move or cry, to hardly even blink. He watched. He missed nothing.

After too long, much too long, Goll stopped wailing, his head sagged forward, and he was still.

WHEN THE MEN left, Peter stood and walked down the hill. He didn't cry, he didn't feel the cuts in his side, the gash across his head, not even the ground beneath his feet. He did not feel. He moved slowly, methodically.

He found Goll's bone-handled knife and cut the moss man down. To Peter's surprise, Goll opened his eyes.

"Be brave, Peterbird," Goll rasped. "Kill the wolf." And that was it. The moss man's eyes glazed over.

Peter slipped Goll's knife into his belt, gathered up his spears, and headed north, away from the village. He had no clear thought of where he was going, only that he was going away from the village, away from the men.

It wasn't long before Peter heard the wolf trailing him. Peter stopped in a clearing, turned, and waited. The one-eared wolf appeared. Its lips curled up like it was laughing at the boy, like it knew it had him.

Peter didn't flinch, didn't hesitate. He dropped the light spear and hefted the stout one to shoulder level. He slipped the bone-handled knife into his other hand, locked eyes with the wolf, and came at the beast in a dead run.

The wolf looked confused.

Peter's eyes flared and he let loose a terrible howl.

The wolf fell back.

Peter threw the spear.

The wolf hunkered to avoid the spear, and when it did, Peter leaped forward and drove Goll's knife deep into its side.

The wolf let out a yelp and took off, but after only a few strides it began to weave and stagger, its hindquarters collapsing, its breath coming out in a harsh, wet wheeze.

Peter snatched up his spear and followed the wolf.

The wolf stopped, unable to do anything but stand and watch the boy coming to kill it, panting as blood dripped from its lips.

Peter's eyes were hard, without hate nor pity, the eyes of a predator. He thrust the spear into the wolf's heart. The wolf thrashed, twitched, then lay still.

Peter stared at the wolf for a long time. His eyes began to well. A single tear ran down his bruised, swollen cheek, then another, and another. Peter fell to his knees before the wolf and began to sob. The tears were for Goll, but they were also for himself, a six-year-old boy without a mother, or a friend, scared, hated, and with nowhere to go.

A SCREAM SNATCHED the child thief from his thoughts.

One of the little kids, a boy, lay on the ground in front of the monkey bars. Two older boys stood over him laughing, not teenagers, just bigger boys, maybe eleven or twelve.

The small boy climbed back to his feet and tried to wipe the mud from the front of his T-shirt. Two chubby girls of about seven or eight ran up and stood on either side of him, braids sprouting from their heads.

"Leave him alone," one of the girls said. She jutted out her chin and planted her hands firmly on her hips. Her friend followed suit.

The handful of children in the playground stopped playing and began to gather around.

"You want me to kick your ass too?" the big boy said and shoved the girl, knocking her to her knees. His pal chuckled.

"Don't you push her!" the little boy shouted, his muddy hands balled into fists, his face full of fear and hate. Peter shook his head, knowing that soon this little boy would be just as mean as these bigger kids, because meanness had an ugly way of spreading.

"What you gonna do about it?"

"We was here first," the second girl shouted as she pulled her friend back up.

"Well, we're here now," the big kid said. "So get the fuck outta here less you want me to kick all your stupid little asses."

When none of them moved, the big kid stepped forward. "You think I'm fucking around? I said—" He saw Peter standing next to the little boy. A confused expression crossed his face as though unsure just where Peter had come from. He glanced back at his pal, but his friend looked just as surprised.

The child thief pulled his hood back and locked his golden eyes on the two big kids, the same eyes that had backed down a full-grown wolf. He didn't say a word, just stared at them.

The big kids seemed to deflate. "C'mon," the kid said to his pal. "Playgrounds are for candy-asses." They left, casting anxious looks back over their shoulders as they went.

"Hey, kid," the little girl said. "You got funny ears."

Peter grinned at her and wiggled his ears. The kids all burst out laughing.

"You wanna play with us?" asked the boy.

"I do," Peter said. "I most certainly do." His eyes gleamed devilishly. "But not today. Today I have to find a friend."

Chapter Seven

Sekeu

Nick sat on the floor with his back firmly against the wall. His aching head felt like it would never stop ringing. He touched his swollen lip and winced. At this point, he felt fairly confident that no one was going to eat him, at least not this morning. He rested his head against the stone works and watched the kids go about their madness.

Half-naked kids darted about in all directions, pushing and yelling, but somehow, out of the chaos, fires were started, torches were lit, bowls were brought out of cupboards, and soon the air smelled of soot and smoke. Nick tried to count the kids, but they moved around too much. He guessed around twenty all together, and was amazed at the ruckus they could make.

Soft morning light flickered along the stone-and-dirt floor. Nick could see a sparse canopy of limbs through the few breaks in the roof.

He scanned the chamber: it was a bit smaller than a basketball court. His eyes returned over and over to the hanging bodies in the far corner. They'd looked so real in the fog, but now, in the light, it was plain to see that they were just straw dummies. Why there should be straw dummies hanging from the rafters was a mystery, but at this point they were the least of his concerns.

The place was a mess: cages and tarps strewn all along one wall, clothes piled up in and on top of old barrels, candy bar wrappers, crumbled cigarette boxes and butts among the straw and leaves, old, blackened chewing gum worn into the stones. The only thing that was neat were the weapons, glistening with fresh oil and hung in nice rows, along with various types of leather armor, helmets, and pads.

Cooking smells caught Nick's attention: a nutty, cinnamon aroma. Nick was surprised when his stomach began to growl. How his stomach could think of food after all that had happened was beyond him. He watched them fill their bowls up with a soupy goop. Was that gruel? Nick wasn't even sure what gruel was, much less what it looked like, but he bet it looked a lot like that stuff.

One by one the kids plopped down onto the benches on either side of a long wooden table and began to eat. Nick still had a hard time believing what he was seeing: wild-haired savages slurping, smacking, yelling, and laughing with large gobs of food in their mouths, several using their hands instead of the big wooden spoons. All the while the little blue people flew about trying to snatch stray berries and nuts.

Another growl came from Nick's stomach. He really wanted a bowl of whatever it was they were eating. But there was no way he was going to beg to be fed, not after the way they'd treated him.

A girl walked purposely over to him. She had the wide cheekbones and a strong jawline of a Native American Indian. Her body was lean and sinewy. At first glance, she appeared to be around his age, but as she neared, he noted the hard set of her face—especially the eyes, they didn't look like the eyes of a child—and it became tougher to guess. Her copper-colored skin was dirty and dotted with scars, leaving no doubt she'd seen her fair share of trouble. Her long black hair was captured in twin braids that ran down her back. Two black wings were threaded through a broad, beaded headband. The feathers swept downward from the sides of her head, the tips touching the tops of each shoulder, giving her a noble bearing. She carried a bowl and a wooden spoon.

She stopped in front of Nick and stared down at him. Her eyes were gold like Peter's, but large and intense. Nick dropped his gaze and stared at the floor.

"I brought you food," she said, and held the bowl out to him.

The nutty smell tugged at Nick but he ignored her.

"Do not be a child. Eat," she said. Her words were stilted, spaced. Nick could tell English wasn't her native tongue.

Nick said nothing.

She gave him a moment longer, then turned to leave.

"Wait." Nick forced the word out.

She looked at him, her eyes hard, uncompromising.

Nick held his hand out for the bowl.

She continued to stare at him.

"Please," Nick said through clenched teeth.

She handed him the bowl.

Nick gave the goop a stir. It looked like chunky oatmeal. He scooped a small clump onto the wooden spoon and gave it a nibble. He noticed a touch of bitter beneath the sweet but it was pretty good.

Careful of his busted lip, Nick began to eat. The gruel was warm and felt good going down; as a matter of fact, it warmed up his whole body.

She sat down, cross-legged, in front of him. "Your name is Nick?"

Nick nodded.

"My name is Sekeu." There was a long pause. "You should know you did well with the red devil. Most kids are too frightened to fight back. I believe there is a warrior in your heart. You just need skills. We will begin training today."

Nick stopped eating. "Training?"

"To become a warrior. To become clan. To become a—*Devil*."

"What?"

"You must learn to fight. To defend yourself and your clan." She said this so matter-of-factly that for a moment Nick thought he might be the crazy one.

"Clan? You mean that bunch of assholes?" Nick jabbed his thumb toward the kids. "You think I want to join their little jerk-off club?"

The kids had pulled swords and spears down from the walls and were

The kids had pulled swords and spears down from the walls and were practicing basic moves—leaps, thrusts, stances, and so on—while others paired off for light sparring. In spite of himself, Nick was fascinated by their speed and agility as they knocked each other back and forth across the floor. *How can they move like that?*

"Peter has brought you here to offer you a chance," Sekeu said sternly. "To become clan, to become a child of Faerie. Do you have any idea what that means? It is a chance at eternal youth, to live wild and free for a thousand years."

Nick stared at Sekeu. "What're you talking about? And where is Peter? Where the hell did that *bastard* go?"

Sekeu's eyes narrowed. "Choose your words carefully, Nick. There are those here that would kill you for calling Peter such." Judging by her face, Nick was pretty sure she was one of them. Nick let out a frustrated sigh.

"Peter is gone to search out more children for the clan," she said.

"What?" Nick could hardly find the words. "You mean to kidnap more kids."

She gave him a sharp look. "Talk to them." Sekeu pointed around the chamber at the kids. "Ask them their story. Peter finds the lost, the left-behind, the abused. Is that not why you are here? Did Peter not save you?"

"Peter tricked me."

"What would have happened last night had Peter not shown up? Where were you going to go, eat, sleep?" Again she pointed to the other kids. "If what they say is true, then how long before you were selling drugs, or as they would put it, before some pimp made you his boy? Or would you have returned home? Do you wish to go back home now?"

Home, Nick thought. He couldn't go home. Not ever. But that didn't mean he wanted to be held captive on some island full of monsters, either. "Just where is here? Just what kind of place is this?"

"*Here* is the isle of Avalon, the sanctuary of the Sidhe and the realm of the Queen Modron, the Lady of the Lakes. *Here* is the refuge for the last of earth's enchanted creatures." Sekeu's eyes locked on his, her voice becoming more and more intense. "*Here* is Devilwood, the domain of Devil Kind, the children of the wolf mask. We are the lost, the wild, the untamable. We are the—"

"Okay, okay," Nick interrupted, rolling his eyes, realizing he was getting nowhere. "Look, you can't *make* me play this stupid game. You got that? I want *no* part of it."

She laughed, a cutting, cold sound. "*Fool.* No one will bother to *make* you. You still do not understand. This is not a gift. It is something you must earn. Peter has brought you here at great peril to himself. What you do from here is up to you. If you wish to leave, then *leave.*"

"I'm not a prisoner? I can just walk out of here?"

"If that is what you really wish."

Nick laughed and shook his head. "Are you kidding me? I'm *so* out of here."

She glared at him. "That is the problem with you runaways. You believe you can always run from your troubles."

"I didn't run away," Nick snapped.

Now she was the one shaking her head.

"Well, I did. But it wasn't like that. Look, you don't know anything about me."

But she looked like she did know, like she'd seen it all too many times before. "One cannot be forced to become a Devil, a child of Faerie. It is a hard enough thing if you want it with all your heart. You must take on the challenge of your own free will or the spirit of the forest will never bind with you."

"Yeah, okay. Whatever. Can you just tell me how I get out of here already?"

She gave him a long, hard look, then pointed toward a large round door at the far end of the chamber.

Nick sat the bowl down and got to his feet. He wiped his hands on his pants, flipped his bangs from his face, and headed for the round door. As he trekked across the hall, one by one, the kids stopped what they were doing and watched him.

A black boy trotted up alongside of him. The kid was a few inches shorter than Nick and missing his left hand just above the wrist. He appeared younger than the others, maybe as young as ten, hard to tell for certain. He had an honest, plain face and kindly eyes, his hair was pulled back into two braids with long blue ribbons woven into their ends. "You leaving already?" he asked in a slight Southern drawl.

Nick kept walking.

"Here." The boy tried to hand Nick the spear he was carrying. Nick pushed it away.

"Kid, it'd be murder to send you out there without a weapon of some sorts. Now you need to listen up. You come across some of them barghest, you be sure not to show no fear. Got that? They sense you're afraid then they'll get after you for sure."

Nick came to the door and stopped.

"Now, hear me," the boy continued. "I'm not playing with you. You're gonna be a-wantin' this." He shoved the spear in Nick's hands.

Nick took the spear and looked at it, positively mortified.

"Oh, yeah. And if the Flesh-eaters track you down, you just drop that there spear and get running. Because," he laughed, "they'll just shove the damn thing right up your ass."

Nick set his hand on the door slat, but didn't slide it over.

"Here let me help you with that," somebody said. This voice was deeper than that of the one-handed kid. Nick turned and found himself looking up into the stern eyes of the tall Devil boy.

"My name's Redbone. Sorry we won't have the chance to get to know each other better." He smiled coldly and yanked the bolt over, pulling the thick round door inward. The wooden hinges whined as the door swung open.

Nick immediately noticed the gouged marks on the outside of the door—long, deep slashes running down the splintered wood.

"Don't mind those," Redbone said. "The barghest like to sharpen their claws there, that's all."

It was gray, musty. Nick could just make out the shapes of a few gnarled stumps and trees, but the rest of the forest fell away into a wall of shifting mist. From somewhere far out, he heard a single howl. Nick recognized that call, would never forget it as long as he lived. It was the same howl that the shadowy hunched creatures, the ones with the orange eyes, had made the night Peter brought him in from the Mist.

Nick found himself incapable of moving.

Redbone put a hand on his back, easing him forward, and started to push the door shut behind him.

"Wait!" Nick cried, slapping a hand on the door. He turned around; they were all staring at him.

"Yes?" Redbone asked, a smirk pushing at the corner of his mouth.

Nick's lips began to quiver. He started to say something, but was too mad, too afraid he would start crying.

Redbone stared at him. "Maybe you'd like to stay and make some friends? You just might live longer with some friends watching your back."

Chapter Eight

Nathan

The child thief watched the park lamps hum to life one by one. Night had come early beneath the incessant drizzle. The deep shadows from the towering tenement buildings squeezed together and there was no longer a soul in sight. Peter refused to admit that another day was lost, he couldn't afford another day, not with the Captain on the prowl in Avalon. He pushed through the row of buildings, onto another, then another.

He spotted two figures dodging lamplights and darting from shadow to shadow. Even across the wide courtyard, Peter could tell that these kids were runaways, could almost smell it. A grin snuck across his face—the game was on.

The child thief trailed them into the stairwell of a large building, slipping beneath the stairs. The stairwell smelled of piss and vomit, mold and stale garbage. He leaned back into the shadows, trying not to inhale through his nose as the two boys conversed in low, anxious tones.

Now that they were in the light, Peter could see they had to be brothers, the older one maybe fifteen or sixteen, the younger one no more than twelve. The older boy had a scrape on his forehead, his left eye was swollen, the knees of his jeans torn and bloody. Someone had beaten him.

"What we gonna do?" the younger boy asked.

"We just gonna tell him."

"No way!"

"Nathan, what else we supposed to do?"

"You think he's gonna believe us?" Nathan said, the anxiety in his voice rising along with the volume. "That was his dope. He's gonna blame us, or think maybe we stole it."

It's the same story, Peter thought. *Drugs.* These days it was always the drugs. But Peter had seen too much, knew too well that men-kind didn't need an excuse to be cruel and murder one another. If it wasn't drugs, then there was always something else.

"Shh," the bigger boy said, glancing furtively up the stairwell. He threw an arm around Nathan. "Chill now. Your big bro got it covered. I'm tight with Henry. He'll work with us. Hell, if he wants to get paid back he'll have to. Now won't he?" The bigger boy was trying to sound cocky, cool, like he had it all together, but Peter knew he was just as scared as his younger brother, maybe more so.

"We can just leave," Nathan said. "Get outta here. To another town maybe."

"Don't you understand? We got nothing, man. Not hardly a damn dollar." A tremor was creeping into the older boy's voice. "You know anybody gonna take us in around here? Especially if Henry's after us? Or do you wanna go back and live with the old man?"

The younger boy shook his head hard. "No. I'm never going back there. *Never.*"

"Look, I got us into this. I'm gonna get us out. Now you just wait here—"

Nathan grabbed his bigger brother's arm. "No, Tony. Don't leave me."

His voice cracked, his eyes welled up. "Please don't go up there. Man, please! Please don't go up there."

"Stop blubbering," Tony said sternly. "You start with that baby shit and I'm gonna leave you for good. You want that?"

The younger boy's face became terrified. "No!" he said and wiped his eyes on his sleeves. "I'm sorry. I'll be cool. I promise."

"I know you'll be cool, 'cause you're the *Coolio*." He rubbed the younger boy's head, and a big smile lit Nathan's face.

"Just wait here," the bigger boy said. "He ain't gonna kill me for one fuckup. I'll be back in a minute and everything will be fine." He held up his fist. "Give it up." Nathan tapped his knuckles against his brother's fist.

"Hang tight, Coolio," the older boy said and headed up the stairs.

PETER LISTENED TO the rain trickling down the gutters as Nathan paced in and out of the stairwell doorway.

It seemed a long time before they heard anything, then a loud shout echoed down the stairwell.

Nathan started for the stairs.

"You don't want to do that," Peter said, coming out of the shadows.

The boy jumped back. "Who are you?"

"A friend."

Nathan squinted at him, then another shout came from above, followed by several angry voices.

The boy forgot about Peter and dashed up the stairs. He made it only one flight up before a scream came from outside, a long, horrified shriek, then a sickening thud in the courtyard. Nathan froze.

Peter grimaced, knowing what that thud meant. He could see by the boy's face that he did too.

"Tony?"

The boy leaped down the entire bottom flight of stairs and shot out of the stairwell. Peter followed slowly behind.

THE BOY LAY sprawled upon the sidewalk, one leg bent awkwardly behind him, his eyes wide, blinking, lips moving but no words coming out.

His head lolled over and Peter saw that the back of his skull was crushed inward, his hair wet with blood.

"TONY!" Nathan screamed, and ran to his brother.

Peter glanced up the face of the building. There, looking down from the sixth-floor balcony, was a man and four older teens. The man pointed at Nathan, said something, and all four of the teens sprinted to the stairwell.

"We need to go," Peter said.

The boy ignored him. "Tony. Tony, man. Ah fuck, no. Tony."

Several people stuck their heads out their doors, glanced over the balcony, then went quickly back in.

Peter heard the teenagers' feet drumming down the stairwell. They'd be down in another moment. Peter placed a hand on the boy's shoulder. "Hey, they're coming. We need to go."

Nathan looked up at Peter, his lips trembling. "They killed him!" A sob tore loose from the back of his throat. "They killed my brother!"

"They're coming for you now. We need to leave."

The boy looked up to the balcony, saw the man, heard the boys shouting in the stairwell. Peter watched the fear leave the boy's eyes, replaced with hatred. The boy jabbed his hand into his brother's coat pocket and pulled out a knife. He popped open the blade and stood up.

"You want to kill them?" Peter asked.

The boy didn't answer. He didn't need to. His eyes said it all.

Peter grinned. "Good. Let's kill them."

Peter darted back beneath the overhang, ducking behind the open stairwell door. He slipped his long knife from his jacket and pressed his back to the wall.

All four teens rushed from the stairwell out into the yard, saw Nathan, and stopped. They looked at the small knife trembling in his hand and began to laugh.

One of them, a short, muscular kid with long sideburns, stepped forward. "You already dead, motherfucker. You just too stupid to know it." He pulled a gun from his jacket and leveled it sideways at Nathan. "Well, what'cha waiting for, badass. Let's see what—"

A blur shot past the teens, a flash of steel, and both the gun and the short, muscular kid's hand flew through the air, bouncing onto the grass.

All the boys' eyes went wide. But none wider than the muscular kid's, as blood began to spurt from his severed wrist. He held his stump away from him as though afraid of it, and began to scream.

The kid next to him made a play for something under his jacket, but Peter didn't give him time to pull it out. Peter had learned that when guns were involved, there was no room for games. You moved fast, stayed a step ahead. In a blink, Peter shoved his knife into the boy's neck and yanked it back out again.

The boy fell to his knees, clutching his throat, and began making a horrible, gurgling sound. Peter's eyes lit up and he let out a laugh like a demented demon. When he did, the two remaining teens took off at a dead run.

"LET'S GO!" Peter called, shouting to be heard over the screams of the kid with the chopped-off hand. "We really need to go."

Nathan looked at him as if he didn't know whether to be thankful or afraid.

Shots came from up above them; dirt sprung up around Peter. The man was shooting at them from the balcony. That got the boy moving; the two of them ducked beneath the overhang. Nathan spotted the gun, the one the muscular boy had dropped. He snatched it up out of the grass.

They heard shouts coming from the building across the courtyard, where the teens had fled. More boys were coming.

"I know where we can go," Peter said and took off.

The boy followed.

Chapter Nine

First Blood

Sekeu led Nick over to the long table. It was spattered in gruel and strewn with dirty spoons and bowls. The blue pixies were swarming about the mess, scrambling to lick up any available crumb. Two boys and a girl were doing their best to fend off the hissing pests while they stacked the bowls and carted them over to a sudsy barrel.

"Your training will begin here," Sekeu said and clapped her hands twice.

The kids stopped, their eyes falling on Nick. These kids weren't covered in body paint, tattoos, or scarring. They lacked the hard angles in their faces, the wiry muscles, and their eyes weren't golden. For the most part, they looked like your average middle-schoolers.

"Nick, this is Cricket."

A girl with sandy, short-cropped hair stood with her hands on her waist and a sassy thrust to her hips. She wore ragged camo pants rolled up to her calves, a pair of well-worn orange high-tops, and a purple tank-top. She had a bald spot on the side of her head, a scar maybe, which gave her a mangy look. She cocked an eyebrow at Nick and smiled.

"And Danny." Sekeu pointed to a pudgy kid wearing dark-rimmed glasses and balancing a stack of bowls. His glasses were wrapped around his head with a strap—it was a sport strap at least, but the strap still made the kid look nerdy as hell to Nick. Danny had gruel in his hair and smeared down the front of his white T-shirt. His brown corduroy pants were pulled up high on the waist, with the legs tucked into a pair of boots. A pixie landed on his head and tugged at the gruel in his hair. "Goddamn it!" he yelled and flicked his head back and forth. The pixie held on but the stack of bowls toppled, crashing down onto the table and floor. "Goddamn it!" Danny yelled again, swatting at the pixie as it flitted away.

Sekeu shook her head. "Danny and Cricket, like you, are unproven. They are New Blood. Once you prove yourself you become clan and only then may you enter the ranks of Devil Kind."

Nick rolled his eyes.

"This is Leroy."

Leroy was a heavyset kid, not pudgy like Danny, but thick-boned and solid through the chest and waist. His short, dark hair lay matted against his skull. He wore a sleeveless sweatshirt and the same sort of stitched-up leather britches as the Devils, but had none of their more extreme adornment.

"Leroy has been with us for a while now. He is still unproven." She gave Leroy a somber look. "We are hoping Leroy will make his challenge soon."

Leroy flushed and his mouth tightened.

"Leroy will see to you. Make sure you get settled in."

Leroy set hostile eyes on Nick.

Without another word, Sekeu turned and left them to their work.

"Get busy," Leroy said and tossed his rag at Nick. It hit the table, spattering chunks of wet gruel across the front of Nick's shirt. "Oh, and for the record," Leroy added, "I ain't your babysitter. So don't come whining to me with your problems. Got it?"

Nick let out a long breath, picked up the rag, and dragged it along the table. The pixies hissed and buzzed his head as he made his way down the length of the table. When he came to the end, he wiped the crumbs onto the floor, then strolled over to the suds barrel, where the girl, Cricket, was wiping out the bowls. He dropped his rag over the lip of the barrel and started to walk away.

"*HEY!*" Leroy called from the far end of the table. "What the fuck? You aren't done. Look at all the crud you left."

"It's *fine.*"

"No, it's not *fine.* You want the fucking pixies crapping all over everything? Get your rag and do it again. Do it right."

Nick glared at Leroy.

"Lose the attitude," Cricket said under her breath. "Trust me, you don't want to push him."

Nick picked up the rag, walked back over to the table, and began to wipe it again.

Leroy came up behind him. "Are you retarded? That's not wiping. How hard is it to wipe a stupid goddamn table?" He snatched the rag from Nick and gave the table a good, hard wipe. "Like this. See? Now do it right." Leroy shoved the wet rag into Nick's chest.

Nick slapped the rag on the table and started to walk away. He made it two steps before he felt a hand on his collar, and the next thing he knew he was yanked around and shoved against the table. Leroy snatched a clump of his hair and pressed his cheek into the rag. Nick tried to twist away but Leroy grabbed his arm and wrenched it behind his back. Nick let out a cry.

Leroy leaned into Nick's face. Nick could see the kid's pulse pumping through the veins along his forehead, felt his hands biting into his wrist, squeezing so hard Nick feared his bones might crack.

"Stop!" Nick pleaded.

"Look, you little shit. I tell you to do something and you better do it. Got it?"

"Yes," Nick said.

Leroy twisted his arm harder. "Got it?"

"*YES!*" Nick cried.

"What?"

"*YES! YES!*"

Leroy let Nick go. "Now wipe the table, fucktard."

"YOU CAN WASH up in there," Cricket said, pointing to a door with a moon burned into its surface. "That's the privy."

Nick wrung out the washrag, hung it across the barrel, and headed to the bathroom. He stepped in and shut the door, pressing his back against it. He clenched his eyes and took several long, deep, hitching breaths, determined not to start crying. He clutched his hands into fists. "Fuck all you bastards," he whispered. "Fucking, fucking bastards."

Something rustled, a clacking sound.

Nick opened his eyes, glancing quickly around the small, dim room. An oval mirror hung from one wall, a network of cracks ran across the surface, fracturing his reflection into a dozen images. A tall window, about half a foot wide, let in a thin slice of light. Enough light to make out an ancient-looking brass pump in one corner and, below it, seated in the floor, a round wood plank. Nick guessed that was the toilet and realized he needed to go really bad.

There was a rope attached to the plank, which ran up through a pulley and down again. Nick grabbed the rope, tugged the lid up, and was greeted by a warm gush of stink. He was in the middle of relieving himself when he heard the clattering again. It came from the hole. He caught movement. Something about the size of a rat, black and hairy, with lots of spidery legs, skittered out from between the stonework. It cocked its head and looked up at Nick with six blank, soulless eyes, then dropped down out of sight. Nick peered into the depths; in the darkness, hundreds of glowing eyes looked back up at him. Nick kicked the lid down, then noticed piles of white goop, what looked to be bird droppings, on the floor in one corner. He glanced up; there, in the rafters, two of the little blue people stared back at him from their straw nest. They drummed their wings, and hissed.

"What the fuck kinda place is this?" he said under his breath as he zipped up. "Just what kind of hell is this?" He caught his reflection—a dozen angry faces looking back at him. He thought he looked like someone from a refugee camp—mud and gruel in his hair, his lip busted and swollen, dried blood streaked down his face. "What've I gotten myself into?" All at once an overwhelming need to see his mother crept up on him. His reflection blurred as his eyes filled with tears.

"No. To hell with her," he said. *This is her fault, all of it. She's the last person I want to see.* He wiped the tears angrily away and stepped over to the pump.

Nick primed the pump, stuck his hands under the spout, and splashed water on his face. The water was cool and refreshing. He washed the mud, gruel, and blood out of his hair and from his face and arms. He looked back in the mirror. *I'll play their game,* he thought. *But first chance I get I'm out of here.*

✦

SEKEU WAS WAITING for Nick when he came out of the privy.

"Come," she said and led him across the chamber. They maneuvered around several groups of Devils practicing with weapons. The air was punctuated with loud shouts and the sharp clacking of wood hitting wood. Again, Nick found himself amazed at the speed and dexterity they displayed. Could he learn to move like that?

He followed Sekeu to the far side of the chamber, to where the straw men—the ones Nick had been so sure were children—hung from ropes. Now, up close, their purpose became obvious: practice dummies. The ground was sandy here. He watched Leroy, Cricket, and Danny practicing various striking maneuvers with short staffs on the straw men.

Danny stopped, completely winded, red-faced, and soaked in sweat. "Hey," he wheezed and wiped his brow. "Is it break time yet?"

"Danny," Sekeu said. "You just started."

Danny's shoulders drooped and he let out a long groan.

Sekeu ignored him, went to the wall, and pulled down a staff. She whirled it around her body in a blur, then stopped it with a snap. She held it out to Nick. "Here."

Nick took the staff.

"Come."

Nick followed Sekeu over to one of the straw men.

"Today you will learn how to strike."

Nick noticed the other New Blood watching, couldn't miss Leroy's smirk.

Sekeu gave the straw man a shove and nodded to Nick.

Nick hefted the staff and got ready. When the dummy swung back, he struck out as hard as he could. The straw man caught him mid-swing, knocking the staff out of his hands. Nick stumbled back and fell on his butt.

Leroy let out a laugh.

Nick's face turned red. He didn't get up.

Sekeu waited.

Nick shook his head. "Why don't we forget about this?"

Sekeu leaned toward him. "You will always be the brunt of brutes unless you make them respect you." She cut her eyes toward Leroy.

Nick sighed, picked up the staff, and pushed himself back to his feet.

"Ready?" Sekeu asked.

Nick hefted the staff. Again Sekeu swung the straw man, again the straw man knocked him down.

Nick crawled to his feet. "Look," he said, shaking his head. "Really, I'm not cut out for this sort of thing. It's just not in me."

Sekeu's ageless eyes searched his face. "Nick, you fought the devil beast today. I saw a brave spirit in your heart. A warrior."

Nick wanted to laugh at her silly words, but the way she said them, the way she looked at him when she said them, as though she truly believed in him. Nick couldn't remember the last time anyone had looked at him like that, *ever.*

Nick let out a sigh. "Okay." He picked up the staff.

The straw man knocked him down again.

"Damn it," Nick said and hit the sand with his fist. "It's too heavy."

"Size does not matter."

Nick got up and Sekeu took the staff.

"First, you must get into an L stance." Sekeu demonstrated. "Weight should be on your back leg. Front leg light. This will keep you maneuverable, but allow you to put the entire weight of your body into the swing.

You push off hard with your back foot and fall into the swing with the front." Sekeu slammed her front foot down to emphasize. "Now, put one hand low on the staff like this. The other midway. When you strike, the high hand slides down and meets the low. This makes power."

Sekeu demonstrated, snapping the staff in the air. Nick could see the staff actually quiver from the force.

"Most important, do not focus on hitting the target. You want to go through it. If you focus on hitting the target, all your force will be lost on contact. But if you focus beyond the target, your blow will carry power.

"There is also timing, but that comes with practice."

Sekeu gave the straw man a shove, slipped into the L stance, her body rocking slightly to and fro as the dummy swung back toward her. At the last moment her body exploded like a coiled viper. The staff connected with the straw man, sending a terrific *"WHACK"* echoing around the chamber. The dummy almost bent double as it flew away from the blow. Loose straw flitted through the air as the slack played out and the straw man jerked on the end of the rope.

"Whoa," Nick gasped.

"You can do it, Nick. But you must practice."

Nick couldn't do it. Not even close. But after an hour with Sekeu, Nick could certainly bring the straw man to a stop without getting knocked down, could hit his mark most every time. These were small steps, but with every blow Nick found himself getting better.

Sekeu moved from kid to kid. Encouraging each of them to focus and push themselves. Showing them tricks and pointing out what they were doing wrong. After some time, Sekeu left them on their own and Nick found himself lost in the repetitiveness of training. Unaware of passing time, unaware that he was actually enjoying himself. And for a while Nick forgot all about high-tops in the mist, blue pixies, Leroy, and the golden-eyed boy named Peter.

SEKEU GATHERED THEM around. Nick, Cricket, and Danny all watched as she pushed the straw man at Leroy.

Leroy struck the straw man a powerful blow, sending the dummy flipping back.

"Good," Sekeu said.

Leroy grinned. "Hell yeah."

"Now, once more."

Leroy gained his stance and hefted the staff, looking cocky, obviously getting a kick out of showing off in front of the New Blood.

Sekeu shoved the straw man toward him, but this time she sent it spinning wildly side to side.

Leroy stumbled back, trying to compensate, and the straw man knocked him to the sand.

Leroy jumped back up. "Hey, what was that?"

"You have to be ready for the unpredictable," Sekeu said. "Danny, why did he fall?"

"Because the dummy hit him?" Danny said with a grin.

Cricket let out a laugh.

Sekeu frowned. "Nick, why did he fall?"

Nick started to say he didn't know, but realized it was what Sekeu had been showing him. "He didn't keep his balance centered," Nick said.

Sekeu nodded. "Very good, Nick."

Leroy flashed Nick a dangerous look.

"Leroy, we have been over this many times. You have great power, but you must not rely on strength alone. If you do not practice what I show you, you will never win your challenge."

Leroy's mouth got tight and small. Nick could see the vein on his forehead pounding.

✦

CLANG, CLANG, CLANG. A bronze spoon banging against an iron pot resounded through the chamber. The smell of cooked onions brought a loud grumble from Nick's belly, made him aware of just how hungry he was.

Nick watched the Devils drop their gear and rush over in mass, pushing and shoving one another as they tussled over bowls and jockeyed for position in front of a huge iron kettle. Redbone and three other Devils appeared to be in charge of the food and they began dipping out generous spoonfuls of some sort of stew.

Danny, who'd been lying on his back like the victim of a heart attack, suddenly sat up, looking alive for the first time all day. "Dinner. My favorite sport!"

Nick leaned his staff against a post and started toward the line.

"Don't even think about it," Leroy said.

Nick glanced at the bigger boy.

"You got work to do."

Leroy pointed to the middle arena, where the Devils had dumped all their gear in their rush for the food line. There were swords, staffs, spears, all manner of helmets and pads.

"Stack the weapons in the holders along that wall." He pointed. "Stack the gear over there. And I better not see you at the table until it's done and done right."

Cricket picked up two staffs and headed toward the racks.

"Uh-uh," Leroy said, shaking his head.

Cricket looked at him, perplexed.

"Nick's doing it all himself tonight."

"That's not fair," Cricket said. "He shouldn't—"

"Shut up," Leroy said.

Cricket began to say more, but bit her lip. She leaned the staffs against the wall and headed toward the table.

"Well, you can stand there all night if you want," Leroy said to Nick. "But you ain't gonna eat until everything's put up."

Leroy waited another minute until Cricket and Danny were out of earshot. "And one more thing, you little suck-up. You ever embarrass me again and I'll make you pay for real. For fucking real." He jabbed Nick in the chest. "Got it, fuckhead?"

BY THE TIME Nick put the weapons away, most of the Devils had already finished eating. He was so tired he almost didn't bother, but the growling in his stomach won out.

He walked over to the iron kettle, shooed away two pixies, then lifted the lid. There were only a few dry clumps of the stew left. Nick scraped off what he could from the walls of the pot, about enough to fill half his bowl.

Leroy sat alone on the far end of the table. Cricket and Danny sat near two Devils in the middle. Cricket looked his way and smiled. Nick sat his bowl down as far away from everyone as he could and collapsed onto the bench.

He couldn't remember ever being so worn out. Yet in a way it was good. He hated to admit it, but the training had been very satisfying. He'd never been much good at sports, especially team sports, never stuck with anything other than skateboarding. It didn't take too many times being the last kid picked before he found the whole team bravado to be a load of bullshit, just another place for kids like Leroy to knock him around.

As the Devils finished up, most of them dumped their dishes in the barrel of sudsy water and began to spread out about the chamber, some migrating over to the shelves of books and comics, others picking up darts, checkers, cards, and various board games.

A soft melody caught Nick's attention, and he watched a girl with dark, curly hair tune a fiddle over by the fireplace. Within a few minutes, two boys joined her, one working out a primitive rhythm on a pair of tall drums while the other plucked at an acoustic guitar. It was just noise at first, then the girl tapped her bow three times and they began to play for real. The chamber filled up with the sweet, haunting wail of the fiddle. The girl played with her eyes closed, as though the fiddle was her voice singing a sad, slow song, then the drum joined in, a deep, steady beat, like a funeral dirge, and finally the guitar, melodic, along the lines of a spaghetti-Western score. Nick was stunned to see these savage kids playing such a beautiful song, and playing it with such heart. He found himself lost in the deep melancholy tune as he ate.

The stew tasted about like the gruel he had for breakfast. As a matter of fact, the only real difference was that the stew contained chunks of mushrooms and wild onions instead of berries. The mushrooms were amazingly sweet and very chewy. Nick plucked one out for closer inspection. When he did, a pixie flew down and dropped to the table just out of arm's reach. This one was a young boy with a jet-black mane of hair. He strutted and cocked his head, staring at the mushroom between Nick's fingers. Nick was struck by how oddly human he appeared. Nick flicked the mushroom to him. The pixie snatched up the morsel, hissed, and flew off. A trace of a smile touched Nick's lips.

Nick watched the Devils going about their evening activities. There was a lively game of poker going on in one corner, punctuated with plenty of cheering and profanity. A kid was working away on a horned-skull tattoo on some Hispanic boy's shoulder, using a needle and string to push the ink under the skin. The boy was biting down on a piece of leather, trying to look tough, but to Nick, he looked like he was about to pass out. Nick was surprised to see several Devils with cigarettes jutting out of their mouths, looking like delinquents as they puffed away. He watched three kids engaged in a light game of hoops, tossing a small ball into a makeshift basket. Even though they were just goofing around, Nick was amazed by how agile and quick they were.

The boy pixie was back. He landed on the edge of the table, a bit closer than before. He stared up at Nick with tiny, slitted eyes.

Nick tossed him a crumb.

"You don't want to do that."

Nick glanced around and found Cricket standing beside him.

"They'll never leave you alone if you feed 'em," she said, taking a seat across from him. A moment later, Danny slid down and joined them.

"So," Cricket said. "Where you from?"

Nick didn't answer.

Cricket leaned over. "Don't let Leroy get under your skin," she whispered. "He treats us all like that. Just take it easy around him. He gets wound up pretty tight sometimes."

Nick didn't need to be warned about Leroy.

"So, where're you from?" Cricket asked again. Nick started to tell her he didn't feel like talking when there came a loud crash.

"You moved your battleship! I saw you!"

"Did not!"

"It was on B-12. Right there. I called it. It counts."

"Does not!"

"You're a no-good *cheat*!"

The room fell quiet.

"It's Redbone again," Danny whispered.

"It's always Redbone," Cricket said.

"Take it back!" Redbone said and pulled a knife.

"*NO!*" a big, blond-haired boy said, and pulled his own knife.

Everyone scrambled out of the way as the two boys squared off in the middle of the chamber.

"Oh, man," Danny said. "Here they go again."

All the Devils dropped what they were doing and formed up a loose circle around the two boys. They began chanting *"first blood"* over and over.

"First blood?" Nick asked.

"Yeah," Cricket said. "It's how they resolve disputes. Whoever draws first blood, wins the argument."

The two boys flicked their knives at each other and began a dangerous dance: weaving, jumping, howling, as each sought an opening. They rushed each other, leaping, spinning, their blades mere blurs as they drove past.

"BLOOD!" screamed Redbone, holding up his blade and grinning. "I drew first blood."

"DID NOT!" cried the second kid.

Everything stopped. Sekeu walked up and examined the boy's forehead. She wiped her thumb on the mark, then held it up so everyone could see the small smudge of blood.

The crowd murmured approval.

"So," Cricket said matter-of-factly. "The thinner the mark, the smaller the amount of blood, the more prestigious the win. Shows superior skill."

The blond kid let loose a string of profanity but lowered his knife. It was over. The Devils returned to what they were doing as though nothing had happened. The band started back up.

"How come they can move like that?" Nick asked. "Doesn't seem possible."

"It's the magic," she answered.

"Magic?" Nick said. "Give me a break."

"No, it's in everything," Danny said. "You're eating it right now."

"What?" Nick stopped eating. "They're putting stuff in our food?"

"Nope," Danny said, and pushed at his glasses. "They don't have to. It's not a potion or fairy dust. Sekeu told me the magic's in everything here: the air, the water. When you eat it, though, you're ingesting it directly. This gunk," Danny wiped a clump off Nick's bowl, "is mostly made up of acorns. But like everything around here, there's magic in them."

"You've noticed their eyes, right?" Cricket asked. "The gold. The magic does that."

Nick noticed that Cricket's eyes had the slightest glint.

"My understanding is when you've been here long enough, that stuff doesn't just change the way you look, it gives you superpowers," she said.

"No, not superpowers," Danny corrected. "Think more like magical steroids. It's part of why they can move so fast."

"What're the side effects?"

"Side effects," Danny scoffed. "What are you talking about? This isn't science, it's flipping magic. Look at Abraham." Danny pointed to a black boy over by the fireplace. Nick recognized him as the one-handed boy that had given him the spear this morning. "Abraham's over a hundred years old. See anything wrong with him? And Sekeu, no one knows how old she is. Some of these other kids have been around since like the sixties and seventies."

"Yeah." Cricket laughed. "Go ask Redbone what an iPod is."

Nick wasn't sure how he felt about sucking down magical porridge. Were they being poisoned? He could feel the warmth in his stomach, feel it spreading. It was kind of a weird feeling when he thought about it, yet good too, soothing. But he wondered what it was really doing to him.

He eyed a spoonful suspiciously, then studied the Devils. *Doesn't seem to be hurting any of them.* He watched a boy leap over his friend, spin around, and do a hook shot all in one bound. *No, not a bit.* Would this stuff really help him move like that? Did he want to be able to move like that? Nick stuck the spoonful into his mouth.

"I don't know about you," Danny said. "But I'd trade this magic mush for a Big Mac any day."

All three of them laughed and nodded.

Leroy came up and they fell quiet. Leroy eyed them. "You know you guys have to clean up."

No one answered.

"Did you hear me?"

"We know, Leroy," Cricket said. "C'mon, lighten up a little."

Danny nodded. "Yeah, it's okay. It's under control."

"Oh, so that's the game. You guys are ganging up against me too?"

"No," Cricket said, letting out an exasperated sigh. "No one's ganging up on you, Leroy. We're supposed to be on the same team. Remember? Look, for once why don't you just sit down with us and talk. Be nice for a change."

Leroy looked unsure. Finally he sat down next to Nick.

"Y'know, it's not like I wanna be the one looking after you guys," Leroy said and stared out at the Devils. "They're making me. Those assholes are always giving me shit."

"They give us all shit," Cricket said. "That's just part of their scene. I think they feel they're supposed to. Y'know, to toughen us up or something."

"Yeah, no sweat," Danny said. "Besides, you'll be one of 'em soon. Then they'll lay off."

Leroy's face darkened.

"How exactly do you get to be a Devil anyway?" Danny asked.

"You have to call a challenge and draw first blood," Leroy muttered. "Or by saving a life, or any act of extraordinary courage. Some bullshit like that."

"Well, how are *you* ever going to make it then?" Danny said with a snort.

"You don't think I'm good enough?" Leroy asked coldly.

The smile fell from Danny's face. "I didn't say—"

"Fuck you, Danny."

"He was just trying to make a joke, Leroy," Cricket said. "Geez, relax for Pete's sakes."

Leroy glared into his bowl. His hand clutched the spoon so tightly his knuckles were white.

"So," Cricket said, "Nick, you were saying?"

"Huh?"

"You were telling us where you were from."

"No, I wasn't."

"Well?"

"Well what?"

"Where you from?"

The pixie boy was back. He landed near Nick, cocking his head left then right, looking up at him with those strange, unblinking eyes.

Nick pinched a crumb of gruel. The pixie eyed it expectantly and took another step forward; when it did, Leroy struck out with his spoon. The utensil caught the small creature with a solid crack, knocking it into the wall behind the table.

"What the hell!" Danny said.

"What is wrong with you?" Cricket cried.

Leroy's eyes narrowed. "Oh yeah. Is that it? That the way you guys wanna play it?"

The pixie's wings sputtered as it tried to get to its feet.

Leroy jumped up and slammed his foot down on the pixie. A horrible crunching sound came from beneath his boot.

A cry stuck in Nick's throat. He stared at the broken shape on the ground, then realized with horror that the pixie wasn't dead. It was trying to crawl out of a patch of blood and gore, its broken wings quivering. To Nick it looked more human than ever as it gasped and writhed in pain.

Leroy stomped down again, and again.

"GOD!" Cricket cried. "What's wrong with you?"

Leroy's face knotted up as he scraped the bottom of his boot along the wall stone, leaving behind a smear of flesh and hair. "Little nasty blue fuckers! Always fucking with me! Everyone's always fucking with me!" He stomped away.

✦

"HE'S CRAZY. I mean like totally batshit crazy," Cricket said. "See the way his eyes got? Like his mind left the room."

They were over by the roots now, as far from Leroy and the dead pixie as they could get. Nick sat on the floor, chin on his knees, hugging his legs while Cricket and Danny leaned against the roots.

"Shit," Cricket said. "It was Leroy who told us we weren't supposed to hurt the pixies in the first place. Said it was one of the laws. They're supposed to be part of the magic of this place or something like that."

"He didn't hurt it," Danny said. "He killed it."

"Hey thanks, Dan-ny. I was there, remember?"

"Probably bipolar or something," Danny said. "Just needs his meds."

"Yeah, well all these kids are messed up one way or another. Hell, I mean we've all been through some shit, right? Leroy's different. It's some-thing deeper."

They were quiet for a spell.

"Y'know," Cricket said, "Abraham told me Leroy's been here awhile. Not just a couple of weeks but a long time. Said Leroy's afraid to make a challenge, that's why he's still just New Blood. Y'know what I think? I think that's the problem. I think that's what's eating at him."

"You're like a regular Dr. Phil, aren't you?" Danny said.

Cricket cut him a sour look.

"Well, I'll tell you what I think," Danny said. "I think old Leroy there ate too many paint chips when he was a baby."

"Maybe we should tell someone?" Cricket suggested.

"Yeah, that sounds like a good plan," Danny snorted. "Cricket, why don't you go do that."

"Why not?"

"Are you kidding? Look around."

Nick watched two Devils taking turns throwing a knife at each other's feet. Another group were carving tribal designs into their arms.

Cricket let out a tired sigh and slumped to the floor.

NICK COULDN'T GET the vision of the pixie's murder from his mind. The little creature had just seemed so human. He guessed all living creatures were the same: animals, people, even pixies, when they're in pain and in fear for their lives—all the same. Nick's eyelids grew heavy. He was ready for sleep, ready to put this long, horrible day behind him. His stomach felt warm, unnaturally warm. He wondered again about the food and what it might be doing to him. But it was mostly a good feeling. He shut his eyes and enjoyed the strange way it spread through his body.

The fire had burned low, and several of the Devils were drifting over to the straw-lined cages. The band stopped playing and Sekeu and Abra-ham were dousing the wall torches.

"I think they're giving us a hint," Cricket said. "C'mon, Nick. We need to set you up."

Nick opened his eyes. "What?" But both Cricket and Danny were headed toward the cages. Nick pushed himself to his feet and followed.

"How's this one?" Cricket pointed to a cage next to hers.

"Sure," Nick said absently and started to crawl in. He stopped when the absurdity of sleeping in a cage dawned on him. "Cricket?"

"Yeah."

"Why do they put us in cages?"

Cricket laughed. "So the pixies can't screw with you all night." She dragged over a cut of canvas. "Here. Toss this over the top. That way they can't pee on you. You can tie the ends down, but it really doesn't matter because I don't think there's a knot they can't untie."

"Yeah, if they get to you they'll suck out all your blood," Danny said. "Happened to a kid just the other night."

Nick looked at him, horrified, then caught the smirk on Cricket's face.

"Uh-uh," Nick said.

Danny laughed.

Nick placed the tarp over his cage and crawled in. He still felt weird about sleeping in a cage, but at this point was too exhausted to care.

"Well, I'm hoping for bacon and waffles tomorrow," Danny said and crawled in his cage. "Shoot, I'd even settle for Cocoa Puffs."

Cricket kept rattling on about something, but Nick barely heard. His eyes felt so heavy. The warmth in his stomach continued to spread, covering him like a blanket, pulling him down into a deep sleep.

The warmth followed him into his dream, turning into the bright sunshine of a balmy summer day. He was in a meadow surrounded by trees, everything turned golden by the sun's brilliant rays. He lifted his face up and put his arms out, letting the heat bathe his whole body.

Giggles caught his attention. A multitude of faerie folk danced and frolicked from one end of the dreamy meadow to the other. Tiny, insect-size people with colorful butterfly wings floated about, pollinating the thousands of multicolored flowers blooming from every vine, tree, and bush. A snort came from the tall grass. Nick saw cat-size centaurs gallop past. Little white-skinned maidens in flowing gossamer rode on their backs, leaping and whooping gleefully. Hoots and howls came from the trees, where purple monkeys leaped from branch to branch. A chorus of bird and faerie song drifted about on the light breeze.

In the dream, Nick drew in a deep breath, filling his lungs with the sweet aroma of flowers and the spice of earth. It was all so wonderful, but all at once he began to sweat and thought a bit of shade would be nice. As he searched for a cool spot, the heat became unbearable and he realized this heat wasn't from the sun, but from his gut. His stomach was burning. Nick wished he could find some water, something to quench the burning. He clasped his belly and groaned, and when he did, the meadow fell silent. All the creatures stared at him and he could see fear in their eyes—fear of him.

Nick didn't want them to be afraid. He raised his hands to calm them and that's when his skin turned black. Right before his eyes, twisting splotches of darkness snaked along his arms, and scaly spots, the color of bruises, bloomed across the backs of his hands. He watched, terrified, as his fingers twisted into jagged black claws.

The creatures fled, leaving him behind. This made him angry, furious. He wanted to hurt them, wanted to chase them down and butcher every one of them.

Nick awoke clutching his gut. His stomach burned, and his clothes were soaked from sweat. He needed some water, but didn't dare go into the privy at night, not with those damn spiders. So he lay there wondering how he ever ended up on an island, in a cage, sharing a fort with Devils and little blue people. Eventually, the heat in his stomach passed, and shortly before morning he fell back asleep.

Chapter Ten

Ginny Greenteeth

Nathan sat on the curb, his face in his hands. He'd been sitting like that for close to an hour.

They were at the docks; the housing projects, the drug dealers, the gangs, all left far behind. The Mist was brewing, swirling up from the bay in front of them, waiting.

Peter wanted to get moving, anxious to get back, but knew better than to pressure or rush the kid. The next step was delicate. The boy had to truly want to follow him or he would never survive.

"I meant it when I said you could come home with me."

The boy didn't seem to hear him. Once out of the housing project, the kid had only talked about his brother.

"It's a really cool fort. You'll like it. I'm sure."

The boy wiped his nose, but didn't look up. "Yeah, that sounds fine," he mumbled. "I got no place else, y'know. With Tony gone I got no one."

"You'll have lots of friends soon. We need to hurry though, before the Mist leaves."

"Okay, man. Just give me another sec." The kid wiped his eyes on the front of his shirt and got to his feet. He saw the mist and frowned. "That's kinda creepy. You sure we wanna go that way?"

"The Mist will take us to Avalon, a magical place where you never have to grow up and no grown-ups are allowed."

Nathan gave Peter a quizzical look. "You're a strange dude. You know that?"

"Do you want to go?" Peter asked.

"Sure, why not."

"Do you go willingly?"

"Sure."

"Well then, you have to say it."

"Say what?"

"Say, 'I go willingly.'"

"Man, you're too much. Okay, I go willingly."

THE CHILD THIEF led, Nathan followed, and the Mist swirled around them. Peter's mouth filled with the chalky taste of the ghostly vapor. It made him think of ground-up bones and fish scales. It hadn't always been that way; he remembered the first time—all those years ago.

After killing the wolf, Peter had continued his trek deeper and deeper into the forest, determined to get as far away from the world of men as he could. The worn raccoon skin was gone, in its place the thick silver pelt of the one-eared wolf. The wolf's head was pulled over his face like a mask. Hard, intense eyes peered out from the dark sockets, alert, scanning the woods for prey and predator alike, but beneath those hard eyes was a six-year-old boy alone in the deep wild woods.

His days were spent following deer trails and creeks, hunting small game. Not knowing where he was going, only knowing what he was getting away from. Near dusk of each day he would seek out a hollow tree or a stone crevasse to curl up within, to try and get some sleep while the larger animals prowled the night.

On the fourth day he felt eyes on him. The forest had begun to change, the trees tightening around him, almost as though herding him this way or that. He heard unfamiliar bird calls, and the whining cries and chirps of insects that sounded all too close to speech.

Other than a few handfuls of nuts and wild berries, Peter hadn't eaten for two days. He found signs of game, heard them, but never saw them. He felt he was going in circles, his uncanny sense of direction somehow thrown off. He tried to think of Goll's voice telling him to be strong and brave, but when he came upon the standing stone, the same one he'd passed several hours before, he collapsed exhausted. He sat against the stone, cradling his legs to his chest, and fought to keep away the tears.

Laughter brought him to his feet. A girl, not much older than himself, stood looking down at him from atop a short rise. She had long white hair and wore a short white gown of such a lightweight fabric that it almost floated around her. She flashed him a mischievous smile, then darted away.

Peter stood frozen, unsure what to do, then heard her laugh again. There was something unsettling about that laugh, something that made him feel it wouldn't be such a good idea to follow her, but curiosity got the better of him and he sprinted up the path after her.

When he crested the rise, she was nowhere to be seen. He heard giggles. There across the way, beside a crumbling ledge, two girls in white gowns were holding hands. They looked like twins. One of them spoke into the other's ear. They glanced at him and burst into fresh giggling. He started toward them and they skipped away behind the ledge.

As Peter ran to catch them, he realized the trees and underbrush were becoming thicker, a maze of bushes and briars, of creepers and vines. He wondered how he would ever find his way back to the trail. He rounded the ledge and caught sight of their white gowns far down the embankment.

He caught up with them in a wide clearing. There were three of them now, identical in every detail. They stood huddled together before a circle of leaning stones. The stones appeared much older than the surrounding rocks. No mold or moss grew on their surface, and all manner of strange symbols ran up and down their sides, and among the stones—*bones*—all sorts of bones.

The girls regarded him through slanted, silvery eyes. Peter could see the tips of their pointed ears poking out from their hair. Their feet were bare and dirty, their flesh so white as to almost be translucent. He could see the spider-webbing of blue veins just beneath their skin. They smiled shyly at him.

Now that Peter had caught up to them, he didn't know what to do and shifted awkwardly from foot to foot. Finally he raised his hand. "Hi."

The girls burst out in giggles again and Peter flushed.

One of the girls slipped over to Peter. She traced a finger along his arm.

"What manner of creature are you?" she asked.

"I'm a Peter," he said.

"What's a Peter? Is it like a boy?"

"Of course, stupid," the other one answered. "Can't you see? He's a boy."

"A boy," the third one chimed in. "A little boy all alone in the forest?"

"What's a little boy doing all alone in the forest?"

"I'm . . . well, I'm," Peter started to say he was lost, but didn't want to be laughed at again. "I'm looking for friends to play with."

The girls exchanged quick, knowing looks.

"So are we!" said one.

"Can't believe the luck," said another, laying a hand on Peter's shoulder.

"We can be playmates," said the third as she slipped behind him, sniffing lightly at his neck and hair.

"What sort of games do you like to play?" asked the first.

Peter shrugged. "All sorts."

"So do we!" said the second.

"Come with us," added the third.

"Where?"

"You'll see."

Peter hesitated. "Are there grown-ups?"

"Grown-ups?" They looked puzzled.

"Oh, you mean men-kind," said the first. "Blood bells no, boy. Not where we're going. Just fun and games."

"Yes," added the second. "Lots of wonderful games."

"Come along," said the third, and gestured for him to follow as the three of them strolled in among the circle of stones.

Peter followed, then stopped. All the hair along his arms stood up, his scalp felt prickly, and a strange tingling tickled his feet and hands. He thought he heard chimes and singing—a lullaby maybe. The sound echoed faintly about the stones.

"Oh, he doesn't want to come," said the first.

"Doesn't want to play with us," said the second.

"So sad," added the third.

"Yes, I do," said Peter.

"He's afraid."

"Am not."

"Not just anyone can come, little Peter boy," said the first.

"Only those who really wish to," said the second.

"Wish it, Peter. Wish it and you can come and play with us," called the third.

The girls slipped into the very center of the ring of stones, to where a flat round stone lay flush with the grass. Their bodies began to sparkle and then, slowly, they faded away, leaving behind a glittering rain of golden dust.

Peter jumped back, staring at the melting flakes of gold.

"Come, let's play," called the girls and laughed; their voices sounded far away as though from the bottom of a well.

Peter glanced about; it was getting dark and cold. He heard the distant call of a wolf, then several answering howls. He didn't want to sleep in a tree again, not tonight. He looked at the stones. Where else did he have to go? He took a deep breath, bit his lip, and walked into the circle.

Nothing happened.

Peter closed his eyes. "I wish to follow them."

Still nothing. He opened his eyes.

"I wish to follow," he said, and this time he wished it with all his heart.

Golden sparkles flashed before his eyes, a silvery mist spun up around his feet, and the forest and stones faded away. For a second he was falling. His stomach lurched and Peter felt sure he would plummet to his death, but instead the mist thickened, became buoyant, and he was swimming through it, almost as though he could fly. He felt wind blowing across his face, and the air was warm and sweet.

The stones reappeared, taking Peter by surprise. He tumbled across a bed of moss, landing with his legs above his head against one of the standing stones.

He was greeted with a burst of girlish laughter.

Peter righted himself and the world around him righted itself as well, only *right* wasn't the word that came to mind. Peter shook his head. The stones were the same as before but the forest—*oh my*, the forest.

There was so much to see he didn't know where to look first. Broad, knobby tree trunks twisted their way upward into a canopy of vivid, colorful leaves, their branches—dripping with vines, flowers, and fruit—reached out, intertwining with one another. Warm, glowing rays of sunlight pushed through the treetops, setting the thin ground mist aglow. Chunky, gnarled roots crawled through the tangled undergrowth, and giant mushrooms poked their speckled heads up from the lush moss and grass. Wild flowers of every shape and variety dotted the trees, vines, and bushes, each seemed to be trying to outdo the next in color and brilliance. But the foliage wasn't what held him spellbound, it was the little people, dozens upon dozens of them. Some barely the size of bees, others as large as cats. Most had wings: bird wings, insect wings, butterfly wings, bat wings. Naked creatures of every imaginable color, some spotted or striped. They buzzed and hummed, giggled and chirped. A thousand little songs forming a gleeful symphony as they chased one another about the small clearing and danced in and out of the beams of sunlight.

The girls were waiting for him along a thin, winding trail. He stepped out of the circle and was struck by the smells; a thousand fragrances perfumed the air. He inhaled deeply, letting the sweet air fill his lungs.

A host of the wee folk flew past his head, then began to circle him, fluffing his hair, plucking at his wolf pelt, the soft humming of their wings tickling him. Peter began to giggle. "Cut it out," he laughed, and tried to shoo them away.

Someone swatted him on the shoulder.

Peter turned around.

"You're it!" cried one of the girls, and all three of them skipped away down the path in a gale of laughter.

Peter grinned, couldn't stop grinning. He gave chase, the swarm of little people fluttering along after him.

The trail wove its way down a gradual slope and the forest began to change. The ground beneath his feet became damp, then marshy. Peter splashed across a muddy creek, then skirted around several weedy bogs. Squat, twisted trees grew up from murky, misty pools, their bark slick, black, and oily, thick moss dripping from their branches. The dim light filtering through their brown, yellowy leaves cast everything in a shadowy amber glow. The delicate scents of flowers and berries were replaced by the sweet, spicy smell of fluff-mud, and the playful birdcalls with croaks and deep bellows.

Peter stopped. He'd lost any sign of the girls. He noticed the little flying people were no longer following him and realized he was alone. Something splashed nearby and Peter jumped. He decided he must've gone the wrong way and started to retrace his steps.

There they were—the three girls, as though they'd materialized out of the musky air. They stood in front of the cascading leaves of a huge weeping willow, just staring at him, their faces somber.

"Where'd you go—" he began, then caught movement behind them. Someone was with them.

The shadowy shape of a woman slipped out from the curtain of leaves.

Peter stepped back, his hand dropping to the hilt of his knife. "A grown-up!" he hissed.

She was stout but curvy, wide through the hips and thighs. The light danced across her face, revealing smoky, heavy eyelids and luminous, swamp-green eyes.

Peter started to run when she called his name, her voice throaty, barely more than a whisper. Yet he heard her well, as though she were beside him. He hesitated.

"You're most welcome here, sweet boy." Her deep, rich voice blanketed him, comforting, soothing, chasing away his fears.

She stepped forward into a soft ray of sunlight, the light glittering off her dark, oily skin. Peter looked closer. Her skin was actually green, the deep dark emerald of evergreen leaves. Her hair was green as well, a darker shade, almost black. It flowed from beneath a skull cap drawn forward into a widow's peak across her forehead. The twisting weaves of hair snaked down almost to her knees and draped across her face like a hood, keeping all but her large eyes in shadow. Her thin, smoky robe clung to her like a spider web, dripping from her in ropy strings, doing little to cover her full breasts and the shadowy tuft between her legs. Bronze bracelets jangled from her wrists and ankles, and a necklace of bone and claws hung about her neck.

She smiled at Peter, strolled over to him, and slid an arm around his shoulders. Her breath was hot, it smelled of honey, and when he inhaled, he felt a drowsy warmth take him.

"Won't you come in?" She gestured to a round hole dug into an embankment beneath a thick overhang of straw and matted moss. Large, pitted stones circled the entrance, each with the face of a brooding beast carved into its surface. Dozens of dried gourds hung around the opening, painted red, with bird-size holes cut into them. Small black bat-winged, men-shaped creatures with long scorpion tails were perched or zipping in and out of them.

It didn't look like any place Peter wanted to go. He shook his head.

"I have fresh-baked gingerbread. All little boys like gingerbread. Don't they?"

The three girls nodded. "Most certainly they do, Mother."

The woman put her full, wet lips to his ear, whispered to him. The words were all gibberish to Peter, a strange song of curt, cutting sounds, but the smell of baking bread and honey suddenly came alive. Peter's stomach growled and his mouth moistened. He licked his lips. He would really like some gingerbread—whatever that was.

"Come along," she murmured and ducked into the hole.

Peter didn't think it would be a good idea to follow the woman into that hole, didn't think it would be a good idea to follow her anywhere, but his mind felt syrupy and slow, and when the three girls took his hands and pulled him along, he followed.

He stooped to avoid bumping the roots and glowing mushrooms as he stumbled drunkenly down the long burrow. The tunnel opened up into a small cavern of black rock and twisting roots. Amber stones burned beneath a stack of branches in a wide earthen fireplace, bathing the cavern in their soft caramel glow.

Peter's foot caught on a hide and he fell sprawling atop a pile of plush furs.

Bones, feathers, beads, dried flowers, and a variety of animal skulls were strung together and dangled from the ceiling on long cords. Fat black toads, great oily beetles, and colorful birds hung upside down from hooks, staring at him with dead, glassy eyes. Scrolls and clay pots lay scattered about on low-lying tables.

Peter caught movement among the crags and crevasses of the cavern, thought he saw shapes crawling within the shadows. Then he spied the pile of little cakes stacked in a clay bowl and could think of little else.

She crawled across the furs, carrying the bowl, sidling up next to him. She slid a bare leg over him and put a cake to his lips. Peter took a bite.

It was sweet and warm, but oddly gooey in the middle. He ate it anyway, then another, wanted more, but was having trouble chewing, having trouble keeping his head up. The room was growing fuzzy, wobbling somehow, like ripples across a pond. One moment he saw dozens of shiny candles flickering down at him, then he'd blink and in their stead would be eyes, hundreds of slanted yellow eyes.

She straddled him, leaning forward, letting her hair drape across his face. She placed a warm hand on his stomach, running her fingers up his chest, pushing the wolf pelt aside. She bent over and sniffed his hair, her breasts sliding along his bare chest as she sniffed his face, down his neck, then pressed her cheek against his chest. He felt the hot wetness of her mouth on his nipple.

Peter felt his loins stir. He saw the three sisters behind the woman, watching, their eyes wide, feverous, drool running shamelessly down their chins.

"My, he is a firm one," whispered the first.

"Rigid as a tent post," chimed in the second.

"We will feed a long time on this one," added the third and all three giggled.

No, Peter tried to shout, but managed only a weak moan. He felt a sharp sting then a burning at his nipple.

"Blood for the children. Blood for all," the sisters said as one.

Peter caught movement above him—eyes, the yellow slanted eyes slithering out from the shadows. Hundreds of them, twisted, deformed creatures, some no bigger than newts, others the size of raccoons. Blotchy gray skin rolled along their bony, cadaverous bodies as they slithered and shimmied toward him, all grinning with long, needle-thin teeth.

He caught sight of the bowl of gingerbread cakes, only they weren't cakes at all, but fat, grubby larvae with little black heads. Again, Peter tried to shout.

The woman convulsed, coughed violently, and sat up. Blood was smeared all around her lips and mouth.

"Mother, what is it?" the sisters asked as one.

She coughed again, a retching cough. She clutched her throat, gagged, and spat up, dousing Peter with a mouthful of bile and blood.

She howled, the horrible sound filling the small chamber.

The creatures froze in place; their eyes terrified.

She stared at Peter while a long string of red drool slid from her lips. "It can't be?" She shook her head. "How?"

She coughed again, spattered Peter's face with more blood.

"Mother, what is it?" the sisters pleaded. "Tell us!"

The woman pushed the wolf cap back from Peter's head. She stared at his ears. "Not a boy," she said, her eyes wide with confusion and fear before they turned hard. "Not a child of the Sidhe either. An *abomination*," she hissed.

Peter felt himself waking up fast, the room coming into sharp focus.

Her hand shot out like a viper, clutching his neck between her rigid fingers, her sharp nails biting into his flesh. "Where did you come from? Did Modron send you? Is this one of her games?"

Peter slid his hand down to his knife, but found the sheath empty.

"Is this her vexings?" she cried, her emerald eyes swimming with malice. "Answer me lest I bite off your boyhood and feed you to the leeches!"

Peter's hand flailed about, hit the clay bowl. He snatched a hold of it and struck her, breaking the bowl on the side of her head, knocking her over. Peter kicked away and almost made it to his feet when her fingers bit into his ankle, tripping him, sending him barreling into the hearth.

She came after him, claws out, lips peeled back, exposing rows of long, green, blood-stained teeth. Her eyes shriveled to tiny pinpricks of glowing green set deep within dark sockets. She snatched a hold of his arm, her sharp claws puncturing deep into his muscle tissue. She raked her other hand across his ribs, tearing into his flesh.

Peter let out a shrill cry and snatched a shard of timber from the fire, cried out again from the heat of it, but held tight as he rammed the burning end into her eye.

She shrieked, a sound so loud that he had to clap his hands over his ears. She flew away from him, crashing across the room, the burning shard stuck deep in her socket, sizzling flames leaping up between her fingers as she clutched at it.

Peter didn't wait around to see what happened next; he dove into the tunnel, scrambling up the shaft as fast as a mole rat.

"Get him!" she wailed. "Get him! *GET HIM!*" she bellowed, and her voice shot up the tunnel, sending leaves, dirt, and bugs rocketing past him in a hot blast.

Every slithering, crawling, and flying thing, the very cavern itself seemed to howl then. And they came for him, all of them, the roots too, grabbing at his arms and legs. The tunnel shrank around him, like the convulsing throat of some giant monstrosity. Things leaped off the walls onto him: bugs, spiders. He felt their stings and bites. He reached the surface and the bat-winged creatures came for him like a swarm of hornets, stinging him with their tails, sending him howling away into the thickets. Peter ran then, ran faster than he'd ever run. He had no idea where he was going, intent only on getting as far away as he could from that woman, that creature, and all the biting, stinging things.

He heard howls and dared a glance back. The three girls were coming for him, running on all fours, great, loping strides, their feet seemed not to even touch the ground, long, pointed tongues lolling out from between sharp canine teeth as they rapidly closed the distance.

Peter broke out of the thicket onto a small path and dashed up the trail. He climbed steadily upward, the bog falling behind as the ground became firm underfoot.

A figure stepped in front of him. A man? Peter crashed headlong into him, both of them tumbling into a small grassy clearing. Peter hopped up, started to flee, and saw more men, five, no, six of them. They pointed long, thin swords at his chest. Peter glanced around, frantically searching for an avenue of escape.

"Whoa. Hold," said the first man, the one Peter had knocked over. "What nonsense is going on here?"

On second look, Peter realized that these were not men, not of the sorts he'd known, anyway. In fact, they were elves, but Peter knew nothing about elves at the time. These elves were much shorter than men, boyish in size, little over a head taller than himself. Long in limb, thin of face, almost feminine with small, golden eyes, mere slits, slanted and set high and wide above sharp cheekbones. They had pointed ears and skin as white as chalk. Their hair hung down their backs in long braids. They wore tight-fitting garments that looked to be made of woven leaves and bark.

"Give him back," came a little girl's voice. The three sisters were standing at the edge of the clearing not ten yards away.

The elves shifted the points of their swords to the girls.

"We brought him through," the girls spoke. "He's ours."

"I think not," said the elf, the one Peter had run into. Peter could see he looked older than the others. His hair was pure white, and there were strong lines about his eyes. The elf got to his feet, drew his sword, and stepped in front of Peter.

The sisters hissed, all three of them raking the air with their claws, as though they couldn't wait to rend Peter's flesh.

"He belongs to me," came a deep, guttural voice from behind the girls.

The elves exchanged looks.

The woman strolled into the clearing, one hand clasped over her eye. "He owes me something." She dropped her hand, exposing the raw, bloody wound of her eyeless socket.

Several of the elves gasped, but held their ground.

"You're trespassing, all of you. Give me one of the boy's eyes and I will allow you to leave unharmed."

"Nonsense," countered a voice from behind Peter.

Another woman entered the clearing. She was a bit taller than the swamp woman, thin-boned and slender through the body, almost frail, her smooth skin so white as to be blue. Her long white hair was tied back and crowned with a ring of holly leaves. She was draped in shimmering white and gold and wore a bronze star attached around her neck by a simple gold chain.

"This is Myrkvior forest," she said. "You've no dominion here. Go back to your hole and rut with your filthy beasts."

The swamp woman smirked. "What do you know of rutting? You with your cold dead cunt."

The white-haired woman's eyes flashed, brilliant cerulean.

The swamp woman laughed. "A barren fertility goddess. No wonder you can no longer hear Father's voice."

A low growl rumbled from the white-haired woman's throat, a sound that made the hair stand up on Peter's arms. She stepped forward, her lips peeled back exposing long canine fangs, appearing more animal than human at that moment.

"Oh, stop your pissing, Modron," the swamp woman said. "If you wish this creature, take him." The swamp woman's face changed then. Peter wasn't sure if he saw sympathy or pity—maybe both. "How many?" she asked. "How many will it take to fill that hole in your heart? You can have all the children in our world and in theirs, but it will never bring your little boy back to you."

Pain, deep pain, fell across the white-haired lady's face.

The swamp woman started away, then stopped. She looked at Peter. "Be careful, little boy. I only want your eye. But she—she'll take your *soul*." The swamp woman spun away and seemed to evaporate into the woods.

The three sisters backed slowly away, not taking their eyes off Peter. Before the last sister left, she pointed at Peter, then at her eye, and jabbed at the air with a hook claw.

THE CERULEAN-EYED WOMAN stared at Peter. They all did. Peter glanced about, looking for an escape.

"Don't be frightened, boy," said the older elf as he dusted off his leggings. "Anyone that stole the witch's very eye has nothing to fear from the likes of us." He gave Peter a wry smile of admiration.

The other elves nodded in agreement and put away their swords.

The old elf extended his hand. "Sergeant Drael of the Lady's First Guard, at your service." His face broke into a broad grin.

Peter liked the elf's smile. He shook his hand and smiled back. "I'm Peter."

"This," the elf extended a hand toward the woman, "is the Lady Modron, daughter of Avallach. The Lady of the Lake and the Queen of all Avalon."

A queen? Peter wasn't sure what a queen was, but judging by the way the elves treated her, it must be something important. He took a closer look. She appeared a bit frail to him, with her fine bones and long, thin neck, yet he sensed strength from her. Maybe it was the confidence in her stride, the way she glided through the forest, the way she looked at all things as though they belonged to her. She was elegant and graceful, but Peter thought her eyes a bit too far apart, her face too long, making her appear animalish, spooky even.

"So, Peter," Drael said. "How did a boy end up in the clutches of Ginny Greenteeth?"

"Who?" Peter asked.

"The witch."

"He's not a boy," the Lady said, appraising Peter. "See his ears. He has faerie in him."

"What is he then?" Drael asked.

The Lady gave Peter another long look. "He's a mystery. A most intriguing mystery." She looked at Peter's chest. "He's been marked."

Peter looked down at himself. He was covered in mud and blood. The cuts in his side were bleeding steadily, the bug stings were red and swelling, and the bite around his nipple was turning black. He'd been so intent on escape he'd not even noticed, but now the wounds began to hurt, the one on his chest burning. His hand did, too. He held out his palm; it was an angry red and dotted with white blisters.

The Lady bent down and lightly touched the edge of the bite wound. Peter flinched and sucked in a breath.

"Come," she said. "We need to take care of that or the poison will spread." She held out her hand.

Peter hesitated.

"It's okay," she said.

Peter took her hand and she led him up the trail. The elves fell in, three in front and three behind. Peter looked up at her as they walked. She smiled at him. Peter decided he liked holding hands with a queen, liked it very much.

The trail led into a lush glade; at its center sat a circular pond surrounded by large, flat, white boulders. A gentle stream cascaded over the stones, sending a soft ripple across the pond's surface. The water was crystal-clear.

Peter caught sight of small, colorful fish chasing one another just below the surface—on second look, he noticed that they had the upper bodies of men and women. The winged wee folk skated across the surface as they zipped about snatching bugs out of the air.

The Lady unhooked the clasp on her shoulder, letting her gown drop. She waded out into the pool until her fingertips touched the water. The sunlight glittered off the surface and danced along her gleaming white skin. She closed her eyes and raised her face to the sun, basking in its warmth.

She spoke a few words that Peter didn't understand and sank beneath the water.

The elves spread out, perching among the surrounding rocks, and watching the woods.

Peter waited for the Lady to surface. He waited a long time. No one could hold their breath that long. He glanced around at the elves, but none of them appeared concerned. He walked up to the bank, caught a flash beneath the water, and saw her, a silvery shape swimming like a fish around the pool. She bobbed up before him and gestured for him to come in.

Peter took off his wolf pelt and tested the water with his foot. It was cool but not cold and felt good on such a warm day. He waded in to his waist and felt something tickling his ankles. The fish people were flittering around his feet, feeding on the silt.

The Lady took his hand and pulled him into the deeper water, until his tiptoes could just touch the bottom. She drifted behind him, draping her arms over his shoulders. Peter stiffened.

"Let go of your fear, Peter," she whispered.

Peter took a deep breath and she took him under, pulling him down to where the water was dark and cold. Peter could just make out the blurry rays of the sun dancing on the surface far above him. His lungs began to tighten and he felt a twinge of panic.

Her arms squeezed about him and he thought of her sharp teeth. Did she mean to drown him?

Her voice drifted to him, a muffled song resonating through the depths. The water began to warm around him. He felt a steady thumping, like a heartbeat, could hear the swish of blood through his own veins and arteries and it was as though he was back in his mother's womb. His pulse began to slow, matching the rhythm, two hearts beating as one. His lungs no longer ached for air. He felt part of her, of the pool, the water itself his lifeblood. Her voice the faintest tickle in his ear, *I am your forest, your earth, your eternity. I am your life. I am your death. I am all things forever and always. Love me. Love me. Forever love me.* He curled into a ball, a floating fetus with the pond his womb. *Yes,* he answered. *Forever.* The womb began to glow, growing brighter, then brighter. His head broke the surface.

Peter spat out a mouthful of water and sucked in a deep lungful of air. He blinked against the sunlight. Where was he? Then he saw the Lady and nothing else mattered. She was the most perfect creature he could imagine, and he couldn't understand how he ever thought otherwise. His heart fairly strummed with her vision, all he wanted to do was gaze upon her forever.

The Lady examined him. "The poison is gone," she said, looking satisfied. "The wounds will heal with time."

Reluctantly, Peter tore his eyes from her and glanced down at his chest. There was only the slightest pink trace of the bite mark left. The slashes in his side were closed and the hundreds of insect stings had vanished.

They got dressed and lay out upon a wide, flat stone to warm themselves in the sun.

Peter was watching a heron drift by overhead when a host of hoots and howls burst from the trees. He sat up. A crew of long-armed creatures came swinging into the clearing. They were a bit larger than raccoons, black manes sprouting around their necks. Their small, dark eyes were close-set and their snouts were long, reminding Peter a bit of wolfhounds. They scampered up to the far bank on short legs and knuckles, slurping noisily as they drank from the pond.

"What are those?"

"Barghest," the Lady said. "Be careful, they can be nasty if given the chance. They'll certainly rob you of anything they can get their hands on."

The creatures hooted and barked as they drank.

Peter cupped his hands to his mouth and mimicked their hooting.

The barghest fell silent, all of them staring at Peter. Peter jumped up and let loose several more hoots. The creatures erupted into a volley of irritated barking, the lot of them leaping away into the trees and disappearing into the woods.

The Lady laughed heartily and the sound was music to Peter's ears.

"That's good, Peter. How'd you learn to do that?"

Peter shrugged, then began to mimic the whistles, hoots, chirps, and calls of the other animals. Soon all the creatures around the pond were cocking their heads quizzically at him.

The Lady laughed long and deep, and even the elves couldn't help but smile.

A strange cry caught their attention. Peter saw a large bird with fiery red plumage glide across the pond and alight in a nearby tree. It surveyed the pond, its brilliant orange eyes standing out in stark contrast to a crown of black feathers.

The Lady let out a soft gasp and leaped to her feet. "Peter," she whispered. "The Sunbird."

It lifted its head and began to sing, and all the creatures in the forest fell silent. This wasn't just a call, but a song made up of whistles and chirps, like nothing Peter had ever heard before.

"Isn't it wonderful?" she whispered.

Peter nodded and glanced at the Lady. She held her fingertips to her lips, her eyes captivated.

As suddenly as it had appeared, the bird took flight and left them.

"Oh, don't go," she said, and sighed. "I've not seen it since I was a girl. That sweet song takes me back to happier times." She was quiet then, her eyes distant.

Peter caught a flash in the sun and something landed on the sandy bank. He leaped up, raced over, and picked it up. It was a brilliant red feather. He brought it back and held it up for the Lady to see. The sunlight shimmered off the fine filaments, and when he twirled it, it sparkled and glowed as though aflame.

The sparkles glittered across the Lady's face. "Oh, Peter. It's beautiful!"

He handed it to her. "It's for you."

"For me? Peter, no, you can't. It is too wonderful a treasure."

"Yes I can."

She took the feather and began to twirl it. A smile of unabashed joy lit up her whole face, and in that moment she looked like a little girl.

Peter cupped his hands over his mouth, and began to whistle and chirp, trying to mimic the Sunbird's song. He didn't get it right, but after a few more tries, he had it and whistled the song all the way through.

The Lady stared at him in utter amazement, then grabbed his hand and clasped it in both of hers. "That's wonderful! You must be part bird."

"Yes, I am," Peter said proudly. "Why, I'm a Peterbird."

"Well Peterbird, you must come visit my court and sing for me. Is it agreed?"

Peter gave a big nod.

"Good." She looked at him, looked at him intently for a long time. Peter wasn't sure what to make of it.

"One more thing." She reached behind her neck and undid the gold chain. She held it out so Peter could see the eight-point star. He noticed it was actually fine threads of tarnished gold spun around a dark stone. "This belonged to another little boy, a very special little boy. He is lost to me. I would like for you to wear it for now. Would you do that for me?"

Again, Peter nodded.

She slipped it around Peter's neck and kissed him atop his head. "My little Mabon," she whispered, so quietly he almost missed it

As Peter held the star, it began to glow slightly.

The Lady saw it too and her eyes began to tear. She reached for Peter and pulled him tight, hugged him for a long time. She smelled of pollen and the sweetness of cool water.

Peter heard her again in his head, or heart maybe, like in the pond. *You are mine. Mine forever.*

Yes, he answered. *Forever.*

"HEY," NATHAN CALLED. "Wait up."

The child thief realized he'd let his mind drift, let the kid fall behind. He knew better, knew that the Mist, given the chance, would get in his head and play games. *Stupid*, he thought. *Careless and stupid.* And now the boy was actually shouting in the Mist.

Peter waited, searching the shimmering wall of silvery light, listening. Had the Sluagh heard? Were they on their way?

"I don't like this," Nathan said. "Just where are we?"

Peter put his fingers to his lips. "Shhh!" Peter whispered. "You have to keep quiet or they'll hear. Now let's go."

"What're you talking about?"

Peter didn't answer; now wasn't the time for talk. He turned, searching for the Path. It was there, just ahead, the thin golden thread sliding and shifting, drifting away as though blown by a hidden wind. You had to stay with the Path or it would leave you behind.

Peter headed for the Path, then realized Nathan wasn't following; the boy was staring at the ground.

"Look!" Nathan said, pointing.

Peter didn't need to look. He knew what it was.

"Those are bones! That's somebody's goddamn head!" Nathan squinted warily at Peter. "What the hell kinda place is this?"

Peter jabbed his finger to his lips. The kid had to be quiet. *Had to!*

"Don't tell me to *shhh*," Nathan said, raising his voice. "I asked you a question. What the fuck kinda place is this?"

Peter gritted his teeth, tried to control his temper, but this kid was going to get them both killed. He glanced at the Path, it was drifting away. He didn't dare lose sight of it, but they needed the kid. Peter stepped toward him.

Nathan stumbled back, jerked a gun out, and pointed it at Peter. Peter halted.

"STAY THE FUCK AWAY FROM ME!" the kid yelled.

Peter heard the distant sound of children's laughter. His blood went cold. The laughter grew louder, joined by wails and moans, the cackling cries of old women. The Mist began to stir.

The kid snapped his head about. "What's that? Huh? What the *fuck* is that?"

The Path drifted farther away, another moment and it would be lost. "Listen, Nathan," Peter said as calmly as he could. "You have one chance. Follow me, right now. Move, or you'll never leave the Mist."

But Nathan wasn't paying Peter any attention. He spun around, left then right, holding the gun out in front of him, his eyes wide and terrified. *"STAY AWAY FROM ME!"* he screamed.

The Sluagh came, first the disembodied heads, flying around, circling the boy, followed by the naked craggy women, holding hands and skipping merrily about, then the beasts, all shapes and sizes, their barks and howls, screams and growls rumbling back and forth across the ghostly wasteland.

"NATHAN!" Peter cried. *"COME! NOW!"*

"OH MY GOD!" Nathan screamed and pulled the trigger over and over. But there was only a dry click as the hammer fell on the dead shells. The kid's face twisted into a mask of confusion and terror. Peter could've told him the gunpowder wouldn't work, not here in the Mist. It never does. And even if the bullets had fired, they wouldn't have done a bit of good.

The spirits, one and all, laughed, the sound booming about the Mist like thunder. The flying heads swarmed the boy, pecking at his hair. He ran screaming, swinging the gun wildly, trying to fend them off as they chased him into the swirling wall of gray mist.

Peter didn't shout to the boy again. It would do no good. Peter found the Path and walked, his face tight, his eyes hard. He watched one foot after the other pound into the soft, powdery ground and did his damndest not to hear the distant echoes of Nathan's screams.

✦

PETER STUMBLED ASHORE and collapsed on the beach. He punched the sand again and again, until his knuckles were raw, until he could no longer hear the boy's cries inside his head. He dug his fingers into the beach, came away with two handfuls of sand, turned and glared at the Mist. *"WHY?"* he screamed and slung the sand into its swirling mass. "Why," he screamed again, knowing the night would hear, the were-beasts and, worse, the Flesh-eaters. He didn't care.

"Flesh-eaters," he spat. "Fucking Flesh-eaters. This is all because of them." He bared his teeth at the Mist. The glint of madness sparkled in his eye. "Someone," he whispered, "needs to remind them to be afraid of the night."

Instead of heading into the swamps and back toward Deviltree, Peter turned and followed the coastline, making his way over the driftwood and rocks beneath the silvery glow of the low-hanging clouds, and it was not long before he heard the soft tread of something trailing him.

Peter slid out his long knife and turned, shouting a challenge, daring the thing to show itself. Nothing did or dared, his madness too plain, and Peter continued on alone until he saw the jagged timber walls of the fort lit up from within by a smoldering watch fire.

He looked out toward the lagoon, to where the skeletons of the great galleons lay half-drowned, leaning off-keel and rotting. Their frames silhouetted against the silver glow of the Mist like the ghostly bones of a sea dragon.

He walked up to the fort wall, mesmerized by the dance of firelight between the jagged timber beams. Atop each of the gate posts sat a boy's head, their mouths frozen forever in the silent screams of the dead, their hair blowing in the brisk wind, the dark hollows of their eyes staring back at him, mocking him, accusing him.

He counted twenty-four of them. "Jimmy, Mark, Davis . . . Bob. No. Bill? Which was it?" He started over again, then again, but no matter how many times he tried, he couldn't remember all their names. As his frustration grew so did his volume, until he was shouting their names, knowing the Flesh-eaters would hear and not caring.

He saw their shapes approach the wall, peering out into the darkness, felt their eyes searching for him.

"DEATH HAS COME," Peter screamed, *"TO CUT YOUR THROATS AND DRINK YOUR BLOOD!"* He threw back his head and howled like a wolf.

The gate opened. Dozens of Flesh-eaters carrying torches and wielding swords and axes stepped out. A figure pushed through them, a tall man wearing a wide-brimmed hat. He slid his sword from his belt, sliced the air with its long, narrow blade, and strolled forward.

Peter slipped silently back into the shadows and disappeared into the night.

Chapter Eleven

Barghest

✦

"Oww! *OWW!*" Nick cried.

"Just hold still," Cricket said. "You're making it worse."

Nick grimaced. During the night, *something*—and Nick had a damn good idea what, judging by the pixies giggling from the rafters—had tied his hair to the bars of his cage.

"Just one more. There," Cricket said. "Y'know, you'll have to learn not to sleep with your head so close to the bars."

Nick sat up, rubbing his hair, and shot Cricket a cutting look. "Thanks, but I think I figured that one out on my own."

"Eww, someone's a sourpuss," Cricket laughed, then stopped abruptly. "Whoa, you don't look so good."

Nick frowned. "Thanks."

"No. I didn't mean it like that. I mean, you don't look *well*. You feel okay?"

"I'm *fine*," Nick said curtly. "Just had a bad dream, that's all."

NICK WAITED HIS turn for the privy, stepped in, and took a hard look at himself in the mirror. Cricket was right, he looked bad. There were dark circles under his eyes and his eyes looked haunted, his face oddly gaunt. He couldn't stop thinking about the nightmare. Unlike most nightmares, this one stayed with him. Not only could he clearly remember every detail, but he still harbored the ill feelings, the horror of what he'd seen and the terrible things he'd done. He knew it was silly, but he checked his hands, searching for any signs that they were turning black or growing claws. It had been that real. He doused his head with the cool water. It made him feel better, but didn't wash away his dread or the dark mood lingering in his chest.

Nick almost ran into Sekeu when he came out. She was busy refereeing breakfast and getting the fires going.

"Sorry," he said.

She gave him a passing glance, stopped, stepped back, and looked at him again. She didn't seem so much concerned as disturbed. "Nick, how do you feel?"

"Okay."

Sekeu eyed him, skeptical. "You are sure?"

"Yeah," Nick said, a bit annoyed. "I'm fine, really."

Redbone came up behind Sekeu and jabbed her in the butt. "Squaw, paleface need'um powwow."

Sekeu spun around, leading with her fist.

Redbone was ready for her and leaped back, but she caught him on the arm so hard that even Nick flinched.

"Oww, Jesus Christ, man!" Redbone cried, wincing and clutching his shoulder. "Geez, I was just kidding around." He shook his arm out.

"What do you want?" Sekeu snapped, looking ready to take his head off.

"Nothing really, except to say we're running low on acorns, and ber-

ries, and mushrooms. Oh, and pretty much every other damn thing." Redbone leaned over to Nick, still rubbing his arm, and whispered, "She got
her muscles from scalping white men, y'know." He snorted and elbowed
Nick, then did a double-take. "Hey, wow. Cat, you don't look so good."

Nick frowned.

"How did you sleep?" Sekeu asked Nick. "Did you have any bad
dreams?"

The image of his skin turning black and his hands twisting into claws
came to Nick. He was about to mention it, but didn't like the way the two
of them were scrutinizing him, like he'd committed a crime. "No," he lied.
"My stomach hurt a little. That's all. I feel fine now."

Sekeu and Redbone exchanged a wary glance, neither looked convinced.

Redbone slapped Nick on the back. "That's just your body getting used
to the different food, man. That's all. It'll pass." But Nick didn't miss the
dark look Redbone shot Sekeu.

It scared him.

✦

THE NEXT COUPLE of days flowed into one another: breakfast, training,
dinner, sleep, breakfast, training, dinner, sleep, round and round. Nick did
his best to stay out of Leroy's way, but the bigger boy took special pleasure
in targeting him, taking every opportunity to give him a hard time. Nick
tried not to let it get to him, losing himself in his training. He found the
drills and long hours of practice to be the one place where he could forget
his troubles. He also found he was getting pretty good with the staff and
spear—his ability quickly outpacing that of both Cricket and Danny. His
progress was encouraging. But more than anything, he wanted to beat
Leroy, and worked tirelessly with Sekeu trying to master every move and
trick. Soon he was pressing her to show him the advanced maneuvers he
saw the Devils performing. He wasn't sure if it was the exercise or the
strange food, maybe both, but either way, his body felt stronger, his timing
and speed increasing with each passing day.

The nights were the hardest, the dark dreams haunting his sleep. Each
night in his nightmares, his skin would turn black and the dread and

rage would grow in his chest. He would wake breathing hard, his stomach burning and murder in his heart.

After breakfast on Nick's fourth morning, Sekeu led him, Cricket, Danny, and Leroy over to the big round door on the far side of the hall.

A few moments later, Redbone and the one-handed boy, Abraham, joined them, toting buckets and potato sacks. They'd put on leathers, tight-fitting, hand-stitched, single-piece garments with pointed boots sewn right into them, held up by a belt strapped high across the chest.

Redbone tugged on a beat-up, black leather jacket. This one wasn't hand-stitched, this was a genuine American motorcycle jacket, complete with spikes, patches, and SYMPATHY FOR THE DEVIL painted in peeling red letters across the back.

Redbone had a sly grin on his face. "Any of you cats up for a break?"

Danny perked up. "Hey, that'd be great!"

"Good," Redbone said. "We're going on a little adventure."

Nick didn't like the way Redbone said *adventure*.

"We are going foraging," Sekeu said.

"Give you a chance to see some of the sights," Abraham added and gave Redbone a wink.

"Dirk and Dash are coming with us," Redbone said to Sekeu. "Be here in a sec. Just as soon as Dirk finds his sword."

"What, again?" Abraham asked. "How do you lose a sword? Kid would lose his butthole if it weren't attached to his ass."

Redbone laughed out loud at that, showing all of his teeth. He seemed to always be wearing that wide, fierce grin. Nick felt that grin combined with the dye, or paint, or whatever it was he rubbed on his skin and hair to make it red, made him look like a real devil. Then there was that ridiculous red bone, the one tied into the topknot of his wild, tangled hair, like something out of the *Flintstones*. Nick figured if he were to ask—which he had no intention of doing—that ridiculous bone would have something to do with his nickname. Up close, Nick couldn't help but notice all the scars on the boy, and wondered how many scrapes and challenges this whacked-out kid had been in. One particularly nasty-looking scar snaked lengthwise right down between his squinty, fiendish eyes.

Abraham, other than his missing hand, had very few scars. It was his golden eyes that made him so striking, contrasting sharply with his dark skin. Nick didn't believe he'd ever seen a person as dark as Abraham; his skin was almost raven-black. Abraham wore a scruffy bowler hat dressed up with black feathers and beads, and a tight-fitting pin-stripe dinner jacket with the sleeves cut out.

Two more boys joined them; one hopping along as he laced up his boot.

"Nick," Sekeu said. "Meet Dirk and Dash."

Dirk's scalp had been shaved; jagged ritual scarring spun away from his eyebrows and along the side of his head. He was a bit shorter than Nick, square-jawed with a hefty build, reminding Nick somewhat of a bulldog.

Dash pushed a clump of blond hair from his face and stared down at Nick. He was almost as tall as Redbone, had a slight underbite, and a head full of long, greasy hair. Bits of bone and metal jutted from his ears, nose, eyebrows, nipples, and Nick didn't want to imagine where the hell else.

Dirk and Dash cocked their heads from side to side and began to click their teeth.

"No," Sekeu said, and whacked Dash.

Dirk snorted.

"Hey," Dash said and jerked a thumb at Dirk. "What about him?"

Sekeu whacked Dirk. Dirk frowned and whacked Dash. Then the two boys were punching each other, and Redbone and Abraham had to separate them.

Ignoring the ruckus, Sekeu went to the wall and tugged over a basket of mangy-looking hides. She handed one to each of the New Blood. "Put these on."

Nick held it out before him, unsure just how one went about *putting on* a hide.

"Just stick your head through that there hole," Abraham said, then added, "They're for camouflage."

What are we hiding from? Nick wondered, but was afraid to ask.

By the time Nick got the hide situated, Sekeu handed him a belt. The belt looked ancient, the leather cracking and flaking. It was wide and studded with rings of tarnished brass. Nick noticed intricate swirling designs all but worn away from the years of abuse.

"You have to earn the right to carry a sword," Sekeu told them as she plucked four spears off the wall. "For now, you are permitted spears."

Nick noted that the Devils carried a long knife on their belts and a short sword slung across their backs. Dirk and Dash brought along spears as well.

Sekeu tossed Nick a spear. It was heavier than the practice spears, the staff a bit thicker. It felt smooth and true in his hand. He admired the sharp, jagged edge of the spearhead.

Danny was staring at his spear with a sour face. "What do we need these for?"

Nick could've answered that one, recalling the claw marks on the door.

"In case we are attacked," Sekeu said.

"Attacked?" Danny stammered. "Huh? By what?"

"Monsters," Redbone said, his eyes serious.

SEKEU SLID THE bolt over and pulled the heavy round door inward.

Nick was surprised to find himself eager to venture out. The last time he was out, it had been too dark to see anything, and the time he peeked out the door, well, he'd been too scared to see past his own shadow. But with all the Devils coming along, all armed to the teeth, he didn't feel scared, he felt an odd excitement.

He glanced at Redbone, Sekeu, Abraham, Dirk, and Dash; they looked alert, dangerous. Not a group he'd want to run into in the forest.

They shuffled out single-file; Nick following Redbone. He took in a deep breath and the musky smell of damp earth filled his nostrils. He peered around the tall boy, eager to see the forest.

The door thudded shut behind them and the heavy bolt clacked into place. Nick stared at the deep claw marks on the door and swallowed loudly. He glanced up and realized that the fort—at least part of it—was actually in a tree, a huge tree that appeared to have grown right out of the stony cliff face, its thick roots and vines twisting around the boulders like a massive octopus. It towered above them and he could see a few lookout stands here and there among the limbs.

They crested a short slope and Nick got his first clear look at the land of Avalon. He couldn't have told you exactly what he'd envisioned, but the scene before him wasn't it.

Gray saturated everything, dull and rutty, like the skin of something long-dead. Where was the thick, flowering undergrowth, the giant trees alive with purple monkeys and floating butterfly people, as in his dream? There were no magical creatures, not even a pixie. For that matter, there wasn't a sign of *any* living creature of any sort. Not so much as a bird or a bug. The landscape laid out before him was composed of barren sooty earth and the carcasses of once mighty trees. Thorny vines snaked around jagged stumps and huge briar patches formed daunting barriers in all directions.

They marched over the rise and down a crooked, uneven trail, crawling over and under the fallen hulks of rotting trees. There came the occasional break in the low-hanging clouds, and Nick could make out steep, rugged cliffs just beyond the forest.

Redbone fell in beside him and they brought up the rear of the troop. He stared at Nick, that weird grin on his face.

Nick smiled back once, hoping this would placate him. Redbone reminded Nick of the crazy folks that talk to you on the street, the ones you quickly learned it was best not to make eye contact with.

A dense fog swept across the trail, momentarily obscuring the path.

Redbone began making low ghost sounds.

"Silence," Sekeu called from the front of the troop.

Redbone stopped at once but his crazy grin never wavered. He gave Sekeu a *sieg heil* salute and winked at Nick.

As they moved along the path, Nick noted a few trees—usually the larger ones—that still held a bit of green in their uppermost branches. Curiosity got the best of him and he asked Redbone in a hushed whisper: "Is the forest dying?"

"Man, all of Avalon is dying," Redbone answered, seemingly pleased as Punch that Nick wanted to talk. "They call it the scourge. Even in the short time I've been here, I've seen this forest go from a thing of beauty to the way it is now. Each time we go out for berries, seems we got to trek farther and farther north."

"How long you been here?"

"Man, that's hard to say. Time's different here, y'know. I do know it was 1974 when I left the human world."

"Whoa."

"That's nothing. That cat Abraham, he left the human world way back during the Civil War. He used to be a slave."

Nick looked at Abraham, disbelieving. "No way."

"Yup, and if you think that's way out, dig this: Sekeu has been here since the pilgrims. She was a slave of the Delaware tribe. Peter stole her right out from under their big fat noses.

"Abraham told me that when he first arrived, this whole forest was still teeming with all sorts of magical little beasties, even the wee folk. Looking at it now, man, that's hard to believe."

Nick saw something move in the mist, a dark, skittering shadow about the size of a rat.

"That's a darkling," Redbone volunteered. "From what I'm told, they've always been a part of Avalon. Nasty life-sucking things. But pretty much the only life you find around here, now. Hell, these days, even the darklings are starting to fade. With all the wee folk gone, they only got each other to eat."

Nick saw another one duck away into the hollow of a log. It looked like a spider but was the size of a cat. *Geez*, Nick thought, and made a mental note to steer clear of any hollow logs or stumps.

They passed a clump of dead bushes, then rounded a bend, and a shallow valley opened below them where brown foliage sparsely littered the trees. As they trekked along the trail, the landscape gradually began to shift and the trees and bushes to fill in. But it wasn't until after about an hour of hiking that Nick finally caught sight of any real greenery.

They forded a wide, lazy creek, crossed a field of tall brown grass dotted with a few wilted wildflowers, and shortly thereafter entered a forest of thick, sprawling trees.

"This is Myrkvior Forest," Redbone said. "It's the oldest woods on Avalon, the very heart of the island. Its magic is strong, but man, look at that." Redbone pointed at the scraggly limbs and gray-and-brown leafage.

"Man, even here the damn scourge is choking the life out of everything."

Nick found no signs of magical creatures, and only heard the occasional lonely birdcall.

The troop halted while Sekeu and Abraham inspected a line of prickly bushes, poking and prodding among the brown leaves.

"Find anything?" Abraham asked.

Sekeu held out two shriveled berries.

"Now that be a pitiful sight," Abraham said, shaking his head.

The group moved along, farther and farther into the tall trees, checking one cluster of bushes, then another, then another. A couple of hours later they halted beneath a grove of short trees. Redbone pulled a limb down for Sekeu to pluck a couple of berries. She dropped them into Abraham's bucket.

Abraham looked into the bucket. "Well now we're getting somewhere. Why that makes eight berries and about twenty acorns so far."

"Enough for my breakfast," Redbone said. "Don't know what the rest of you jive turkeys are gonna do for grub."

Abraham let out a long, defeated sigh. "Once you could've filled all our buckets up from just this one bush here. If this keeps up we'll be eating thorns sure enough."

"What the fuck?" Dirk said. "Last week there were plenty of berries here."

"Shit," Redbone said. "It's like it's going faster. Every time we have to search farther and farther into the forest. Man, what're we gonna do when we run out of forest?"

"Enough talk," Sekeu said sharply, her face tight. She walked quickly away, continuing down the trail.

The rest of the Devils exchanged somber looks and followed.

A SMALL DEER broke cover. It was thin and mangy. It leaped across a wide, shallow creek, up a slope, and disappeared into the brambles.

Redbone snatched Danny's spear away from him and started after the deer.

"*NO!*" Sekeu shouted.

Redbone ignored her.

"THE LADY'S WOOD!" she cried.

Redbone stopped. He looked up and down the creek, his face confused.

"Oh, good Lord," Abraham said, his voice incredulous. "She's right. That's Cusith Creek. Why, I didn't even recognize it. Not with all them leaves and flowers gone."

"Impossible," Dirk said. "The scourge in the Lady's Wood?"

"If we don't bring something back we're gonna starve," Redbone growled. "I say we go after it."

"You go," Abraham said. "I'm in no mind to throw my life away for a spot of venison."

Redbone stared after the deer.

"The elves will kill you," Sekeu stated with certainty. "The trees have eyes and ears." She pointed to three bird-size faeries watching them from a high branch.

THEY FOLLOWED THE dark creek downstream, stopping occasionally to examine the bushes along the banks. The sun never came out from behind the clouds, but the day had grown warm and humid.

"Hey," Danny huffed, wiping the sweat from his brow. His face was bright red, his T-shirt soaked. "Any chance of a break?"

Sekeu kept plodding onward, her eyes relentlessly searching the bushes and underbrush.

"Y'know," Abraham said, "break might not be such a bad idea. Be a mite awkward if we were to kill the New Blood on their first day out."

Sekeu stopped, took a hard look at Danny, then scanned the surrounding tree line. "Rest here. I will go check oak grove. Dirk, come."

Nick collapsed atop a large, flat stone next to the shallow creek and watched Sekeu and Dirk disappear into the woods. He let out a tired sigh and joined the rest of them in dousing his head and getting a long drink. The sweetness of the water still amazed him.

"Can't believe the scourge has spread to the Lady's Wood," Redbone said. "Man, I would've never dreamed that possible."

"Seems to me, it's accelerating," Abraham said. "I do wonder if Peter has any idea."

"Y'know," Dash said, "Peter should've been back by now."

"Just hope he ain't got himself in a spot he can't get out of," Abraham said.

"There's no such thing as trouble that dude can't get out of," Redbone said.

"I just hope he brings some more Snickers," Dash said.

"Man, there ain't much I miss about the world," Redbone said. "But I gotta say I sure miss the food. Remember that time Peter brought back six boxes of Ray's pizza?"

"Do I ever," Abraham said, and a big smile lit up his face. "Why I dream about that most every night."

Danny's eyes grew big. "Pizza! Wow, that'd make my decade."

"Don't tell me you're getting tired of acorns and mushrooms already," Redbone said, and nudged Danny. "Man, you gotta wait 'til you've been here as long as me before you start griping about the food."

"So where *is* Peter?" Nick asked.

"Catching kids," Redbone said with a laugh.

Nick couldn't believe they were laughing. "That's funny?"

Redbone's smile faded.

"It's not right," Nick muttered, half-under his breath.

"What's not right?"

Nick didn't answer, he just shook his head.

"I said, what's not right?"

"What do you think?" Nick said. "The bastard kidnapping kids. That's what's not right."

Redbone struck Nick. He moved so quickly Nick didn't even see it coming, hit him in the chest, knocking him into the creek.

Abraham was up and between them in a blink, holding Redbone back. "Whoa. Ease back now. Let it go. He's New Blood, remember?"

Redbone glared at Nick then glanced around at the other New Blood. "Let's get one thing straight. I don't want to catch any of you badmouthing the *man*. That jive don't fly with me." He walked over to Nick, grabbed him by the collar, and pulled him up out of the creek. He propped Nick back up on the rock, then plopped down across from him, leaning forward and locking his crazy eyes on him.

"You need to understand a thing or two," Redbone said. "So I'm gonna lay it on you. Back before I came here I lived upstate with my old man. Got tired of the sorry fuck beating the snot out of me every other day. So I upped and lit out for the big city. In less than a week, I was sleeping in a cardboard box, stealing, and turning tricks just to eat. You've any idea how bad that is? I had to do things I can't even talk about still. I was thirteen. *Fucking thirteen!*

"One night this pimp gets a hold of me. Bastard tells me if I wanna work *his* street, I gotta pay. *Pay?* With what? I didn't have enough dough to buy food. How was I supposed to pay this hustler? So I don't. Sure enough he catches up with me and beats the crap out of me. I mean really beats the crap out of me. Left me in a Dumpster, spitting up blood. Man, at that point I wanted to die.

"Week later I'm back at it, because that's all I got, see. Only now, no one wants anything to do with me. Y'know why?" Redbone's eyes bore into Nick. "Because I got this gnarly scab on my mouth and I was all scraped up from the beating. So I'm mostly stealing shit and eating out of garbage cans. He caught me on his turf again. I wasn't getting any action. I was just there, y'know. Made no difference to this motherfucker. He drug me into an alley, stuffed garbage in my mouth so no one could hear me screaming, and pulled out his knife. Says he's gonna fix me for good and gives me this." Redbone traced the scar running down his face. "Would've killed me, but that's when Peter showed up. Y'know, the guy you were just badmouthing? Before that asshole even knew what was happening Peter cut him *wide* open. Laid him out! That's one son'bitch that'll never hurt another kid, *ever.*

"Peter doctored me up the best he could and brought me back with him. So let me lay it on you straight. I love that pointy-eared dude. He did more than save my life. He gave me a life. Gave me a family. I know what I'm about, 'cause it's all real simple here. We're clan. We're Devils and we look after one another."

Abraham and Dash nodded along.

"And if you think my story's bad," Redbone continued, "man, you ain't heard shit. Get Abraham to tell you what it was like to be a runaway slave sometime. Ask him about the life Peter *saved* him from. Hell, ask any of them kids back at the fort. Every one of them gots a hard-luck story that'd bring tears to your eyes. Plenty a lot worse than mine. And there's not a single one of them that wants to go back. Because we've all had our share of dealing with fucked-up parents, stepparents, priests, cops, pimps, pushers, crackheads, all those fuckers out there. That world out there, I say they can keep it, man.

"Peter's given us another chance. That cat has put his life on the line for me. For you and for every kid here, time and again. The sooner you get your mind right about that the better off you'll be. Are we straight on that?"

No, Nick thought. *We're not.* But he nodded anyway.

"Good," Redbone said. "Because I like you. And I'd hate to have to kill you."

Nick wasn't sure if Redbone was kidding, was pretty sure he wasn't, pretty sure this kid *would* kill him if Peter asked him to, and judging from what he had seen back at the fort, probably any of them would. He glanced at Abraham, Dash, Leroy, even Cricket and Danny. He could see it in all their eyes. They were completely taken in by Peter's ruse. It was as though Peter was some sort of messiah to them, come to take them to the promised land.

"This is a magical place," Abraham said, addressing all the New Blood. "You wouldn't know it. Not by the way things are now. But when I first come here these forests were lush, teeming with life. Every kind of fruits and nuts you could imagine. Why there were wild bananas hanging off the trees . . . a true paradise."

"And it'll be again," Redbone stated with absolute conviction. "That's where we come in. Where *you* come in. Together we're gonna drive away the Flesh-eaters and then." His eyes glimmered. "Then, we'll be the Lords of Avalon."

"Flesh-eaters?" Cricket asked.

Redbone hesitated, cut his eyes to Abraham.

"Tell us," Cricket prodded.

"Yeah, well," Redbone muttered. "Let's just say they're the ones causing all this trouble and leave it at that."

"What are they?" Cricket persisted.

"Hush up, now," Abraham said. "Here comes Sekeu. She's in a foul enough mood already. She'll scalp the lot of us if she hears us talking to New Blood about Flesh-eaters. Peter will tell you. Let you in on everything soon enough."

Why can't we talk about these Flesh-eaters? Nick wondered. *What are they hiding?* Nick thought about asking Sekeu, then saw her face and decided now wasn't the time.

Sekeu held out her hand: four gray acorns.

"That there's from Oak Grove?" Abraham asked.

She nodded.

"What're we gonna do?"

"I say we slip across the creek," Redbone said. "Make a quick raid into the Lady's Wood."

Abraham looked at him as though he'd lost his mind. "You do have a death wish."

"The elves are too vigilant," Sekeu said.

"Well, that leaves the witch's swamp," Redbone said.

They all fell quiet.

"Well?" Abraham asked, looking at Sekeu.

Sekeu shook her head. "What other choice do we have?"

THEY FOLLOWED THE creek downstream until the land began to level out. The water turned brown and led into a marsh of high, gray reeds. The reeds gave way to squat twisted trees with slick, black, oily bark, their branches dripping with thick moss. The path became soggy then muddy, grabbing at their feet. The trees pressed in around them as the path wove around weedy bogs and stagnant ponds.

Nick didn't like it; other than an occasional bellow, the swamp was still and silent, the air musty and stifling. Even Redbone had fallen deathly quiet, all of them creeping along, weapons out, keeping a tight watch on the trees and murky pools. Nick felt as though he was in a sideshow spook house, knowing something would pop out at any second. He was worn out, his feet sore, and the dread was wearing on his nerves. He decided he'd had all the adventuring he needed for one day, and found himself actually longing to be back at the fort.

A cry came from behind and Nick spun about in time to see Danny sliding down a short embankment and into a pool of black, viscous mud.

"HELP!" Danny cried as he clawed at the slippery bank. The mud bubbled up around him. It was up to his waist in no time and appeared to be pulling him down.

Redbone leaped over, grabbed a root in one hand, and snatched a hold of Danny's wrist with the other. Dash and Dirk were there in a second and it took all three of them to finally pull Danny out.

"Hey Danny," Redbone said. "Next time you decide to drown yourself, try not to make so much noise. Okay?"

Danny looked like he was about to cry. He'd lost both his boots and was covered from the neck down in stringy, oily mud. The mud gurgled loudly behind him and he scurried away from the bank.

"Maybe we should take them back," Abraham said to Sekeu.

"There," Sekeu said, and pointed to a cluster of spotted mushrooms growing beneath a thick, thorny hedge.

"Few more over here," Dash said. "We should spread out. Might just find enough."

Sekeu nodded in agreement. She pointed at Nick and the other New Blood. "You four look here. Abraham, stay with them. The rest of you spread out. But keep in sight. We must be quick. She will find us if we linger."

"OUCH," NICK SAID, and stuck his finger in his mouth. That was about the hundredth time he'd been pricked so far. The only mushrooms they'd found were growing beneath the thornbushes. Nick guessed these were the ones the deer couldn't get to.

"Me too," Cricket said. She held up the back of her hand. She was a couple bushes down the slope, but Nick had no problem seeing the scratches. Danny actually looked like he was enjoying himself for the first time all day. He was on all fours, knocking at a mushroom with his spear.

"It's kind of like hunting Easter eggs," Danny said. "Don't you think?"

"Just shut up and keep picking," Leroy said.

Abraham came over to Leroy and dropped a handful of mushrooms into his sack.

"We do need to hurry," Abraham said, looking worriedly up the hill. "The fog's gettin' up."

Nick glanced up the hill and could just make out the shape of Sekeu and Redbone digging around on the ridgeline.

Something splashed nearby; Abraham heard it too. The fog was indeed getting thicker. At first, Nick thought he was just imagining things, then a wave of fog drifted into the clearing and all but obscured Danny.

"No sir, this ain't right at all," Abraham said. "We need to git. I'll fetch Sekeu. Now, don't any of you go nowhere." He sprinted away up the hill.

The fog continued to roll in.

"Nobody told you to stop," Leroy said.

"Can you see them?" Cricket asked.

"Not anymore," Nick said.

"Got it!" Danny said, holding up a big yellow mushroom. "Man, would you look at the size of this thing?"

"Shit, I can't see a thing," Cricket said.

"I said get back to work," Leroy growled.

A small break opened in the fog. Nick spotted Abraham nearing the ridge, then the hair shot up on the back of his neck. Behind Abraham were four, maybe five hunched shapes, right on his heels, and whatever they were, they *weren't* human.

Nick was in mid-shout when a horrible screech cut him off.

It was Danny. He was on the ground and on top of him was a—*monster.* It had red fur, was no larger than a cat, and reminded Nick of a hyena but with long arms and clawed fingers that were even now digging into Danny's arm and shoulder. It whipped about a long tail with a wet red stinger protruding from the end, and it began slamming the stinger repeatedly into Danny's neck and face.

"OH, SHIT!" Nick cried. His sack fell from his hand, sending the handful of mushrooms tumbling down the slope.

Danny's face went bright red, his mouth opened wide as he gasped loudly for breath. He toppled over backward, twitched violently, then lay still, his eyes staring up at nothing.

Another hyena-thing dropped from the tree above Cricket, knocking the spear from her hand. This one was much larger, closer to the size of a German shepherd, a thick mane of black fur circling its head. It too had a whip tail, but this one lacked any sort of stinger that Nick could see.

Cricket screamed and swung wildly with her bucket, driving it back. She tried to get around it, but it kept her pinned between the thorn bushes, hissing and snapping its teeth.

Leroy, not five strides away from her, seemed frozen in place, his eyes big, his mouth agape, clutching his spear between his white-knuckled fists.

"*HELP HER!*" Nick shouted. But Leroy only continued to stare.

Cricket hit the monster with the pail. It jigged side to side, darting to and fro. Nick saw the smaller, red-haired creature creeping up from behind her. If somebody didn't do something now, Cricket would be as dead as Danny.

Leroy stumbled backward and fell.

Nick rushed out from the bushes, not even feeling the thorns dig into his legs, not thinking about anything but driving those monsters away from Cricket. He snatched up his spear and rushed the beasts, leaping past Leroy as Leroy scrambled up the hill on all fours.

The red creature leaped on Cricket's back and jabbed its stinger into her neck, over and over. Cricket let out a pitiful cry and tumbled over.

"*NO!*" Nick screamed, and slammed the spear into the red creature's ribs, knocking it off Cricket and driving it into the dirt.

The red creature shrieked and thrashed, black blood spewing from the wound.

The black hyena-thing let loose a howl that almost caused Nick to drop his spear. The wail sounded human, sounded full of rage and anguish.

Nick yanked his spear free and leveled it at the hyena-thing.

The monster locked eyes with Nick and began to beat the ground in front of it. It bared its fangs and tore up clumps of dirt and leaves, slinging them into the air.

It means to tear me apart, Nick thought, and wanted to run, but knew if he turned his back, even for a second, the creature would have him. His heart thundered in his chest. *This is beyond me, I can't do this.* But there was a new voice in his head; Sekeu, telling him to hold steady, to focus. Nick slid into the L-stance, fixed his trembling hands on the spear. *One shot,* he thought, *that's all I'm gonna get.*

The hyena-thing let loose an earsplitting screech and came for him, ripping across the ground in a crazy zigzagging charge, hooting and howling.

Focus, Nick thought, taking quick, short breaths, fighting to hold steady. The monster leaped and Nick swung, putting a snap on the spear just as Sekeu had showed him. The blade caught the beast in the neck, cutting its throat wide-open.

The creature slammed into Nick, spattering him in black blood and knocking him to the ground. Nick shoved the convulsing body away and tried for his feet, but before he could get up, something landed on his back. The smaller, red creature, its claws sunk into his shoulder, its stinger whipping toward his face. Nick managed to get his arm up and the stinger ripped across his forearm.

Nick cried out as searing pain shot up his arm. He twisted free and kicked away from the beast. It twitched and clawed at the dirt but didn't get back up.

Nick clasped his wounded arm to his chest; he could feel the burning spread up his shoulder. His face began to grow warm, then hot; his throat tightened. Nick dropped his spear and fell over on his back, gasping for breath as his throat continued to constrict. He caught a glimpse of Cricket. She was pale and still, her eyes lifeless.

The red beast lay on its side, twitching. Leroy, his face a mask of fear and revulsion, rushed up and slammed his spear into the monster's body over and over, and kept repeating, "Oh shit! Oh shit! Oh shit!"

"THEY ARE HERE!" Sekeu shouted, running out of the fog, taking in the scene in a glance and sliding down next to Cricket. She leaned over, putting an ear against the girl's chest.

Abraham, Dirk, Dash, and Redbone came running up. Redbone was splattered in black blood. A nasty slash ran across his shoulder and chest, his breath coming hard and fast through clenched teeth, sword in one hand, knife in the other, both dripping with blood. He locked wild, fierce eyes on the two dead creatures.

"I killed them," Leroy said quickly. "Killed both of them." He looked at Cricket and Danny. "I tried to save them. Things just happened so fast. I did what I could."

Redbone met Leroy's eyes; his mouth a grim line. He slipped away his knife, clapped a bloody hand on Leroy's shoulder, and shook the boy. "Those are barghest, man. Right on, Leroy!"

Leroy grinned weakly and cut his eyes to Nick.

What? Nick thought. *"No!"* he tried to shout, but his throat was too tight and he broke into a fit of painful coughing.

A howl cut through the fog; it came from everywhere, from the very ground. The fog itself began to darken like a storm cloud.

"The witch," Sekeu said.

Chapter Twelve

Lady Modron's Garden

Peter stared at the bodies. In the soft glow of dawn he could see that the earth was still dark from their slaughter. There were four of them, Pooxits, distant cousins to the centaur, only much smaller, coming no higher than Peter's knee. They had the bodies of cats, and the torsos of monkeys. They'd always reminded Peter of little people with their dexterous fingers, chattery speech, and lively, expressive faces.

He could see where the Flesh-eaters had burned them out of the nearby brush, there were slashes in the dirt of a struggle and tracks where they'd been dragged over to be skinned and butchered. Their bones lay scattered about the dirt; Peter couldn't help but notice the teeth marks on the bones.

He found their heads and hands in a ditch, tossed aside like garbage.

Their eyes—glazed and jellied—stared up at him, the horror of their deaths still plain to see. Peter had heard the screams of those caught by the Flesh-eaters. Be they elf, centaur, gnome, troll, faerie folk, or even Devil, it didn't matter, the Flesh-eaters showed no mercy. They skinned them alive, butchered, and ate them. *Better to die by my own hand,* Peter thought, *than ever fall into theirs.*

Other than a slight tightening of the jaw, Peter showed no emotion. He turned and pressed on, heading north. The Flesh-eaters' path of razed, brutalized land spread out before him as far as he could see. He skirted the remnants of a village. The burned-out huts jutting up from the dead, ashen earth like so many jagged teeth. A stack of broken skulls were piled against one wall; their hollow eyes followed him as he passed. *It is time to end this,* Peter thought. *One way or another, it* must *end.*

He glanced heavenward. Somewhere above the low-lying clouds, the sun lit up the sky. He could tell the day was going to be warm, could feel the humidity building. He scanned the gray mud and burned husks of long-fallen trees and wondered if the sun's face would ever grace this tortured landscape again.

Peter crested a long, sloping hill, found himself staring into the eyes of a god, and realized where he was. "Avallach's Shrine," he said and dropped heavily onto a boulder. He gazed at the broken ruins. He could see the marshlands below. Deviltree wasn't far now, just past the swamps, but he wasn't looking forward to crossing through the witch's land, not during the day. *Not while I still have my eyes,* he thought, and grinned a nasty grin.

He regarded the god's head, a giant thing of carved granite easily the size of a barrel. It had been knocked from its base at the neck and lay on its side as though listening to the earth. Its face was marred, hacked, and hammered, but even so the eyes still held their strength.

The rest of the great statue still stood, its hands forever clasped to its chest. A ring of craggy stumps spiraled out from the statue—all that remained of the vast apple orchard. When Peter closed his eyes, he could still see those trees, hundreds of them, their white blossoms flittering in the warm sunlight of that faraway day.

PETER SAT BESIDE the old elf upon a large field stone. He cupped a hand across his brow, shielding his eyes from the midday sun as he looked up at the giant statue. The statue's eyes were set deep within the shadow of its thick furrowed brow, staring ceaselessly out over the orchard.

Apple blossoms drifted lazily by, glittering in the sunlight, gathering in every crease and fold of the statue's drapery. The apple trees surrounding the statue hummed and buzzed with honey bees, birds, and the ceaseless chatter of sprites and faeries.

Peter followed the Lady's every move, found he cared to do little more. She stood before the statue, a slender hand resting upon its foot, looking up into the stern face.

"That's Avallach," the old elf said. "God of healing, Lord of Avalon. He's left us, his mortal time on earth long past. He now reigns in Otherworld, leaving his children to watch over Avalon."

"Uh-huh," Peter said distractedly.

"The Lady Modron is one of his children."

"The Lady?"

"Yes."

"Did her mother leave her too?"

"Mother? I don't believe the Lady had a mother. Not in the way we might think of, anyway. Avallach created his children from the elements at hand. The Lady's spirit comes from the rivers, lakes, and streams. Water will forever be her lifeblood. Her brother, the Horned One, was created from living sacrifices of flesh and blood, while her sister, Ginny, the witch, was grown from the earth like a tree."

Peter glanced over at him, concerned. "The witch is her sister? How can that be? The witch is so wicked."

The elf laughed. "They're gods," he said, as though that explained everything.

Peter looked puzzled.

"They're Nature and one must always be wary of Nature. They play their roles, keeping the balance of Avalon. None of them would flinch at killing any who should threaten that balance. Why even the children of faerie are not immune from their ire. The Horned One will smite any who enter Avalon uninvited. The witch, well you're well aware of what the witch does to outsiders. The Lady guards us all with her Mist. Even among the Sidhe, only a very few can walk the Mist."

Peter watched the Lady lay her cheek against the stone and close her eyes. "I like the Lady very much."

"Yes," the elf sighed. "She is hard not to love. She is like the earth itself. But," he lowered his voice, "one must always be wary of gods and goddesses, lest we become too entangled in their desires and schemes."

174

The elf fell quiet for a while.

"Did you know that the whole world was once Faerie?"

Peter shook his head, half-listening.

"Yes indeed, before men-kind came along." The elf's voice sobered. "Men have disturbed the balance, putting the children of Avallach to the test. All we have left now is this island. The new gods are pushing out the old. Soon, I fear, there'll no longer be room for Earth's first children . . . anywhere. That is why the Lady comes here. To seek her father's counsel. Whether he hears or not, none of us know. Judging from her face I don't believe he does. But that's the business of the gods. My business is to keep the Lady safe."

"Safe?" Peter glanced up at the elf. "From what? The witch?"

"No. I don't believe the witch would harm her, or even could. They might not like each other, but they need each other, the way the land needs water and water needs land. But there are others that would."

Peter looked concerned.

"The Lady's spirit is immortal, but she's not. There are those, even in Faerie, that would feed on her flesh. If her mortal form were to pass she'd no longer be bound to the earth, to Avalon, then where would we be?

"But that won't happen. Not while I'm part of the Guard," the elf stated with obvious pride. "It's my duty to see to it she comes and goes without fear of beast, or witch, or little red-headed freckle-faced boys." He smiled.

Peter leaped to his feet. "Can I join the Lady's Guard?" He thumped his chest. "I'd make a great guard. Why, I'm not afraid of that witch, or wolves, or bears, not anything."

The guard laughed and patted Peter on the head. "Maybe, one day."

✦

"WE'RE HERE, PETERBIRD," the Lady Modron said. "My garden."

It had been a long trek from the statue to the garden. They'd passed through forests and glades, crossed creeks and streams, but to Peter it had seemed no time at all as he walked beside the Lady, as she told him about all the sights and creatures they came upon.

The sun edged toward the horizon, painting the sky and surrounding forest a brilliant gold. The trees about the garden were tall and straight, with pale blue bark and leaves.

They proceeded up a walkway of alabaster flagstones framed by two long, slender wading pools. Tall standing stones stood sentinel in their still waters. The walkway led to a lofty archway cut into a towering white stone ledge. Wide bands of gold veined the stone, glittered in the waning sunlight, sending dazzling beams sparkling off the long pools. A gentle waterfall spilled onto the crest of the archway, dividing the waterfall into twin falls that cascaded down either side, forming the head of each pool.

A field of wildflowers spilled over the banks of the pools, filling the air with the sweet perfume of nectar and evening dew. Wild faeries and sprites perched upon every reed, lily, and stem, some even straddling the backs of bored-looking bullfrogs. They filled the dusk with their song as they watched the Lady pass.

The Lady and her procession approached the archway and two young elves pulled the tall doors open. The boys bowed to the Lady, giving Peter curious looks as he passed.

They entered a short passageway of polished, iridescent stone, the palest shade of green. The walls were framed by stone pillars in the shape of trees that looked to have grown right from the floor, their branches weaving into a spidery canopy. Music drifted along the corridor, accompanied by raucous laughter, squeals, and grunts. Peter glanced down the hall and

saw a tall, handsome boy with a heavy brow and dark, brooding eyes strid-
ing purposely toward them.

"Someone does not look pleased, my Lady," Drael whispered.

The Lady sighed. "When ever does he?"

The boy was much taller than Peter, eye level with the Lady. Peter
guessed him to be several years older than himself. His dark hair was
cropped in a bowl cut just above his ears, oiled and shiny, not a strand
out of place. He wore a quilted jacket, trimmed in gold, with long puffed
sleeves, made from a finely woven fabric. He had on black stockings and
gold shoes with pointed toes. Peter could not find a speck of dust, nor a

trace of dirt anywhere on the boy.

The tall boy dismissed Peter at a glance and addressed the Lady.

"Modron, you were supposed—"

"Ulfger," the Lady interrupted. "Not today. I do not need this from you
today."

"You were supposed to be here hours ago," he continued, his voice stern
and serious. "Have you forgotten your duties?"

"No, Ulfger," the Lady said with noticeable irritation. "I have *not* forgotten my duties. And I will not be drawn into this today. Not today."

"The fate of Avalon hangs in the balance, yet the council spends its
time drinking, gossiping, and exchanging rude riddles." He stared accus-
ingly at the Lady. "They need leadership."

"Ulfger, it is not your place to tell me—"

"It *is* my place, Modron," he said, making no attempt to hide the con-
tempt in his voice. "This frivolity and buffoonery . . . it is why Avalon is
dying."

"Oh, Ulfger. Why must you do this? You're a boy. You should be having
fun, running wild, getting into mischief. You—"

"No! That, Modron—*that* is the very problem. Avalon needs *order* and
discipline." He clenched his hand into a fist. "Needs an iron hand to combat
men-kind's aggression. Without it we are destined to become extinct."

The Lady looked at him sadly. "Those are your mother's words. Even at
death's door, she can't keep her long nose out of things. And look what she
has done to you. At an age when you should be at your most carefree, you
are bent beneath the weight of her nettling and conniving."

Ulfger flushed. "No, that's not true."

The Lady shook her head. "This is my fault, I should have stood up to her, should have insisted you live in the forest with your father. Your mother has done everything in her power to kill the wildness within you. I am fearful the Horned One will not know his own son."

Ulfger's eyes fell to the floor. He turned away, but not before Peter caught the wounded look on his face.

The Lady took Peter's hand; they pushed past the handsome boy and strolled down the hall.

✦

THEY PASSED BENEATH another arch and entered a great domed hall. A small circular pond lay at the center of the hall, cut into the stone floor. The pond glowed brightly—the very water was phosphorescent—filling the whole hall with a soft, greenish glow. A crescent moon, stars, and winged fish were carved into the dome. The light swirled over the designs, making them appear to swim around the ceiling.

A dozen curved tables circled the pond. Plates and bowls of wild game, bread, boiled carrots, beets, and potatoes littered the pitted, well-worn surface, their spice filling the chamber. Peter inhaled deeply and his stomach grumbled.

"I believe someone's hungry," the Lady said.

Peter grinned up at her and nodded.

A man set down his goblet, pushed back his chair, and propped a cloven hoof on the edge of the table. He wore no clothing, only a thick leather yoke with large brass bells. His small, boyish body appeared to be that of a shaggy goat from the waist down. His skin was blood-red, his hair black. A long, pointed goatee curled upward off his chin and two short horns poked up from his sloping forehead, each with a small gold bell jangling from its tip. "You're late," he growled.

"And a good end of day to you too, Hiisi," the Lady said, a smile pushing one corner of her mouth. "Nice to see everyone waited."

A boar with long, curving tusks, dressed in a brilliant crushed velvet tunic complete with ruffles, held up a drumstick. "Like one swine waits for another," he said through a mouthful of food, then snorted.

There were at least forty folk in attendance, mostly elves, their thin, spindly bodies draped across their high-backed chairs, their movements and gestures elegant and graceful. There were many other strange beings that Peter had never seen or imagined. Four plump men—easily as wide as they were tall and not a one larger than a chicken—with big red noses and cheeks and tiny black eyes that looked like they'd been pushed into their faces, sat upon tall stools wearing outlandish feathered caps and passing a large jug of wine back and forth. A flock of winged faeries sat crossed-legged on the table top, sharing a bowl of fruit. These were different than the ones Peter had seen in the forest; foremost, they were clothed, wearing britches and jackets or wispy gowns, and were well-mannered as they ate from tiny plates and sipped from tiny cups.

There were various other impish creatures, some more beast than manlike. Peter noticed two elven women, one with skin as black as coal, the other pink as roses. They lay coiled in each other's arms, their eyes closed as they kissed and licked each other's mouths, their hands lost beneath each other's dresses. A child—an infant really—with a single red horn jutting from its forehead puffed away on a pipe, his eyes heavy as though lost in a dream. There were at least three faerie folk passed out on the floor, one of them snoring loud enough to be heard even over the ruckus.

Sour-faced servants moved in and out of the chamber, carrying trays, pouring wine into goblets, and complaining loudly to each other all at the same time. Over in one corner four stout faerie folk with bristly beards that fell all the way to their knees were playing flutes and plucking at string instruments, creating a whimsical melody.

Several servants came in and hastily laid out a table setting before an elegant, high-backed chair. The chair was by far the tallest in the room, formed of delicate white roots and branches. It appeared to have grown straight from the floor, its limbs reaching upward, weaving together into a symmetrical arch that nearly touched the top of the dome. The uppermost limbs sprouted into an umbrella of draping leaves. Tiny sprites played in the leaves, their multicolored lights blinking on and off.

The Lady leaned over to Peter. "Wait here with Drael." She strolled to the chair. The band stopped playing and most of the attendees rose as she was seated. The Lady smiled and inclined her head. The dinner guests dropped back into their chairs, returning to their food and conversation as though nothing had happened.

Hiisi, the red-skinned man, sat on the Lady's left. He leaned over. "My Lady, Tanngnost has asked to speak."

The Lady let out a sigh. "Can I not at least eat first?"

"He's just returned from the lands of men-kind. If he doesn't get to speak soon, I fear he will simply burst."

"Oh, dear. I wouldn't wish our beloved Tanngnost to burst, not here in my chamber anyway. I guess we have little choice but to let him say his bit."

Hiisi stood and banged his fork against his goblet. Most everyone ignored him. "Tonight, Council," he said. "A dear old friend has graced us with his pungency. I've composed a rhyme in honor of this most un-notable occasion. Shall I?"

Several heads shook in dire disapproval, but the Lady smiled. "Why yes, dear Hiisi. By all means, proceed."

Hiisi smiled, flicked his eyebrows, then cleared his throat. "I bestow a special troll. One who is dear to heart when he is apart, and hard to bear when he is near. But his lack of charm does no harm. Yes, the harbinger of doom and gloom is back in the room." He inclined his head across the table to a tall figure cloaked in long, tattered gray robes. "Back from his daring jaunt across the lands of men-kind, I give you no other than— *Tanngnost*."

The troll, who didn't look as though he appreciated his introduction in the least, stood up to a spattering of weak applause. He appeared more beast than man, much taller than the elves, taller even than any man Peter had ever seen. He was stooped and appeared ancient but not frail; solidly built, like a stag. His legs were those of a great woolly elk, while his upper body resembled that of a man. A mane of sand-colored hair rolled down his shoulders in thick tangles, framing a long, goatlike snout. Golden, intelligent eyes peered out from beneath thick, drooping brows. Broad horns curled outward from the sides of his head, and thick tusks jutted from his mouth.

Under most circumstances, such an imposing beast would have frightened Peter, but something in this creature's bearing spoke of graciousness, even refinement.

The troll bowed to the Lady, cleared his throat. "I am at your service," he said in a deep baritone. "It is truly an honor to attend the ever-fair Lady Modron, daughter of Avallach, Great Lady of the Lakes, Goddess of—"

"Yes, yes, don't you start with all that silliness," the Lady said, waving her hand as though shooing a fly. "You'll not flatter me. You want something or you'd not be here my dear Tanngnost. Something besides the feasting; which I see you've done your share."

The troll dropped a guilty glance at the five dirty plates stacked before him.

"What ill tidings do you bring today?" she asked. "Go on, spill the beans. Get it over with."

Tanngnost inclined his head. "Lady, you mustn't slay the messenger."

"A very wise old saying indeed," Hiisi interjected. "Unless of course that messenger so happens to be a minder, meddler, and manipulator of other people's business."

This brought plenty of snickers from around the tables.

Tanngnost gave the Lady a long-suffering look. "Modron, if I may be so bold? How did the visit with your father go today?"

The table fell quiet and all eyes turned to the Lady.

The Lady's face clouded.

Tanngnost let out a regretful sigh. "I see."

Somber murmurings hummed around the tables and several folk began to speak at once.

"Why has Avallach abandoned us?" the boar called out, his words slurred. "Why now, when we need him most?"

"Why does he not hear us?" an elf demanded.

"He is dead," shouted a smallish gray man with donkey ears.

"No, not dead. Avallach cannot die you ass. He is just gone."

"We're lost without his hand," someone cried from under the table.

"We've angered him," added a peevish green man with leaves for hair.

"We must placate him."

"A living sacrifice!" a rosy-cheeked lady cried out.

The plump folk all raised their mugs and cheered at that. "Blood, blood, blood."

"AVALLACH IS GONE!" the Lady spoke, her voice commanding, not loud, yet somehow rising above the ruckus. She came to her feet, eyes gleaming, her shadow growing tall, darkening the room. She looked both beautiful and dangerous, and for a moment, Peter was afraid. The room fell quiet. "It is time we all accept that." She looked from face to face, daring any to challenge her. "We are his children. But do we wish to be children forever? It is time we face our trials on our own."

No one spoke for a long minute.

"Aye," the boar said, setting a hand on the table to steady himself. "That's very stoic and all, my Lady, but where does that leave us? I mean really? What are we supposed to do with that?"

"It means it's time to stop waiting for Avallach to save you," called a boy's voice.

All eyes turned to find Ulfger standing in the doorway. He walked in and stood next to the Lady. "It's time to end the decadence and debauchery. To think about something other than wine and lust and song. It is time for Avalon to embrace order and discipline or *die*."

The boar dismissed him with a wave of his hand. "With all due respect Lord Ulfger." The boar let out a short burp. "I'd rather not be preached to by a boy."

"Maybe it would do you some good to give him a listen," the troll said.

"Those are not even his words," the boar stammered as he refilled his goblet. "We all know he's merely a mouthpiece for his mudder, muther— his *mother*."

Ulfger stiffened and the Lady set a hand on his shoulder.

"And where is your father, Lord Ulfger?" the boar growled. "Where is the mighty Horned One? Why does he not come and talk with us?"

"That is not his way," Tanngnost said. "You know that well enough."

"I know he's not here," the boar said. "Just what does it take to bring him out of his deep dark forest cave?"

This was met with expectant nods and lively quibbling, and again the chamber disintegrated into bickering.

The Lady's shoulders slumped and she sat back into her chair. Her eyes drifted away as though she were somewhere else. She looked very sad to

Peter, and he wanted to go to her, wanted to do whatever he could to cheer her up. Then her eyes found him and she smiled. She came to her feet. "Today I was sent a gift."

The room quieted as one by one the occupants looked her way.

"Maybe it came from Avallach, maybe it sprouted from a cabbage. Either way, a most wonderful delight." She pointed to Peter.

All heads turned to Peter. He blushed and slid behind Drael.

"This boy fell into the clutches of Greenteeth herself," she said. "Did he wait for Avallach to save him? No, not him. This brave child single-handedly burned out the witch's eye and escaped from her very lair!"

An astonished gasp came from every attendee at the table. Several stood to get a better view of Peter.

"Lord Ulfger is right. We can no longer afford to wait for Avallach. Like this boy, we need to save ourselves. We need to take all the wonderful gifts that Avallach has bestowed upon us and make good use of them.

"Peter," the Lady called. "Don't be bashful. Come here and sit beside me."

The old elf nudged Peter and Peter dashed over to the Lady's chair. The Lady pulled him into her lap.

"Where did he come from?" the boar asked.

"From the lands of men-kind," the Lady said. "Through the stones."

Hiisi poked one of Peter's feet. "What is he?"

"A human boy, I think," the Lady said. "But look." She flipped back his hair, exposing the pointed tips of his ears. "He seems to have some faerie in him as well."

They all leaned forward.

"Modron," Ulfger said. "What does he have to do with—"

"Tanngnost?" the Lady asked. "How can such come to be?"

"Most curious," Tanngnost said. "I've never seen the like. Have you?"

The Lady shook her head. "I didn't know it was possible."

"Does he not remember his parents?"

"Not his father," the Lady said. "His mother was human. It was she that left him to die in the forest."

"Men-kind are such cruel beasts," the boar huffed.

"So, the faerie in him comes from his father," Tanngnost remarked absently and stroked his hairy chin.

"Modron," Ulfger said. "This is exactly why nothing ever gets done. We need to discuss—"

"Maybe one of the satyrs," the boar suggested, and everyone looked to the red-skinned, horned man.

Hiisi grinned. "Well, I've certainly fucked my way through every young maiden I could catch. But to my knowledge, all I've ever left behind in those sullied maidens was the flush of orgasmic delights."

An old faerie lady with drooping wings and powdered cleavage nudged the boar. "If the satyr's seed could sprout, why we'd have a couple million pointy-eared mongrels running about. Aye." She winked at Hiisi and let loose a cackle.

"He can travel between the worlds?" the troll asked.

The Lady cut the troll a suspicious look. "Tanngnost, don't start your scheming. I'll not have you using this boy toward your ends."

Tanngnost looked taken aback. "My Lady, I would never dream such."

The Lady laughed. "Of course not, and Hiisi would never diddle a virgin."

This drew several snickers.

"Besides," the Lady said. "You cannot have him. He has told me he wishes nothing more than to serve in my Guard."

"You'd be lucky to have one so brave," said Hiisi.

"I would. Not only is he stouthearted, but talented as well," the Lady said like a proud mother. "Peter, let them hear the forest."

Peter beamed, drinking in all the attention, their curiosity making him bold. He started with a frog's croak, then the chattering of a squirrel, a hooting monkey, then lifted his head and howled, the sound resounding off the dome. He played through a dozen birdcalls and ended with a rooster's crow.

The hall burst into laughter and applause. If Peter had grinned any wider his face would have split in two.

"Modron," Ulfger growled. "Please, there are important matters to—"

"All in good time, Ulfger," the Lady said. "But first, I want you to hear something. It might do your spirit good. Come, sit here beside me."

Ulfger shook his head, but sat down.

"Now, Peter," the Lady whispered. "The Sunbird."

Peter drew in a deep breath, sat up straight, cocked his head back, and began the song. The hall fell silent, even the servants stopped, all of them listening in stunned silence as his song echoed and resonated around the chamber, the acoustics of the dome amplifying the tune and the green ambient light of the pool brightening in response.

Peter finished and looked around, expecting more applause. Instead he was met by faraway eyes, half-opened mouths, some of them even weeping. Peter wondered what he'd done. He glanced at the Lady, unsure. Saw that she too had tears in her eyes.

"That was beautiful, Peter," she said and her wonderful smile fell on him and he knew he'd done well.

"Truly breathtaking," the old faerie lady blurted out, dabbing away at her eyes.

"Ulfger," the Lady said. "Does his song not touch your heart?"

Ulfger looked as though he'd drunk sour milk.

Hiisi stood up and began to clap, the rest followed his lead, all except for Ulfger, who sat stoned-faced, digging his nails into his palms.

✦

PETER WAS BROUGHT a plate of food. One sullen-faced servant actually smiled at him and slipped him a honey pie. Peter ate his fill and then some, and soon the drone of warm conversation, the soft music, and hypnotic glow of the pool made him drowsy. He rested his head against the Lady's breast.

The Lady slipped her arms about him and began to softly twirl his hair. She smelled of pond water and honeysuckle, and these scents, like his mother's sweet milk of so long ago, filled him with contentment. He was where he belonged, by the Lady's side, for always and forever.

Hiisi slid over a few chairs and began to flirt with a blushing elven maiden. Tanngnost came around, taking a seat next to the Lady. He leaned over and spoke low. "My Lady I would speak with you."

The Lady sighed. "You cannot stand the sight of me being happy, not even for a moment. Can you, you fretful old goat?"

Tanngnost shook his head sorrowfully. "There is nothing I wish more than your happiness. But . . . things are worse than we feared."

"Yes, I know. I read that much in your eyes."

Tanngnost let out a sigh. "These are ill times, my Lady."

"The men-kind?"

"Christians. They're determined to rid the land of any who worship the Horned One. Murdering all the druids, burning the temples, sometimes whole villages, and knocking over the standing stones."

The Lady's face hardened. "This god of peace and love certainly likes to bathe the land in blood."

Ulfger's eyes lit up; he leaned over. "Now is the time to take the folk of Avalon to war! Now, before it is too late. Now while we still have allies in the world of men-kind."

The Lady looked at him sadly. "Ulfger, why are you in such a hurry to abandon your youth? The weight of the world will be on your shoulders soon enough, then you'll yearn for these days. What I wouldn't do to have one carefree day of my youth back."

Ulfger grimaced. "Modron, I don't see what my age has to do with any of this."

Peter looked up. "The bad men? Are they coming here?"

"No, Peter," the Lady said. "Not here. They can't come here. I would never allow it." She handed him a cream puff and sat him on the floor.

"Ulfger, do me this favor, take the boy here out into the yard with the other children. Go and play."

Peter's ears perked up. There were other children to play with?

"I am not a nursemaid," Ulfger snapped.

"I mean *you*, Ulfger. *You* go and play. Run around. Build something. Break something. Climb a tree. Get dirty. Get in some trouble. Have some fun."

Ulfger looked at her as though she'd lost her mind.

"Just try it. For once. For me?"

"No. I wish to hear of Tanngnost's travels."

"You will hear everything in good time. Your mother will see to it. For now, I wish you to take Peter to the courtyard."

Ulfger didn't move, just stared at her.

"Ulfger, please. We can talk later. I promise."

Ulfger looked as though someone were twisting a knife in his gut. "Fine," he said, forcing the word out through clenched teeth.

The Lady touched the tall boy's arm. "Ulfger, I hope to Avallach that you wake up and see what that woman has done to you. I hope you see it before all of your youth is lost."

Ulfger turned and headed for the door. Peter glanced at the Lady, unsure. She nodded and he followed the boy out from the chamber.

PETER CAUGHT UP with Ulfger in the hall. The tall boy stood studying an intricately woven tapestry. The scene was of a massive, caped lord holding a long black sword and wearing a helmet with great elk horns jutting up from either side. The helmet covered his face, but his eyes glowed out from the visor.

Peter heard the distant calls of children coming from somewhere down the way. Peter cleared his throat. "Um . . . Ulfger."

The tall boy didn't respond; his eyes lost in the tapestry.

"Hey-ho, Ulfger," Peter called.

"You will address me as Lord Ulfger," the tall boy said, without taking his eyes from the tapestry.

"Lord Ulfger, can we go play now?"

"This is my father," Ulfger said. "The Horned One. He rules the forest." Ulfger moved down to the next tapestry. "And this . . . this is my mother." He inclined his head toward the portrait. A thin-faced woman with piercing eyes glared back at Peter. He felt the woman's eyes were judging him, staring right through him.

"Queen Eailynn, of the elven line of Norrenthal."

Peter thought he detected a sneer in the tall boy's tone, and wasn't sure if the boy revered the queen or resented her. Maybe both, he thought.

"Their lineage makes me a lord." He looked at Peter as though expecting something. "When I come of age I shall rule all of Avalon."

"Sure. Okay," Peter said, nodding. "Can we go play now?"

"Try, 'Lord Ulfger, may we go play now?'"

"Lord Ulfger, may we go play now?"

Ulfger stepped over to the next tapestry. Peter recognized this one right away; it was the Lady. In her portrait she looked kind and strong, her eyes bright and glowing.

"Modron is a creature of whim and fancy, song and sentiment," Ulfger said, looking troubled. "She was never meant to lead."

Peter glanced wistfully down the hall. He really wanted to play with the other children, and didn't understand why they had to stand here looking at these boring portraits.

"She tries," Ulfger continued. "There are moments when she seems capable. Tonight, there at the round table, I thought she would rally—make them see what was at stake. But no, her mood shifts like the wind, distracted by something as trivial as a singing child." Ulfger stared at Peter, his dark eyes boring into the boy. Peter squirmed, and glanced nervously up and down the empty hall.

After a moment, Ulfger asked, "Do you adore her?"

Peter nodded.

"Do you wish for her love?" He leaned toward Peter, his voice became harsh, more intense with every word. "Her attention? Her motherly doting?"

Peter stepped back.

"Of course you do. What choice have you? She has most certainly caught you in her spell. But heed me. You're naught but a distraction, a substitute for her poor lost Mabon. She's but trying to plug that ever-bleeding hole in her heart." He let out a long breath. "She was stronger before her great loss, before her son was stolen from her. Now she is always pining for her Mabon. That is why she spends so much time at Avallach's Shrine, not for the sake of Avalon. *No*, it is her hope that Avallach will tell her where she can find her son." Ulfger all but spit this last bit out.

"So now she brings her little surrogate child to the court. Has him sing us a pretty ditty." He gave Peter a peculiar smile. "And the fools beam, and applaud, and shed sentimental tears then go back to wine, feast, and frolic while Avalon sinks beneath their very *feet*!" He gritted his teeth. "When I come to rule I will put an end to their debauchery. Faerie shall become a force to be feared. Ulfger, a name spoken in frightful whispers. We will make men-kind remember their place and will hide behind the Lady's Mist no longer."

"Ulfger, I mean, Lord Ulfger," Peter said. "Can we go play now?"

Ulfger bristled. "Play? Play? To run around with the boys and girls laughing and giggling. Is that all you can think of?"

Peter nodded wholeheartedly.

Ulfger sighed. "Come."

"HOW DO YOU become one of the Lady's Guard?" Peter asked.

Ulfger looked down at him and smirked. Walking right next to him, Peter realized how big the boy was. He was already taller than the elves, but unlike them, he was thick-boned and solid through the chest, more like the men Peter had seen.

"First you have to learn respect for your betters. You can start by addressing me properly. My title is lord. As in, 'Lord Ulfger, may I' or 'May I, Lord Ulfger.' Can you grasp this simple bit of etiquette?"

Peter gave him a quizzical look but nodded.

"No! You do *not* nod to me. *Never* nod to me. That is only allowed among peers. Understand?"

Peter shrugged.

Ulfger stopped. "Are you simpleminded? Shrugging is the same as nodding. Try again."

"Try what again?"

"No!" Ulfger growled. "It's, 'Try what again, Lord Ulfger?'"

Peter could hear the spirited shouts of children and tried to peer around Ulfger.

"Now say *it*."

"*It*, Lord Ulfger."

Ulfger let out a breath of frustration. "You'll be lucky if they allow you to guard the maid's chamber pot."

"Chamber pot?"

"Never mind," Ulfger huffed, and pushed open the gate into the courtyard.

It was night, but the courtyard was lit with hundreds of orange lanterns. Well over a dozen elven children—boys and girls of all ages—were climbing and racing around a group of standing stones. Several had blunt wooden swords and spears and were busy raiding and defending the stones.

"Hey, it's that kid!" a boy shouted. "The one who took the witch's eye."

They all came running over to get a closer look at Peter, circling him but keeping their distance as though scared he might bite them.

"Lord Ulfger?" a girl asked. "Is it true? Did this boy really burn the witch's eye out?"

"So the story goes, if you choose to believe such tales."

"He doesn't look so tough," a boy said.

"He has hopes of entering the Lady's Guard," Ulfger said.

The children burst out laughing.

Peter looked to Ulfger. "Lord Ulfger, why's that so funny?"

"Because you're an uncouth mongrel that doesn't know the first thing about courtly etiquette. Why, look at the way you're dressed. Who would want such a dirty little monkey escorting them anywhere? Do you know how to march? Have you ever even seen a formal parade? Do you know the first thing about titles, ceremonies, manners? There's more to being a guard than just being brave."

Peter's eyes dropped. He hadn't realized being a guard could be so complicated.

"Don't worry yourself," Ulfger said. "You will make a fine manure boy. Now go play your mindless games with the rest of them." He glared at the children. "Now, everyone leave. Get out of my sight."

The boys and girls all scampered back to the rocks. Peter ran along after them, glad to finally get away from the tall, brooding boy.

THE BOYS AND girls stood around Peter, staring at him as though he'd just hatched from an egg.

"Weren't you afraid?" a freckle-faced girl asked. Her front teeth were so big that she reminded Peter of a rabbit.

"Afraid?" Peter laughed and stuck his chest out. "No, not at all." He pulled his wolf hood up. "I'm the wolf slayer. I fear nothing."

"How'd you do it?" a boy asked. His head was shaven and he had dirt crusted around his mouth, making Peter wonder what he'd been eating.

"You really want to know?" Peter asked.

The kids all nodded.

"I'm warning you, it's a very scary tale. Are you sure you want to hear it?"

They leaned in, nodding eagerly.

"Well, okay, I'll tell you then. I was walking alone in the swamps when she jumped out of a hole, blocking my path. She was a horrible sight, all covered in scales and horns, her hair a nest of snakes. Her teeth were green and as long as knives. She came for me, drooling and snapping her teeth."

The kids exchanged quick, nervous looks, some putting their hands up to their faces.

"Anyone else would have screamed and run, I'm sure. But not me. I snatched out my knife." Peter picked a stick up off the ground. "And drove her back." His face twisted up into a snarl as he made jabbing motions with the stick. "I chased her back down her stinking hole. Her den was full of demons and monsters. She set them on me. My knife broke on their thick hides and I had to beat them away with my bare fists. The witch jumped on my back, hissing, clawing, and snapping her long teeth. I threw her across the room, and grabbed a limb from the fire, jabbed it into her eye like this." He bared his teeth, jabbed the stick at the air, and twisted it back and forth. "I could have killed her, but she began to cry, begging me to spare her life. It would have been cowardly to have killed her then. So I let her live." He raised one finger, squinted. "But I gave her fair warning. Told her if she should ever, *ever*, attack another child, I would come back and cut out her black heart."

The kids stared at him wordlessly. Finally, the buck-toothed girl whispered, "Wow." Several others echoed her sentiment, all wide-eyed.

The buck-toothed girl scooted over next to Peter. "You certainly *are* brave," she said and gave Peter a flirty smile.

Peter blushed and grinned. "Heck, I did what I had to do."

The boy with the shaven head frowned at the girl, then gave Peter a hard look. "Yeah, well, I don't believe anyone is *that* brave."

Peter shrugged.

"If you're so brave let's see you catch a Fire Salamander."

"A what?"

"Fire Salamander," the boy repeated. "You'd have to be very brave to catch one of those. Their bite is as fifty hornet stings."

"Why would I want to do that?"

The elf boy's eyes gleamed. "Because I *dare* you."

The other boys and girls looked at Peter expectantly.

"Well, if I knew where one was, I'd do it in a heartbeat," Peter said, then realized all the kids were suddenly grinning. "What?"

The elf boy's smile reached from ear to ear. "I can show you where a bunch of them are."

"Oh . . . hmm," Peter said weakly, caught the girl's eyes on him. "Sure, okay. Show me then."

The elf boy led Peter up to a small garden pond. Wildflowers and marble stonework surrounded the pond; wide lily pads floated along its surface. Set among the lilies were crystal globes the size of pumpkins, giving off a sparkling, golden luminance.

The kids stopped at the knee-high hedge.

"That's the Lady's orb pond," the girl said. "We're not allowed past here."

"Yeah," agreed the boy. "If Ulfger catches us in there he'll have us lashed."

Peter chuckled.

"No, really," the girl said.

Peter hesitated, glanced back down the slope. He could see Ulfger's back. The tall boy sat upon a bench among the trees, his head down, looking lost in thought. Peter felt sure he could sneak up to the pond and back without drawing any notice.

"He's scared," the elf boy said. "See, told you he wasn't so brave."

Peter stepped over the hedge, not missing the looks of admiration. He puffed out his chest and strolled boldly up the short walk to the pond's edge.

Peter had no problem finding a salamander—they glowed. A plump red one floated just below the surface in front of him, its short legs dangling beneath its long body. It was about as long as Peter's forearm, from nose to the tip of the tail. Peter wondered what the big deal was. He'd caught his fair share of frogs, and frogs were fast. The thing looked about as fast as a slug.

He stepped out onto a rock, keeping one foot on the bank, straddling the salamander. He figured the best way to avoid getting bitten was to snatch it up from behind the neck, like you would a snake. Peter slowly eased his hand into the water, trying to come up behind the creature. The salamander didn't move, didn't seem aware that Peter was there at all. Peter's hand hovered above its neck. He swallowed loudly, wondering just what fifty hornets' stings might feel like, hoping not to find out.

Peter grabbed the salamander. Caught it cleanly about the neck, whipped it out of the pond, and held it high for the kids to see. The kids clamped their hands over their mouths in amazement; even the elf boy with the shaven head looked impressed. All at once the salamander came to life, wiggling and squirming, slipping loose of Peter's grasp. Peter caught hold of its tail and realized his error the second it bit him—pain shot up his arm. Not fifty hornets, more like a hundred and fifty.

Peter screamed.

He screamed and tried to sling the creature off his arm, lost his balance, and fell backward into the pond, hitting one of the globes. The globe smashed into another and both of them exploded with a loud, hollow boom. There came two brilliant flashes of light followed by a flume of smoke. But Peter didn't care about the globes, didn't care about Ulfger, the only thing that mattered was getting the stinging monster off his arm. He slapped wildly at it, but the thing only clamped down harder. Finally he grabbed it around the neck and twisted it loose, leaving six deep puncture wounds in his arm. Only then did he hear the tall boy shouting at him.

"WHAT HAVE YOU DONE?" Ulfger cried, his eyes full of outrage. "Get out of there! *OUT! OUT!"*

Several of the children had run away, but most stood stock-still, mouths open, staring in stunned disbelief.

Ulfger yanked one of the wooden play swords away from a boy, pointed it at Peter. "Come here," he demanded.

Peter had no intention of coming anywhere near Ulfger and made a run for it. Ulfger leaped after him, snatching hold of Peter's wolf skin. Peter twisted away, leaving the pelt dangling in Ulfger's fist. Peter made it only three strides before finding his way blocked by the courtyard wall. Ulfger pressed in and Peter realized he was trapped.

Ulfger's eyes flared. "Do you have any idea what you have done? Those globes are over a thousand years old!"

Peter flinched. "I didn't mean to."

Ulfger bared his teeth. "Discipline. There is no discipline. It is time Avalon wakes up. And it starts now, right here." He jabbed the wooden sword at Peter. "You will be flogged. And you will learn to obey. You will—" Ulfger stopped. His eyes narrowed. He pointed the sword at the necklace around Peter's neck. "How did you come by that?"

"Huh?" Peter glanced down at the star.

"How did you come by that?"

"The Lady gave it to me."

"She gave *you* Mabon's star? Why?" he said, then, in a harsh whisper, *"Has she truly lost her mind?"* A kind of madness entered Ulfger's eyes. He slowly shook his head from side to side. "No, she would never do such a thing. You're a liar. *A LIAR!*" he shouted. "A liar and a thief. Give it to me, *NOW!*"

Peter clutched the star in his hand and shook his head.

"You will do as you are ordered!" Ulfger reached for the necklace.

"NO!" Peter cried, and grabbed Ulfger's wrist, catching the shocked looks on the other children's faces when he did.

Ulfger's dark eyes flashed, his lips trembled, his nose creasing into a sneer. "You dare," he hissed. "Dare lay your nasty hands on me?" He jerked his arm away then slapped Peter, hit him so hard that Peter reeled and stumbled to the ground.

Peter started to get up, then Ulfger's knee stabbed into his back, knocking the wind from him, the weight of the large boy pinning him into the ground. Ulfger grabbed a handful of Peter's hair and shoved his face into the dirt.

"You will learn your place!" Ulfger cried and Peter felt a sharp sting across the back of his legs. Again and again hot pain bit into the back of his thighs and buttocks as Ulfger beat him with the wooden sword, the sound echoing off the courtyard wall.

The children stared, horror-stricken.

Peter screamed and Ulfger pressed his face harder into the ground. Peter choked on the dirt and grass.

"ULFGER!" someone cried. "What are you doing?" It was the old elf. "Lord Ulfger, he is the Lady's guest!"

Ulfger pointed the play sword at Drael. "Have you forgotten your place, old man? Has everyone forgotten their damn place today?" Ulfger struck Peter another vicious blow.

The old elf rushed forward and grabbed the sword.

Ulfger stood up, jerking the sword out of the elf's grasp. "Are you mad?" Ulfger's eyes flared. "Are you out of your fucking mind?" He struck the elf in the face with the butt of the sword. The elf stumbled back, clutching his nose, and sat down hard.

Peter glared at Ulfger. Goll had taught him there was only one way to deal with a wolf. A low animal growl came from deep in Peter's throat, and the children backed away.

Ulfger prepared to strike the elf again when Peter howled and charged. He leaped upon the bigger boy's back, screeching and shrieking as he dug his claws into Ulfger's face. Ulfger tore at Peter's arms and spun around, trying to dislodge the wild boy. Peter bit into Ulfger's ear and Ulfger screamed as blood spurted down his neck.

Peter snarled and shook his head back and forth until he tore Ulfger's ear free.

Ulfger slung Peter from him. Peter hit the ground and came up in a roll, his eyes wild, blood smeared across his face, his fingers twisted into claws, ready for more.

"WHAT IS GOING ON!" The Lady stood at the courtyard entrance, Tanngnost and Hiisi by her side. Several of the dinner guests came up behind them, all of them staring in wide-eyed bewilderment at the two boys: Ulfger with his hand clasped to the side of his head, blood pouring through his finger, and Peter in his loincloth with Ulfger's ear still clamped in his mouth, blood running down his chin and chest.

Peter spat the ear onto the ground.

Ulfger stared at the ear, at *his* ear. "Guards," he called weakly, then, at the top of his lungs, screamed, *"GUARDS!"* He shoved past the Lady, into the hall. *"GUARDS! GUARDS!"*

Hiisi helped the old elf to his feet.

"Drael," the Lady called, and put an arm around the elf. "Drael. You're bleeding."

The elf clutched his nose, trying to stifle the blood. "My Lady, I'm not sure what happened. The boys had some sort of a spat. Ulfger was set to kill the boy—to truly *kill* him."

The Lady looked at Peter. "My poor child." She went to him, wiping the blood from his face with her robe, then taking him into her arms. When Peter felt the warmth of her embrace, he began to cry.

"We have to get him out of here," Hiisi said. "Ulfger will have him killed."

The Lady didn't answer, just held Peter. Hiisi gave Tanngnost a fretful look.

"I can take him," Tanngnost said. "But we must hurry."

They heard the distant call of guards.

"Out the back way," Hiisi said. "Through the gardens. I can delay the guards. My Lady, you have to let him go now." Hiisi and Tanngnost gently pulled Peter from the Lady's arms.

The Lady shook her head. "No, I wish him here, with me. He's mine. He belongs to *me*."

"He'll be in good hands," Hiisi said. "Peter, go with Tanngnost. He's a grouchy old goat, but has a good heart."

The Lady clasped Peter's hands in hers. Peter saw the tears in her eyes. She hugged him one last time and Peter inhaled deeply, determined to never forget her sweet scent. Then the troll took him away into the night.

✦

ALL THE COLOR of that long-ago memory evaporated, replaced with the endless gray, the mud, the rot. Peter tried to remember the sweet scent of the Lady but could not.

He stood and headed north, toward the witch's marsh, leaving behind Avallach's head forever listening to the earth. As he made his way down the trail, through the burned-out remains of the great apple orchard, he dared to dream of a day when the Flesh-eaters—those twisted, murderous demons—would at last be driven from the land. Then the apple trees could come back, the hills would again be green, the forest alive with the song of wild faeries, and he'd be able to sit alongside the Lady once again.

He decided to follow the dark waters of Cusith Creek, skirting along the western edge of the swamp; this would allow him to swing by Tanngnost's hut. If there was any news, Tanngnost would know; the old troll never failed to be in everyone's business. But there was more to it than that. Something Peter hardly recognized, and would certainly never admit. He'd come to rely on Tanngnost, his advice, his knowledge of history of the Avalon. He was the one fixture Peter could count on, the only stable element in his life over the long, tumultuous years in Avalon.

He reached the lowlands and the ground became soft. The witch's land had fared better than others so far, but even in the short time he'd been away, the deadly fingers of the scourge had crawled deep into her bogs. Peter moved stealthy, carefully darting from stump to stump. He didn't want to meet the witch, not today.

Peter heard approaching footfalls, someone coming fast. He slid out his knife and ducked down behind a clump of bulrushes.

A tall, hunched figure came into view, strolling right down the trail, swinging a gnarled staff. "Tanngnost," Peter said under his breath, and grinned. The troll bore a thunderous frown.

Peter waited until the troll was almost upon him, then leaped out. *"BOO!"*

Tanngnost swung his staff around, quicker than Peter had anticipated. Peter dove to the ground to avoid getting hit.

"Peter! You . . . you . . . you impish little shit!"

Peter laughed, laughed so hard he had to clutch his stomach.

Tanngnost gave him a furious look, grunted, snorted, huffed, and smacked him soundly on the rump.

"Oww!"

"Someone needs to beat some respect in you. Despicable mongrel. And just what has taken you so long. Had me worried sick." He glanced behind Peter as though looking for someone. His face softened. "It didn't go well."

Peter sobered up. He shook his head.

The troll let out a long, deep sigh. "Peter, I'm sorry. And I hate to add to your misery, but I've ill tidings of my own. It seems Avallach has deserted us this day. The Flesh-eaters are burning—"

"Shhh," Peter said. "Did you hear that?"

"Peter, the *Flesh-eaters*—"

"Shhh, listen." Peter took a few quick steps down the trail, cocked his head left then right. That'd been a scream, he was sure of it.

Tanngnost followed him.

Again, from somewhere in the swamp. Shrieking. It sounded like a boy. Peter's blood went cold. The only boys on the island were his Devils. He took off at a full run, leaping heedlessly across bogs, and roots, and mud—knife out, eyes wild, a deadly grimace across his face.

Chapter Thirteen

Men-kind

The fog swirled around them. The howls came closer.

Nick picked up his spear and used it to push himself to his knees, trying to breathe through his burning throat, trying his best not to fall over.

Sekeu, Abraham, Redbone, Dirk, Dash, and Leroy formed a loose ring around Cricket's and Danny's limp bodies.

Howls and moans circled them, coming from all directions. Dark shapes with orange eyes shot past. He braced the end of his spear in the dirt and aimed the point outward.

Giggling—it sounded like little girls—came from all sides of them.

Sekeu's eyes were wide. And for the first time, Nick caught a flash of fear even on Redbone's face.

The fog thinned, and there in front of them, not twenty feet away, stood a little girl with long white hair in a flowing white gown. She smiled at them and tittered.

"Look," she said, "little boys and girls come out to play."

"How precious," someone answered. Nick glanced behind and saw another girl.

"Precious indeed," called a third girl, this one on his left. The girls appeared to be identical in every detail.

"Such nice hides. Mother will surely make us new shoes."

"Shoesies-poosies. I want a necklace of shiny white teeth."

"And earrings, don't forget earrings. One can *never* have enough earrings."

"*YOU JUST TRY!*" shouted Redbone, and banged his blades together. "*GONNA FUCK YOU UP!*"

"Oh my, such a tiger!"

"Little boys shouldn't use such language."

"Should rinse his mouth out with a good swig of hot piss."

"Most certainly," the girls agreed. And from behind them, a line of beasts crept forward out of the fog. Nick guessed there were easily fifteen, maybe even twenty more of the hyena beasts that had attacked them earlier, what Redbone had called barghest. Nick didn't see any more of the red ones with the poisonous tails, only the larger, dog-size ones with black, bristling manes.

The barghest circled the kids, growling, slapping the earth, and tearing at the loose leaves. Some of the larger ones lunged at them, darting in and away, getting bolder with every charge.

The Devils kept their guard, trying to hold the beasts at bay.

"*WHAT DO WE DO?*" Leroy cried, spear clutched tightly to his chest, his eyes darting in every direction. The barghest were everywhere. "*WHAT DO WE DO?*"

"Why, you die, silly," said one of the girls and all three girls laughed.

Two large barghest rushed Nick, knocking the spear from his hands and yanking him out of the circle. Their claws bit into his arm as they dragged him away from the group and into the fog.

Redbone let out a war cry and came for Nick, cutting and jabbing, chasing the two creatures back. Two more rushed in from behind, one slashing at Redbone's face. Redbone ducked the blow; when he did, the other raked its claws across his thigh, tearing a gash into his pants and flesh. Redbone yowled, struck out, but the barghest were already away.

"STAY TOGETHER!" Sekeu shouted.

But it was all they could do to keep the claws and teeth at bay. The barghest were slowly splitting them up.

A long howl came from somewhere in the swamp. The sound carried over the den of clacking teeth, hoots, and growls—a fearsome howl—and Nick wondered what new horror had beset them.

A figure burst into the ring of barghest, smashed right through them like a cannonball, little more than a blur of arms and legs as he spun and jabbed. Nick caught a flash of steel, and two beasts hit the dirt, one with its gut cut wide open, the other clutching at its neck.

"PETER!" Sekeu shouted.

And there he was. With no more than his long knife, driving into the beasts, all teeth and wild eyes, never in one place for more than a second as he slashed and screamed, stabbed and howled. The beasts scattered before his blazing eyes and horrifying grin.

Peter drove in, snatched up Nick's spear, and sent it flying at the nearest girl. The girl's eyes flashed in outrage. She moved incredibly fast, but not fast enough. The spear hit her slightly off-mark, slicing through her hair, the staff slapping her shoulder and ricocheting against her jaw. She let loose a shrill screech, clutched her face, and spun away into the fog.

"DEVILS, TO ME!" Peter cried.

Big grins lit up the faces of all the Devils. They answered his call with wild screams of their own and attacked, driving the barghest back. The horde broke and fled, seeming to melt away into the fog.

"NOW!" Peter shouted. *"GET THE KIDS. WE'RE AWAY!"*

Peter and Sekeu picked up Cricket, rolling her over Peter's shoulder. Dirk grabbed Danny's arms, Dash his feet, and Redbone got an arm around Nick, dragging him along. They moved quickly back down the trail.

"Peter," a chilling whisper sliced through the fog. Nick felt the word in his very bones.

There, just ahead, a single shadowy figure blocked their way.

The party halted.

"Peter," Sekeu whispered. "Do we run?"

"No," he said, letting Cricket slide gently to the ground. "There's no running from her."

The shadow melted away from the figure. Nick saw it was a woman, a shapely one, her skin glistening green and her hair long and dark, almost black. Her face remained in shadow, but within that shadow one eye lit up like a blazing emerald, and her full, dark lips parted into a triumphant smile, exposing a row of long, sharp, green teeth. Nick didn't need anyone to tell him that this was the witch.

The three little girls skipped out from behind the trees and stood in front of the witch. The barghest crept out from the swamp, flanking Nick and the Devils. But that was not all. Nick heard rustling, clicking, and crackling. The sound was approaching them from all sides. The very ground came alive; the carpet of dead leaves jittered and danced. Then Nick understood, and the hair pricked up along his arms: bugs, creepy-crawlies, thousands, maybe tens of thousands of them, big oily beetles, long segmented centipedes, scorpions, roaches, and spiders as big as his fist. They swarmed down from trees, up out of holes, skittering toward them like a living carpet of stingers, snapping pincers and clacking mandibles. They circled the party, approaching to within five feet, twisting and crawling over one another, the ground boiling with black, shiny bugs.

The witch sauntered forward a few steps, tracing the outline of her thighs with long, black fingernails as she gently swayed from hip to hip. "Little thieves, stealing from my swamp," she called, her voice low and husky.

The three little girls shook their fingers at them.

"Naughty."

"Naughty."

"Naughty."

"Peter darling," the witch cooed. "You owe me a little something." She pulled back her hair, exposing the scar of her left eye socket. "One chance, sweet Peter. I'll give you and your little playmates one chance. Give me one of your eyes and you can all go free. Peter dear, what say you?"

Peter let out a wild laugh, a crazy crowing, like madness had taken him, then suddenly stopped. His face tight, hard, he locked his eyes on the witch. "I say we cut heads from necks, empty guts from stomachs, and slice arms off bodies." He leaped forward and stomped a huge green beetle, its yellow guts squirting out from beneath his boot.

The witch's face twisted into a snarl, her one eye narrowed to a slit. "You will regret—"

"HOLD THERE!" came a cry from far off down the trail. "Hold, hold I beg."

Nick watched a tall, stooped goat-headed beast come trotting up the trail waving a gnarled staff.

"Excuse me, Ginny," he said as he pushed past the witch, moving up the trail, careful not to step on any of the bugs as they skittered from in front of his large hooves. He halted between the two parties, leaning on his staff, trying to catch his breath. "So sorry to interrupt your little squabble," he said curtly. "But there are pressing matters at stake."

The witch rolled her eye. "Don't interfere, Tanngnost. I've no patience for your meddling. Today I will have my eye."

"Come and take it!" Peter snarled.

"ENOUGH!" Tanngnost shouted, and slammed down his staff. "Whisperwood *burns*! While you fools try and kill one another, Avalon falls."

The swamp fell quiet.

All the malevolence fell from the witch's face. "That's not possible."

"Yes, it most certainly is," Tanngnost said. "If you'd drop your dramatic stage dressings you could see for yourself."

The witch frowned. "If this is one of your games, Tanngnost, it is your bones that will be stage dressings." She raised her hands, closed her eyes, and muttered a string of curt, sharp commands. A warm breeze rose, blew through the swamp, and the fog began to clear. After a moment, Nick could see the gray clouds above and, yes, faintly, the dark stain of black smoke. Something was indeed burning.

"You need only climb upon Mag Mell Hill to see," Tanngnost said.

"That can't be," Peter said. "The trees in Whisperwood can't be burned."

"That's what I thought," Tanngnost said. "But somehow they *are* burning. And need I tell you, once Whisperwood is gone, there's nothing to hold the Flesh-eaters back, this swamp or maybe Devilwood will be next. Soon they will be burning your precious bog, Ginny."

The three little girls looked up at their mother with worried faces.

The witch seemed to diminish somewhat, the fire gone from her eye.

Tanngnost took a deep breath. "Hear me and hear me well. You must put past grievance aside and join together. If not, all of Avalon will be lost."

"What?" The witch's eye flashed. "Are you suggesting we fight alongside these thieving brats? These *human* children? Why, they're no different than the Flesh-eaters. A taint on the land. They too must be driven out."

Tanngnost slammed his staff down again, his eyes flared. "How dare you!" he growled, his words harsh, cutting. "They've earned their place among the faerie fold. Paid with their blood and lives fighting alongside the Horned One at Merrow Cove. And where, Ginny, were you that terrible day?"

The witch waved him away as though she didn't hear, but Nick caught the pained look on her face.

"Avallach's gone, the Horned One is gone," Tanngnost said. "It is up to us now. The fate of Avalon is on our shoulders."

"Oh, stop your ranting, old goat. I've had all the preaching I can stomach." She inclined her head toward Peter. "Tell me, Peter, does your precious Lady own your soul yet? Do you dream of suckling at her teat every night?"

Peter's eyes squeezed down to slits. "Watch how you speak of her."

"Ah, I see that she does." The witch let out a knowing laugh. "Now, be gone, the lot of you. I'll not tolerate thieves in my swamp. And you, Peter, the next time I see you, I will have your eye."

Peter pointed his knife at her. "Why wait? Here, I'll bring it to you." Peter cut the air with his knife and started forward.

The troll grabbed him by the collar. "Peter, don't be an imbecile."

"Tanngnost," the witch said. "You ask too much. I shall never fight alongside such rabble." She spun around and started away.

"But Mother," one of the little girls said. "Aren't we going to eat them?"

"Hush up and come along," the witch hissed and left, melting away into the trees and brambles. The bugs lost their purpose and began skittering away in all directions. The barghest leaped up into the trees and made a noisy exit. The little girls stayed a moment longer, staring at Peter and the Devils with wide, blinking eyes, then shrugged and skipped away.

✦

"THERE," THE TROLL said, pointing down the valley at the billowing smoke rising from the trees far below.

Peter stared. "I don't understand. I don't see how—" He stopped. "The Captain. The barrels." He spat. "The fucking barrels."

"What?"

"The Captain must have brought up oil. They're using oil."

Nick sat against a stump. He could smell burning wood, but all that mattered to him at the moment was being out of the swamp and away from Ginny Greenteeth. The troll had led them across Cusith Creek and to the top of this small rise to survey the fires.

Nick took another swig of water from the pail, but no matter how much he drank, his throat still felt parched and raw.

Cricket was sitting up now, propped against a stone. Danny lay next to her in the grass. Cricket didn't look so well, but she was better off than Danny. His neck and face were red and swollen and he was floating in and out of consciousness. His glasses hung around his neck by the strap, one lens cracked and the frame bent.

The troll had said that they'd be all right, that the Red Tails liked their blood warm and their poison was meant to paralyze, not kill. He'd told them that other than the puncture wounds, there should be no lasting effects, and in a couple of hours they'd be good as new. Nick didn't feel like he'd ever be good as new. His head hurt, his face felt hot and swollen, and the cut on his arm burned.

Peter and the troll had been arguing ever since they left the swamp, something about the Flesh-eaters, about the witch, about the elves. All of it about fighting and killing and Nick didn't like the sound of any of it. As far as he was concerned, he was done. He wasn't fighting with or against anyone. He intended to get well and make Peter take him back.

Abraham walked over and joined Leroy by Cricket and Danny.

"You know," Abraham said. "You saved their lives. That's something to be mighty proud of."

A coy grin crossed Leroy's face before he shrugged self-effacingly. "It just happened, y'know. Don't remember even thinking about it."

"And that there's the true test. When you're willing to risk life and limb for your fellow Devils without so much as a thought about yourself." He placed a hand on Leroy's shoulder. "You know what this means?"

You could tell by Leroy's grin he knew exactly what it meant.

"You'll be gettin' your own sword and knife now. You're gonna be accepted as clan, gonna be a *Devil*!"

Leroy smiled like a crocodile and cut his eyes over to Nick. He caught Nick watching and his smile faltered. Leroy picked up a bucket and walked over to Nick.

"How're you doing on water, buddy?" Leroy asked and squatted down next to him. "You feeling better? Had me worried for a bit there."

"You l—" Nick croaked and winced, his throat still too swollen and raw to speak.

"Don't worry about it, Nicky," Leroy said. "You can thank me later."

Fuck you, you son of a bitch, Nick thought and glared at him.

Leroy glanced over his shoulder; the rest of the Devils had all drifted over by Peter, studying the smoke. Leroy leaned closer to Nick. "Look," he whispered. "Don't go getting worked up. A lot happened fast. It was all really confusing. You might remember things a bit different than me. That's all. Nothing to make a big deal over, right? Are we good?"

Nick narrowed his eyes to slits and gave Leroy the finger.

Leroy's nostrils flared, his mouth puckered like he'd bitten into something sour, the same face he'd made when he'd stomped the pixie. He grabbed Nick's hand and squeezed his fingers together. "You better listen," he hissed. "I waited too fucking long for this. Put up with way too much shit. You say or do anything to fuck this up for me, I'll kill you." He twisted Nick's fingers. Nick winced, gritting his teeth against the pain.

"I'm not kidding. I'll come to you while you're sleeping and stab you in the face. Slit your fucking throat!"

Nick could see he wasn't kidding.

"You got it? You got it?"

Nick nodded and Leroy let him go.

Nick turned away, staring down at the grass through a blur of tears. *Let it go*, he told himself. *Doesn't matter.* He was getting out of here. Right? Leroy could call himself a Devil, could wear a feather and call himself Yankee Fucking Doodle for all he cared. Nick was done with him, done with all of this madness.

"I'LL CATCH UP with you at Deviltree," Peter said.

"Peter," Sekeu said. "This is madness. You must not go to Lady's Wood. Elves will kill you."

Peter glanced at Tanngnost; the troll waited for him at the trail head. Peter let out a long breath and smiled. "I have to. You know it. We've only days left. The Flesh-eaters are on their way. The magic is failing. The scourge is eating up the last of the forests. What do we have left to eat? Soon we'll be eating each other, like them." He nodded toward the smoke.

"We'll all go then," Redbone said.

Peter shook his head. "Can't. Elves would never allow it. Only chance I have to convince them of my allegiance to the Lady is to go alone."

"Ulfger will never fight beside you," Sekeu said.

Peter nodded. "Yeah, and I'll never fight alongside him either. But that doesn't mean we can't coordinate our efforts. He'll have to see this. All of us are at the end. If we fall, so do they."

"Well, at least let me come," Redbone said. "Y'know, as your official diplomatic dignitary. To carry your cane and top hat." He grinned.

"Nope, but you can help carry Danny back." Peter returned his grin.

Danny was sitting up now, but didn't look like he could walk yet or anytime soon. His eyes were puffy and his swollen neck made him look like a bullfrog.

Tanngnost thumped his staff impatiently.

"Later alligators," Peter said and sprinted up to the troll. Together they entered the Lady's Wood.

"Okay Peter," the troll said. "The very life of the Lady and Avalon depends on this. You must, *must*, be on your best behavior."

"I'm always on my best behavior."

"Promise me you'll leave the past behind."

Peter's face hardened. "Some things can never be left behind."

Tanngnost sighed. "Peter, that feud was all so long ago."

Peter fell quiet; it had indeed been *so* long ago. He'd only seen the great oaks shed their leaves twenty times by then, yet still, he hadn't grown into adulthood and not a single whisker grew from his chin. But he had grown into a lean, rangy youth. Tanngnost called him the wild boy of Myrkvior, told him it was his human blood that kept puberty at bay, told him he would never be able to grow into manhood. Tanngnost explained this in grave terms, as though it were a curse—a dreadful vexing. But Peter had danced about the troll's hut, overjoyed to know he'd never have to turn into one of those horrible, hairy, brutish men. He'd spent those days delighting in his eternal youthfulness, all the great forest his playground—at least, that is, until Ulfger found him.

✦

PETER RECALLED HOW hard his heart had raced. He'd known better than to enter the Lady's Wood. How many times had Tanngnost warned him, told him that Ulfger had given the elves orders to kill him on sight? He'd contemplated turning back, then caught sight of the Spriggan. The nasty little goblin was in the brush, just across the creek. It waved its prize: a knife—*Peter's* knife—taunting, teasing, well aware that Peter wouldn't dare follow it into the Lady's Wood.

"You little thief," Peter cried, and leaped up, splashing across the creek, forgetting all about Ulfger and his murdering elves. The Spriggan's eyes popped open in surprise. It turned tail and dashed up the trail.

Peter lost sight of it in the thick underbrush. He scanned the pine needles, tracking the goblin's trail, so intent he didn't notice the figures slipping up on him from behind.

Peter caught the soft crunch of pine needles, turned, expecting to find the Spriggan, instead saw a spear flying directly for his chest. Peter threw himself backward. The spear shot past, nicking his shoulder and bouncing down the thin path. He hit the dirt, rolled, and was back to his feet all in a blink. His instinct was to run, but then he froze. There were three of them, two were elves, but it was the third that held him in his tracks.

The figure towered over the elves, taller even than most men Peter had ever seen, thick through the chest and arms, but it was his eyes that held Peter. Peter would never forget those dark, brooding eyes.

"Ulfger," Peter hissed, as he tried to comprehend how the tall boy had turned into this huge, brutish man. The Ulfger before him sported a bristling goatee tied into a knot, and thick, dark eyebrows. He wore a red-and-gold tunic with a black elk head emblazoned upon the chest, black leather britches, knee-high boots, and a long broadsword at his side. He'd let his hair grow long, parted it along his crown, letting it fall straight down the sides of his head to cover his ears. *Or his one ear*, Peter thought.

Ulfger stared at him, looking like a man who has just discovered a pot of gold. He let out a low laugh. "It can't be. Avallach has brought me a gift. And look at you." He laughed again, louder. "Still a miserable snot-nosed brat." He shook his head, sneered. "It's your human blood. Avallach curses those who don't belong here."

Ulfger signaled and the two elves slid out long knives and ducked into the woods on either side of the trail.

Peter backed away, keeping a close eye on the elves and searching for a path of escape.

"It is plain you have no sense," Ulfger called. "Or you would have left Avalon long ago. Though I have to admit, it pleases me deeply to find you here, to find you still alive. Otherwise I would not have the pleasure of killing you."

Ulfger drew his sword and strolled toward Peter. Peter couldn't miss the way the muscles rippled along the giant's arms, the way he carried the massive broadsword as though it weighed nothing. Peter suddenly felt small and vulnerable, and for the first time found himself envious of growing up, jealous of such strength and might.

"Keep to his flanks," Ulfger shouted in a deep, thunderous voice. "Don't let him around us. Remember, he's *my* kill!"

Peter caught sight of the spear, the one the elf had thrown at him. It lay on the trail near his foot. He caught it under his toe and kicked it into the air, catching it and sending it hurtling for Ulfger.

Ulfger hardly blinked, simply slapped the spear out of the air with his sword. The giant let out a laugh. "Good, a bit of sport will make this more enjoyable!"

Peter turned and ran. He lost sight of the elves in the brush, but knew they were keeping pace. He heard Ulfger crashing along the trail behind him. Peter's heart drummed in his chest; again he felt the fear, that of the hunted deer. The same fear as when the men had chased him back to Goll's hill—it was almost as though he'd never stopped running.

The trees thinned on one side of the trail. Peter could see a swamp and reeds below, down a sharp ravine. *The reeds,* Peter thought, *I can lose them in the reeds.* He left the trail, sprinted toward the drop. An elf leaped into his path. Peter didn't have time to do anything other than crash directly into him. Peter heard a wounded *uff* as the two of them tumbled. Peter came out on top and tried to break away. The elf grabbed his arm and clung on. Peter jabbed a thumb in the elf's eye, tore his arm free, got one foot under him when a big, black boot connected with his midsection. Peter left the ground, slammed up against a tree. He heard Ulfger's laugh, caught sight of the giant's grin, then Ulfger punched him in the face, right between the eyes. Peter reeled, lost his feet, and sat down squarely.

Ulfger snatched Peter up by the hair. He pulled out a notched hunting knife, held it up to Peter's face. "Let's start with an *ear,* shall we?"

Peter grabbed Ulfger's hand, and bit deep, felt cartilage crunch beneath his teeth, and tasted blood.

Ulfger yowled, yanked his hand away, lost his grip on both the knife and Peter. Peter snatched up the knife and slashed out wildly. Ulfger stepped back, had his sword in his hand in a flash. The two elves fell in on either side, knives ready.

Ulfger flicked the blood off his thumb, glared at Peter. "Enough games."

Peter threw his knife. The blade bounced harmlessly off Ulfger's shoulder, but bought Peter a needed second. He leaped for the ledge, slid, and rolled down the ravine, crashing into the mud and reeds. He glanced up, saw the elves skidding down after him, Ulfger following.

Peter splashed into the reeds, pushing between the tall, misty stalks, trying to lose himself within the maze of stems and shallow black pools. Pushing farther and farther until he could no longer hear Ulfger's curses.

The mist thickened and Peter began to question his way; he'd done a very good job indeed of getting lost. He kept moving and his instincts paid off as the terrain began to change, the ground became gray and firm, and the reeds thinned out. But the mist continued to thicken and Peter found himself within a wall of swirling fog, unable to see farther than twenty paces in any given direction, afraid to take another step lest he became lost forever.

His head throbbed. His brow was swollen and sore from where Ulfger had punched him. His ribs hurt with every breath. He gently probed them and winced, wondered if they might be broken. The mist felt as though it were moving in on him, suffocating him. He closed his eyes, trying to calm himself, trying to figure out what he should do, and it was then he caught a familiar scent. He inhaled deeply—just a trace of honeysuckle and pond water. *The Lady?*

Peter felt a slight warmth against his chest and opened his eyes. The necklace—Mabon's star—began to glow and Peter caught a faint glimmer ahead in the mist. He approached; before him, a dusting of gold glittered just above the clammy gray earth, gently weaving and flowing, like a lazy creek. Peter remembered the Lady spoke of her Mist. *Is this her doing?* He followed the Path.

Peter found thoughts of the Lady dominating his heart; at one point, he could swear he heard the distant echo of her voice calling, only it wasn't his name, it was—*Mabon.*

How many times had he snuck up to the Lady's Garden? How many times had he lain hidden near Avallach's shrine in hopes of a single glimpse of her? And in all those years, only once had he seen her, there in her courtyard, talking and laughing with Hiisi. When she'd laughed, Peter had smiled while tears fell from his eyes, his desire to be near her so vast his whole body ached.

The mist began to thin and Peter heard the lapping of waves and got his first whiff of the sea. The gray earth and mist gave way to a drizzly, pebble-littered beach. He stood facing a rocky ledge. The ledge was topped with scraggly spruce and pine. Peter saw no sign of tropical lushness, no sign of faerie kind whatsoever. The air here was cold and damp, sharp smells bit at his nostrils. He heard strange birdcalls. Yet, somehow all of it was familiar and it dawned on him just where he was. He felt a chill, and not from the harsh wind. Peter realized he was back in the world of men-kind.

PETER CLIMBED TO the top of the ledge and looked back. The shifting mist clung to the shore, giving no sign or clue to the magical kingdom hidden in its midst. His first instinct was to head back into the Lady's Mist, to return to the safety of Avalon's forest. He shook his head, grimaced. *There's no safety there,* he thought. *Not for me. Not anymore. Ulfger will hunt me relentlessly.*

He looked up the coast, the endless miles fading into the winter grayness—a world of men. *What's here for me?* he wondered, and again grimly shook his head. *Death, or at best a life of hiding in holes, like Goll.* Peter fought back the tears. *Is there no place for me?* He wiped angrily at his eyes. *I have to go somewhere, at least for a while. Maybe one day Ulfger will grow tired of hunting me and I can return. Maybe, but not now, not this day.*

Peter headed over the rise, felt a tugging on his heart, and stopped. It was *her,* the Lady. Even here, he felt her. It was as though she was part of his soul, and the thought of never seeing her again was almost too much to bear. "I will come back." *And if I have to kill Ulfger, I will find a way.*

He moved inland, crested the ledge, and a wide, sprawling valley opened before him. Peter caught a telling trail of smoke far below, could just make out a cultivated field and a cluster of buildings. The old fears snuck up on him. He could almost still hear the sounds of the men and their dogs chasing him through the woods, surprised by the intensity of those long-ago memories. He suppressed a shudder, took a deep breath, and pushed his chest out. "They'd best be wary of me," he stated. "I'm a creature of Faerie. A shadow in the dark. I will cut their throats as they sleep."

He clutched his belt and remembered he no longer had even a knife and that the world of men was full of wolves, bears, and hill cats. His lips tightened into a thin line and he started down the slope.

The shadows were growing long by the time he found the road. The dirt overturned with fresh horse tracks, plenty of them, and Peter heard Tanngnost in his head, the old troll warning him of his foolishness. But Peter trailed the road, keeping to the bushes, slipping soundlessly from tree to tree, the way he did when trying to sneak up on the wild faeries. He smelled smoke and then stumbled upon the body.

It was a young woman. She lay on her back in the ditch, the torn remnants of her dress trampled into the mud. Her legs splayed wide apart, the horrible wound between her legs crusted with blood and bared to the world. Deep slashes riddled her small breasts and dark bruises stood out against the pale skin of her thin neck.

Peter clenched his jaw and stared into her unblinking eyes. Looking closer, he could see she was barely more than a child. He wondered what sort of games she'd liked to play, wondered what a child could've ever done to deserve such a death. Peter felt his dread give way to anger, to hate. He remembered why he never wanted to grow up, never wanted to turn into one of *them.*

The rays of the late-afternoon sun cut across the tops of the pines and the shadows began to deepen. Peter left the girl and continued to trail the road.

The next body Peter found was that of a man hanging from a tree. He was badly burned and a crow pecked at the charred flesh hanging from his cheek. A sign hung around the man's neck, painted with a white cross. Tied to his feet were the heads of a woman and two children. Peter saw no sign of their bodies.

He could see the village now, could just make out the gray shapes in the deepening shadows. The acrid smell of smoke saturated the air.

He came upon a man lying in the middle of the road, the side of his head crushed, his blond hair clotted with blood. He still clutched his spear. Peter crouched next to him and pried the spear from his stiff fingers and a knife from his belt. Across the road lay a scorched pasture; in its center, a smoldering pile of burned bodies. Peter guessed there were close to fifty

213

bodies and every one that he could see had been decapitated. A company of crows cawed and pecked at the choicest morsels. He heard Tanngnost again, telling him to leave now, but Tanngnost had also told him that curiosity would be his undoing. Peter smiled at the memory of the fretting old troll, stood, and headed toward the village.

Peter crept along the ditch, keeping low and to the shadows. He slipped past a burned-out barn, only its blackened framework still standing, then came upon three wolves feeding on the body of a woman. Her protruding belly had been slit open and their snouts were wet from gorging on its contents. As Peter neared, the wolves lifted their heads and gave him a warning growl. A tiny infant's leg hung from the jaws of one of them. Peter gave them a wide berth and continued into the village.

Most of the structures had been burned to the ground. Here and there, a few timbers still smoldered; other than the distant cawing of crows, the village was still and quiet.

Peter slipped within the burned hulk of a stable, crouched in the shadows, surveying the town from between the slats.

A huge cross of freshly hewn timber had been erected in the center of the square. A man hung limply from its beams, a rope stretched taut across his neck, chest, and beneath each arm. Great iron nails had been driven into his hands and feet. He wore a long robe adorned with dancing animals and swirling symbols of the sun, moon, and stars. His robe had been slit up the front. Thick rivulets of congealed blood ran down the insides of his legs, forming a dark pool on the ground. Peter could see that his genitals had been butchered and stuffed into his mouth. No less than thirty heads hung from the cross: men, women, and children. In the deepening shadows, several of them appeared to stare at Peter, as though they might start talking to him at any moment. Peter didn't like it, didn't like anything about this place, decided there was nothing here for him, after all, decided it was time to leave. But he heard the heavy tromp of hooves heading his way, then the deep voices of men, and ducked back down.

Two men came into view, leading a horse. The horse pulled along a line of tethered children. The men were wearing chain mail beneath matching blue tunics with white crosses on their chests; short swords hung from their belts. Peter counted eight children; older children, for the most part.

Their hands were bound behind their backs and a rope was looped around each of their necks. They were covered in soot and mud; several were bruised and bleeding from ugly wounds. They had despondent, haunted eyes, the eyes of children who'd seen too much.

"So, there you are," came a man's call from somewhere behind Peter. Two more soldiers came out of the woods, heading right for his hiding spot. Peter felt sure they were talking to him. He froze, not so much as breathing. But they tromped right past. There was a girl between them. She was tall, long in the leg, but still a girl. She wore a simple, rose-colored dress, spattered in mud, one sleeve torn away. They pushed her roughly along ahead of them and joined the men by the horse.

"We found a few of them hiding up on the hill," one of the soldiers said. He was stout and bald, one of his legs was shorter than the other and he walked with a pronounced lurch. "The others got away, but we got the one we wanted." The man grinned.

The other two soldiers took an appraising look at the tall girl and returned his grin. A wiry man with a black cap and a toothless maw said, "No harm in a little sport while we wait for the baron."

The men chuckled.

A fifth man came out of the woods from the south and met up with them. He was shorter than the others, but with thick, muscled arms and a dark, bristling beard. He wore a helmet, while the other men did not, a white plume stuck up from its crest. "No luck south," he said. "I'm done hunting these brats. It's a waste of effort, I say. Why, they make terrible servants anyway. You can whip them till your arm falls off and still not beat the wildness out of them. If the baron wants the rest of them, I say he can root them out of the woods himself."

They all nodded.

"Aye, sir, they're like rats, the way they hide in holes and under rocks. Spend a month and not find them all."

"Truth be, the winter will get the rest of them anyway."

"Where's the baron and the guard, sir?" the toothless man asked. "Where'd they get off to now?"

"They'll be back soon enough," the bearded man said. "The scouts located another heathen village in the hills. Just a few huts really. The baron took the guard. They intend to do a bit of converting."

They all laughed.

"Perhaps, sir, some fun while we wait?" the bald soldier said, and shoved the tall girl forward.

The bearded man looked the girl up and down, nodding. He pulled off his helmet, then his gloves, dropped them to the ground. He gently touched her cheek with the back of his finger, then grabbed a handful of her long, auburn hair, and tugged her head back. Peter got a good look at her face. Her eyes were light green and full of fear, her mouth wide and thick-lipped.

"Little witch child," the bearded man said, and ran a hand down her neck, squeezed her shoulder. "Do you drink blood and dance around your horned god? You do, don't you?"

The girl said nothing.

His hand trailed down her waist, down her leg. He squeezed her thigh. "Why I bet you crawl around on your hands and knees before him, naked and grunting like a pig. Then bare your ass to the forest beasts, don't you?" He shook her. "Don't you?"

The soldiers all snickered, and the toothless man pawed at his own lips.

The bearded man smirked and pushed his hand under her dress, shoving it hard up between her legs.

The girl let out a cry and slapped at him, raking her nails across his face. The man let go of her hair, tried to grab her wrist. She tore loose and ran for the trees.

Peter jumped to his feet, hands tight around his spear. *Demons,* he thought, *men-kind are all demons.*

The toothless man leaped after the girl, caught her by the hair, spun her into the dirt. Two others fell upon her, pinning her arms to the ground.

The bearded man touched his face, looked at the blood on his fingers, and spat, "You little cunt." He strolled over to where they held her on the ground, undid his belt, letting his trousers drop. He knelt between the girl's legs, pushing her dress up over her hips.

Peter slipped from his hiding place, crept toward the men in a low crouch, knife in one hand, spear in the other.

The girl spat at the bearded man, tried to kick him away from her.

He struck her twice in the face, splitting open her lip, then punched her hard in the stomach. She let out a choked gasp and stopped kicking. "That should take the devil out of you," he said. "Now, two mugs of mead to the man who can make her squeal the loudest. Who's in?"

They all grinned and grunted.

Peter hefted his spear, gauging the range as he prepared to throw, then saw a figure come running out from one of the houses, heading right toward the soldiers.

It was a boy, one of the pagan folk. He couldn't have been older than twelve, carrying a spear at waist level and rushing the men at a full run. The boy's eyes were wide; Peter could see he was terrified. Yet still he came.

The bald soldier saw the boy, let out a shout of warning, but a second too late. The spear drove into the bearded man's back, punched out his chest.

The bald soldier made his feet and struck the boy, knocking him down. He yanked out his sword, brought it up, and that was when Peter threw his spear. The spear hit the bald man in the back of the neck, tore out through the front of his throat, driving the man face-first into the mud.

Peter let out a howl and was on the next soldier before the man could free his sword of its scabbard. He jabbed his knife into the man's side and ripped it across his gut, tearing upon his stomach. The man's entrails poured out from the wound, steaming in the winter chill. He let out a low groan and dropped to his knees.

The two remaining soldiers came for him. Peter easily ducked a swing meant for his head, and another for his chest. These men were big and strong, but Peter was faster, so fast that these lumbering giants seemed to be moving in syrup. He drove in beneath one swing, bringing his knife up into the man's crotch, felt the blade punch deep into the man's groin. The soldier let out a horrified wail and Peter's eyes *gleamed*. He liked the sound, craved it.

There was only the toothless man left. He looked from his dead and dying comrades to Peter, stared at him as though he were a demon, some pagan god seeking vengeance.

A wicked grin spread across Peter's face. These huge, brutish men who had struck such terror in his heart, had haunted his nightmares for an age, turned out to be little more than blundering beasts. The battle had turned into a game, the most exciting one he had ever played. Peter licked his knife and let out a low growl.

The man turned and ran.

Peter whooped and raced after him. He caught up to him in a heartbeat, leaping upon his back. He plunged the knife into the soldier's neck, tore open his throat, and rode him into the dirt. Peter watched the man's lifeblood gurgle and bubble from his open throat, watched until the man's eyes glazed over.

A weak whimpering drew Peter to his feet. One of the soldiers still lived. The wounded man was clutching his groin, trailing a wide swath of blood as he tried to crawl away. Peter picked up a fallen sword, and advanced. To his surprise, the pagan boy snatched up a spear and rushed the wounded man. Peter stopped, watched as the boy drove the spear into the man's back, not once, but over and over. The boy kept jabbing well after the man had stopped moving. *"BASTARDS!"* the boy screamed. *"FUCK-ING, WICKED BASTARDS!"* Finally the girl made him stop. The boy began to cry, his whole body racked with sobs.

The girl looked at Peter. "Who are you?" she asked.

The boy stopped crying, pushed the girl behind him, and pointed the spear at Peter. His red-rimmed eyes were laced with fear, but the spear was steady. "What do you want?"

Peter studied the boy. The boy might be scared but he was ready to fight him to the death, it was plain on his face. Together they'd just killed five men. Peter glanced over to the children tied to the horse. They had the same hard eyes as the boy. *Eight of them there,* he thought. *Ten all together, maybe a handful more hiding in the hills. Desperate, dangerous children without a home. Plenty of swords and spears lying about.* Peter tapped his chin. *Wonder what Ulfger would think if a clan of wild kids sprouted up in his forest?* Peter grinned.

Peter dropped his knife and stuck his sword into the dirt. He took a step forward and planted his hands on his hips. "My name's Peter. I'm looking to make some new friends."

The boy stared at him in wonder.

The girl spoke up. "I'm Wendlyn."

Peter walked right up to the point of the boy's spear. Stuck out his hand. The boy looked from Peter's hand to Wendlyn. She nodded. The boy lowered his spear and slowly stuck out his own hand. Peter took it, shook it mightily, and smiled, and the boy and the girl and the other children all smiled back, because Peter's smile was a most contagious thing.

"Say," Peter said. "I know a place we can go. It's a heck of a lot nicer than here."

"PETER, THIS IS madness. You *must* take them back!" Tanngnost said.

"No," Peter replied and crossed his arms. "They're my friends."

"You've no idea what you're doing. No idea. The Horned One will never allow their kind here."

"Come see our fort," Peter said, waving for Tanngnost to follow him down the trail.

"I *will* not. I'll not have anything to do with this folly. Peter, if Ulfger finds out, the elves will hunt you down. They'll kill all of you."

Peter whistled and five kids dropped from the trees, spears in hands, teeth bared. Their wiry nude bodies were covered in war paint. They surrounded the troll, growling and glaring at him with wild golden eyes.

"Let them try," Peter said. "We'll feed them their own noses." He raised his spear and howled.

The kids howled back, began to clack their teeth together and jab the air with their spears.

The troll rolled his eyes, then batted one of the spears away. "Don't point that at me you little wart," he snapped at a small boy wearing a raccoon skin over his head like a mask.

"These are our woods now," Peter said sternly. "They belong to us, the *Devils*. From here to Goggie Creek is now Devilwood. Any who enter risk our wrath."

Tanngnost let out a sigh and shook his head. "Devils? You mean half-wits. Peter, there's so much here you don't understand." The troll glanced at one boy a bit older than the rest. "The magic of faerie can be poison to their kind. If any of these children are too old, they'll turn. Have you any idea what that means?"

Peter gave the troll a suspicious look.

"The magic can twist them, turn them into murderous demons."

"Don't try to scare me. It won't work. Not this time."

"Peter, you have enemies enough. People with too many enemies don't live long. I'll not stay around to see you hanged." Tanngnost stomped away.

PETER HEARD THE whistle, snatched up his sword, and leaned around the tree. The whistle meant Ulfger was coming. Peter did a quick check; the Devils were all in place and well hidden.

We're ready, he told himself, and realized his hands were shaking, but not from nerves—from excitement. He listened to his heart pounding away. *I'm alive, more alive than I've ever been. The game is on, the greatest game ever. I've thirty Devils now. Thirty brave, deadly warriors.* How long had they practiced and prepared for this very moment? Two seasons, three? These children were done with drills, done with living in fear—of men, of elves, of *Ulfger.* These feral children would run no more. They were ready to fight, ready to kill. They were Devils now, and this scrap of scraggly wood was *their* forest.

Ulfger came into view, leading a squad of eight well-armed elves. They strolled right down the main trail just as Peter knew they would, Ulfger no doubt believing he was about nothing more dangerous than a fox hunt. *Well,* Peter thought, *this fox intends to bite.*

When they were within twenty yards, Peter stepped out into the trail and leveled his sword at Ulfger.

"This is Devilwood. This is *my* forest," Peter shouted. *"LEAVE!"*

Ulfger halted and lifted a gloved hand. The elves moved up on his flanks. He looked Peter up and down and sneered. "Seems Myrkvior has become infested with vermin. Surrender yourself and the other pests and I promise you leniency."

Peter could see they carried no nets, ropes, or other bindings, only swords and spears. He knew Ulfger's leniency amounted to nothing more than a quick death.

"Perhaps you didn't hear me," Peter said. "Or is it hard to hear with just one ear?"

Ulfger glowered. "The time for fun and games is over, little runt." He pulled a long, wide sword from his scabbard, spun it once, and started forward. The elves began to fan out.

Peter whistled and the woods came alive with howls. Kids dropped out of trees and sprung up from the bushes, leveling spears, swords, and hatchets at the elves, all thirty kids snarling and clacking their teeth.

The elves looked about wildly, their thin, narrow eyes filled with shock and surprise. The Devils jabbed at the air, pressing them back into a tight knot.

Ulfger spun around and around, appeared stunned, confused, as though trying to comprehend how the tables could've turned so quickly, so utterly. He clutched his long sword with both hands and stumbled backward into the elves.

"You have to the count of four to drop your weapons!" Peter cried.

"*ONE!*"

The elves glanced at one another.

"*TWO!*"

The Devils hefted their spears, ready to throw. There was no playfulness on their faces, no mercy, only the eyes of children that had seen more than their share of brutality and death.

"*THREE!*"

The elves tossed down their spears.

"What are you doing?" Ulfger cried.

Three Devils shoved their spears to within an inch of Ulfger's face.

"It's your call, Ulfger," Peter said.

Ulfger's sword trembled in his hands. His face twisted into a knot of rage, his dark eyes glowering. He threw down his sword with a cry of frustration.

"Take all their weapons," Peter said. "We can use some good elven blades."

They kept the elves under guard as several smaller kids swarmed around and relieved them of their swords and knives.

"Thieves," Ulfger said, and spat. "Nothing but the lowest caste."

Peter jabbed his blade beneath Ulfger's chin. "Take off your clothes. Everything."

"What?" Ulfger's dark eyes flashed.

"That's 'What, *Lord* Peter,'" Peter said. "As in 'May I *Lord* Peter' or '*Lord* Peter, may I.'"

Ulfger glared at him.

"Oh, don't you remember the drill?" Peter asked. He could see by Ulfger's face that he did.

Peter pressed his sword point into Ulfger's neck, just enough to prick the skin. "Take off your clothes, *now.*"

Ulfger tugged off his boots, then his tunic, a thin shirt of mail, his pants, until finally he stood before them all completely nude.

The Devils snickered and jeered. Ulfger's face flushed red, his lips trembling with outrage. "You . . . will . . . regret this."

Peter smacked the side of his face with the flat of his sword. Ulfger reeled, almost lost his feet. He spat and wiped his mouth, looked at the blood on his hand.

"You forgot to address me as *Lord Peter.*"

Ulfger squinted.

Peter raised the sword. "Do it now! And maybe, just maybe, I will let you leave with your balls still attached."

"Lord Peter," Ulfger forced out between clenched teeth.

"Good, now turn around. I owe you something."

Ulfger no longer seemed capable of speaking. He just shook his head.

Peter flicked the blade across Ulfger's cheek, opening a small cut. Ulfger flinched, let out a weak cry.

"If I have to ask again, you'll lose your other ear."

Ulfger turned slowly around.

Peter reared back his sword and hit Ulfger across the buttocks with the flat of the blade. The loud clap echoed off the trees. Ulfger let out a cry. Peter hit him again, then again. The kids winced with every blow. Ulfger let out a sob, stumbled forward, and fell to the dirt.

"This is Devilwood," Peter said and leaned over next to Ulfger's ear. "This is *my* forest. The next time you set foot in these woods I will shove my sword all the way up your ass." Peter kicked Ulfger hard in the buttocks. "Now *get* out of here!"

Ulfger pushed to his feet and limped down the trail. The Devils chased after him, hooting, howling, and barking, as they pelted him with pinecones and dirt clods, chasing him all the way to Goggie Creek.

✦

A SHARP CHIRP brought Peter back to the present. He caught a flash of green: faeries—three of them—leaped off a branch and flew away up the trail.

"I believe news of our visit precedes us," Tanngnost said with a wry grin. "Keep your eyes open: the welcoming committee should be arriving soon."

Peter glanced about the terrain, spotted a rocky ledge just off the main trail. "We should wait over there," Peter said. "Those rocks will give me a good head start if I need to leave a bit early."

The troll nodded and the two of them strolled toward the ledge.

"All will be fine," Tanngnost said. "So long as you keep your head about you and don't antagonize him. He can't possibly raise his sword against you, not after his own father granted you a place among faerie fold. He's honor-bound to at least hear us out."

"Honor? Ulfger has no honor."

"Ulfger does have honor—in many ways it is his greatest undoing. He's tied to what he believes is his duty, no matter how distorted that may have become. He'll honor his father's clemency. But I don't have to warn you to be careful. You know he'd love to kill you. And if he can find a reason to claim you a threat to Avalon, or to the welfare of the Lady, he will try."

"From what you've told me, the Lady's little more than his prisoner."

"Peter, you distort my words. I never implied any such gibberish."

"You said he never allows visitors or for her to leave. When was the last time you saw her outside her refuge?"

Tanngnost's great furry brow creased. "I can't say exactly. I don't know if she ever leaves."

"See!"

"I don't believe that's Ulfger's doing, though. When the Great Horned One died, part of Modron seemed to have died as well. I saw her once, briefly, sometime after the great battle. She didn't recognize me. Not sure she even saw me; she stared through me as though asleep with her eyes open. And now the elves tell that she has grown listless and weaker still. Sadly, she neglects the Mist, and as you well know it has become infested with the Sluagh. They feed on it. Feed on . . . *her*." The troll was quiet for a moment. "I fear if she loses her will altogether, the Mist will fall. Then that will be the end for all of us." Tanngnost pulled at his long chin whiskers and drifted away into his own thoughts. "Um, what were we talking about?"

Peter smiled. "About what an *ass* Ulfger is."

"Ah, yes. That's right. What I meant to tell you is that whatever Ulfger's failings, you must never forget that he's the son of the Horned One. That he, and only he, can wear the Horned Helm and wield Caliburn."

"But the sword was broken."

"Even broken, the blade holds enough power and poison to help us drive the Flesh-eaters into the Mist."

"You never told me *that*! What are we waiting for?" Peter's voice became excited. "Where do they keep it? I'll steal it. Why, if I had the sword I'd drive the Flesh-eaters away myself!" Peter's eyes lit up.

"Peter," Tanngnost huffed, and rapped twice on the boy's head. "Do you ever listen? Did you sleep through all my teachings? Have all my pearls of wisdom been wasted on a dingbat? Caliburn was forged by Avallach and given to the Horned One to protect Avalon in his stead, to drive outsiders away."

"I *know* that," Peter muttered.

"Its touch is death. Only those of ancient blood lines can wield it. And of those, who is left?"

Peter shrugged.

"Don't be a dunderheaded halfwit," Tanngnost said. "*Ulfger.* Only *Ulfger* remains. Not even the elves can touch it without being burned. And one of impure blood such as yourself? Why, it would burn you from the inside out!"

Peter frowned.

"Peter, whether you like it or not, we need Ulfger. And we need to do our best to convince him to join us."

"Well, all I know is if you're putting any faith in him then *you're* the dunderheaded halfwit. Ulfger's a coward. It'll be just like at the Merrow Cove."

"No, not a coward. Trapped in the past. Ulfger inherited his father's physical prowess but not his will. He cannot rise above his father's ghost. It wasn't his choice to stay behind at the great battle. His father had him swear an oath to defend the Lady and her garden against whatever should pass. Ulfger still holds to that and will not leave her forest. Even with the destruction of all of Avalon at hand, he believes it is his duty to remain with the Lady."

Peter let loose an ugly laugh. "He hides behind duty like it is his mother's apron."

"That may well be, but—"

Peter put up his hand and cocked his head. "They're here."

Just on the top of the rise stood Ulfger, flanked by twelve narrow-eyed elves all carrying swords and spears. The elves' leathers were the color of the forest and well-worn, while Ulfger still wore the gold-and-red tunic. The tunic was a bit threadbare now, but it still bore the black elk-head crest.

"A meddler and a human-born," Ulfger called. "And neither welcome here. Trespass in the Lady's Wood carries but one punishment . . . *death*."

Chapter Fourteen

Clan

Nick swallowed a spoonful of porridge and winced. His throat was still sore, but the troll had been right. Except for a throbbing in his temples, he felt better. Cricket and Danny winced as they ate, as well, but they were all so hungry they finished every bite.

The wounds were still hard to look at, but Sekeu had rubbed some sort of smelly ointment on them and the redness and swelling were subsiding.

"What do you guys know about these Flesh-eaters?" Nick asked.

"Not much," Cricket said. "They won't tell me a thing. Just that we'll find out when we're ready."

"Just what the hell is that supposed to mean?" Nick said. "I don't like all these secrets. Doesn't that bother you guys? I mean—"

Leroy sat his bowl on the table and plopped down beside Nick.

"Crazy day, huh?" Leroy said, his tone upbeat, almost cheerful.

Nick looked away in disgust, staring into his empty bowl. Nobody spoke for a long moment.

Cricket sighed. "Abraham told me about what you did, Leroy." She stuck out her hand. "Thanks."

Leroy's face lit up. He shook Cricket's hand. "Hell, the whole thing was just crazy, that's all."

Danny tried to straighten his glasses, pushing at the broken frame as he weighed the situation. He didn't put out his hand but he did say, "Thanks." And it sounded to Nick like he meant it.

"Hey," Leroy said. "I know I can be a real shit sometimes. But . . . if you guys can cut me a little slack . . . I mean, what I'm trying to say is I'd really like to start over with you guys. What'd you say? Friends?"

Cricket and Danny took a moment, nodded to each other, and finally both of them said, "Friends." Nick remained quiet.

"I'm going to be a Devil now. Devils look after each other," Leroy said, and stuck out his hand to Nick. "Right, Nick?"

Nick didn't look at him. He just poked at his bowl with his spoon.

"*Right,* Nick?" Leroy repeated, now with a noticeable edge to his voice.

No, Nick thought. *I don't have to play this part anymore. I'm done being dicked around, done with Peter and his games, and I'm most certainly done with Leroy.*

Nick got up from the table and went over to the roots, leaving Danny and Cricket looking perplexed, and Leroy very unhappy.

NICK CLOSED HIS eyes and let the warmth from the porridge spread through his body. He was sure things weren't over between Leroy and him, but he'd deal with that later. Right now his head hurt and he wanted some space to sort things out, but he only had a minute before Cricket and Danny came over and sat with him.

"Soooo?" Cricket asked.

Nick was silent.

"So what's the deal with you and Leroy?"

"Nothing."

"Yeah, right," Cricket said. She looked like she might burst at any minute. "C'mon, you gotta tell me. What'd he do now? Huh, what?"

"Nothing," Nick said curtly, and wondered why everyone seemed bent on driving him crazy tonight. "Just drop it, all right?"

"Man, what's up with you?" Cricket said. "Leroy saved your life. Seems you could cut him some slack. Think about—"

"Do you guys miss home?" Nick cut in.

"No," Cricket said, without hesitation. "Not a bit. Things were really fucked up at home. My dad—" She stopped, looked like she wanted to add something more, then shook her head. "Deviltree *is* my home now."

Nick wondered how bad it could be that Cricket felt safer here, among these cretins, than with her own family.

"I miss Cocoa Puffs," Danny said.

Both Nick and Cricket rolled their eyes.

"I'm not trying to be funny," Danny said, as he tried to straighten his glasses. "Wouldn't you kill for a bowl right now? Or maybe some microwave popcorn? What I really miss is freaking toilet paper. Never would've thought toilet paper was man's greatest invention. Y'know what else? I miss my Gameboy. I also miss my stupid little dog. She's a pug named Piglet. She had something wrong with her nose and made a snorting noise all the time. Just like a little piggy. Funniest damn thing. That little monkey-faced dog snored louder than my dad, too. We had to shut her in the downstairs laundry at night so that we could sleep. I sorta miss my friends at school. I miss my mom and dad, I guess. But," he laughed, "most of all I miss my goddamn Gameboy."

Nick and Cricket stared at him. Finally, Nick asked, "Danny, why'd you run away in the first place?"

"Huh? Oh, because I set the school on fire. After I saw all the fire trucks and police cars, I thought it might be a good idea to get out of town."

"You did what?" Cricket and Nick asked at the same time.

"Well," Danny said defensively, "I was pissed at that sour old tit Mrs. Kerry. She's the one that took my Gameboy."

"So you burned the school down?" Nick asked.

"Yes. No. Well sorta. I tried to. I only managed to burn up a bunch of bushes and part of the roof before——"

"That's great, Danny," Cricket interrupted. "How about you, Nick? Why'd you leave?"

"Because I had to."

"Why?"

"It's complicated. Some guys moved into my grandmother's house. Turned into a bad scene."

"How bad?" Cricket asked.

Nick rolled up his sleeve, showed them the burn on his arm.

Cricket looked at him. "That's bad."

"Well, I've got my mom to thank for that one."

"Your *mom* did that?"

"No, but it was her fault, it was her idea to rent out the rooms in my granny's house. Hell, it was her idea to move back to Brooklyn in the first place. We used to live at Fort Bragg, down in North Carolina, but after my dad died Mom decided we needed to move in with Granny. Said it was because money was tight. That was the same excuse she used to talk Granny into renting out the downstairs rooms. And that's how Marko and his pals ended up in our house. Marko's the one that burned me."

Nick shook his head. "I mean I could see that those guys were shit the first time I met them. Right? But Mom, she was so glad to have some tenants, she just bent over backward for them. Turns out these guys are fucking street-level drug dealers and here's my mom making them feel right at home. I mean, can you believe that?

"Soon we had these kids coming and going, running dope all over the place. A regular operation working out of our back porch. By then even my mom had caught on. I mean it wasn't like these guys were going out of their way to be discreet. They pretty much acted like they owned the place."

"Didn't she call the police?" Cricket asked.

"No, that's just it. She wouldn't. We got in an argument about that. She said Marko had told her if she called the cops, he'd make sure it looked like she was in on it. If that happened the state would take me away from her, or seize Granny's house. Bunch of crap like that. I think Marko had laid it on thick. Had scared her to death. Anyway, Marko must've got wind of our argument, because it was shortly after that him and his pals gave me this." Nick tapped the burn mark.

"So you left?"

"You bet. I fucked up their setup and got out of there."

Cricket looked at him, horrified. "You left your mom and grandmother behind . . . alone in that house with . . . *them*?"

"No . . . I mean, yeah. I left them, but don't make it sound like I *deserted* them."

"Nick, that's terrible. Think about how scared your mom must be without you there."

"She's the one that brought them in!" Nick said angrily. "She's the one that wouldn't call the cops. What was I supposed to do? Stay there and put up with Marko's crap? The guy was going to kill me."

"Nick, think about it. They probably told her they'd hurt you and your grandmother if she did anything or told anyone. There's no telling what-all they said to her." Cricket shook her head. "That poor woman is in such an awful situation. What's she going to do? I can't believe you just up and left her there like that."

"You don't understand. You weren't there. It's not like you think. It's—" He stopped. "Never mind. Just never fucking mind!" Nick got up and stomped away, crossed the chamber, and went into the privy. He pushed the door shut and dropped the latch. He pressed his back against the door, ignoring the clicking and rustling coming from the toilet. He stared at his reflection in the broken mirror and saw a dozen angry faces glaring back at him.

Fuck her, he thought. *She doesn't know what the fuck she's talking about. I didn't abandon my mother. I'd never do that.* He tried to push away the thoughts of his mother alone with Marko, but could think of nothing else. He saw her face. Could see Marko and his pals: Marko's bulging, bloodshot eyes, his beastly grin, could still hear the way they'd laughed when they'd burned him. If they didn't mind burning him, what were they capable of doing to her, to Granny? With him gone, they could do anything. *God,* he thought, *she must be so scared.* And on top of all that, Granny could barely even get out of bed these days. Mom's got nowhere to go. No other family, no one else to help her. *What've I done?* His face clenched up and an ugly sob escaped his throat. He pressed his face into his hands and began to cry.

"Mom," he whispered. "I'm so sorry. I'm so damn sorry."

✦

ULFGER DREW HIS broadsword from its scabbard. His thick, muscled arms twitched, seemed to ache to cut the boy in two. He took a step down the path, toward the ledge where Peter stood, hands on hips, legs wide, glaring down at him.

"You were warned, runt," Ulfger said. "I will have your head."

Tanngnost shuffled between them. "Lord Ulfger, if I may—"

Peter whipped out his long knife. "Come and get me, you one-eared fuck!" he shouted and let loose a wild hoot.

"Peter!" Tanngnost cried and shot the boy a nasty look. He wished Peter wouldn't make it his mission to remind potential allies of prior mutilations.

"You can count on it," Ulfger growled, and spat in the dirt.

"We didn't come to fight!" Tanngnost cried, wondering how things could be spiraling out of control so quickly.

"TAKE HIM!" Ulfger shouted.

The elves all drew their swords.

"FOOLS!" Tanngnost thundered, and slammed his staff down, his powerful booming voice echoing through the forest. "Squabbling among yourselves like children. It is little wonder that we're losing this war! Now put your swords away, all of you!"

The elves hesitated, looking to Ulfger.

Ulfger's dark eyes fell on Tanngnost. "Mind your place, old goat. You give no orders here."

"Forgive me, Lord Ulfger," Tanngnost said and made a slight bowing gesture. "But please, just hear my say."

"I've had enough of your schemes, your distortions, your half-truths."

"The Flesh-eaters are burning Whisperwood," Tanngnost said.

Surprise showed even across the elves' stone faces.

"Liar," Ulfger said. "Whisperwood can't be burned."

"Find a vantage point and you can see the fires for yourself."

Ulfger narrowed his eyes.

"Peter being here, armed with nothing more than a knife, is proof enough," Tanngnost said. "Do you believe he'd take such a risk were the need not dire? If the Lady were not in imminent danger? Not to mention setting aside his pride and old grievances to appeal to you?" The troll took in a deep breath. "He may be lacking in diplomatic skills, but his sword and life are sworn to the Lady. If he is willing to take such risks, can you not at least hear us out?"

"Go on then, speak your bit," Ulfger conceded. "Then *I* will decide if he lives or dies."

Tanngnost clutched his staff, struggled to stifle his temper. "No, Lord Ulfger," he said levelly. "Not today you won't. Need I remind you that it was your father that granted him a place in Avalon? He has earned the right with his own blood and the blood of his clan. If you should harm Peter here and now, under these circumstances, it will be nothing short of murder."

Ulfger's eyes flared. "Say your bit and be done," he growled.

"Don the Horned Helm," Tanngnost said. "Take up your rightful place and lead us into battle. The Flesh-eaters have grown weak. With your father's sword leading we can drive them into the Mist. The Lady's Guard, the Devils, even the witch and her horde, all of them, they will rally around the Horned Helm. They will follow *you*, Ulfger. *You!*"

Ulfger flinched and took a step back. He glanced about almost like an animal searching for an escape. "Whisperwood is not my concern," he muttered.

"Do you believe they will stop with Whisperwood?"

Ulfger was silent for a long moment. "My duty lies with the Lady. I'll not leave my post on the whimsy of some interlopers."

"You hide behind long-dead oaths!" Peter shouted from atop the ledge.

Ulfger glowered up at the boy.

"If you wish to speak of duty then carry the sword," Peter said. "Fight the Lady's enemies before it's too late."

"Do not even pretend you have the right to talk to me, child thief," Ulfger hissed.

Peter sheathed his knife, leaped down the ledge, and headed up the path toward Ulfger.

"Tread lightly young Peter," Tanngnost warned.

Peter strolled boldly past Ulfger and right up to the line of elves. "And have the Lady's Guard given up as well? Are there none who would stand with the wild children of Deviltree against the Lady's enemies?" He waited, looking from face to face, then lowered his voice. "Tomorrow, at dawn, the Devils will be at Red Rock. We intend to drive the Flesh-eaters from Whisperwood. If we have to fight the Flesh-eaters alone, we will. But remember, if we should fall . . . *so will you.*"

The elves' faces betrayed no sign, no emotion.

Ulfger clapped, laughing. "I see now. You've come here to amuse us with your jests. Unless you truly believe there are those among the Lady's Guard foolish enough to follow a little boy, a mere child who plays at being a warlord, into battle."

"Playing?" Peter grinned. "Sadly, even play-fighting the Flesh-eaters is more than the son of the Horned One can claim."

Ulfger stopped laughing; his face became hard, his dark eyes cold. "My father's clemency has spared you today, runt. But by my name, should I see you again in these woods there will be no banter, only your swift death." Ulfger turned and headed back up the trail. The elves lingered a moment longer, staring at Peter with their narrow, cold eyes, then they too disappeared up the trail.

✦

THREE SHARP RAPS hit the door. All the Devils stopped what they were doing; looked at one another, then to the door.

A large kid named Bear opened the peephole and a big grin lit his face. He threw the slat over and pulled the round door inward. "Well, well," he said. "Look what the Devil dragged home!"

Peter rushed past, to the middle of the chamber, raising his knife high. *"BLOOD IS CLAN AND CLAN IS BLOOD. ALL HAIL THE LORDS OF DEVILTREE!"*

The Devils dropped whatever they were doing, leaped to their feet, and shouted, *"BLOOD IS CLAN AND CLAN IS BLOOD!"* They rushed toward Peter.

Nick could feel the excitement in the air like an electrical charge. The

Devils danced and clamored around Peter as though he were the Messiah. Even the usually reserved Sekeu beamed like a schoolgirl.

The tall, lumbering troll came in quietly behind Peter and shut the door. No one appeared to notice, nor care. He made his way around the kids and eased himself onto a bench near the roots. He sat with his long face in his large hands, looking haggard and defeated.

Peter tried to speak, but the kids were all talking at the same time. Peter raised his hand and waited for the chamber to quiet down.

"I'm sure you're all aware that things have become dire. The Flesh-eaters burn Whisperwood. It's time for bold action and brave deeds."

Their faces grew somber.

"That is why I took it upon myself to enter the Lady's Wood, convinced Tanngnost that it was time to set aside old grievance and try to bring the clans together."

The troll rolled his eyes.

Peter thumped his chest. "I braved the Lady's Wood, stood alone before Ulfger and his horde of elves with nothing but my knife. And I challenged Ulfger, dared him to stand with us against the Flesh-eaters."

The Devils held their breaths, leaned forward.

Peter spat on the ground. "The *coward* refused."

Some of the kids booed, there were shouts of "who needs him," but Nick also saw several troubled faces.

"Don't fear. For I have a plan." A devilish smile lit Peter's face. "Such a wicked plan. The Devils will have their day of glory, this I promise." Peter raised his knife above his head and shouted: *"FOR WHO ARE THE TRUE GUARDIANS OF THE LADY?"*

The kids erupted. *"THE DEVILS!"*

"AND WHO ARE THE TRUE LORDS OF AVALON?"

"THE DEVILS!"

Peter held his hand up until the chamber again quieted. "As I'm sure you've all heard by now, the Devils stood against the witch today."

They cheered.

"Held their own against Ginny Greenteeth's entire horde!"

More hoots and cheers.

"Not only that, but one of our New Blood has proven himself worthy.

In defense of his clan, he singlehandedly killed *two* barghest and saved the lives of three New Bloods." Peter's voice dropped. "Devils . . . *prepare!*"

Two Devils ran around the chamber, dousing the torches and lanterns until only a single torch burned on the central pillar above Peter's head.

Sekeu handed Peter a tattered gray wolf pelt. Peter slipped it over his head like a hood, so that his eyes peeked out from the mask. Peter hopped up onto a stone at the pillar's base. He threw his arms up with a theatrical flourish. The chamber fell dead quiet. "Bring me the body of *Leroy!*"

Leroy looked both delighted and terrified. Redbone and several of the Devils grabbed him and jostled him over to Peter.

The Devils formed a semicircle, all facing Peter. Sekeu brought Peter a knife and sword, both in scabbards and tied to a wide, studded belt.

Peter slid out the knife, held it before Leroy's eyes, letting the flicking torchlight dance along its sharp edge. "Leroy, do you give your blood to the Devils?"

Leroy looked at the knife and hesitated, finally letting out a timid "Yes."

"All have heard . . . he gives his blood willingly," Peter cried.

The Devils began to clack their teeth.

Leroy glanced about, eyes wide. Nick could see he was breathing fast.

"Hold out your hands," Peter said, his golden eyes grave, almost angry.

Leroy slowly brought up his hands. They were trembling. He winced.

Peter laid the hilt of the knife in Leroy's palm, clasped Leroy's hand in his, so that together they held the knife.

"This belongs to you now," Peter said in a hushed, reverent tone.

Leroy's face flushed with relief. He looked at the knife, overjoyed.

Sekeu handed Peter the sword and belt. Peter knelt and buckled the belt around Leroy's waist, then stood, clasping Leroy on each shoulder. "Welcome brother. Welcome to the clan of Deviltree."

Leroy beamed.

"One has put his life on the line for his clan!" Peter shouted. "Stood face to face against two barghest! His reward is our brotherhood. Mark this day as the day Leroy earned the right to wear a sword, earned the right to be called a *DEVIL! LONG LIVE THE CLAN OF DEVILTREE!*"

The Devils exploded in cheers and hoots. They snatched Leroy up onto their shoulders and began to parade him around the chamber, chanting his name.

"I will claw out his eyes," Nick hissed and clenched his hands into tight fists, digging his nails into his palms. "Burn his face. Stab him. Stab him. *Stab*—" Nick clamped his teeth together tightly. What was he saying? He shook his head, tried to clear away the acid, the venom. What had come over him? What was he thinking?

He watched them tromp by, saw Leroy laughing and beaming with joy.

Hatred swept over him again. He felt the frustration and anger welling up within him, and all at once a flush of heat bloomed in his stomach. The venom climbed up his throat. *That fucking shit. Dig out his eyes. Tear his flesh. Stomp his skull into the stones!* Nick clutched his head. *No*, he thought. *Fuck it. I don't give a fuck.* But another part of him did care, cared very much.

The pounding in his head grew worse. He wondered if it had anything to do with the poison from the barghest. It felt more like in his dream, right before he'd turned into that demon thing. He needed something to drink. He glanced about, caught the troll watching him. He sucked in a deep breath. *Let it go*, he told himself. *Get some water, cool down.*

He got up and poured himself a mug of water, then headed over to the table, as far from everyone as he could get.

The troll gave him a concerned look as he passed.

Nick stared at the table, did his best to ignore the celebration. There was a nut pinned between the boards of the table, and he began to pick at it. Something, anything to keep his mind off Leroy, off the violence pounding in his head. The nut popped free. He batted it between his hands. *It's been a long day, that's all*, he thought. *Shit, between almost getting killed, and all this bullshit with Leroy, well, being in a bad mood is understandable. Right?*

Two pixies alighted on the table, well out of arm's reach, and watched the nut.

Tonight Nick found he could hardly stand the sight of the little blue people. He swatted at them with the back of his hand. "Scat."

They stuck out their tongues and wagged their butts at him. Nick felt the heat grow in his stomach, the venom in his throat. He rubbed his head. *What's wrong with me?*

Peter was talking to Leroy now.

Nick stopped rolling the nut.

Peter was obviously congratulating Leroy. Pumping his hand up and down and patting him on the back. Leroy was all grins.

Nick's lip quivered and his fingernails dug into the table.

One of the pixies flicked Nick's ear, while the other tried for the nut. Nick swatted violently at them. They flitted out of the way, giggling.

Nick couldn't hear what Leroy was saying, but it was obvious by his exaggerated pantomimes that he was describing how he'd killed the barghest.

The heat in Nick's stomach began to burn, just like in the dream, and just like in the dream, he felt murder growing in his heart. Not just for Leroy, but for everyone.

One of the pixies yanked a tuft of Nick's hair while the second one snatched for the nut again, and Nick felt the venom take him.

He howled and hurled the mug at the pixie. It struck the pixie in mid-air, knocking it to the ground. The mug clanged across the stone floor.

The hall fell silent.

The pixie screamed, and the cry of pain brought Nick back. Nick watched it fluttering, trying to get up. It was hurt. Had he done that? Yes, he knew he had. But how could he have done such a thing? How could he have lost control like that?

He heard Cricket gasp and looked up; everyone was staring at him.

Redbone slid out his knife and started toward him.

"No," Peter said.

"What?" Redbone said. "He needs a lesson. Needs a mark."

"No," Peter repeated.

SEKEU CLEARED HER throat. "Nick will have to be killed."

"No," Peter said.

Tanngnost let out a sigh and thought, *This will not be easy.* He looked out over the ever-thinning canopy of leaves. The watchtower had always been a good place for counsel, a place to clear the mind. The bit of moon glow that found its way through the low-hanging clouds glistened silver off the dewy limbs. He saw a few fireflies, and thought back to when the trees had been lush and the night alive with the glimmer of a million tiny faeries. Tanngnost hooked his pipe in his mouth, inhaled deeply, then exhaled, watching the smoke drift away on the light breeze. "She's right, Peter. There's no other choice."

"No," Peter repeated.

"He's turning," Tanngnost said. "And if we wait until it's too late, it'll be worse for all of us. If the kids see him turn—worse, if they see us kill him, think what that will do for morale. We need to act now."

Peter pursed his lips and shook his head adamantly.

"Nick is showing all the signs," Sekeu said.

Peter didn't answer. He pulled his legs up to his chest, wrapped his arms around them, and put his chin on his knees.

Ever the contradiction, Tanngnost thought. *One moment a cold-hearted killer, the next a sentimental boy, always the eternal optimist despite a lifetime of tragedy. Of course, that's his glamour. The very thing that draws the children to him, makes them love him despite so many contradictions.*

"Nick is having the nightmares," Sekeu said. "I hear him at night. You can see darkness in his eyes in the morning."

Peter's brow tightened.

"You saw him tonight," she said. "He is having trouble controlling his anger. You know that is the last sign before they turn for good."

Peter looked up. "What, because he swatted a pixie? Who hasn't? The little pests will run over you if you don't."

"No, Peter," Tanngnost said. "That wasn't a swat. I was watching him. The darkness had him. He meant to kill that pixie."

"I found one dead the other night," Sekeu said. "Someone had crushed it."

Peter looked at her. "What? No."

"Yes."

"He'll beat it," Peter said. "We've had others that went through it: older boys, just starting puberty, their bodies always fight the magic."

"Yes," Sekeu said. "But they do not go so far. One night, maybe two of bad dreams and stomachaches and that is all."

Tanngnost sucked in a deep breath. "We can't risk another Roger." There, he'd said it. "Not now. Not with everything at stake."

Sekeu gave Peter a hard look. Peter's face clouded. He looked away into the night sky.

Tanngnost knew it was cruel to bring up Roger. He hated having to, but he had to get through to Peter, and with Peter sometimes this was the only way. Roger had been too old. Like with Nick, it started with the stomachaches, the dreams, then he began to have violent outbursts. One moment Roger seemed fine, then he'd lose control. He'd have that same confused look that Nick had: trying to understand why. Horrible thing to have to watch. Roger turned while out gathering berries. Sekeu told them one minute Roger was picking berries the next he attacked another New Blood, stabbed Sam over and over in the face, neck, and stomach. Sekeu had been the one to kill Roger, then had the task of putting Sam out of his misery.

"Peter, I will not allow it to happen again," Sekeu said, and the coldness of her tone chilled Tanngnost. "If he shows any more signs I *will* kill him."

"No. I brought him through. If he turns, *I'll* be the one to kill him."

"And if you are not there?" Sekeu asked.

Peter set hard eyes on Sekeu. "If it happens again . . . kill him," Peter said bitterly. "Make it quick, but kill him. Tell Redbone, but none of the others."

Sekeu nodded; she looked relieved.

Peter hit the banister with his fist. "We can't lose him. We need him. If we're to defeat the Flesh-eaters we'll need all of them."

An uncomfortable silence fell between them. Tanngnost took another pull on his pipe. "Then it's decided?" Tanngnost asked. "About the Flesh-eaters?"

Peter nodded. "What other choice do we have? Food's almost gone. We can either try and drive the Flesh-eaters back or fight Greenteeth and Ulfger for the scraps left in their woods."

"You spoke of a plan—a *wicked* plan I believe?"

Peter frowned. "Oh that." He cleared his throat. "Well, I'm still working on that." He stood and began to pace back and forth. "Picking them off one at a time is no longer an option. We will never drive them back that way. There're just too many of them, too few of us, and too little time. We need a new strategy."

"What do you propose?"

Peter nodded to himself, as though trying to convince himself of something. He crossed his arms over his chest. "An all-out assault."

Tanngnost raised his shaggy eyebrows. "Peter, you know they're too many to—"

"We're out of time. If they break through Whisperwood all will fall. What other option is there? Tell me?"

Tanngnost could think of nothing.

Peter looked at Tanngnost with grim, determined eyes. "It is the end, old friend. One way or another, it's the end."

Chapter Fifteen

Merrow's Cove

Nick *felt the heat swim through his veins like venom. The skin along his arms prickled then began to burn, to shrivel and turn black right before his eyes. Claws grew out of his fingers, tore right through his flesh. He let out a long, painful wail then saw them—three little faeries no bigger than birds—and his wail turned into a deep, hungry growl. The faeries crouched in the crook of a tree, quivering, frozen in fear, fear of him. He smiled, felt his lips peel back over jagged teeth, and snatched up two of them. Slowly, he squeezed them. Their eyes bulged and he felt their tiny bones crack and snap in his hand, their shrieks music to his ears. He bit off their heads, grinding their flesh and bones between his teeth, squeezed their runny guts into his mouth. Nick reached for the last one, the little boy. The* *boy screamed, only it wasn't a little faerie scream that came out, but his scream, Nick's. Nick heard himself screaming and screaming, with fear, with pain, with overwhelming loss.*

Nick awoke with a start, drenched in sweat, his stomach burning. This time the nightmares didn't fade. They'd been all too real, too vivid. He could almost still taste them.

Nick didn't want to go back to sleep, afraid the dreams would return. He wondered why he was the only one that seemed to be having night-mares. He looked at Danny. The boy was sleeping like a baby. Danny had come in only a day or two before him.

Nick unlatched his cage and got up. The first light of dawn was creep-ing through the windows, setting the thin mist aglow. None of the oth-ers were awake yet. He saw a few pixies flittering about here and there, scrounging around searching for crumbs. They kept a wary eye on him. *They're scared of me*, he thought. This should've been good, but it made Nick feel as though something was wrong with him, like he had a disease, something contagious, something horrible.

Nick stretched, surprised that his muscles weren't sore from all the hiking yesterday. If anything, he felt spry. He clenched his fist. He felt strong. He assumed it was the gruel. It really *was* doing something to him. And again, Nick had to ask himself just what that might be.

He walked to the privy; the night chill still hung in the air and the cool stones felt good beneath his bare feet. He entered, heard hissing, and saw the two pixies nesting just above him in the rafters keeping a wary eye on him. Nick ignored them, dousing his head under the pump, and drank deeply, slowly washing away the fire in his stomach, the horrible taste from his mouth, then came back out into the chamber. He sat at the end of the long table and watched the morning light gradually fill the great hall. He stared at the straw men hanging in the shadows. They still reminded him of dead children.

He found his thoughts returning again and again to his mother. In those last few years he'd come to almost hate her. How? Why? Where had that hostility come from? Why was he always pushing her away, always making things so difficult? So many of their fights seemed so stupid now, so trivial.

Absently, he stroked the soft fur of the blue rabbit's foot and recalled the days after his dad's funeral. He'd been ten then. Each night that week, a couple of NCO wives would drop off a few dishes for dinner. Sometimes they would bring along their children as well. Each bestowing their condolences, wishing his mother the best in the coming months, making his mother promise if she needed anything, anything at all, to please just call. They could never stay long though, they had kids to take to soccer or to swim team, or groceries to pick up. They'd leave their Styrofoam takeout trays and head back to their homes, their lives, their *husbands*, leaving Nick and his mother alone in a room full of wilting flowers and sappy sympathy cards.

It was then that it truly sank in that his father wouldn't be coming home. Would never again walk through the door, plop down on the stairs, and gripe about his day while unlacing his boots. Would never again grab a beer out of the fridge, swat his wife on the butt, and ask what the heck was for supper. Never again jab Nick in the gut and ask him if he'd beaten up any little girls at school. From now on, it would be just Nick and Mom.

Those first nights his mother had held him, rocking him gently as he cried himself to sleep. But now, while sitting in this gloomy chamber of stone and roots, he wondered just who had held her, who'd rocked *her*, wiped away *her* tears, told *her* everything would be all right? What had that been like for *her*, suddenly facing life as a single mom? With no one to turn to but an ailing mother in Brooklyn.

And there were other matters, things grieving widows should never have to deal with. They could no longer stay on base, so she needed to find a place for them to live. And to add to that, the accident that had killed his father was under investigation, the Army claiming negligence on his father's part. Nick understood little of the details, only that it had something to do with their benefits and meant his mother was suddenly desperate to find a job.

And how had I helped? Nick asked himself. *What did I do to make things easier? I argued, I complained, and I fought with her about everything. And worst of all I blamed her for it all.* He could hear his own whiny voice griping about his school, his room, his shoes, his stupid fucking *shoes*. God, how he hated the sound of it in his head.

What had been wrong with him? Did he really believe he was the only one suffering? The only one hurting? Had he truly been that blind? Nick rubbed his forehead. Somehow everything had gotten jumbled up, twisted, that's all. The loss, the hurt, the anger, all of it. Now it seemed so clear. So goddamn painfully clear.

"I'm gonna come back, Mom," he whispered. "Gonna make up for it. I promise. Just hang on. Please hang on."

Nick pressed his hands into his face and tried to rub away the strain, the grief and regret. He heard a creak and looked up. Peter, Sekeu, and the troll were coming down the stairs from the loft. All three of them were

staring at him. Nick had the feeling that he was being scrutinized, almost examined.

A smile lit Peter's face. "Hey Nick. You doing okay?"

Nick stood up. "Peter, we need to talk."

Peter walked over and placed a hand on Nick's back. "And we will, Nick. Most certainly. But not now. Too many things afoot." Peter's golden eyes gleamed wickedly. "There's blood to be spilled and throats to slit." Peter threw his head back and crowed like a rooster, crowed until everyone in the chamber was on their feet.

✦

KIDS LINED UP in front of the privy. Fires were set, torches lit, porridge put to boil; you could feel the excitement as the Devils rushed about getting the day going. Nick got his bowl and took a seat next to Cricket and Danny.

Danny looked in his bowl and frowned. "That's all we get? There's hardly enough to fill the bottom of my bowl."

"What are you complaining for?" Cricket asked. "I thought you hated this gunk."

"Wow, would you look at that!" Danny said. He was holding his glasses away from his face, pulling them off and on, and squinting. He looked straight up.

Cricket and Nick looked up too.

"Danny?" Cricket asked. "What the hell are you doing?"

"How . . . about . . . that," Danny said. "I can see better *without* my glasses now. This magic porridge might taste like bark, but man, is it *goood* for you." He stood up, turned sideways, and pulled his shirt up. "Check this out." He patted his stomach. "My gut's almost gone."

"You're sucking in," Cricket said.

"Am not. I'm turning into a lean mean killing machine."

"Puh—lease!" Cricket said, slapping the table and letting out a laugh.

"Y'know," Danny continued, "if we could figure out the ingredients to this slop, we could make like a couple million bucks back home."

"We're not ever going back home," Cricket said, and as the profoundness of her words hit them, they all fell quiet.

"I am," Nick said. "I'm getting out of here."

Cricket and Danny stared at him.

"What do you mean?" Cricket asked.

"I mean, I'm going home." He paused. "I have to get back to my mom. One way or another, I have to."

"How you gonna do that?" Danny asked.

"I don't know yet."

A sad smile crossed Cricket's lips. She reached out and clasped Nick's hand. "I'm sure there's a way."

"*DEVILS*," Peter called. "Gather round. There is a tale to tell!"

✦

PETER TOOK A deep breath. The Devils clustered about him in a semicircle, sitting on the stone floor, atop their cages, or leaning against tree roots, goading and picking at one another. He looked from face to face: Cutter, who'd walked through the Mist without so much as a word; Huck, who'd actually laughed at it; Dirk and Dash, who were always fighting with each other but were never apart; Ivy, with her beautiful curly hair and one lazy eye from where her mother had kicked her for wearing makeup; Amos, the Amish boy who was banished for being too profane. How similar they were to the Devils from the first age, before the great battle, to those boys and girls who'd died so valiantly.

Peter leaned over to Tanngnost. "They're ready, as ready as they'll ever be. Are you?"

The old troll huffed and pushed himself to his feet. "No, but I'll do my best." He walked in front of the Devils, drew himself up to his full height, and stamped his staff once, hard, the sound reverberating about the chamber. The chattering died down.

"This is not an easy tale to tell," Tanngnost began, his deep baritone filling the chamber. "Maybe if the words had been passed down to me from another. But this isn't some ancient dusty legend, this is a real-life tragedy, and I was there to witness it. I saw the carnage, heard the screams, smelled the blood, and have no desire to relive the horror once again. I've done that enough in all the nightmares that've plagued me since. But you are being asked to put your lives on the line for Avalon. You deserve to know the truth, to know what you're fighting for. So it is time to tell the tale once more."

The troll cleared his throat. "We've New Blood among us. For those of you to whom this story is new, it should enlighten you and hopefully inspire you. For those who've heard it not once but many times, it should serve as a reminder of who we are and why we carry on. For me, it's important to pass down the events of that terrible day so that the deeds of those who died are not forgotten. This is a tale of evil, of death, and of heroism. It is my tale. It is your tale. This is the tale of the Flesh-eaters."

The hall fell quiet; all the kids leaned forward.

"Before forever ago, the very earth itself was alive, a place of mystery, nature, and magic. It was the time of the first races, when gods still walked among us and we rejoiced in their miracles and wonderment. Men-kind shared this world for but a blink, then, sadly, they became *enlightened*, found science and religion. The new world of men left little room for magic or the magical creatures of old. Earth's first children were driven into the shadows by flame and cold iron, by man's insatiable need of conquest.

"Those who could escape men-kind's persecution gathered around the Lady of the Lakes, Lady Modron, daughter of the Great Avallach. She released the Mist to hide and guard Avalon, and the isle became a refuge, a sanctuary from the human world.

"There is a sacred spot within Avalon—the Haven. At its center lies Avallach's Tree. Its roots bind all of Avalon together. It is said that Avallach's blood courses through its roots. The Tree is the heart, Avalon is the body, the inhabitants the soul, all three woven together, one living entity. One cannot be without the other. You are all part of this union."

Tanngnost looked out past the kids. His eyes focused beyond the hall.

"It was some time after the betrayal of King Arthur and his round table of villains that Avalon began to drift away from human civilization. The isle left the Britains, drifting for an age along the frozen coasts of the Atlantic, until finally finding a home in the land now known as the Americas. This was a golden time for Avalon, for we were far away from men-kind's intolerant god. This new land was still wild and full of magic, much like the early ages of earth. The native people of the Americas were one with nature, both revering and fearing its magic.

"So, as time passed, we came to trust the peace, believe we were safe from the evils of human civilization. The Lady called the Mist back into the lakes and once again the magical people had the stars and moon to dance under at night and the sun to bask in during the day. The native people came and paid reverence to the Lady. We shared our magic with their shamans and traded crafts, harvests, and wild game, just as we had with the druids of old.

"Then the ships came."

Tanngnost paused, took in a deep breath.

"One day I looked out toward the horizon and there, in Merrow's Cove, three tall galleons lay at anchor. Three ships full of men, women, children, dogs, pigs, fowl, goats, disease, and vermin. Their stench reached deep into the forest.

"I watched them wade ashore in droves, boatload after boatload. Close to three hundred men and women landed, fouling our streams with their filth. Their priests planted a cold iron cross on the beach and tainted our land with their blessings. We'd fled to the farthest corner of the world to escape their tyranny and yet somehow, here they were on the very shores of our sacred Avalon.

"All the magical creatures took flight at the sight of them. We hid far into the woods and watched from the hills. We hoped they'd take what they needed and leave. But instead they began to set up camp, and soon another ship came and then another. Five ships sat in our harbor. How many more were on their way? We had no way of telling.

"The folk of Avalon held council with the Lady. The Lady sent a fellowship representing many of the faerie folk to meet with the men, to let them know that this was our land and ask them to leave. The delegation was led by Hiisi, the Lady's lifelong friend and closest confidant. And I was proud to see my brother Tanngrisnir there representing the trolls of Avalon. Dressed in their best finery, they all marched under the banner of the Lady that day, each carrying a gift of fruit gathered from the Lady's own garden.

"We watched from the woods as the delegation went forth. A group of women were washing in the stream and when they saw the troop approaching they began to shout and scream then fled back into their camp.

"The delegation halted. They seemed unsure of what to do.

"Dozens of the men began to gather along the edge of the camp, shouting and yelling at the group. This went on for some minutes, then all at once several loud pops and plumes of white smoke erupted from the camp. I didn't know it at the time, but it was musket fire. Several of the delegation collapsed and didn't get back up. The rest ran for the woods. Hiisi fell over clutching his chest. Tanngrisnir picked Hiisi up and tried to carry him away. But the men from the camp came for them with swords and pikes. The delegation was unarmed, as they had come only to talk and parley. Those that were not fleet enough were run down and slain before our eyes. I watched my own brother stabbed over and over. They killed them right in front of us. We fled into the hills, all terrified for our lives."

Tanngnost cleared his throat and continued, his voice thick with emotion.

"The Lady released the Mist to protect our shores, to hide Avalon, lest even more ships should come. The Mist boiled up from the lakes and rolled out of the forests and hills like dragon's breath. By that night the Mist had surrounded the island and covered the sky. I've not seen the sun or moon since."

Tanngnost stopped, seemed unable to continue.

Peter leaped up and began to pace the floor. "That was only the beginning of the dark days ahead," he said and cocked his head as though hearing something far away. "When I think back to that time, it is the drums I hear." Peter thumped his chest. "I can still hear them in my heart. For the

Lady called on the Great Horned One to come out of the forest and crush the men, to drive them from our shores and into the Mist. He came from out of the deepest darkest wood, his eyes flaming beneath the Horned Helm. He beat his war drum and called all the folk to arms. He called for them to remember how to use their horns, teeth, and claws, to remember how to be terrible, to remember what it is like to darken the earth with the blood of men-kind.

"And hear this!" Peter stuck out his chest, his face beamed with pride. "The Horned One came here . . . to *Deviltree*! The Lord of Avalon came to *us*! He called for our swords! Offered us a place among the faerie fold in return for our allegiance.

"Do you know why?" Peter looked across the faces. "Because the Devils knew what it means to fight for your place in this wicked world. Because none had fought harder to escape the evils of men and none were hungrier to rid our land of their stink. The Horned One knew this well. He, the Horned One, danced with us around the fire that night as we sharpened our knives and teeth.

"Our hearts were ignited. All the island was united beneath the Horned One's banner. Seelie and Unseelie alike dug out their weapons of old, dusted off their shields and armor, sharpened their swords and spears. We painted our faces and all that night we beat our drums, howling and wailing. Hoping to put the fear of ancient ones back in the hearts of the men and drive them into the Mist. The warriors of Avalon gathered at the edge of the forest and awaited dawn's first light. But the invaders didn't leave. Instead they dug trenches and hid within them.

"When the first glow of dawn lit up the misty morning, the Great Horned One walked out of the forest and stood before us like a mighty oak. The morning light glistened off his majestic antlers. He beat his fist twice upon his chest and raised his mighty sword, Caliburn, high above his head. Horns rang out all along the forest line. When he brought the sword down, we charged.

"Elves, gnomes, minotaurs, centaurs, all manner of faerie folk, trolls, even the goblins had answered the Horned One's call; never before had such an army been seen. I'll never forget that day, as ageless enemies put aside their differences to come to Avalon's defense. We were here to save our very world. I knew there'd be a thousand songs sung about this legion and was proud to count myself among them. My senses were alive, never had the dew smelled so fresh and the air so crisp. I raised my sword, howled, and followed the Horned One into battle."

Peter snatched a spear from the wall, pointed it at an imaginary foe. "We charged, well over five hundred strong. Such a sight we made, rushing down upon the enemy with weapons high and banners waving, and such a sound, like thunder, as we beat our swords and spears against our shields. And none howled louder than the Devils. We were hungry to paint the tide red with the blood of the invader. We bore down upon their camp and yet still they waited in their trenches. We thought them too scared to meet us on the battlefield. We were from a different age. We knew nothing of modern warfare, of fighting with muskets and . . . *cannon*."

Peter's voice dropped. "All five ships gave us a broadside. The thunder of those cannons was so loud that at times I swear I can still hear their echo. I saw limbs torn from bodies. Bodies turned to meat. Whole heads disappeared in a spray of blood." His voice broke. "Never had I thought such carnage possible.

"Those not killed or maimed in the first volley were lost in shock, not knowing to run or fight, unable to even understand what was happening. Too many just stood there with wide eyes and were cut down as volley after volley ripped through our ranks. The air came alive with their screams, their cries of pain and terror. But," Peter said, his voice swelling with pride, "not the Devils. No, we did not lose our wits. It was *us* that stood beside the Horned one, *we* that did not waver. He continued to push ahead and we followed. The men behind the trenches stood and began shooting their muskets. And it was only then that the Devils began to lose our numbers. The Horned One was hit repeatedly and still he continued forward. He climbed the embankment and attacked.

"They paid the price then. The men screamed and ran from his blazing eyes and terrible sword as he waded through them, cutting them down by the dozen. The Devils rallied and came to his side, and that was when we heard the thunder, when the very earth erupted beneath our feet as cannon shot exploded all around us.

"When the smoke cleared, the Horned One was lying still upon a mound of scorched earth, his body blown to bits, around him the bodies of our clan." Peter slammed the spear down across his knee, splintering the staff into two pieces. The Devils started. "The men had killed the Great Horned One. They slaughtered my *clan*."

Peter's chin fell to his chest. He closed his eyes and could still see their faces, their mangled, shattered bodies, smell the stench of charred flesh. The rest was a jumble: Sekeu helping him back up the beach, thick, choking smoke, pain, the endless ringing in his ears, the two of them stumbling toward the forest, trying not to slip in the pools of blood and gore as they climbed over the bodies of the dead and dying.

Tanngnost spoke up then, low, but the hall was so quiet not a word was lost. "The story didn't end there. If only it had. Those that survived fell back into the hills, crawling into holes, dens, and caves, or any place they could find to hide away and lick their wounds.

"We waited for the men to leave. We hoped and begged the ancient gods to chase them off, but they did *not* leave. Instead they built their fort, cleared the land to plant crops and build pens for their livestock. And worst of all, they erected a Christ church, defiling the very sanctity of Avalon.

"Large platoons of men began entering the forest, never venturing far, but killing any creatures they found. And they ate what they killed. Not just the wild game, no, they ate the magical ones as well. And this, you might have guessed, is how we came to call them *Flesh-eaters*.

"Then they began to burn the forest. Why? I can only guess at the madness of these demons. To create a barrier between them and us perhaps? Whatever the reason, they've become obsessed with clearing the whole island of our kind. To burn down every tree, burn out every hole and den where we might live or hide. Year after year, they burned more and more.

"At first we thought we could outlast them. Thought maybe they'd wither and die, as men-kind do in the human world. But dying is not so easy in Avalon. We've no sickness or disease here, at least not of the kind found in the human world. And we don't age the same either. Peter has been here since before the Romans entered Britain. Myself, I do not know. Men-kind were still hairy beasts wearing furs and stone weapons when I

253

was young. Some creatures live for millennia without aging at all. As you can see, I have grown old while Peter never seems to age. Sekeu and Abraham have been here over a century and have barely changed. That's just the way of faerie. This same magic, unfortunately, also keeps the Flesh-eaters alive.

"But the magic does more than extend the Flesh-eaters' lives. Because Avalon is enchanted, only those with a magical nature can live here in harmony. Children like yourselves are full of magic, but the men have turned, they've lost their magic to the fear and hatred they harbor for all that they can't explain, control, or understand. And so the magic twists them, blackens their hides. They sprout claws and horns and turn into the demons they truly are.

"So we began to understand our plight. Something had to be done or Avalon would be destroyed and lost forever. Some went to the Lady, hoping she could unite the remnants of Avalon, but her grief was too great—the loss of Hiisi, the Horned One, and so many magical creatures had driven her to despair. The elves told that she withdrew within the Haven, slept in the pond beneath Avallach's Tree. She'd become inconsolable and it took all her remaining will just to keep the Mist alive. Soon, Ulfger forbade any to visit her.

"By then, the men no longer had reliable gunpowder, but even without their musket and cannon they were far too numerous and formidable for a direct assault. There were a few vain attempts at organized resistance, but without the Horned One, they quickly fell apart due to mistrust and squabbling. The various folk of faerie withdrew back into their own territories. Ulfger took leadership of the Lady's Wood for himself and forbade any to enter or leave. Avalon had become a wake.

"Decades passed and the Flesh-eaters became bolder and bolder, their forays penetrating deep into the heart of Avalon. They met little resistance and it became obvious that it was only a matter of time before they would discover Avalon's last sanctuary, the Haven, and thus the Lady and Avallach's Tree."

Peter sprang forward, the fire back in his eyes. He pointed the spearhead at the kids. "And that, Devils, is where you came in. Time moves faster in the human world and during our strife the world had moved on.

Great cities had sprung up, a civil war engulfed the America land, and as usual it was the children who suffered. I found the orphaned, the abused, the lost and starving, gathered together those who wished a chance at a better life and were courageous enough to fight for it and brought them here.

"It wasn't long before Deviltree again rung with the shouts and cries of sparring warriors. The Devils were back and ready to reclaim Avalon. Tanngnost set out seeking allies, those brave enough to stand with us. He went to the witch, to Ulfger, but all they did was laugh. 'What,' they asked, 'could a handful of throwaway children do against the Flesh-eaters? How could children dare hope to succeed where the Horned One had failed?' They laughed at us while huddled in their dying beleaguered forest.

"Well, the Devils did not hide. No, we went to war!" Peter said, slapping the flat of the spearhead into the palm of his hand with a loud smack. "We played by our own rules, setting ambushes, tricks, and traps, going after the Flesh-eaters' crops and stockpiles. We harried the men at every turn, and soon it was the Flesh-eaters that were afraid—afraid to come into the forest, afraid to leave their fort at night. The tide began to turn and there was hope for Avalon once again. All because a group of ragtag children that nobody wanted or believed in came together and fought for the Lady. Because *you*, the Lords of Deviltree, would not give up. Will never give up!"

Peter stood, feet planted wide, chest out. "My tale doesn't end there, for the end has yet to be written." He pointed with the spearhead. "You are the writers of this tale now. How it ends is up to each of you. You're the Lords of Deviltree, the deadliest, most courageous warriors Avalon has ever seen. The proud defenders of the Lady and Avallach's Tree. Make no mistake, it will not be easy, but if you are stout of heart, are valiant in your deeds, if you are dedicated to ridding Avalon once and for all of these demons, then this story will end well. For the world of faerie is strong and resolute. Mark my words, once the Flesh-eaters are gone Avalon *will* heal itself, and from that day on you'll be the true Lords of Avalon. Your tale sung for a thousand ages!" Peter raised the spearhead and shouted, *"BLOOD IS CLAN AND CLAN IS BLOOD. ALL HAIL THE LORDS OF DEVILTREE!"*

"BLOOD IS CLAN AND CLAN IS BLOOD!" the kids screamed and

jumped to their feet, waving their fists and pogoing into one another. Peter leaped among them, spurring them on, thrilling in their furor as they shouted and howled.

All but one: a boy with dark circles under his eyes, and green shoes, sitting in the back by himself.

✦

NICK STOOD WITH Peter, the troll, and the other New Blood upon the watchtower. It was another silvery gray day beneath the ghostly clouds of Avalon. He could see across the treetops, across the fog clinging to the lowlands, and across rolling hills and ragged cliffs. Between breaks in the haze he could just make out the perimeter of the island, the impenetrable Mist forming a solid wall of whiteness at the shoreline.

Peter pointed to a jagged line of devastation that ran the width of the island, to the black smoke rising from along the edge of the forest. "The Flesh-eaters are burning down Avalon tree by tree, even as we stand here."

Nick stared at the blackened scar dominating the landscape but didn't really see it; his thoughts were tangled around Tanngnost's words: "The magic poisoned the men, darkening their skin, growing scales and claws, turning them into demons." *Just like in my dream*, Nick thought. *What does that mean then? That I'm turning into a Flesh-eater?*

Peter placed a hand on Nick's back. "Do you see, Nick?"

Nick started; he hadn't been listening.

Peter pointed. "There, that inlet. That's the Merrow Cove. And just up past that ridge, there. That's where the Flesh-eaters' fort lies."

Nick could see it now, a cluster of black specks surrounded by some sort of fortification. He could also make out what must be the rotting skeletons of the ships in the cove.

"From there all the way to the black smoke, all used to be a lush forest, home to a million faerie folk."

The burned lands ran the width of the island, and came inward from the coasts. On one side of that line, nothing but ravaged land, on the other the dying forests of Avalon. There was so little left, and much of what remained was gray and withered.

"All the gray you see is the scourge," Tanngnost said. "It's the result of so many of Avalon's trees and inhabitants being killed. There's no longer enough magic to support the wilds and more delicate creatures, so the wilderness is dying, essentially starving to death for want of magic. Once the forests are gone, where will we live?"

And that's what this all comes down to, Nick thought. *They want us to fight their war.* Somehow seeing the fires made it all too real: kids fighting and dying. Nick shuddered. He tried to imagine what that would be like, tried to imagine himself being handed a sword and actually fighting a man to the death. There was no way he could ever do such a thing, just no way. *Just what have I got myself into? And how am I going to get out of this?*

"Hey," Danny said. "Why don't we get some guns? A few AK-47s outta do the trick."

There were plenty of nods.

"What's an AK-47?" Peter asked.

"Y'know," Danny replied. "An automatic rifle. A machine gun."

"Oh, I've brought back guns over the decades," Peter said. "But they don't work after going through the Mist. The powder gets messed up or something. Flashlights and radios don't want to work either. Even brought over a Gameboy—I really wanted one of those. But nothing electrical works here. I don't know why, but I think the Mist gets to them. Mucks them up."

"What? Gameboys don't work here!" Danny's shoulders slumped. "Ah man, no way. That just sucks."

Nick scanned the length of the island. "Where are we exactly?" Nick asked, shaking his head. "I mean this island. There's no way it can fit in New York Harbor. And even if it could, don't you think someone would notice a big fluffy cloud drifting about?"

Peter made a face like such a thought had never even crossed his mind and looked to Tanngnost.

"I've often wondered the same," Tanngnost said. "Many of us have. I know before the Mist returned, we could see the surrounding lands. The natives used to come to us on canoes, so they could see us too. Maybe the Mist does more than hide us, maybe it takes us into a different time and place. This would explain why time moves so much slower here. But this is merely a guess. I certainly can't begin to understand the ways of Avallach."

Then another thought struck Nick. "Wait," he said. "The Lady controls the Mist, right?"

"Sure," Tanngnost said. "She's a water goddess. She's one with all the bodies of water."

"Then why doesn't she lift the Mist?"

Peter looked horrified. "Lift the Mist? Then more men would come! Why would she ever want to do that for?"

"So the Flesh-eaters can leave." *And*, Nick thought, *so I can go home.*

"Leave?" Peter gasped, looking at Nick as though his head was screwed on backward. "The Flesh-eaters aren't gonna leave. We could send them golden swans to carry them home and they'd only slaughter and eat them. Murder is all they know. They're monsters!"

"Yes," Nick said. "But if they're killing Avalon, isn't it worth the chance?"

"Maybe early on," Tanngnost put in. "Perhaps then that might've worked, before the magic twisted them, before the new world became so populated. Maybe if the Lady had not been so consumed by grief she'd have done things differently. Maybe not. For the Lady is not all-knowing. Far from it. She sees the world in ancient terms. A creature ruled by sentiment and emotions. Regardless, it is too late now. The only way out is to destroy them before they destroy us. Can you see that, Nick?"

Nick nodded, but he wasn't sure, wasn't sure about a lot of things on this island.

"Enough talk," Peter said, and his eyes flashed. "It's time to turn you three into killers."

✦

"PETER," NICK SAID. "I need to talk to you."

"Not now," Peter replied. "We've much to do."

Nick grabbed Peter's arm. "No, it has to be now!"

Peter looked at the hand holding him, then into Nick's eyes. He could see it, the darkness. "Careful, Nick."

Nick let go. "Peter, please."

Peter caught the hard look from Sekeu. He winked at her, then hung back with Nick as she and the others headed down the stairs.

"Peter, I need to get back."

Peter stared at him absently.

"Back home," Nick said.

"Home?" Peter's nose wrinkled up. "You mean back to the *human* world?"

"My mother needs me."

"You're just homesick. That happens. Look, there's a lot around here that takes getting used to. But—"

"No, it's not that. I *have* to get back to my mother. *Have to!* She's in danger. There are a couple of bad men living in the house with her. I told you about them—Marko, remember?"

"The drug dealer? I remember. I thought you said that was all your mother's mess?"

"Doesn't matter. What matters is she's in trouble. And if I don't get back there . . . well, they're going to hurt her. Maybe already have."

Peter could hear the strain in Nick's voice, could see the growing agitation in his eyes, caught the boy clenching and unclenching his fists.

"If anything happens to her, I don't know what I'll do. I have to get back. Okay? Okay?"

He's on the edge, Peter thought, *need to be careful. Maybe Sekeu's right. Maybe it would be best to kill the boy before it went too far.* "Okay, Nick," Peter said calmly. "We can work something out."

Nick's face flooded with relief. "Really? Good. Good. When can we go?"

"Day after tomorrow."

Nick narrowed his eyes at him.

"You have to do me a favor first," Peter said. "You help me, then I help you. How does that sound?"

"You want me to fight."

"No, you don't have to fight. I'd never ask that of New Blood. But I need you there, need you to help in other ways."

Nick stared at him. "This isn't one of your games? One of your tricks?"

Peter acted wounded. "*Nick*, of course not."

"I want you to swear. Swear on the Lady's life that if I stand with you, you'll help me get back through the Mist."

"I swear," Peter said, knowing very well the odds were against either one of them ever seeing the human world again. "Heck, I'll go one better. I swear I'll come home with you and help you take care of Marko."

Nick searched Peter's face, clearly seeking any sign of deceit. Peter now saw the resolve and determination, the same qualities that brought this boy through the Mist. *There's deep strength in this boy,* Peter thought. *If anyone can beat the darkness it'll be him.*

"You would do that?" Nick asked. "Come back with me?"

"Only if you promise I get to be the one who slits their throats," Peter said.

A grim smile snuck across Nick's face.

Peter spat into the palm of his hand and stuck it out to Nick. "Deal?"

Nick spat in his own hand and they shook. "Deal."

✦

NICK, DANNY, CRICKET, and Leroy gathered around Peter in the chamber. Peter hefted his short sword and twirled it from one hand to another. "Flesh-eaters are made of hard stuff," he said, his voice dropping down low. "The magic has twisted them. Perverted them. Turned them into monsters, into . . . *demons.* Their skin has turned into thick scaly hides, hard to cut or penetrate. Their vitals have shriveled within their bodies, hard to find." He clutched his stomach. "I've seen them take a stab in the gut and keep on coming. They're strong too. If they catch hold of you they can rip your innards right out of your bugle hole. Sound scary? It shouldn't. Because fighting is about being fast and clever, and they're *neither.* The faster fighter will always beat the brute. So all you have to do is learn the right tactics, keep on your toes, and you will take the day. Shall we get started?"

The kids looked at each other, unsure.

"Good," Peter said. "Then line up."

Leroy, Nick, Cricket, and Danny all lined up.

"We're not asking you to fight tomorrow. We need your help in other ways."

There were several audible exhalations of relief.

"But war is unpredictable. So we're going to show you some basic tricks in case you find yourself in a bad spot."

Sekeu and Redbone handed each of them a short sword.

"In times past," Peter said, "New Blood would never be given swords. But dire times call for dire measures. Swords and spears have always been our weapons of choice. The live wood of Avalon is too soft and fleshy for accurate arrows. We use short swords and light spears as they play best to our strengths of speed and cunning. And by cunning I mean we play the game our way. We use their height against them. We get in and out, low and fast. We do not engage them. We do not try to kill them. Our goal is to maim. We go for their weakest spots." Peter pointed to his own limbs. "Their legs and arms, especially their ankles and knees. Ankles are thin and close to the ground, hard to protect. This," Peter pointed to the long tendon on the back of his foot, "is your Achilles tendon. If you cut this tendon, they cannot walk. Once they can no longer walk, they're done."

Peter pointed to the straw dummies. "We've lots to show you. Find a straw man and let's get started."

Sekeu paired with Nick, Peter with Danny, and Redbone with Cricket.

Nick hefted his short sword, swung it about, getting the feel of it in his hand. The blade was heavy but well balanced.

"Okay," Sekeu said, and pushed the straw man toward Nick.

Nick prepared himself. Keeping in mind all the things Sekeu had taught him about proper footwork, he sprang forward and back, timing his strikes. He found that many of the same principles of the staff and spear applied to swordplay. He was able to stab the dummy several times without losing his footing.

Sekeu raised an eyebrow. "Good footwork," she said. Compliments were hard won from Sekeu, and Nick was surprised at how much her approval meant to him. He couldn't help but smile. "But you must focus on using the edge of the sword. Not so much stabbing. A Flesh-eater can take many stabs and keep coming. If you must stab, be aware. Your blade can get caught in their hide. So it is best to make quick, strong strikes. You want to cut muscle, sever tendons."

Sekeu spent most of the day with Nick. Nick found it impossible to think in terms of cutting flesh, of actually fighting, but instead lost himself in the craft of swordplay, determined to master the disciplines Sekeu was teaching. He'd be fighting for more than his life tomorrow; he'd be fighting to get back to his mom. Nick went at the straw man with a zeal and vigor he'd not known before, determined to learn all he could.

He also found himself amazed by how much his speed, dexterity, timing, even his endurance had improved. The hiking and training was some of it, but he knew the porridge was playing its part too. *Danny's right,* he thought. *If we could bottle that gunk and take it back, we'd make a fortune.*

Peter called for a break for the kids to don pads and helmets. They were given wooden swords wrapped in cloth.

As they waited for Danny to finish tying his pads, Nick watched the Devils sparring. He was still amazed at their mastery, but found he could now see the technique beneath the speed, could recognize the forms and tricks for what they were. Could sometimes predict or read a move before it was even acted upon.

"It's one thing to hit a moving target," Peter said, "quite another to hit a moving target that's trying to hit you. Leroy," Peter pointed to one side of the round sand pit. "Over there."

Leroy hopped up and took his place.

"Danny, here." Peter pointed to the opposite side of the ring.

Danny looked around as though there might be another Danny in the chamber.

"Move it, Danny," Peter called and clapped. "Quick. Quick."

Danny pushed himself up with a huff and shuffled over to his place.

"Leroy here is a Flesh-eater and it's *your* flesh he's after," Peter said.

Leroy flared his eyes at Danny, grinned, showing all of his teeth, and nodded.

Danny slumped his shoulders, looked up at the ceiling, and let out a long groan.

"That's the spirit, Danny," Peter said, rolling his eyes. "Look, this is fun. It's like tag. All you have to do to win is whop the lunkhead over there on a leg, arm, or head. Fun, huh?"

Danny groaned again.

"Leroy, remember," Peter said. "You're a Flesh-eater. You're only to respond to his attack. Light contact. We're not trying to hurt each other. Got it?"

Still wearing his sadistic grin, Leroy nodded agreeably.

"*GO*," shouted Peter.

"Get him, Danny Boy!" Cricket cried. "Go get him!"

Danny gave her a baleful look, let out a loud sputter through his lips, and began circling Leroy.

Leroy put up his guard and waited.

Danny circled and circled, and would probably have continued all day if Peter had let him.

"Danny, you trying to make him dizzy? Get him," Peter shouted. "*AT-TACK!*"

"C'mon wuss," Leroy said. "Let's see what you got."

Danny lunged. Leroy easily sidestepped and smacked Danny hard on the shoulder with the side of his sword.

Danny dropped his sword. "*OWWW!*" he cried. "Dammit, Leroy. Peter said *light contact*. What part of *light contact* don't you understand?"

Leroy shrugged. "Sorry, dude."

"It's your life, Danny," Peter shouted while clapping his hands. "Grab the sword! *MOVE, MOVE, MOVE!*"

Danny picked up his sword and charged, clenching his eyes shut and swinging wildly in all directions. Leroy knocked Danny's sword down and hit Danny hard on the butt as he barreled past. Danny went sprawling into the sand.

Nick caught the dispirited glance between Peter and Sekeu. Redbone put his face in his hands and shook his head. Leroy was laughing so hard he could hardly stand.

Danny's face was bright red. He punched the sand with his fist, picked up the sword, and got slowly back to his feet.

"Danny, remember your training," Peter said. "You can't charge a Flesh-eater. You have to find his weak spots, use cunning."

Danny's eyes grew large, his mouth dropped open, and he pointed at something behind Leroy. "Whoa, what's that?"

This time Peter put his face in his hands.

Leroy smirked. "You'll have to do better than that, fat-ass."

Danny dropped his guard, looked defeated, and started to turn away, then, with all the grace and cunning of an armadillo, he spun back around and made a low swing at Leroy's ankle. He missed completely, and Leroy delivered a solid whack to the side of Danny's helmet.

Danny made a weak bleating sound, dropped his sword, and cradled his head in his hands. His face cinched up and Nick could see he was trying not to cry.

"Oh, don't be a baby," Leroy said. "I barely touched you."

"GO TO HELL!" Danny yelled and threw his sword at Leroy. The sword missed by a wide berth and Leroy started laughing again.

Peter gave Leroy a dirty look.

"What?" Leroy said, and shrugged. "I'm a Flesh-eater."

"You're an asshole," Cricket said.

Peter pulled Danny to his feet and threw an arm around him. "What'd you say we let someone else have a turn?"

Danny tore off the helmet, threw it in the sand, then plopped down heavily next to Cricket.

"Nick," Peter called. "Ready to give it a shot?"

No. Getting into the ring with that psycho is about the last thing I want to do. Nick let out a long breath, strapped on his helmet, and got to his feet.

Nick met Leroy's eyes. Leroy cocked his head back and smirked, but below that smirk Nick saw something else, something dangerous. *He's out to get me,* Nick thought.

"Okay, Nick," Peter said. "Tag him. Leg, arm, or head. Got it?"
Nick nodded.

"Leroy," Peter said sternly. "*You* keep the contact down. Got it?"
Leroy only grinned.

Nick slipped around the ring, keeping light on his toes. He made quick jabs and short jumps in and out, testing Leroy's defenses just as Sekeu had shown him. Leroy followed his every move.

"GET HIM NICK!" Cricket called.

"Yeah," Leroy laughed. "Get me, twinkle toes."

Nick lunged, making a low slash for Leroy's ankle. Leroy countered, blocking the blow with such force as to knock Nick off-balance. Leroy followed around and caught him on the arm, a solid smack that sent Nick into the sand. Even though the swords were padded, Nick had to grit his teeth not to cry out.

"Up, Nick!" Peter called. "Back on your feet. *QUICK!*"

Nick rolled to his feet. There was no doubt now, Leroy meant to hurt him—would hurt him. Nick felt old fears and self-doubts assail him. *No, Nick thought, I won't let him intimidate me. I'm the one that stood and faced the barghest. If I can kill a barghest, I can take this jerk. Just need to focus. Stay focused.*

Nick met Leroy's eyes and held them. Leroy must've seen something in that look, because his smirk fell away.

"Okay," Peter said. "Keep it light and fun."

"Go Nicky!" Cricket yelled. "Get him!"

Nick saw Leroy slide into a wider stance, planting his feet in the sand for leverage. He noted how tightly Leroy clutched the sword and knew Leroy planned to really clobber him this time.

Okay, Nick thought. *He's stronger than me. I'll never win with force.* Sekeu had shown him a simple maneuver: a feint and counterattack. She'd said it was very effective against an aggressive opponent. But it was one thing to execute the maneuver on a straw man, quite another on some shit trying his best to break your bones. *If it doesn't work,* Nick thought, *he's going to nail me.* He glanced at Sekeu. She seemed to read his thoughts. She smiled and nodded.

Nick used his eyes and body language to telecast a low attack. He made sure Leroy caught him eyeing his ankles. Then Nick went in quick and feinted a low swing. Leroy bought it completely. He swung down hard, anticipating Nick's attack, his full momentum behind the block. The instant he committed, Nick switched, surprised by his own speed. He had a second to catch the stunned look on Leroy's face, the utter disbelief, as the boy stumbled forward off-balance. Then Nick struck. A tremendous crack echoed across the hall as his sword hit the back of Leroy's helmet, sending him face-first into the sand.

There followed a long space of silence as everybody just stared.

Peter blinked a couple of times and finally managed a breathless "Wow."

"WOOHOO!" Danny cried. "You killed him!"

No, Nick thought. *No such luck.*

Leroy sat up, face red and covered in sand. He spat and looked stunned, but not as stunned as Nick. Nick was amazed, not so much by the fact that he'd managed to outplay Leroy—Leroy, after all, was just a big lunkhead—but that he'd once again pushed fear from his mind and focused on what had to be done.

Peter recovered his spirit. "Did you guys see that? That's exactly what we've been talking about. You have to rely on your speed and trickery. You have to make them fight *your* fight."

Redbone pulled Leroy to his feet. "You all right?"

Leroy jerked away. "Of course I'm all right," he said harshly. "Little

prick barely touched me. Lucky shot. No big deal."

Nick thought that it was a big deal, and judging from Leroy's face it was a very big deal.

Peter clapped his hands together. "That's enough for now. Time for grub."

The Devils all headed for the table, leaving Leroy and the New Blood behind. Leroy shucked off his arm pads, untied his helmet. He walked over to them and pointed at the sparring equipment. "Clean this shit up," he growled. Then he pushed his face into Nick's, glaring into his eyes. Nick held the bigger boy's eyes, determined to stand his ground. A slight smirk nudged the corner of Leroy's mouth. He shoved his helmet into Nick's chest. "Put it away," Leroy said, and stomped off.

In the movies or on TV, that would've been the end of it. The bully gaining a little respect for him, and, if not eventually becoming his friend, at least leaving him be. But Nick knew that's not how things worked in the real world. In the real world, you might get a lucky lick in, but boys like Leroy, they never forgot, never forgave, and then somewhere, somehow, boys like Leroy always got you back.

THE FOLLOWING MORNING Nick sat as far away from Leroy as he could and watched the Devils prepare for the raid. He'd had the dreams again, as bad as before, maybe worse. Each morning the darkness in his heart was harder to shake off. He studied his arms, expecting to find some sign of the dark scales and claws. It was all too real in the dream: the screams,

the blood, the carnage. Nick put his face in his hands and rubbed his eyes.
I don't want to turn into a monster.

Cricket came along with her breakfast and sat across from him.

"How you doing there, Nicky?" Cricket asked, worried.

"Never been chipper," Nick mumbled.

Danny wandered over, a bowl in one hand, rubbing sleep out of his eyes with the other. "What's the plan?"

"Don't know," Cricket said. "Nobody said."

"Sure are up early," Danny grumbled. "Still dark outside."

A low, tense murmuring filled the chamber as the Devils went about strapping on weapons, applying war paint, and dressing for battle. Nick noted the rather eclectic assortment of arms and armaments. Alongside the more traditional medieval styles, there were a German kaiser helmet, a tank helmet, an old-style leather football helmet, aviator goggles, at least two samurai swords, a Civil War cavalry saber, ninja stars, a pitchfork, and several pairs of brass knuckles. Most of the kids wore the one-piece, rawhide leathers with the pointed boots sewn into them, but several also had on leather jackets from Nick's world, customized with spikes and studs, looking to Nick like a gang of psychotic punk rockers.

Sekeu came over. With her war paint on, she truly looked the part of an Indian on the warpath. "Come," she said.

Nervous, the New Blood followed her to where the Devils were getting dressed.

Peter had two short swords strapped on his back, the belts crisscrossing his chest bandito style. A black splash of war paint covered his face, and his golden eyes gleamed out from the paint. He pulled his swords free, clanged them together, and all the Devils lined up on either side of him. Including Peter, there were twenty-three warriors.

Peter took a step forward, crossed his swords upon his chest, and set his gleaming golden eyes on Nick, Danny, and Cricket. "Today the Devils go into battle. We go to stop the burning of Whisperwood. There'll be bloodshed. Oh yes, plenty of death to go around this great day." He smiled wickedly. "But a soul simply has not lived until they've heard the screams of their dying enemies." Peter cocked his head and looked deep into their faces. "Who among you will make the Flesh-eaters scream?"

The New Blood shared a quick look.

"Any who stand with us today will become Devils the moment they walk out that door. For such a courageous deed would make any worthy. We've a world to win. Eternal youth, and all the glory of faerie awaits our victory. Search your hearts, find the courage to take life on. Now, who will share this grand adventure with us? Who will become a Lord of Avalon?"

This was it, Nick knew: the point of no return. It was all too real now and suddenly he was unsure. Was this a death march? Did he dare trust this insane boy? The last time he'd followed Peter, he'd ended up in the Mist fighting for his life. Did he believe today would be any better?

Nick glanced from Danny to Cricket. They looked as scared as he felt. This wasn't a game, not this time. They were going off to kill men. You can call them Flesh-eaters or whatever you like, but they were *men*. By the gravity in the air, Nick suspected some of these kids, maybe a lot of these kids, wouldn't be coming back. Nick wondered if he might stand a better chance trying to get back home on his own.

None of the New Blood stepped forward. They stared at the ground, fidgeting and shifting from foot to foot.

Leroy stood beside Peter, his head cocked back. *Like a real tough guy,* Nick thought. Leroy was decked out in full Devil garb, proudly holding his sword and looking full of himself.

Cricket gave Nick a nervous, sidelong glance. Nick met her eyes and shook his head. "You don't have to do this," he whispered.

She made a pained face that said she did. "This is my family now," she said and walked over. Peter hugged her and all the Devils clapped her on the back.

Then it was Nick and Danny. Danny was biting his lip. His brow cinched up.

Danny glanced at Nick. "Peter says we won't have to do any fighting."

"Do you believe that?"

Danny shrugged his shoulders, took in a deep breath, like someone about to jump off the high diving board for the first time, then followed Cricket.

They were all looking at Nick then. The silence of the room weighed on his shoulders. He caught the smirk on Leroy's face. That smirk said Nick was a chump, a wuss, a regular fucktard. But Nick didn't care about that, not anymore. It was his mother that mattered. He thought of her alone in that house, and in the end he knew he had but one choice. Nick locked eyes with Leroy and stepped forward. When he did, Leroy's smirk fell from his face; as a matter of fact, Leroy looked like he'd just swallowed a bug.

A cheer rang out. Peter dashed forward and embraced Nick in a bear hug. Then they were all patting him on the back, ruffling his hair. And at some point, among the cheering, the backslaps, and grins, Nick forgot to be scared, forgot to be mad, realized he was grinning too. *I've lost my mind*, he thought, *I've totally lost my mind.* And it was amazing how good it felt.

"Three cheers for our New Blood!" Peter cried.

One and all, they cheered.

THE DEVILS' ALOOFNESS evaporated. Nick felt the warmth of a true brotherhood as the whole clan worked quickly to deck the New Blood out in battle gear. Even the most ferocious of the Devils pitched in, laughing and joking as they helped them lace up boots and strap on belts and armor.

They'd painted lines of dark green straight down Cricket's face, and when she pursed her lips and lowered her head, she looked wicked and dangerous.

Unfortunately for Danny, he'd allowed Redbone to apply his war paint. "He's a war cat," Redbone declared. But complete with black snout and whiskers, Danny looked more like a war panda. No one could look at him without letting out a snort. It only made matters worse when Danny began to pout, for then he looked like a pouting panda.

After seeing what they'd done to Danny, Nick decided it might be prudent to slip over to the mirror. At first, Nick thought it was some trick, because the boy in the mirror wasn't him. Standing there instead was a savage with dark swatches of black paint running down both sides of his face. The savage looked lean and hard, but it was the eyes that Nick found most disturbing, piercing, haunted eyes, sparkling with gold. Was that really him? What had they done with the nerdy boy with the funny shoes? Nick wasn't sure how he felt about this.

Peter came up behind him. "Nick, this is for you." Peter handed him a short sword.

Nick slipped it out of the tattered leather scabbard. The blade was thin and elegant, so smooth as to shimmer, but on closer inspection, Nick could see the faintest runes inlaid up and down the metal. When the graceful designs caught the light, they sparkled like tiny diamonds. Its edge was so sharp that he nicked his thumb just by touching it. "Wow," Nick said.

Peter beamed. "It's a true elven blade. One from their glory days of long, long ago. It's so strong and sharp that it can cut through steel. These are very rare, Nick. Oh, and it has a name, of course—because those silly elves have to give everything a name. It's called Maldiriel. I want you to have it."

Nick looked at Peter. He didn't know what to say. Why had Peter given this to him? He hadn't given any of the other New Blood such gifts. "Mulderal?"

"No, Maldiriel," Peter corrected.

"Maldiriel," Nick repeated.

"Maldiriel?" Redbone echoed, then laughed. "That's a girl sword."

Peter frowned and gave him a cutting look.

"A girl's sword?" Nick asked.

"No," Tanngnost put in. "Not a girl's sword. But the sword itself is female."

"My sword has a gender?"

"Man, you gotta dig them elves," Redbone said. "They're a fruity bunch."

Nick looked at the sword again, at all the slender, graceful lines. It did look rather feminine. "Well, girl sword or not, I like it," he said. "Thanks."

Peter's smile returned, big and broad. "Sure thing," he replied, then slipped over to help Danny get his belt in place.

Nick held the blade up and snuck another peek into the mirror. He decided that he did indeed like what he saw, liked it very much. And for the moment, he let himself relax, to set aside the dark thoughts and fears, and just reveled in how cool he looked decked out in the odd leather

Devil suit, with its sewn-in boots and high, belted waistband, his hair in a greasy tangle, war paint running down his face, and a *flipping* elven sword named Maldiriel. *Too cool.*

"Let's go," Peter called, and the Devils began to file out the door.

Nick snuck a last peek, still not believing what he was seeing. He touched his blue rabbit's foot to his lips, then ran along after them.

PART III

The Flesh-eaters

Chapter Sixteen

Flame

They trekked silently down the trail, all lost in their own thoughts, the ageless silence of warriors making peace with their fears as they marched into battle.

Nick glanced over at Redbone. Redbone winked at him, his perpetual grin growing into an impish smile. Nick looked behind him at the handful of Devils pulling up the rear, every face greeting him with kinship and comradery. Nick had never experienced anything like it, and as much as he hated to admit it, he was beginning to enjoy being a Devil. He even wondered if this was why so many people loved team sports, this sense of coming together under one banner against a common foe.

The forest changed as they continued their downward track through the gray and dying trees. The land turned ashen and soggy underfoot.

The fog thickened, clinging to the ground. The trees seemed to shrink, to wither, bending beneath their own weight, their jagged limbs clawing the sky like drowning men.

After about an hour's march, a tangy burning smell assailed Nick's nostrils. *Smoke, fires,* he thought. *The Flesh-eaters can't be too far away.* And suddenly it was all too real. It's one thing to hit a straw dummy and pretend you're fighting monsters, quite another to know that monsters—ones even Redbone and Sekeu were wary of—were not only real but nearby.

Peter gestured the Devils to him, and they gathered around. He put a finger to his lips and whispered: "We must be silent. Follow my hand signals. Stay close."

Nick's heart sped up and he had to force himself to slow his breathing. *How close?* he wondered. His eyes darted everywhere, trying to peer through the ground fog; every rotten bush and stump suddenly looked liked a monster. Nick wrapped his hand tightly around Maldiriel's hilt, wondering yet again what it would be like to actually face a man with a sword, hoping to God he wouldn't have to find out.

Peter raised a hand and they halted. He slipped up ahead, surveying the terrain before waving the Devils to follow. Silently, they pushed through a mesh of undergrowth until they could see down a steep slope into a valley. Peter signaled to stay low.

Between the rolling waves of low-lying clouds, Nick scanned the burned and ravaged land. His blood went cold, there below them—*Flesh-eaters.* From where he lay, they were little more than ant-sized dots milling about near the burning trees. Nick's mouth suddenly felt dry as he watched them moving in and out of the black smoke.

He glanced at Peter. Peter's face was grim as he took in every movement. *Strange to see such severity on Peter's face,* Nick thought. No boyish mischief here; what Nick saw looked wild and scary—*deadly.*

PETER TOOK IN a deep breath. *So many.* He hadn't counted on so many—at least sixty or seventy Flesh-eaters that he could see. There'd be more, and somewhere among them—the Captain. A direct assault would be a gallant way to die, but Peter wasn't looking for a way to die. He wanted to drive them out of Whisperwood and save Avalon. He fought to keep his despair hidden. If he lost confidence in front of the Devils, all would be lost. He now understood why Tanngnost had tried so hard to bring the clans together in one coordinated attack. And, as much as he hated to even think it, if Ulfger would bear Caliburn, they could drive the Captain and his Flesh-eaters into the Mist this very day.

Peter realized he was grinding his teeth, and took in a deep breath, letting it out slowly. Now wasn't the time for maybes and what-ifs; he must stay focused. One way or another, they had to stop these demons.

There, the barrels. He watched the figures march back and forth between a pair of barrels and the trees. He slipped up closer, squinted. *So, it must be oil after all.* He nodded to himself. Then maybe there *is* another way.

Peter signaled them back. They gathered in a small ravine. Peter squatted on his haunches and they followed his example.

"We're after the oil," Peter said in a hushed tone. "Whisperwood isn't a typical forest even by Avalon standards. Most of the trees are living beings, each with its own spirit. They see and hear and even whisper to one another." *And long ago, before the Flesh-eaters came, they used to sing to each other, and there was no song more beautiful.* "Beneath their thick bark is flesh and blood. Those trees won't burn by torch alone. The Flesh-eaters are brushing oil on them to set them ablaze, burning them *alive.*

"They can't have much oil left, not after all these years. They must be desperate, to be using the last of their reserves. If we knock over those barrels and dump their oil, it'll put an end to the burning of Whisperwood.

"We don't have enough Devils to push through that many Flesh-eaters, so this is what we're going to do. We're going to draw them away from the oil with an attack by a main force and send in a small squad to knock over the barrels.

"The Captain knows our tricks. He'll not be easily fooled. We have to make this a real assault, or he won't give chase. He knows we've the advantage in the forest, and will be reluctant to follow us into the woods. So we'll have to take the fight to the edge of the fields. Try to draw the Flesh-eaters in. Hit and run, hit and run, avoid a full engagement at all cost. We won't be able to do much damage and neither will they, and that's what I want. Remember, all that matters is that we distract them long enough for the squad to dart in, get past whatever guard is left, and knock over those barrels.

"Sekeu, you're in charge of the squad. Redbone, Abraham, Leroy, and Nick, go with Sekeu."

Peter caught the anxious looks on Leroy's and Nick's faces. He looked them square in the eye and smiled confidently. *They have to know you believe in them, or they won't believe in themselves.* But a darker voice knew this would be dangerous, that he was sending two of them after the barrels in the hopes that at least one would make it. He held little hope either would return. "You're not to engage unless you have to. Your role is to focus on the barrels. Sekeu, Abraham, and Redbone will take care of any guards. Nick, Leroy, I'm giving you two the most important task of this whole operation. I wouldn't pick you unless I knew you could do this. Are you with me?"

Nick and Leroy still looked unsure, but they both nodded.

"Good. Sekeu, take your group and circle around to the east side of the clearing. Wait under cover until you hear us attack. We'll come in from the west side. You know the drill: get in and out as fast as you can.

"Danny, Cricket, you're coming with me." Cricket also looked nervous, but Danny looked absolutely petrified. Peter caught his hands trembling and thought the boy might start crying at any moment. *He's not ready.* Peter wondered if he should leave the boy behind. *No, now is not the time to play it safe.*

"Danny, Cricket, you're going to do fine. Your role is simply to make our numbers look more impressive. Hang back, make a lot of noise, and stay well clear of the combat. Think you can do that?"

They both agreed, but Danny still looked petrified.

"Remember, our goal is to draw them away from the barrels. As soon as the barrels are knocked over, we all run into the forest. If anyone from either party gets separated, we meet back here. You can see this outcropping of red boulders from just about anywhere in the valley."

Peter stood up and let a wicked smile slide across his face. "Time to play."

The Devils grinned back. "Time to play."

PETER

SEKEU

ULFGER

THE
CAPTAIN

✦

PETER WATCHED SEKEU and her crew slip away through the brambles and disappear into the ground fog, then led his own group down the west slope toward the burning fields. The going was slow and treacherous as they wove their way silently around the wet rocks, mud, clingy briars, and roots.

Near the bottom of the valley, just as the land began to level out, Peter caught the distant shouts of Flesh-eaters at their labors. While trying to decide the best path forward, he heard it: a click, somewhere to their flank. Peter signaled and the Devils dropped to a crouch.

Another pop, coming from somewhere toward their front. He heard it again, then again. He scanned the drifting grayness in front of him, searching for movement, but saw nothing. He was sure someone was heading their way, a scout or a sentry, maybe even a small troop. *No,* thought Peter. *Not now.* If they were discovered before Sekeu could get into position, all would be lost. Their only chance would be to try to make short work of any enemies before they blew their cover. Peter reached for one of his swords, then stopped, suddenly feeling cold steel against the back of his neck.

"What have we here?" came a sharp whisper.

Peter slowly turned, expecting to look into the eyes of his executioner. Standing behind him at spear's length was the old elf, Drael. Drael lifted his spear and smiled. "You weren't going to go play without me, were you?"

Peter's face lit up with disbelief and pleasure. "Drael, you came! By the gods, you came!" Peter couldn't grin any wider. He leaped to his feet and embraced the old elf. "It's good to see you again!"

Drael clucked his tongue and five more elves materialized out of the smoky woods, each armed with three throwing spears. They'd traded their traditional green tunics for gray and had their long hair tied back, out of their slanted icy eyes.

"I heard word you entered the Lady's Wood seeking allies. I bring five of the Guard's finest." He extended his hand toward the elves. "I just wish

I could have convinced more to join with us. The elves find it hard to break an oath, even in the face of madness. I am afraid the rest of the Guard will follow Ulfger to their doom. My allegiance lies with the Lady, not a crazed Lord. I'd rather die here today, among warriors, than cower within the Lady's Wood. What do you say, do we fight this day?"

Peter clasped the old elf's shoulder. "You are a true friend."

"And you, my friend, are a crazy devil."

"Then we go?"

"Yes, Peter. We follow your lead."

Peter moved out and the Devils and elves fell in line. Peter had to blink back tears. Not just from seeing the face of an old friend, but because they'd come to fight with *him*, to follow him against such hopeless odds; this in itself was a victory. They weren't enough, he knew, but he felt better knowing he had six elven swords at his side. He bit his lip. *We must win this day.*

THE CRY CUT through the fog, a sound of pain, agony, and helplessness. A sound so human that Nick found it impossible to believe it could be a tree. Tree or not, Nick wanted to run as far from the cry as he could get. But he didn't run; instead, he gritted his teeth and forced himself onward against every instinct, following Sekeu as they slithered on their bellies through the mud and brambles toward the clearing.

Nick stopped to wipe a clot of mud from his mouth. He glanced back, and though Redbone was only a few paces behind, Nick could barely make him out. Sekeu had them cover themselves from head to toe in a greasy muck of mud, leaves, and bark. Now they blended into the land, all but invisible among the ash and smoke. They'd circumvented the clearing and were now creeping forward from the east side. As they neared, Nick could hear rough shouts and make out movement through the brambles.

Sekeu signaled them up and Nick slid forward with slow, steady movements, as she had instructed, avoiding any quick moves that might draw attention. Abraham and Leroy crawled into position on one side of Sekeu, and Nick on the other. A moment later, Redbone, his absurd grin in place, slipped in next to Nick.

The guards raised a cry and came for them. Peter guessed there were at least sixty of them, leaving behind only three men that he could see to guard the barrels. *Good,* Peter thought, and he allowed himself to believe the day might end well after all. "Here they come," Peter shouted. "Hold steady."

A yell came from a tall man with a thin mustache and goatee, wearing a leather doublet and a wide-brimmed hat with a tattered feather. Peter's blood went cold. It was him, the Captain. The Captain ran up to the ragged formation, meeting them midfield. He raised his sword and ordered them to halt. The guards stopped.

What's he doing? Peter kept a close watch, knowing the Captain was a hard man to stay ahead of. How many times had this man turned the tables on him? More than he cared to remember.

The Captain formed the men up into ranks, shouting and pointing this way and that with his sword. Peter's heart sank as the Captain sent one line of about twenty guards back toward the barrels. The Captain shouted again and the remaining ranks resumed their advance, charging Peter's group at a steady run.

Peter glanced at the barrels; he could no longer see the boys, but knew they must be behind the slope and probably unaware of the shift in defense. *Fast,* he thought, *they have to be fast or all is lost.*

✦

SEKEU TOOK THE lead, Redbone next, followed by Leroy, then Nick, with Abraham covering their rear. Nick had seen the guards gather and go after Peter. *It's gonna work. It's gonna work. It's gonna work,* Nick told himself, as though he could will it so. He kept his eyes fixed on the treacherous tangle of roots, mud, and branches as he wove his way up the slope. He leaped atop a stump and dared a look forward. There, just ahead, *the barrels!* He heard a shout and spotted three guards heading right for them.

Sekeu bounded off a log and into the first guard, knocking the man's pike aside and cutting all the way through his arm at the elbow. Both the guard's forearm and the pike flew into the brambles. The guard screamed and spun away, but didn't quit; he drew his sword with his remaining arm, but before he could swing, Redbone came up behind him and cut one of his legs out from beneath him. The man tumbled. Redbone and Sekeu kept going without so much as a backward glance. Nick gritted his teeth and jumped over the squirming guard, horrified that the man was still trying to get to his feet.

Sekeu and Redbone charged the next two guards, pushing them back before a whirlwind of strikes and blows, like offensive linemen clearing a path for the running back. Nick and Leroy dashed through the melee, heading toward the barrels.

There was now only the peg-legged hunchback left between them and the barrels. Leroy made the rise first and stopped cold. Nick ran into him, started to curse, then saw the scene: a large troop of guards were chasing Peter's band into the trees, but that wasn't what had stopped Leroy in his tracks—below them, not fifty yards away, at least twenty guards were heading directly for them: hard-looking men moving fast.

A minute, Nick thought, they had maybe one minute before those guards would be upon them. Nick yanked out his sword and yelled, "Go!" He gave Leroy a shove and the two of them ran as hard as they could for the barrels.

The hunchback held a wide, curved sword in one hand and the oily ladle in the other. He showed them a few crusty black teeth and shouted, "Com'eer you little fucks, let Henry cut out your eyes and shove 'em up your asses."

Nick feinted a hard swing to the man's head, intent on using the trick that'd worked so well on Leroy the night before. But the hunchback caught Nick's sword at the hilt, knocking the weapon out of Nick's hand. Nick would've been dead for certain, but the hunchback shifted his attention to stopping Leroy. He swung the ladle, catching Leroy in the back of the head and sending the boy sprawling into the dirt.

Nick snatched up his sword and swung as hard as he could, hitting the man in the shoulder, the elven blade opening a nasty gash and knocking the hunchback off balance. His peg leg caught a root and he tumbled down the steep incline, cursing all the way to the bottom.

Nick dove for the barrel, ramming his shoulder into it. It barely budged. *"SHIT!"* he cried, and tried again. It didn't move.

A spear slammed into a stump next to Nick. The guards were almost on them, a few even now scrambling their way up the steep, muddy slope. Nick was about to give up and run when Leroy reached the barrel. They both shoved. The barrel tipped but fell back. *"AGAIN,"* Nick cried, and together they rammed their shoulders into the barrel. This time it tipped and over it went, splashing the hillside in slick oil as it careened down the incline, taking several of the guards with it.

Leroy and Nick leaped for the second barrel, only to be confronted by a thick-set guard. Red eyes blazing, he raised a huge cutlass and came at them. Nick tried to run, only to collide into Leroy, knocking both of them to the ground. The guard let loose a victorious whoop, then a sword blade tore through his throat from behind. The man dropped his weapon, clasped his neck, and crumpled to the dirt. And there, behind him, stood Abraham. *"THE BARREL!"*

Nick and Leroy jumped up and slammed into the remaining barrel. Half-empty, this one rolled right over, almost taking Nick with it. It bounded and spun down the slope, knocking down at least three guards and dousing several others in the oil. But the men were quick to their feet and at least a dozen of them were scrambling up the hill right through the patch of oil.

Abraham kicked the cauldron over, sending the hot oil right into the face of the foremost guard. Nick could hear the man's skin sizzling as the oil burned out his eyes, hear the man's choking gargle as he tried to scream through a mouthful of boiling oil.

Abraham snatched up a timber from the fire and stood over the slope. The guards saw the flame, the oil clinging to the hillside and to themselves, and at once understood their fate. Abraham tossed the flaming timber onto the oil-drenched hillside.

There was a moment when nothing happened. Everyone, Devils and guards alike, were frozen for a prolonged heartbeat, then a blue flame bloomed, dancing across the surface of the oil. Nick saw the horrified looks in the men's eyes, the look of knowing one's ultimate demise, and knowing it would be bad. The oil burst into bright red flame and Nick was running, running away from the twisting, burning men, running away from their horrible screams.

THE FLESH-EATERS WERE almost upon them.

"Positions," Peter cried, and the Devils and elves melted back into the forest, shifting from swords to spears, taking cover among the trees and ledges. Peter was well aware that the Devils would never stand a chance against the Flesh-eaters in open-field combat, not against the long pike axes, thick armor, and heavy weapons of their enemies. But if they could draw them in among the smoke, among the trees, where maneuverability was key, they could play a lethal game of hide-and-seek until every last Flesh-eater was dead.

The Captain halted about thirty yards out, just shy of effective spear range, and quickly formed his men into four rows of ten. Peter had hoped for a chaotic mob of Flesh-eaters mindlessly charging into the woods. He hadn't counted on the Captain rallying his men so quickly.

"What are you waiting for?" Peter whispered. "Come get us."

But the Captain seemed in no hurry. He scanned the terrain. Peter could see he was carefully planning his next move. Peter didn't like it. If given the chance, he knew, the man would turn the situation to his advantage.

The Captain barked a quick succession of orders, and two lines of men broke away from the main body, heading outward, toward Peter's flanks.

Peter leaped up, strolled boldly out into plain sight, and set his foot upon the breastplate of one of the dead guards from the skirmish.

The Flesh-eaters halted, all eyes on Peter. Peter brought his sword down, cleaving the dead man's head from his shoulders. He snatched the head up by the hair and raised it for all to see, then spat into its face.

Curses and shouts of outrage rose from the lines. The formation wavered as several Flesh-eaters broke ranks and came for Peter.

"HOLD," cried the Captain. "HOLD I SAY!"

All but one of the guards halted; a shirtless man with a large ax.

"STAND DOWN, BOYLE!" the Captain cried. "STAND DOWN!" But the man kept heading toward Peter.

"YOU'LL PAY FER THAT ONE!" the crazed-eyed man screamed. "YE LITTLE DEMON BASTARD! AYE, YOU'LL PAY!"

Peter swung the head and launched it toward the man. An instant later, one of the elves slid out from behind a tree and flung his spear. The Flesh-eater dodged the head, but not the spear. It caught him in the neck. He slid to his knees and sat there clawing at the shaft, gasping and gurgling until he finally fell over.

Peter showed them his teeth, then let out a long, hooting laugh like a wild monkey.

"Back in line, before I flay your hides!" the Captain yelled. "Form—"

A low thud rolled across the field, and a bright glow bloomed over by the barrels. A plume of dark smoke billowed upward and the screams of men burning alive filled the air.

The Captain's controlled composure lit up with outrage. He gave Peter one last look that promised he would make the boy pay, then raised his sword and shouted, *"FOOTMEN, TO THE CENTER! TRIPLE TIME. BEFORE ALL IS LOST!"* Forgetting about Peter and his band, the Flesh-eaters disintegrated into a ragged line and ran back toward the barrels.

A cheer went up behind Peter. The Devils broke cover, yelling and shouting, exchanging high-fives and laughing like schoolboys.

"We did it," Peter said breathlessly. He tried to see beyond the smoke and flames, searching for any sign of Sekeu and her group. There was nothing more they could do for them now other than wish them luck.

"AWAY!" Peter shouted. "To Red Rock."

✦

ANGRY SHOUTS CHASED after Nick as he wove his way through the tangle of roots and branches. He dared a glance back and saw the flaming hillside, black clouds mushrooming into the air, and men engulfed in fire clawing at their own flesh. At least six guards had made it through the flame and were rushing down the path after them not a hundred yards behind. Nick recalled Peter saying they were slow. *Slow must mean something different in Avalon,* Nick thought, because these men were covering some ground. He heard shouts and saw another group of men, at least a dozen strong, trying to cut them off.

Nick's foot snagged on a root, he stumbled and slid to one knee. Sekeu caught up to him, yanking him back to his feet. Their eyes met for the briefest moment and Nick caught her smile, and that smile was worth more than all the praise, back slaps, and cheers he could ever receive. It told him that he'd done good—no, that he had done great, and that he was one of them now. She shoved him on his way and together they ran hard for the tree line. And there, among the screams, the confusion, the terror, Nick realized he was grinning. He was starting to like being a Devil, like it very much.

Redbone made the trees first, Leroy and Abraham darting in right behind, followed by Sekeu, then Nick. There came a sense of relief upon entering the woods, but as Nick crashed into the brambles, as the vines and thorns slowed him to barely a jog, his relief turned to dread. Too soon he heard the men crashing into the woods behind them, their large bulks bulldozing through the underbrush and gaining quickly.

The ground began to soften underfoot, turned to mud, then Nick was splashing through ankle-deep marsh, trying hard to keep up with the rest of the group. The scourge-ridden trees began to knot around them, their mossy limbs blotting out the sky above. Redbone led them onto a thin trail of firmer ground and they wove their way around treacherous pools of muckish black water.

The trail led into a ledge of crumbling clay and overhanging roots. Redbone, Abraham, and Sekeu leaped high, caught hold of the roots, and scrambled up out of the ravine, disappearing over the ridge. Leroy ran up the ledge, grabbing onto a root, but the root tore loose and he fell backward into Nick. Both boys tumbled into the knee-deep bog.

Nick tried for his feet but found his legs tangled in the thorny marsh weeds. He kicked viciously only to tangle himself further. He clawed at the muddy bank, but the greasy mud slid through his fingers. Something grabbed hold of his leg; for a horrible moment Nick thought it was some swamp creature before he realized it was Leroy. Leroy—splashing and panicking—clawed his way on top of Nick, pressing him into the mud, shoving Nick's face below the black water as he crawled over him. Leroy planted his foot into Nick's shoulder and kicked away. Nick got his head up in time to see Leroy catch hold of a clump of marsh grass and pull himself out of the muck.

Nick stuck his hand out. "Leroy! Hey Leroy!"

But Leroy wasn't looking at Nick; he was staring back through the trees in the direction of the shouting men, his eyes wide with terror.

"*LEROY!*" Nick screamed as he tried to claw his way out of the gooey mud. "*HELP!*"

Leroy glanced at Nick and for a second the fear left Leroy's face, his eyes got mean, and a nasty smirk curved his lips. He rolled to his feet and scrambled up the ravine. Sekeu was at the top of the ledge, waiting for them, and Leroy almost knocked her over as he barreled past. Sekeu stared down at Nick.

Nick could hear the shouts of the men closing in. *"HEY! HELP!"* he screamed, waving to Sekeu, then saw it in her face: she wasn't going to help him.

Sekeu started to leave. She stopped and Nick caught her expression change: something close to anger, but not at him, at herself maybe. She moved then, bounding back down the ravine in a single leap, snatched her sword free, and leaped into the muck, tugging Nick as she hacked away the tangle of swamp weeds. She said something to him; Nick thought it was "You better best it, Nick." But he couldn't make any sense of it in the confusion. Then he was free, the two of them scrambling to escape the muddy pool.

Nick made high ground first, turned to help Sekeu, and saw the spear come flying through the air right at them. Before Nick could so much as shout, the spear hit Sekeu, stabbing deep into her upper thigh, knocking her to the ground. Sekeu clutched her leg and cried out. Nick could see the point jabbing all the way through her thigh, could see her muscle tissue like a slab of raw beef. The blood filled the wound and began to gush down her leg.

Six men came racing through the trees waving their cutlasses and axes, their faces twisted into snarls.

Sekeu wrenched the spear from her leg with a scream of pain and rage and threw it hard and true. It sailed across the marsh and caught the lead man dead in the chest, knocking him into the bog.

Nick grabbed Sekeu and pulled her to one knee. Sekeu tried to stand but fell, and they both tumbled to the ground.

"GET OUT OF HERE!" Sekeu cried, and shoved Nick away.

Nick stumbled back and realized with horror that he had to leave her, after she'd come back for him, he now had to leave her—*had to. RUN!* his mind screamed. *RUN!* Yet he didn't—*couldn't.*

Three of the Flesh-eaters came bearing down upon them. Nick grasped clumsily for his sword, jerking it from its scabbard and almost dropping it. He pointed the blade at the Flesh-eaters. Suddenly, it felt like a lead weight in his trembling hand, all his training forgotten in his terror.

The forward man read this and a murderous grin lit his red eyes. He reared his ax back and came for Nick.

"Oh, God!" Nick cried. "Oh, Jesus!"

Abraham shot past Nick, coming in below the man's swing, thrusting his sword up into the man's rib cage. The man's eyes went wide, the ax flew from his hands, the blunt edge of the blade slammed into Nick's chest, jabbing into his ribs and knocking him down. Abraham made to spin away, but the man caught Abraham's arm and the two of them landed in the bog with a loud splash.

A war cry filled the air. Redbone flew past Nick and drove into the next two Flesh-eaters feet-first, knocking the first into the second. Redbone was up in a bound, hacking the first across the face as the man tried to get up. The second was quicker, and a sweeping slash of his cutlass all but

knocked Redbone's blade from his grip. Redbone circled, driving the man back, and that's when Sekeu—still on her knees—slashed his hamstrings. The man fell over, digging at the slimy mud as he slid into the bog.

Redbone charged forward, blocking the advance of the remaining two Flesh-eaters.

Nick clutched his chest; his hand came away wet with his own blood. *I'm going to die,* he thought, then heard a retching gasp, saw Abraham struggling with the Flesh-eater in the bog. The huge man clutched the boy about the neck. Abraham clawed at the man's thick, leathery hands as he fought to keep his head above water. Nick met Abraham's terrified eyes as he sank beneath the dark water, and Nick forgot about dying. He had to stop this man. No matter what, he *had* to stop him.

Nick leaped at the huge Flesh-eater, bringing his sword down with all his strength. The blade sank deep into the top of the man's shoulder, lodging into his collarbone. The man groaned but, to Nick's horror, didn't let go of Abraham. Nick tried to tug the sword loose, but it was wedged into the man's leathery flesh, black blood oozing out around the blade. Nick could still see Abraham's eyes, the bubbles escaping his mouth.

NO! Nick thought and felt a sudden burning flush of heat in his stomach. Venom shot up his throat like stinging vomit, flaring in his head—*thundering.* A sound he didn't recognize escaped his throat, raw and animalistic.

Nick saw nothing but the man, every ounce of him focused on the back of his skull, at the shiny, lumpy black scalp. *Smash it! Crush it! Turn it into pulp!* Nick yanked violently at the sword, jerked it back and forth until it ripped free. Nick reared back and swung, swung with all the rage and venom burning within him. Maldiriel slammed into the man's head just above the ear, peeling most of his scalp from the bone. Nick struck again, and again. He felt the skull crack beneath his blade, felt the flesh yield, felt the hot blood and gore splatter across his face. It felt good and Nick's smile grew with every bite of his sword. The man slumped over and Nick's blade caught nothing but air, sending him careening face-first into the bog. He sucked in a mouthful of muck, yanked his head up, and coughed violently. There in the bog, right in front of him, was Abraham. The boy stared up at him from beneath the dark water with dead, unblinking eyes.

The world came back into focus then, the burning subsiding a degree. Nick grabbed Abraham and dragged his head and shoulders up onto the muddy bank. *"ABRAHAM!"* Nick shouted and shook the boy. But Abraham only stared back at him with those dead eyes. "Oh, God!" Nick cried. "Oh no. Oh no. No. *No!*"

A cutting laugh caused Nick to look up. Ten more Flesh-eaters came out of the trees, spreading out, picking their way through the bog, and blocking off any chance of escape.

Nick found Sekeu's eyes on Abraham, her lips tight and grim.

The two Flesh-eaters before Redbone slid back into the ranks, leaving the wild boy panting and looking unsure what to do. He glanced back at Sekeu down on one knee, swaying unsteadily, the pool of blood growing beneath her. His eyes found Abraham and his ferocious grin fell away, all that was left was pain. Redbone's mouth tightened into a hard line. He returned his attention to the Flesh-eaters, slapping the flat of his bloody sword against his palm and growling.

The Flesh-eaters laughed until a howl echoed through the bog. This howl didn't sound human. More howls followed, coming from all around them—from *above* them. Nick noticed the tree limbs shaking as shadowy shapes leaped along the branches.

The Flesh-eaters exchanged quick, fretful looks. They seemed uncertain which direction to turn, whether to fight or flee. They were spread out over the bog, vulnerable, and Nick could tell by their faces they knew it.

The swamp erupted in eerie cries and moans. The Flesh-eaters spun about, faces tight with terror. Four barghest dropped from above, landing on one Flesh-eater and knocking him to the ground, tearing into him with their jagged claws and teeth. Two men started forward to help, only to have a dozen more barghest drop onto them. What followed was a frenzy of claws and teeth, flailing arms and screams as the men's stomachs and throats were torn open.

The remaining men turned and ran, stumbling and falling as they tried to navigate the treacherous bog. A long shriek cut across the marsh. The men stopped. There, blocking their retreat, stood the witch's daughters, looking almost like angels with their white swirling gossamer gowns, pale skin, and long, flowing hair. Before Nick's eyes, the girls shifted, their hands sprouting hooked claws and their faces stretching into snouts. They smiled at the men, exposing long, jagged teeth, then came for them, three white streaks bounding across the bog as though their feet never touched the ground. All three hit the first man, knocking him off his feet and tearing out his throat.

The last men panicked, running recklessly away from the girls, thrashing through the muck and quickly becoming entangled in the marsh weeds. They made for easy pickings as the barghest swarmed over them.

Still on his knees, holding Abraham, Nick watched the barghest descend into a killing frenzy. The sky darkened, the air felt charged. Nick turned and found himself looking up into the single emerald eye of the witch.

"You look lost, child," she said, her smile revealing long, green teeth.

aven

Tanngnost was waiting for Peter at Red Rock. The old troll pushed himself up to his feet and strode quickly forward, his face anxious. "Well?" he asked. "Well, tell me. Quickly, boy. Tell me. How did it go?"

Peter brushed past him, searching the small plateau. "They're not here?"

"Who?" Tanngnost asked.

"They should've been here by now. They should've beaten us back."

"Peter, tell me what happened?"

Peter stopped. He clutched the troll by the arm, his golden eyes full of fire. "We won the day, Tanngnost! Such glory. If only you could've seen it. We cut them down. Dumped their oil and burned them alive!" A devilish grin lit Peter's face. "Their screams . . . such a *sweet* sound. This day goes to the Lady." Peter's smile fell away. "But there are still Devils unaccounted for." He turned away from Tanngnost. "Spread out," he shouted. "Keep your eyes and ears sharp."

Devils and elves spread about the rocks while Peter paced restlessly from one ledge to the next, scanning the tree lines for any sign of Sekeu and her small band. *What's taking them so long?* he wondered and watched the black smoke billowing upward into the gray clouds. *Such a victory,* he thought, still not believing they'd driven the Flesh-eaters back. Peter looked at his old friend Drael. *And the elves, they'd come. Had fought under my lead. We'll not stop. We'll strike again this very night. Raid their fort. Keep at them until every one of them is dead.*

"We got trouble!" Huck called, pulling his sword out.

Peter dashed over to where Huck leaned out over a steep ledge, the Devils and elves quickly joining them. There, coming around the bend, a host of barghest marched out of the trees, heading right toward them. *Barghest, here?* Peter wondered. *That makes no sense.* Then he saw the three girls. "Witches," Peter hissed and drew his own sword. "If they want trouble, then trouble they will get!"

"Wait," Tanngnost said. "There, Redbone, and—"

Peter looked again. Between the trees he saw Nick, then Leroy and Redbone. They were carrying Sekeu and there was no missing the blood-soaked cloth wrapped around her leg, nor the way her head lolled listlessly from side to side. *No,* he thought. *Not Sekeu. Not after all we've been through.* Peter put away his sword, leaped down the rocks, and raced toward them. He ran right past the barghest without so much as a glance. He reached Sekeu and stopped.

Leroy and Redbone laid her limp form gently to the ground.

She's so pale. Peter glanced at Redbone. "How bad?"

Redbone looked at pains to answer, but only shook his head.

"She's dying," one of the sisters said.

"Yes, we can smell her death. Won't be long now," the second added.

"Poor little dear," the third put in dryly while twirling a strand of her long white hair about her finger.

Peter dropped down to Sekeu, clasping her hand in his. He looked at the wound. *So much blood.* He touched her cheek with his fingers and her eyes fluttered open.

"Sekeu," Peter said. "Hey, hang on."

"Abraham," she said in a weak whisper.

Peter realized Abraham wasn't with them.

"He fought bravely . . . saved me," she said. "Nick too . . . he stood with me."

Peter could see it took great effort for Sekeu to talk. "Shhh," he said and touched her lips.

Sekeu closed her eyes. Hot tears blurred Peter's vision.

Tanngnost came up and knelt next to Peter. He looked Sekeu over.

"Help her," Peter pleaded. "Do something. You have ways. Your potions. Your medicines. *Do something.*"

The old troll shook his head. "She's lost too much blood, Peter. There's nothing to be done."

Everyone fell quiet.

"Yes there is," Peter said, his voice resolute. "There's something to be done. Most certainly." He took Sekeu in his arms and stood. "The Lady. The Lady can save her."

"WE'VE BEEN SEEN," Drael said, pointing to the green faeries zipping away into the Lady's Wood.

"Peter," Tanngnost said as they crossed Cusith Creek and entered the forest. "This is folly. You know it is."

"Folly," echoed one of the girls.

"Death and dismemberment for all," added the next.

"A jolly good time," said the third.

Peter ignored them, hugging Sekeu tightly to his chest and marching steadily onward.

Tanngnost looked behind at the line of Devils, elves, witches, and barghest. *Quite the parade,* he thought. Not since the Horned One had such a host marched together. He couldn't help but admire Peter's ability to bring these longtime bitter enemies together. But nothing good could come out of entering the Lady's Wood with such a host.

Tanngnost pushed up to Peter, spoke low, so as not to be overheard. "Peter, Ulfger will try and kill you this time. You know this. Please, Peter, for the sake of Avalon, reconsider." But one look at Peter's hard, stubborn face told Tanngnost he was wasting his breath. *When Peter sets his mind to a thing,* Tanngnost thought, *far be it from reason to stop him.* "Even if you could see the Lady," Tanngnost went on, "she's too weak to help. It has been too many years since—"

Peter halted. They all did. Ulfger stood blocking the path, flanked by fifteen heavily armed elves. Ulfger wore his full battle gear: fine leather mail hung in jagged rows beneath a chest plate of dark steel, armored gloves ran up his forearms, thigh-length boots, and a cape of bear fur draped across one shoulder.

Ulfger hefted a battle ax and glared at Drael and the rogue elves. "Your treachery has cost you your place. You're to leave at once and never step foot in these woods again." Then Ulfger set his dark, brooding eyes on Peter. "Child thief, I've no such mercy for you. My patience for your games is at an end. I gave you clear warning. Your sentence is death."

Peter gently lowered Sekeu to the ground, stood, and took a step forward. He didn't look at Ulfger; instead he addressed the elf guards flanking the giant man.

"Today," Peter said, speaking loudly, "this group of kids you snub your noses at came together with your kin, and with the witch's brood. Together they stood against the Flesh-eaters. Together they cut them down, burned them alive, reminded them that Avalon still has *teeth*! Their bravery, their blood, their lives have won Avalon this day and maybe many more." Peter set his unrelenting glare on each elf. "Where were you?"

Tanngnost was surprised at the power of Peter's words on the stolid elves. Most were unable to meet Peter's eyes. Some of them flinched visibly beneath his gaze. He caught several sidelong looks between them.

"This girl," Peter gestured to Sekeu. "She bled for the Lady today. And a brave boy by the name of Abraham died defending Avalon. Where were you?"

"No one is listening to your prattle," Ulfger said with a dark laugh.

"All I ask," Peter said, continuing to address the elves, "is passage to the Lady, to bring this wounded warrior, this defender of Avalon, before her. Who among you would deny her this honor?"

"*NEVER!*" Ulfger shouted. "None may see the Lady. Much less such vile rabble."

Peter turned his eyes on Ulfger. Tanngnost could see Peter struggling to contain his rage. "The Lady is not yours to command," Peter said through clenched teeth. "The Lady belongs to all of Avalon. Or have you forgotten the words of your own father?"

Ulfger's eyes flared dangerously, his knuckles went white around the shaft of his ax.

"This *rabble*," Peter said, sweeping his arm toward his companions, "have earned the right to see the Lady with their blood. How Ulfger . . . how have *you* earned the right?"

"Kill him," Ulfger ordered.

Several of the elves dropped their hands to the hilts of their swords, but they didn't draw, seemingly unsure what to do.

"Lord Ulfger!" Tanngnost shouted. "Open your eyes! Can you not see that all the clans have come together? It is your time. Don the Horned Helm. Lead Avalon to victory!" Tanngnost lowered his voice. "Lord Ulfger, I beg you to think before you act. The fate of Avalon rests with you."

"Have you grown senile in your old age?" Ulfger sneered. "I've already given you my answer. The Lady's Guard will never fight alongside this vileness. And are you such a fool that you would trust the secrets of the Haven to this rabble? Why not just lead the Flesh-eaters to the Lady yourself?"

"At least they've earned that trust," Peter said.

Ulfger turned to his guard. "I will not say it again. *Kill* him!"

The elves didn't move.

"What are you waiting for?" Ulfger cried. He stared at them, and still they stood. Then, one by one, each stepped *away* from Ulfger.

Ulfger's face first showed disbelief, then twisted into outrage. "What *treachery* is this?" he snarled, his face turning red as his brow clenched together. "Have you forgotten your oaths? Has all of Avalon gone mad?" He shoved the nearest guard forward, nearly knocking the elf to the ground. "*NOW*," he shouted. "*KILL HIM! KILL HIM!*"

The guards stood their ground.

"*TRAITORS!*" Ulfger screamed. "*ALL OF YOU . . . TRAITORS! IT IS LEFT TO ME TO DEFEND THE LADY!*" He hefted his ax and came at

Peter with a wild overhand swing, leaving Peter no chance to pull out his sword. Instead Peter did the one thing Ulfger least expected. He leaped forward at the giant, dashing inside the blow intended to cleave him in two. Peter kicked the back of Ulfger's knee as the man barreled past, sending him tumbling into the dirt. Ulfger landed hard, the ax flying from his hand.

Ulfger let out a shrill cry of rage, scrambled for his ax, and was met by the spear tips of all fifteen elven guards, their cold eyes backing up the promise of their razor-sharp spears.

"Enough, Ulfger," Drael shouted. "Enough."

Ulfger stared at Drael, his mouth open, then his eyes became distant as though staring through the elf, as though seeing someone behind him, above him, some ghostly spectra only he could see. His whole body began to tremble, his dark eyes wide and crazed. "Why . . . why must you always hound me?" Ulfger cried, his voice cracking. "I gave you my oath. My oath!" He clutched at the earth, leaving deep claw marks in the soft dirt. "I will protect her, of course. How many times must I swear it?"

The elves exchanged nervous looks.

"Come." Tanngnost waved the troop onward. They made a wide berth around the giant man as he continued to paw the dirt, following Drael as the old elf led them up the path toward Lady Modron's Garden.

"I believe his butter has curdled," said one of the witch's daughters.

"Gone loopy lou lou," added another.

"Worms in the woodwork, indeed," said the third.

"Time to go see Auntie," said the first.

"I hope she has cake," put in the second.

"I hope she has bunnies," said the third. "I like bunnies."

"Bunnies, yum," said the first. "I'll have two."

THE ELVES LED them along a rocky, fast-running creek. Peter carried Sekeu, pressing forward at a steady jog. The Devils followed right behind Peter, and a bit further back came the barghest, running along sideways on their knuckles. They looked playful and curious as they hooted and raced along the trail. It was hard for Nick to believe they were the same vicious beasts that had almost killed him. He caught occasional glimpses of the three girls as they skipped, almost floated, through the woods, their white gowns still streaked with black blood. He couldn't suppress the shudder as their light giggles echoed about the forest.

Cricket and Danny fell in with Nick. Danny was sweating and breathing so hard Nick wasn't sure he'd make it much farther. His panda cat makeup had run all down his face, adding to the harrowed look of his eyes. "I've had it," Danny huffed. "I'm done. Done with all this stupid bullcrap."

"Hang in there, Danny-O," Cricket said, her voice pumped with excitement, like this was all some sort of big adventure. She patted him on the back. "You're doing good."

Danny stared at her as though she'd lost her mind then turned to Nick. "Nick," he gasped. "When you're ready to go home . . . be sure to take me with you. I mean it." Nick could tell that Danny did indeed mean it; the boy sounded like he might start crying at any moment.

"I don't want to die here," Danny muttered. "I just want to go home."

"So, what happened out there?" Cricket asked Nick.

Nick didn't answer; the fever in his stomach still burned, the murderous urges still clawed at him, just like when he woke from the nightmares. Only this time the burning didn't fade—if anything, it was growing worse. His head began to throb.

"Hey, Nick," Cricket said cautiously. "You okay?"

Nick wished she'd leave him alone. He needed some time to himself, time to try and sort things out and get his mind straight.

Cricket started to say something else, then quickened her pace, fell in line with Leroy, and began quizzing him. Leroy was more than happy to give his account, going on and on about how he'd knocked over the barrels, about burning the Flesh-eaters alive.

What about how you hid in the swamp while Abraham was murdered? Nick felt the heat in his stomach flare. Anger was working its way back into his chest; he could feel it pulsing in his neck. *It had felt so good,* Nick thought, *smashing in the Flesh-eater's skull. The spray of brains. So good.* He looked at the back of Leroy's head. *How would it feel to smash Leroy's brains in?*

Leroy was still going on about knocking over the barrels.

He ran, Nick thought. *Ran away and left me there to die. He ran. He ran.*

The thought burned in his mind until it just forced its way out. "He ran," Nick growled.

"What?" Cricket asked.

"He *ran*."

Leroy's eyes blazed.

"Ran away and hid."

Leroy shoved Nick. "You better shut the fuck up!"

"You left us."

"I said shut the fuck up." Leroy made to shove Nick again when someone grabbed him by the arm and jerked him around. Leroy stumbled and almost fell.

"Tell them, Leroy," Redbone said. "Tell them where you were when Abraham was dying."

Leroy glanced about like a caged dog, unable to meet anyone's eyes.

"One. One extra sword," Redbone said. "Could have saved Abraham."

Leroy shook his head, opened his mouth, but said nothing. He backed away from Redbone, away from all the hard stares. He looked unsure what to do with himself, and drifted back among the barghest.

A sudden burning sensation stung the wound in Nick's side. He clutched the cut, felt the hot wetness. He pulled his hand away and stifled a cry. The blood, *his* blood, was dark, almost *black. What's happening?* he wondered. Another voice, a not very nice one, said, *You know what's happening.* His head was drumming now, pounding hard. He stumbled and would have fallen but someone grabbed him, put an arm around him.

"Steady there, Nick."

Nick saw Redbone's wild grin through wet, blurry eyes.

Redbone's grin faltered. "Hey, man. You okay?"

"Yeah," Nick said. "I'm . . . fine."

Redbone glanced at Nick's blood-soaked leathers. "Fuck, man. You took one hell of a lick."

"I'm fine," Nick said, harsher than he'd intended. He pulled away from the wild boy and quickly covered the wound with his hand.

"Okay, man. That's cool. Just be sure to let me know if you need a hand." Redbone started to say something more, hesitated, seemed to be searching for the right words, finally he blurted out, "Look, man, just gotta say. You earned your blades today. There were six of them bad dudes coming down on your ass, but you stood with her. Stood when you could've run. That takes more than guts. Let me tell you, that's something deeper." He clasped Nick on the shoulder. "Just want you to know, brother. You need me, I'm there." He gave Nick another of his crazed grins before heading up to check on Peter and Sekeu.

For a moment Nick forgot the pain, the burning in his stomach. There was no denying what he'd seen in the wild boy's eyes. Redbone was his friend, the kind of friend that would stand by him to the end. Nick found himself blinking away tears.

The river narrowed, became clear and fast, splashing and swirling against the large boulders and rocky bank. They'd left all signs of the scourge behind; most of the trees here still had their leaves. They came to a series of large flat stones strung out across the river and leaped from one to the other to cross the current. The three sisters didn't use the stones, their tiny feet plucking at the rushing water as they danced right across the waves.

The foliage on the far bank was fuller. Nick spied the occasional flower and caught sight of several faeries watching them timidly from up in the trees. Nick admired their brilliantly colored wings. *Yes,* he thought, *so very pretty. How delicious to feel their tiny bones cracking in my hands.* Nick shook his head. *No,* he thought. *Stop.* But that *other,* that deeper *him,* didn't want to stop.

THE TRAIL BROADENED into a long courtyard. Murky wading pools stretched along either side of the path. A few shriveled lily pads and water weeds poked up here and there. Standing stones covered with brown, dried moss stood in intervals down the pools, several had fallen and lay half-submerged on their sides. Ahead, a tall archway cut into a towering white stone ledge with a gentle waterfall spilling onto its crest. The ancient wooden doors were barred shut.

Peter let out a sound as though he'd been punched in the gut. "How?"

"She took the path to the Haven and never returned," the old elf said. "The garden wilts without her hand."

They entered a courtyard and Peter slowed, staring at a pond. Scattered among the algae and weeds were the shattered remnants of several golden globes. Peter stopped. He looked pained, disheartened.

Tanngnost came and stood beside him. "Sometimes it is the smaller things that hit the hardest."

They continued through a series of courtyards until they came to a large overgrown field surrounded by wild hedges and crumbling arches. Nick counted ten arches. The elf led them toward the back of the field, to a small, unassuming arch half-hidden behind a straggly hedge. The arch was in the shape of a dragon's mouth; several of the teeth had broken and lay scattered in the weeds.

They passed through and the trail narrowed, weaving its way through dense underbrush, towering trees, and giant boulders. The path ran upward along the bottom of a steep cliff until coming to an abrupt end against the sheer walls of a box canyon. The walls towered so high above as to leave the troop in deep shadow.

The canyon smelled of damp earth and rotting things. Vines as thick as a man's leg pushed up from the earth, their stems—spiked with treacherous thorns—twisted and coiled up the face of the stone like a nest of snakes. A simple apple was carved into the stone at eye level.

The old elf gave the Devils and barghest a hard, probing look. He turned to Peter and the troll. "Are you sure?" he asked.

Both of them nodded.

"The oath?" the elf asked. "The rites?"

"We've no time for oaths and silly ceremonies," Peter said impatiently. "Just open the thing."

The elf looked to the troll.

"They are Avalon now," Tanngnost said. "There are no others. We have to trust them."

Drael still looked unsure but stepped up to the stone, placed his hand atop the apple, closed his eyes, and spoke a string of strange words.

Silence hung in the air as the troop held their collective breath. Nothing happened for a long moment, then the thorny vines began to rustle, slowly slithering, coiling unto themselves like vipers preparing to strike, creeping back until a circular groove—almost as tall as the troll—was revealed in the stone.

The old elf pushed on one side of the circle, several of the elves quickly joining him. There came the slight grinding of stone as they pivoted the circle inward, revealing a short tunnel. Nick could see light coming through from the far end. The opening was large enough for one person to enter at a time, and one by one the troop filed through.

Nick hesitated; something about the entrance made him—or some part of him—uneasy. He waited until the last barghest passed, before approaching the tunnel. The vines rustled as he neared, almost as though watching him. Nick took a deep breath and ducked in; as he did, a vine struck him, hitting him hard on the forehead, just missing his eye. Another snagged his ankle, almost tripping him, while several more struck at him like biting snakes. Nick jerked his foot free and dashed through the tunnel.

Redbone was waiting for him. "You okay, man?" Redbone squinted back down the dark tunnel. "You look like something's after you."

"Uh, no . . . nothing," Nick said breathlessly. "Just . . . got spooked. That's all."

They continued to follow the elves and soon came upon a steep, rushing creek. The water was crystal-clear and smelled sweet. The forest flourished as they made their way up the steady incline. Soon there were flowers sprouting from vines and bushes, and soft moss carpeting the trail. Nick caught sight of a pair of small spotted deer and heard the peeping of tree frogs. A soft hum buzzed past his head as several dozen faeries zipped about the troop, chirping and doing loop-de-loops. A feverish shudder coursed across Nick's skin, a fresh flush of heat bloomed in his stomach. His fingernails bit into his palms as an overwhelming need to tear the little creatures to pieces all but consumed him. He felt if he could kill them, the pounding in his head, the heat in his stomach would finally cease. *No,* he thought. *Stop it. Stop it before it's too late.* He clenched his fingers into fists, pressed his hands tight against his thighs, fighting to keep them under control.

The wound began to burn again, worse than before. He clutched his side, felt the heat. He made sure no one was watching, then looked at his hand. His blood was darker now, almost black. *"Fuck!"* Nick whispered.

A barghest, much smaller than the others, loped up alongside of him.

The creature only came up to Nick's knee. It gave him a curious look and chirped.

"Get the fuck away from me," Nick hissed, and grinned.

The barghest cocked its head from side to side, then scampered away.

"Dig your beady little eyes out with my thumbs," Nick said under his breath. The heat in his stomach began to burn, to climb up his throat, the pressure behind his eyes to throb. "Tear your flesh from your bones." *Yes,* the Other in him said. *Do it! Do it now! All the pain will go away. Just do it. Do it. Do it now.* And at that moment, Nick believed that Other, truly felt that killing the barghest would make the pain go away, felt it in his very core.

The troop pushed around a bend and Nick was confronted by dozens of tall, thin waterfalls, their silvery waters cascading down a mountain face of pure white stone. Nick tilted back his head but couldn't find the top of the falls. The water appeared to be falling from the low-lying clouds themselves. The mist was cool, soothing, and smelled like spring. Nick inhaled deeply and felt a reprieve from that Other, from that deeper self. For a moment, he stood there and just lost himself in the spectacle of the beautiful falling water.

The elf led them to a smaller fall, the one farthest back. An inconspicuous path ran along a small ledge and disappeared directly into the falls. The water crashed down with such force it was obvious they could go no farther, but the old elf walked directly into the falls and vanished from view.

Peter hesitated a moment, then followed. One by one, each of the party entered until it was Nick's turn. Nick could see it wasn't a trick, there was just enough space behind the falls to slip past, but it was still unnerving to blindly walk into the misty shadows. Nick took a deep breath, stepped through, and found himself in a short tunnel, the walls shimmering with an emerald light the color of the sea.

The tunnel led into a large cavern that opened to the sky. Jagged cliffs leaned in on all sides. Thick, glowing bands of gold veined the white stone, bathing the cavern in a soft golden light. Before him, a magnificent Eden spread out from ledge to ledge, at least the width and length of a soccer field.

The Devils, barghest, even the elves, all stared in wide-eyed wonder.

"The Haven," Tanngnost said.

"I see bunnies," said one of the witch's daughters.

"My, my. Lots of bunnies," said the second.

"Yummy for your tummy," added the third.

✷

NICK'S BREATH ESCAPED him. Before him lay a circular pond, delicate ripples crisscrossing its mirrorlike surface as tiny sprites, barely larger than bees, danced along its banks. An apple tree with white bark and leaves stood upon a tiny island in the middle of the pond, the centerpiece of the whole garden. Vibrant red apples hung from its delicate limbs and its leaves shimmered.

"Avallach's Tree," Peter whispered.

"Yes," Tanngnost said, and even his voice was awed. "The very heart of Avalon."

A birdcall drew Nick's attention away from the Tree and he took in the rest of the garden. Dozens of brooks fed into the pond, their sparkling waters bubbling over smooth, crystal-clear stones. Grass and clover of deep greens and blues, as rich as though it were painted, rolled across the glade, while lush ivy and muscadine vines dripped down from the delicate trellises and along the ledges and cliffs that walled the sanctuary. Wildflowers spilled across the grounds like waves in an ocean, splashing along the edge of every stone and tree. Massive, moss-covered standing stones leaned heavily, their ancient pitted surfaces covered in runes and carvings of brooding faces. Brightly painted birds flew above, along with all manner of sprites, pixies, and tiny faeries. Wee folk of every sort peeked out from behind stones and giant toadstools. And on and on, there were so many sights, smells, and strange creatures about that Nick found it impossible to focus on any one thing for more than a second.

"My Lady," Peter called softly, his voice reverent.

Nick followed Peter's eyes to a tapestry of brilliant white vines, flowers, and leaves nestled together upon a throne of leaning stones on the far side of the pond. The overall effect was that of an elegant woman in a long gown. Nick realized that many of the leaves were actually white butter-flies, some slowly opening and closing their wings, while others fluttered to and fro, giving the illusion that the tapestry was moving.

"She's in the pond," Dash said, and all the Devils pressed forward, try-ing to see her.

"I see her," said Redbone.

"Where—*oh!*" said Cricket.

Nick searched the murky water, he didn't see her, but he did see small winged fish with the upper torsos of boys and girls darting back and forth, chasing one another just beneath the surface. Then he understood, and he saw her, saw her well. In the reflection, all the white flowers, leaves, and butterflies came together to form the Lady. And, just like any illusion, once he saw her, it was impossible to not see her.

He glanced back up and there she sat on the throne, unmoving like a marble statue, staring with heavy, unblinking eyes at the Tree. Her head nestled among the flowers, the vines and leaves spilled around her, cradling her. Her skin was so white as almost to glow, her neck long and graceful, her lips full but pale, her cheekbones high, her eyes set wide apart, almost too wide, giving her a slight animal countenance. And when Nick looked at those eyes, those dull, glassy eyes, he could see just how fragile, how very vulnerable she really was. And as the heat bloomed in his gut, as it turned to fire, as his blood turned black and pumped through his veins like venom, he thought, *It will do me such good to kill her.*

✷

"LADY MODRON." THE name escaped Peter's lips in a weak breath. *She's too thin*, he thought and couldn't push away the fear that she might be dead. He looked into her eyes, those ceaselessly staring eyes, and found no sign of life, nothing.

He walked softly up to her and laid Sekeu down upon the spongy moss at her feet. He cleared his throat. "My Lady," he said gently.

She continued to stare past him, through him—not so much as a blink.

Peter followed her gaze to the Tree, still amazed to be in its presence. He noticed that many of the leaves were wilted, that some of the limbs were bare and looked to be dying. He wondered how much longer Avalon had.

He fell to one knee, reached out, and laid his hand on the Lady's, gently, as though his touch might break her. Her hand felt cold. "My Lady," he whispered. "Lady Modron. It's me. Peter."

Her face never changed.

"Lady," he said again, then again.

Peter felt a hand on his shoulder, heard Tanngnost's deep sigh. "I'm sorry, Peter. I was afraid of this. She still lives, but is gone from us, withdrawn deep within. Keeping the Mist alive, but little more."

"I cannot remember the last time she spoke," Drael said. "Maybe to Ulfger. I don't know. For he forbade any of us to come near."

"Peter," Tanngnost said softly. "I fear she's beyond us."

Peter continued to hold the Lady's hand, to stare into her eyes—to *hope*. He felt a warmth against his chest—the eight-point star. He pulled the necklace over his head and examined it. The faintest glow pulsed from the star's center. "No, she's still with us." He reached for the Lady's hand, carefully turning it upward, and laid the star in her palm. The star brightened.

"Lady," he called. "My Lady."

The Lady's eyes closed, then slowly reopened. She looked at the star. Her lips moved; no sound came out, but Peter had no problem reading her lips. "Mabon," she'd tried to say. Her hand closed around the star. "Mabon," she repeated, her words little more than air. Her eyes became distant again, then slowly closed, and she was still.

Peter waited, but the Lady showed no more signs of life.

"My Lady. It's Peter."

Still, there came no response.

Peter stood, cleared his throat, and began to hum softly, then sing, slowly building up the song as his voice cleared. He found the old tune, the song of the Sunbird. And as he sung, as his rich voice echoed off the tall cliffs, the birds and the faeries lent him their voice and soon the tune drifted throughout the garden.

Peter watched a lone tear roll down the Lady's face. She opened her eyes. This time she saw him. "Peter," she whispered and reached out, touching his cheek. "My little Peterbird? You flew back to me."

He nodded up and down as tears blurred his vision. Her caress touched so much more than his skin. He felt it to his very core, felt a warmth swell up inside him. As though they were still in that pond, so long ago.

"Flew all the way here from Otherworld just to sing me a song," she said.

Peter nodded absently.

Her eyes found Drael, then Tanngnost. She frowned, her face confused. "You've come back too. Or have I finally passed beyond? Ulfger told me you were all dead."

"No, my Lady," Tanngnost said. "We're not dead. Nor are you."

Peter barely heard them, their voices muffled by the beating of his own heart. He put his hand to his cheek; it still tingled from her touch. It was all too much; after a thousand million wishes, he was finally back by her side. He felt his heart might burst, felt his own will had been stolen and he was now incapable of anything more than just staring at her, wishing only to bask in her presence forever.

She looked about the garden at the Devils and the barghest. Her eyes fell on Sekeu lying motionless at her feet. "Peter, who is this?"

Peter tore his eyes away from the Lady, saw the injured girl on the grass, and wondered who she was.

"My Lady," Tanngnost said. "A lot has happened since the battle at Merrow Cove. Avalon still holds. Peter has rallied the clans. Today he led—"

Sekeu, Peter thought. *Sekeu's dying.* And the world all came back into focus. "She needs your touch," Peter interrupted. "She was wounded protecting Whisperwood."

"One of your Devils? She fights for Avalon?"

"Yes," Peter said. "She fights for you. She bleeds for you."

"Help me to the pond," the Lady said, pushing to her feet.

Peter and Drael rushed up, taking the Lady's arm around each shoulder. Gently, they eased her down a set of stone steps into the pond. She drifted away from the shore and slowly sank beneath the water.

A light mist spread across the surface and the water began to clear, slowly revealing the stony bed below. The Lady resurfaced and now there was a vibrancy to her eyes, sparkling brilliant cerulean.

"Bring me the girl," she said, her voice clear and strong.

Peter picked Sekeu up. She felt lifeless in his arms, but she let out a slight moan and he dared to believe that maybe, maybe, there was still hope. He carried her down the steps and floated her into the arms of the Lady.

The Lady pulled Sekeu below, swimming away toward the Tree. The mist thickened, swirled about, blocking the view below. The golden veins along the cliffs dulled, the cavern darkened, then the mist began to glow, casting an eerie green underlight onto the faces of the elves and Devils.

They waited, the Devils shuffling nervously from foot to foot, scanning the mist.

Peter searched for movement, a splash, a ripple, any sign that Sekeu was okay. *It's taking too long,* he thought. *Maybe the Lady's too weak?* And he had a terrible thought. *Could this be too much for her? Could it kill her?* He wondered if he should dive in, try and find them before it was too late.

The Lady broke the surface and Peter was terrified by what he saw. The Lady's flesh had become gray, almost translucent, he could see every vein.

"Take her," the Lady gasped, struggling to keep Sekeu's head above the surface. Peter splashed forward and pulled Sekeu to him just as the Lady sank below the water. Peter hesitated, unsure what to do.

"It's all right, Peter," Tanngnost said. "Water's her element. The pond's the best place for her now." But the old troll looked anxious.

The mist lost its glow, the water became murky. Peter would probably have continued to stand there had Sekeu not let out a gasp. He rushed her to the bank. Redbone and Drael gave a hand and they laid her in the grass. The dressing was gone from her leg. The wound was still there, a long, deep cut, but there was no bleeding, no redness. It looked on the mend. There was color in Sekeu's face.

Sekeu spat out a mouthful of water, coughed, then her eyes fluttered open and she smiled weakly. "I saw Mother Moon and the stars. They were beautiful."

✦

NICK STOOD IN the shadow and watched the Lady. She sat slumped on her throne, letting the flowers and vines cradle her as she listened to Tanngnost go on and on. Peter stood at her side. *Fawning,* Nick thought, *like a little boy.* The color had returned to her skin, but she looked weak, worn out, except her eyes, they were alive, piercing—the eyes of a goddess. They scared Nick and he made sure to stay well clear of her gaze.

A laugh stole his attention. The Devils were exploring the garden, picking nuts and fruit. The Lady had insisted they eat their fill and gather what they could for their stocks. While the Devils stuffed their berry-smeared faces, the barghest rooted beneath logs and stones for fungus and grubs, hooting and barking at each other. A small white rabbit dashed by, followed quickly by the three sisters, giggling as they chased it into the bush. Sekeu sat on the bank. She still looked weak but was sitting up on her own now and eating away at the clump of muscadines Redbone had brought her.

The faeries zipped about, gathering armloads of flower petals and dropping them atop the barghest, chirping and giggling as the beasts growled and grumbled. Nick saw smiles, heard laughter, and it made the heat in his gut turn to fire. *Oh, how fucking charming. How fucking magical.* Nick's heart drummed, the hot black blood pulsed in his head, the pain overwhelming, like a nail being driven into his brain. It was her, the Lady. She was doing it. *Kill her,* the Other wailed in his head. And Nick no longer argued, no longer protested. Him, the Other, his deeper self, they both shared the same burning black blood, they both wanted the pain to stop.

Nick slipped the knife from his belt and edged toward the Lady, careful to stay in the shadows. But no one was watching him. *Stupid fucks,* he thought. *All too busy stuffing their faces and having a merry gay old time.* He clasped the back of the throne to steady himself, trying not to swoon as the pain grew so bad that the edges of his vision blurred. He could see her profile, the elegant curve of her neck.

He clutched the weapon, thought how good it would feel sinking into her soft flesh. *Yes,* he thought, *make the pain go away. The Mist too. Make all of this horrible nightmare disappear.* He raised the knife, preparing to drive it into her neck.

She turned, such a simple, graceful movement, and locked her eyes on him—her hard, icy eyes. They held him, looked into him, deep into his very core. Nick heard the Other inside him wail. He couldn't move, couldn't so much as blink as the tears began to roll down his face.

She grabbed his wrist, and though she was thin and frail to look upon, her grip was like a vise, her touch cold, penetrating. Nick let out a small cry and the knife fell from his hand.

Peter and the troll exchanged a quick look and Peter was there at her side. "My Lady, what?" he asked, glaring at Nick, looking ready to slit him open.

She didn't answer, just pulled Nick toward the pond, and Nick found it impossible to resist her will. Before he even had a chance to draw a breath, she dragged him beneath the dark water, pulled him down along the bottom. He knew she intended to drown him. The Other in him screamed, and this time Nick screamed too. His lungs filled with water and he had a moment of confusion, expecting pain, expecting to choke, to drown, but instead the water was sweet. It filled his lungs like a breath of spring air, dousing the heat in his stomach and the throbbing in his head.

Nick felt a pulse, but it wasn't his. It came from all around him. He made out several large twisting shapes spiraling downward, disappearing into the depths. He realized he was beneath the apple tree and that these must be its roots. He laid his hand on one, could feel the pulse, warmth sloshing as it pumped through the thick root like a great artery.

She held his hand as they drifted downward. A soft glow came toward them, enveloped them, and everything came into focus. There were stars, the moon. He saw Avalon, not as it was now, but how it used to be. He was swimming above the forest like a fish, through the valleys and glades. He saw the sparkling lights of a million faeries, nymphs dancing around tall standing stones, centaurs galloping across pastures of wildflowers, and trees of every color glistening in the silvery moonlight. He saw the magic running beneath all things, a glittering aura, a fragile element that needed protecting. He reached for the magic and it reached for him, blooming in his chest like love. He heard her voice, like a song, faint and faraway. *I am your forest, your earth, your eternity. I am your life. I am your death. I am all things forever and always. Love me. Love me. Forever love me.*

Yes, he answered. *Forever.*

315

She pulled him upward, toward the moon; it grew and grew, then, all at once, he broke the surface. He gasped, coughed, and took in a deep lungful of air.

Peter and the troll were at the steps, anxious and worried.

The Lady left Nick clinging to the bank, drifted away, disappearing beneath the dark water. *Don't go,* Nick thought and reached for her; the garden blurred, wavered. He felt dizzy, could want, wish, think of nothing but the Lady. *Forever.*

Chapter Eighteen

Caliburn

✦

Ulfger passed beneath an arch with massive elk horns set into its peak, climbed the winding steps as they curved around the sheer face of the granite ledge. His thighs and his lungs burned, yet he didn't stop until he came face to face with the Hall of Kings, high above the valley.

A domed chamber loomed before him, beckoning him, daring him to visit with the dead. He stumbled forward, catching himself in the arched doorway, the sweat pouring down his face in rivulets as he gasped to regain his breath. The stained-glass ceiling bathed the chamber in a soft emerald glow while the large oval windows provided the dead with a view of the valley below.

The bones of seven elven kings moldered within the seven stone sarcophaguses spread out in a ring before him. In their center sat a longboat. Ulfger glared at the dead kings, then slowly brought his eyes up until they were level with the boat's deck. The boat stretched nearly twenty feet lengthwise; at the bow reared a ferocious dragon figurehead, its red ruby eyes staring out the largest window, looking ready to sail away into the low-lying clouds.

The boat had been built to be put to sea and set aflame, to take the Horned One to the Otherworld, to Avallach. But Ulfger had forbidden it. He'd made the elves bring the boat and the Horned One here. He'd not allow the Horned One to leave him, not while there were still Flesh-eaters on Avalon.

"I'm still here, Father," Ulfger said, his voice shaky, appeasing. He inched forward. "They've betrayed you. Every one of them. But not *me*. *I* remembered my oath. I alone am worthy of your blessings." He leaned heavily against one of the tombs, studied the face of the elven king carved in relief on its lid. He traced a shaky hand down the noble features. "Traitor," he hissed. "All of you . . . *traitors*!" He sneered, raking his fingers across the eyes, scratching furiously at them, but his fingers had no effect on the cold marble gaze. Hefting his ax, Ulfger brought the blunt side down with a tremendous blow, smiting the face and cracking open the sarcophagus lid. He shoved the lid to the floor and stared into the hollow sockets of the dead king. "You dare to look at me that way?" Ulfger's face twisted into a knot of rage. He snatched the skull from its cradle and dashed it to the stones, grinding the bones beneath his heel until there was nothing left but dust and teeth.

He spun away, brought the ax down on the next tomb, then the next, and the next, bashing them apart, kicking and scattering the bodies until the chamber was littered in rotting tapestry, robes, armor, and crumbling bones. He tripped on the leathery carcass of some ancient lord, and went sprawling into the rubble. He lay on his back, panting, a fine layer of bone dust pasted to his sweaty skin. His eyes darted wildly about until finally coming to rest on the boat. His lips began to quiver. "I'm not a coward," he said and the tears rolled down his cheeks, cutting dark paths through the bone dust. "I'm not a coward. I did not choose to stay behind. You made me swear, Father. Have you forgotten? None cried louder for war than I!"

He rolled over and crawled across the floor, raking through the bones until he reached the boat. He got a hand on the railing and pulled himself up, clinging to the side board as he glared into the face of the Horned One.

A fierce death grimace greeted Ulfger. The Horned One lay draped in a wooly elk fur, his parched, leathery skin pulled taut across his bones. Several necklaces of tusks and bronze rings hung in a tangle about his neck. The broken blade of Caliburn lay across his chest, clasped in his huge bony hands. The Horned Helm sat low on his head, dark sockets peering out from within the slanted eye slits. The dark hollows bore into Ulfger, accusing him.

"Do you hear me? Have I not proven myself? I alone still stand . . . still defend the Tree."

The dark sockets mocked him with their silence.

Ulfger's eyes fell to the sword and a sneer pushed at his face. "I *am* worthy, Father," he whispered and slowly reached out until his hand hovered above the hilt. He glared at the tiny sharp spikes lining the grip, spikes that would bite into his hand and, if he were unworthy, would poison and burn him from the inside out. His hand began to shake. "I . . . *am* . . . worthy," he hissed between clenched teeth and tried to force his hand upon the hilt, force himself to pick up the sword. Tears streamed down his face as his whole arm began to shake, then a wretched howl escaped his lips and he yanked his hand away, clutching it to his chest.

He slid back down to the stones, cradling his hand like a baby. "Why did you leave me behind, Father?" He heard it then, laughter, coming from all around him, echoing about the chamber. They were laughing at him, his father, the kings, all of them. He clasped his hands to his ears, and still he heard it, louder, as though they were all in his head.

He let out a weak cry and half-crawled, half-stumbled toward the large open window. He hit the ledge, fell forward, just catching himself. He hung there a moment, staring down from the dizzying heights, and thought about letting go. *How sweet it would be, to be finished with all this torment.* And he might have, but something caught his eye, something that made the laughter stop and his blood burn. There, far below, parading through the courtyard as though he lorded over all, was the child thief himself, leading his band of traitors and brats.

Ulfger's knees buckled and he sat down hard on the window ledge. They'd seen the Lady. *No*, he thought, *there's more going on here.* Somehow, they'd awakened her. Because the girl was better, there was no denying that. He'd seen her before, when she was close to death, and only the Lady could've saved her. He saw the baskets and sacks of fruit. "Thieves, burn forever," he hissed. "You've tainted the Haven. Desecrated the heart of Avalon. And she, Modron, has aided you. Has betrayed Avallach himself."

Ulfger stomped back to the boat. He glared into his father's face, into those deep, dark hollows, into that fierce death grimace. Ulfger matched that grimace. "You, you favored the runt as well. Called him to stand by your side in battle, yet would deny me. Deny your only son? How is it that he is worthy when I am not? How? How, you hateful beast? Tell me! *TELL ME!*" Ulfger snarled and thrust his hand forward, grabbed the sword, tearing it from the Horned One's grip. He felt its bite, the sharp jabs as the spikes pierced his palm. The marks began to burn. "*GO ON!*" he screamed. "Burn me! I dare you! But nothing will keep me from my duty, from avenging Avallach. *NOTHING!*"

The heat continued to flow into his body, but it didn't burn. The broken blade became light in his hand as a feeling of power possessed him. He felt his chest swell as the heat pumped through his heart, his veins and muscles. "See, Father. I am worthy. Avallach honors me! *ME!*"

Ulfger grabbed the helmet by one of the antlers and tore it from the Horned One's head. He placed it on his own head and stared through the slanted slits at his father, at the ravaged remains of the once mighty warlord. He heard laughter, but this time it was his own. The Horned One's head fell against the side board and looked sadly back at him.

A wind whipped up, blowing the bone dust across the stone floor. Ulfger felt his senses awaken. *What is this?* he wondered, realizing he could sense the life around him: a couple of deer in the woods below, a host of faeries battening down for the evening, and . . . *them*. He could sense *them*, Peter and the others. Sense their spirit, their feelings, their joys, excitement, their . . . *fears*. Then he understood more, that he could touch them, not physically, but with his mind.

He grinned. "Child thief, you will pay. You will know what it is to suffer, and to lose all you love."

✦

PETER FELT AS though he were in a dream, as though his feet barely touched the ground as they marched back through the Lady's Wood. He found it impossible to believe all that had happened this day, from driving the Flesh-eaters back to ridding Avalon, once and for all, of Ulfger's poison. But it was the Lady who dominated his thoughts, ruled his heart; he could think of little else. He closed his eyes and could still smell her scent: honeysuckle and spring water.

"Peter," Redbone called and pointed. "Look!"

Peter stopped and stared, dumbfounded. They all did.

They'd come at last to the border of Myrkvior, to Cusith Creek, back to the scourge-ridden woods. Everyone stared at the trees, at the fresh green buds that had sprouted out along a few of the gray limbs, and the occasional bloom here and there among the dead weeds.

"Tanngnost, what does it mean?" Peter asked.

Tanngnost set Sekeu carefully down. He'd carried her the whole way back. The troll might be old, but he was still a troll and, to him, she appeared to weigh nothing. Sekeu hopped over to a rock and took a seat. Peter thought it'd be a while before she'd be able to fight, but she looked on the mend and he couldn't help but smile. *Almost lost you*, he thought, surprised to find himself blinking back tears. *Been through too much, me and you. We're going to finish this thing together.*

Tanngnost touched one of the buds. "It means that the Lady's back," the troll said. "We have hope again."

"The Lady did that?" asked Cricket.

"Yes," Tanngnost said. "Peter has reawakened her spirit. She will tend Avallach's Tree. If we can stop the burning, she might be able to stop the scourge."

"And," Peter added, "when we drive them into the Mist, when we kill them all, then she will heal all of Avalon! Right? Return it to its splendor!"

"Yes, most certainly," the troll agreed.

"We must strike again!" Peter said, his voice brimming with excitement. "As soon as we can. We can't allow them to burn another tree!" He looked to the old elf. "Drael, what of you? Will you meet us at Red Rock, come dawn?"

"I tell you this," the old elf said. "The Lady's Guard will sit on the sidelines no longer. We'll be there, Peter. That you can count on." Every elf nodded in agreement, their stern faces and hard eyes all the oath Peter needed.

"Good," Peter said, clasping the elf on the arm. "Good." He could hardly contain the urge to let out a crazy whoop. He turned to the three girls. "Will you stand with us? Can we count on Ginny's children?"

The barghest looked to the girls.

"Will there be lots of blood?" asked the first.

"Enough noodlely guts for all?" asked the second.

"And eyeballs, don't forget eyeballs," put in the third.

"Oh, yes," Peter said, and returned their wicked smiles. "Brains too. Plenty to go around."

"I want to go!" said one.

"Me too!" chimed in the second.

"Oh, most certainly then," said the third. "But Peter?"

"Yes?" Peter said.

"You'll have to ask our mother first."

"Yes," said the second. "Mother doesn't like for us to play with strangers."

"Will you come ask her for us?" asked the third, with big, imploring eyes.

"I will," Peter said. "Right away." He addressed Drael. "Tomorrow then, Red Rock?"

"Agreed," Drael said, and the elves started away, back into the Lady's Wood.

"Leroy, Danny, Cricket, Nick. You guys grab all the stock and head back to Deviltree. We'll be there as soon as we can. Tanngnost, can you take Sekeu and go with them?"

Tanngnost looked troubled. "Most certainly, but—"

"There's always a but, isn't there?" Peter said.

"Peter, a word."

"Only one? Why do I doubt that?"

Tanngnost frowned, tugged Peter over into the woods. "Peter, you needn't go. The witch will come. The girls, they're her eyes and ears. They are just playing a game—"

"I know," Peter interrupted. "I have to go back to the swamp. I have to find Abraham's body before the Flesh-eaters do. I can't stand the thought of his head on their fort."

Tanngnost was quiet for a moment. "Yes. Yes, of course."

Peter started away.

"Peter."

"What now?" Peter said with a sigh.

"What about Nick?"

"Tanngnost, when did you become such an old woman?"

The troll gave him a sour look. "You saw him," he said defensively. "The darkness, it had him, *completely*."

"The Lady touched him. She healed him. You can see it in his eyes. Stop worrying so much. All is coming together. Avallach has smiled on us." This didn't seem to placate the troll. "Okay, keep a close eye on him if it makes you feel better."

"Peter?"

"What?" Peter said, exasperated.

"You were the one that brought them all together. You did that. If I didn't know you to be such a cretin, I'd believe the Horned One's spirit lives in you."

Peter smiled warmly at his old friend. "Is that a tear? It is. Why, Tanngnost, you *have* turned into an old woman." And Peter laughed, and when he did, all the Devils grinned, because Peter's laugh was a most contagious thing.

"HOW MUCH FARTHER?" Danny asked, for the third time in the last ten minutes.

No one answered.

"How come I have to carry the apples?" he groaned. "They weigh a goddamn ton. Cricket's only got mushrooms. How come she gets mushrooms? Mushrooms weigh like nothing. That's not fair. Hey Cricket, how about we switch for a while. Huh? How about it?"

Cricket shook her head.

"Ah, c'mon. C'mon. C'mon."

"Geezy fucking weezy, Danny," Cricket cried. "Do you ever stop bellyaching? Here, take the goddamn mushrooms already." She jerked the sack of apples from him and shoved the mushrooms into his gut. "Just stop whining for five flipping minutes. All right? Okay?"

Danny nodded sheepishly.

Cricket stomped away up the trail.

"Hey, Cricket?" Danny called.

Cricket didn't answer.

"You're a real sweetheart."

She flipped him the bird.

Danny looked at Nick, bounced the bag of mushrooms between his hands, lifted his eyebrows, and grinned.

Nick recognized the trail; Deviltree wasn't much farther. He'd be glad when they made it; the bag of fruit and nuts he carried wasn't light, plus the day was fading, the shadows growing dark. Nick didn't really care to be out in the night.

There were no signs of new buds here, nothing but endless gray. Still, he sensed a current beneath the gray. *It's the magic,* he realized—the Lady had opened his eyes to the magic. The hills around him felt like a winter woodland just before spring.

The dark feelings, the heat in his stomach, were completely gone. He felt the fatigue of the long day, but his spirit was alive, as though the magic of Avalon and his body were at last in harmony. His thoughts kept drifting back to the world behind the falls, the flowers, the magical animals, the sweet smells, the hundreds of little faerie folk . . . the *Lady. "The Lady,"* he whispered; she consumed his thoughts—her cerulean eyes, her silky hair, her pale skin, so white as to almost be blue. Visions of her soothed him. He felt . . . what? Love? *Yes,* he realized, like a mother's love.

Nick stopped dead in his tracks. A stab of guilt jabbed his chest. *"Mom,"* he said. He realized with horror that he'd forgotten about his *own* mother. She'd not just slipped his mind, he'd completely forgotten her. She seemed a distant memory, someone he'd known forever ago. It was as though the Lady had, had—*what?* Pushed his mother from his mind? Had taken her place somehow? He concentrated on his mother's face and this helped clear his mind. All at once the Lady's words came back to him, raw and bare: *I am your life. I am your death. I am all things forever and always. Love me. Love me. Forever love me.* A chill ran down his spine. *She's done more than healed me,* he realized. *She's woven a spell.* He cut his eyes left and right, felt sure someone, something, everything, was watching him. Nick realized he had to return *soon,* because Avalon was a seductive place. Because goddesses were obviously jealous creatures that didn't compete for devotion, not even with mothers. Nick had no doubt that if he didn't leave soon, he'd never leave, and after a while all the memories of his mother would be lost forever.

Someone jabbed him. "You better keep your mouth shut."

Nick started. He'd been so lost in thought he hadn't noticed Leroy come up behind him. The others were ahead. Nick began walking again.

"Did you hear me?" Leroy said, speaking low.

Nick ignored him.

Leroy's face twisted into a sneer. "Hey, I'm talking to you, asshole." He jabbed his finger into Nick's chest. "You ever bring that bullshit about Abraham up again and I'll *kill* you . . . fucking *kill* you!"

A flash of Abraham's face, his terrified eyes as he choked to death beneath the black water came to Nick, all because Leroy hadn't taken the two seconds to pull him out of the bog. Nick felt anger—no heat in his stomach, no pounding in his head—just good old reliable rage, it swelled up in him and all he could see was Leroy, big, stupid Leroy standing there sneering at him.

"Fuck you!" Nick spat and slammed his sack into Leroy's chest, slammed his fist into Leroy's face, catching the bigger boy high on the cheek, knocking him to the ground. Both Nick's sack and Leroy's hit the ground, spilling fruit and nuts all across the trail.

Leroy put a hand to his cheek, his eyes wide. Whatever he'd expected from Nick, this was definitely not it. His hands clenched into fists and he started for his feet.

"*ENOUGH!*" Sekeu cried from behind them. She stood on one leg, leaning against Tanngnost.

The troll cast hard eyes on Nick, scrutinizing him.

"He attacked me!" Leroy said. "Look at him, he's crazy."

Sekeu's eyes blazed, but she wasn't looking at Nick, her glare rested on Leroy. "You do not have the right to even talk to him. Not after what you did."

Leroy's mouth fell open. "What? No . . . you got it *wrong*! That bastard." He jabbed a finger at Nick. "It's his fault. He knocked *me* into the bog. He's trying to pin this on me. Can't you see that?" The way Leroy said it, Nick felt sure he truly believed it had happened that way.

"No," Sekeu said, her words cold and flat. "That is not what happened."

Leroy shook his head, his mouth worked, but he seemed unable to speak.

"You should be shamed, Leroy," Sekeu said. "You should keep your head low."

Chapter Nineteen

Murder

The shadows deepened and night came to the Lady's Wood. Ulfger stood as still as a statue at the edge of the forest. He closed his eyes and opened himself to the night. He sensed the fish in the wading pool, the frogs, a lone fox, a pair of doves sharing a limb and cooing to each other. He sensed the bond between the birds, the love of lifelong mates. He pushed at them, told them to be afraid of each other, and felt the fear grip them, heard them flap away in different directions, as fast as they could fly.

Ulfger smiled and turned his attention to the elven barracks, the ornate longhouse that stood sentinel in the courtyard next to the Great Hall. The elves were back. He could sense all twenty-one of them within the wooden structure. They were not so easy to read as the animals, but he felt their excitement as they prepared for battle.

A door opened. A ray of torchlight flickered across the courtyard. Four elves came out with canteens strapped over their shoulders and headed down the path past the wading pools. Ulfger followed them to the ancient well and watched them filling the canteens. He hefted the broken blade and strolled toward them, not even bothering to hide his step. The elves caught sight of Ulfger and pulled their swords. Ulfger swung, meeting two of the swords mid-strike, smashing effortlessly through their block and cleaving both of their heads from their shoulders.

One of the remaining elves landed a blow across Ulfger's midsection, but his armor deflected the cut. The other slashed across his upper arm, cutting deep into the muscle. Ulfger felt the heat of the wound and locked his eyes, his fiery eyes, on the elves and in that moment he found their fear, seized upon it with his mind, managed to hold them with it long enough to slam his sword onto the head of the forward elf, cleaving his skull in two, dashing the other in bits of blood and brains.

He grabbed the remaining elf around the neck, dug his fingers into flesh, and picked him up as though the elf weighed nothing. He could so easily snap the elf's neck with one twist but instead he brought the black blade to the elf's eye. The elf saw the poisonous edge and clawed frantically at Ulfger's hand.

"Why do you squirm so?" Ulfger asked. "If you are true to Avallach, the blade won't burn you." He touched the edge to the elf's cheek, made the slightest nick. The cut immediately began to blacken, to sizzle, to burn away from the bone like acid. Ulfger felt the heat beneath his hand as the poison spread inside the elf, felt the gurgling as the sizzling blood bubbled up the elf's throat, pouring from his mouth, nose, eyes. Ulfger held him, enjoying every last tremor until at last the elf was still.

Ulfger dropped the elf, then examined the cut on his own arm. He was surprised to see that the wound wasn't deeper, that there was no blood. It had been a strong strike. Then he noticed that the wound was shrinking, healing before his eyes. "I'm . . . I am truly a *god*!" he cried. "I *am* the Horned One." He sucked in a deep breath of the night air. "Time for the child thief to meet Avallach's true son."

✦

ULFGER WALKED THE path through Devilwood without fear. He sensed the rare creature and when he did, he told it to be afraid, and the beasts fled before him. "Dread me," he whispered. "Dread my coming!"

He searched the wood, looking for signs or trails that might lead him the right way, but more and more he relied on his senses, closing his eyes and seeking. Finally he caught the faintest glimmer, like a spark far in the distance, and as he homed in on that spark, he began to feel them, closer and closer until he stood before Deviltree.

"The child thief's not here," he snarled beneath his breath. *But she is, his dark-skinned bitch. I sense her pain.* A smile slowly snuck across his face. *To take her from him. Cut her into pieces, leave her head upon the spit, after all that fuss to save her. Why, that would bring him to his knees.* He laughed. *Give him a taste of what it is to lose that which is dear.*

Ulfger pushed on the door. It was solid and locked tight. He circled the tree, but found no way in. He just needed someone to slide the bolt. He wondered if he could make one of the children do that. If he could just push them, like with the doves.

He closed his eyes and reached out with his mind, felt for them, grasping for a hold. He found the troll sleeping in the loft above. Ulfger quickly moved on. The old troll was full of tricks and unknown secrets, and Ulfger was afraid he just might touch him back. He located a girl, but she was too deep in sleep; next to her a boy, but he too was in a deep slumber. Ulfger found another boy, this one entrenched in dreams, the boy's mind fairly danced with them, and no matter how hard Ulfger tried he couldn't break through. He moved on, growing impatient, probing, searching until he found something else, something very intriguing: a boy by himself in a small room. This one wasn't asleep, not by far. This one's mind was open—*wide open.* Ulfger could feel the anger boiling off this boy, so much rage and hatred, both for himself and for *them.* The child was mad with it. And Ulfger realized this madness left him open, and so vulnerable.

Ulfger sent a thought, pushed it into the boy's head. *Open the door.* The boy didn't respond. *Open the door.* Nothing. *Open the door.*

Ulfger's brow tightened with frustration. And then all at once he understood the nature of this great gift Avallach had bestowed upon him. He couldn't control minds, after all, couldn't make people do things they didn't want to. He could only push them, push the workings that were already in place, such as fear, or hatred, or jealousy. He probed again and found something good, something he knew he could use.

Murder, he thought and pushed the notion at the boy, and to his surprise, to his utter delight, it only took that nudge, that tiny whiff, and murder blossomed.

Nick dreamed, and for once the dream was peaceful. He played in the Lady's Garden, chasing the wild faeries while the Lady sat upon a throne and watched. A warm breeze blew lightly across a pond, it smelled of honeysuckle and spring water. The faeries giggled and flew up into a tree. Nick flew after them and perched alongside them. It was then that he realized that he'd sprouted wings, that he wasn't any larger than a bird, and, odder than that, he was fine with this. What could be better than being a faerie in the Lady's Garden? The Lady smiled at him, like one of her children. Nick was happy, content, and wished for nothing more.

Nick heard someone call his name; the voice was familiar but he couldn't place it at first, it was so far away. It was that other woman, he realized, the one he'd left behind. Nick felt a tickle in the back of his mind, something he needed to do for her, but he couldn't be bothered to think about her, not now, he was just too busy playing.

A shadow fell across the grounds. A round wood door stood in the garden. Nick heard scratching coming from behind it. Something wanted in, wanted in badly. Nick looked to the Lady; she looked frightened. A shrill cry cut across the garden, something in great pain; it rang in his head, louder, and louder—

Nick awoke; for the first time since he'd arrived, he wasn't covered in sweat and his stomach didn't burn. Yet he still felt uneasy. He glanced at the round door. He couldn't shake the feeling that something sinister was on the other side, waiting to be let in.

There was no sign that Peter and the Devils had come back yet. He wondered how late it was. Cricket and Danny were asleep in their cages, the long day looking to have caught up with them. They'd moved Sekeu's cage over near the fireplace. He watched her twist fitfully in her sleep; her face appeared troubled, as though she were having a bad dream. Nick glanced to Leroy's cage—it was empty.

Nick caught a faint sound, a squeal. It came again, a strained laugh or maybe a cry, hard to tell. Again, a faint sound, but this time Nick recognized it as a scream, something in pain. It came from the privy.

What the hell? he thought and crawled from his cage. It was eerie with all the Devils gone. He listened, could hear the troll's snores coming from the loft above, then the squeal, a long squeal. It sent a chill up his spine and he wondered how such a small sound could be so terrible.

Nick crossed the floor to the privy. The door was slightly ajar and a thin, flickering light escaped through the crack. Nick laid his hand on the door and started to push it inward, when it flew open and he was face to face with Leroy. But it was as though Leroy didn't even see him; the boy's eyes were looking past him toward the round door.

"He's here," Leroy whispered and shoved past Nick.

Before Nick could say or do anything, another painful squeal came from the privy. He glanced in, and his eyes went wide. There, on the stone next to the toilet pit, was a single crumbled pixie wing, a strand of bloody blue flesh dangling from the end.

The sharp squeal again, like a mouse in the teeth of a cat. It came from the toilet pit. Nick didn't want to look, but he inched forward anyway and peered down the shaft. He saw two blue pixies tangled in the stringy black webbing, one a boy, the other a girl with a mane of wispy white hair. The girl appeared unharmed, but the boy looked dead, his body broken as though he'd been crushed, two bloody gashes on his back where his wings had been torn away.

The girl let loose a chilling scream and the blue glow of her skin pulsated, lighting up the shaft, and Nick saw them, far down the pit among the shit and stink, hundreds of black spiders, the blue radiance glittering off their tiny, cold eyes. He could hear their clatter as they scrambled up the web. The girl screamed again and fought to free herself.

The spiders reached the boy, swarmed over him, and the boy let out a shrill wail. "Oh, God!" Nick cried, upon realizing the boy still lived. "Oh, *good God!*" The spiders tore the boy from the web, pulled him down into the pit, and he disappeared beneath their black, oily bodies.

The spiders came for the girl.

Get her out, Nick told himself. *Now! Hurry!* "NO!" he said harshly. *She's too far down. There's no way. No—way!* Yet he found himself down on one knee, his hand hovering above the pit. "No! No!" he spat through clenched teeth. Then the spiders were on her. She screamed and Nick plunged his entire arm into the pit, tearing down through the gummy webbing. He grabbed the pixie and in doing so also grabbed a handful of spiders. He could feel their hard, hairy legs and soft, soggy bodies as they writhed in his grasp, felt their hot secretions spurt into his hand as he tugged them from the web.

A jab of pain, like a wasp sting, hit his palm, then another and another. He cried out, but didn't let go of the girl. He sat up quick, yanking his arm and the pixie from the pit. Long, syrupy strings of web stretched and snapped as he pulled away. The spiders clung to his hand like leeches, their flat, tick-like bodies creased and wrinkled, glistening with sticky, milky goo. He dropped the girl to the stones and frantically slapped and clawed the spiders from his arm, leaping to his feet, trying to stomp them as they skittered about like crabs, darting back into the pit.

Angry red welts dotted his hand and wrist. He wiped at his arm, trying to peel away the smelly webbing. He noticed the pixie; she too was covered in filth and webbing. Her wings trembled and her eyes were full of terror, but she looked like she might be okay.

Nick heard Leroy's laugh.

Leroy walked into the flickering lantern light, stopped, and peered in. Nick saw that Leroy held a sword, then realized it was Maldiriel. Leroy smiled a strange, vacant smile and walked on.

"What the fuck?" Nick said under his breath and rushed from the privy.

It took a second for Nick's eyes to adjust to the darkness. *Where did he go?* Nick saw Leroy in front of the fireplace. He stood over Sekeu's cage. And then, like it was nothing to him, like he was simply poking a bundle of hay, Leroy brought the sword up and shoved it down through the cage into Sekeu's neck.

Sekeu's eyes flashed open; a terrible gurgle escaped her throat.

"NO!" Nick screamed and charged, ran as hard as he could, but felt as though moving through syrup as Leroy tugged the blade free and brought it down again, and again, and again. Blood gushed from Sekeu's neck as she flailed against the cage, struggled to escape, but she was trapped, like an animal for slaughter. The sharp blade cut into her arms, her hands, her chest, then into her face.

Nick hit him, slammed into Leroy at a full run, knocking the bigger boy against the mantel. Maldiriel flew from Leroy's hand, clattered across the stone. Nick snatched the sword up and came for Leroy.

Leroy looked dazed, confused, then caught sight of Nick, saw the bloody sword in Nick's hand, and his eyes went wide. *"STAY AWAY FROM ME!"* he shrieked.

"WHAT'S GOING ON?" came a deep, booming voice, and Nick was confronted by a blinding flame. Nick stopped, blinked, then saw Tanngnost standing before him with a torch in one hand and an ax in the other; behind the troll stood Cricket and Danny, their faces ashen and horrified.

The torchlight revealed more than Nick ever wanted to see. Blood bubbled from the slash in Sekeu's throat as she tried to speak. A wet, sucking sound came from the wounds in her chest. She met Nick's eyes and seemed to be begging him to help her. A clot of blood spat from her lips and she was still, her unblinking eyes frozen on his.

Leroy raised a shaking hand and pointed an accusing finger at Nick. "He . . . killed . . . her. I saw it. Saw it all. He's crazy. I tried to warn you. He's fucking *crazy!*"

Nick glanced at the sword in his hand—*his* sword, at the blood smeared across its blade and dripping onto the stones. *Splat, splat, splat,* like a telltale heart.

"Nick?" Cricket called weakly.

Nick didn't feel his fingernails cut into his palm as he clenched his hand into a fist. Didn't hear the inhuman growl that escaped his own throat or even realize his lips were peeled back into a snarl. He set his eyes on Leroy, took a step forward, then another, his head hung low, like that of a mad dog. "Murderer," he said, low and harsh. *"Murderer!"*—the ragged words tearing loose from deep in his throat. *"MURDERER!"* he screamed, his face full of rage.

"GET BACK!" the troll cried, pushing Cricket and Danny away. "He's turned! The darkness has him!"

Leroy scrambled behind the troll and ran for the door. Nick leaped after him, so intent on catching him he didn't see the troll bring the ax around until the last second. Nick ducked, sliding beneath the blow. The ax hit the mantel, smashing the edge to bits.

"DON'T LET HIM OPEN THE DOOR!" Nick screamed, his face a knot of frustration. Couldn't they see that Leroy was heading toward the door, that he was going to let whatever was out there in?

The troll swung again, knocking the sword from Nick's hand and driving Nick into the wall.

Leroy was at the door, sliding the slat free.

Nick faked left and jumped right, causing the troll to stumble into one of the benches. Nick darted past in time to see Leroy shove the door open and flee into the night.

Nick stopped, sure some indescribable horror was about to appear in the doorway. But the only horror coming for him was the troll with the ax. Nick caught sight of Cricket and Danny, caught their condemning looks.

"NO!" Nick shouted, shaking his head. *"IT WASN'T ME!"*

The troll didn't even pause, just came on at a full charge.

"IT WASN'T ME!" Nick shouted again, then ran, the troll's heavy footsteps chasing him out the door and into the swirling night fog.

✦

WHEN NICK FINALLY dared to stop, he wished he hadn't. While running, he'd been too occupied avoiding the roots and thorns, ledges and pits, to worry about anything else. But now, as he leaned heavily against the trunk of a fallen tree, as the sound of his own breathing slowed down, he began to hear the night, to hear the things *in* the night.

The woods themselves creaked and moaned and Nick thought of the way the trees in Whisperwood had talked to each other and wondered if the trees around him now were speaking. If they were telling the things with claws, and fangs, and stingers, that he was here, wondered if they were telling that other thing, that dark thing, that he was alone.

Nick strained to see within the deeper shadows. He could feel that other out there, still probing for him in the night. Nick reached for his sword and realized he'd left it behind. But he did have his knife. He pulled it out. It felt small and insubstantial in his hand.

I can't stay out here, he thought. *I have to go back. I can clear this up. Right? No,* a deeper voice warned. *No, you can't.* He knew what he'd seen on the troll's face, in Cricket's and Danny's eyes. The troll had said he'd turned. *Turned into what?* A Flesh-eater, he guessed. He'd seen the way they'd been watching him. It wasn't hard to put together. Now they believed he'd murdered Sekeu. *Peter will kill me on sight.*

He started forward then stopped. *Where am I going?* "Home," he whispered. *I've got to get home, back to my mom. One way or another.* He shook his head. *I can't even find my way out of these goddamn woods. How am I supposed to make it all the way home? I'm screwed,* he thought. *Completely screwed.*

He heard something in the distance, back the way he'd come; sounded like footsteps. *Were they after him already? Peter and the Devils?* He wasn't going to wait around to find out. He pushed down the slope and realized he'd no idea which direction he was heading, that he could be heading back to Deviltree, for all he knew. Then *it* was there, just ahead, in a small clearing illuminated by the luminescent ground fog. A tall figure draped in a long, woolly cape. It wore a helmet with wide, curving antlers. It held someone—*Leroy.* It appeared to be talking to the boy.

The horned creature turned its head toward Nick. Its eyes glowed from deep within the visor. The eyes, those burning eyes, fixed on Nick, and when they did, a fear so crippling gripped him that he fell to his knees.

"Run little rabbit. Run."

Nick found he could move again. Scrambling on his hands and knees, he clawed his way up the slope, stumbled to his feet, and ran.

PETER LED THE Devils homeward to Deviltree. As he jogged through the night, he tried to keep his mind focused on tomorrow, away from thoughts of Abraham. The witch had helped them find him. The boy's decapitated body hung from a tree out in the burning field, naked, mutilated. The witch had almost been kindly to Peter in his grief. It was her land, her swamp that the Flesh-eaters had so boldly trespassed. She was ready to fight, anxious for blood. So it was all set. *Tomorrow,* Peter thought. *Tomorrow we end it.*

They crested the trail and Peter saw Deviltree below. He stopped. The door to the fort stood open, Tanngnost's tall figure silhouetted in its frame, an ax in his hand.

What now? Peter wondered and sprinted down. As he neared, he caught sight of the troll's anguished features and slowed to a walk.

Tanngnost tried to speak, but seemed capable of only shaking his head, yet his eyes told Peter all he needed to know. Peter tried to shove past. The old troll grabbed him. "Peter," Tanngnost called. "Peter, wait. You should—"

Peter tore loose and pushed into the chamber, saw the blankets, the blood on the floor, on the walls. He saw Sekeu's copper-colored hand curling out from beneath the blankets and fell to his knees. He reached for her hand, hesitated, afraid to touch her, then slowly clasped her hand in his. It was cold.

"Sekeu," Peter whispered and started to pull the blanket back from her face. Cricket put her hand on the blanket. "No," she said sternly.

"Peter," Tanngnost said, his voice tender. "It was the darkness. It took Nick. I'm sorry. It just happened . . . so fast."

"The darkness?" Peter asked, almost choking on the words. "No, that's not possible!"

The troll looked pained. "I know this is hard. But . . . I was there. I saw it with my own eyes. We all did. Nick's out of his mind, Peter. He attacked Leroy. I've never seen such rage."

"But how?" Peter asked, his voice cracking. "How? You were there. The Lady . . . she healed him. She drove it from him. You saw it. Tell me you saw it!"

"The Lady . . . well, she's so weak. Maybe it didn't hold. Maybe—" Tanngnost looked baffled. "Peter, I don't know. I wish I had an answer."

"No," Peter said, shaking his head. "No, it's not the darkness. I won't believe it."

Leroy came stumbling through the entrance, his back to them, staring at something out in the woods. His back bumped into the door and he quickly shoved it closed, fumbling to slide the heavy slat into place.

"Where is he?" Tanngnost asked.

Leroy jumped; the slat slid from his hands, landing on the stones with a solid thud. He spun around and glanced wildly about the room. His eyes fell on Sekeu, went to Peter, and became wide, afraid. He backed into the door. "Nick killed her!" he said.

"Yes," the troll said. "Where did he go?"

"He's in the woods," Leroy said quickly. "I tried to stop him . . . but he has a sword . . . *his* sword and I don't . . . didn't." Leroy's eyes kept shifting back to Sekeu. "If I had a weapon I would've stopped him. I tried to stop him."

"Where in the woods?" Tanngnost pressed. "Which direction was he going?"

"Toward Goggie Creek."

"Peter," Tanngnost said. "We have to catch him *now*. Right now."

Peter didn't answer.

"Peter, don't you understand? We can't let him fall into the hands of the Flesh-eaters. He knows where Deviltree is. Knows our numbers, our plans. They'll get him to talk. Everything's at stake. Peter, he knows where the Haven lies!"

Peter's eyes fixed on Sekeu's long black hair spilling out from beneath the blanket. He touched it, ran his fingers through it. *Sekeu, how?*

Redbone brought Peter a spear. The Devils were lined up behind him. They looked anxious. "We're ready," Redbone said. "Peter?"

"Just go," Tanngnost said to the group and herded them toward the door. "Hurry, before it's too late. Take everyone. You'll need every pair of eyes. Danny, Cricket, you too." He snatched spears off the wall and pushed them into their hands. "Take no chances. Remember, this isn't Nick. This isn't your friend. Nick's gone from us—what's left is a monster." He raised his voice. "Kill him on sight. Whatever you do, don't let him fall into the hands of the Flesh-eaters."

Peter heard all this as though from somewhere far away.

The troll sat down next to Peter.

Peter continued to stroke Sekeu's hair as his thoughts stumbled over one another. *How could I have let this happen?* He pressed his hand to his temple. *Because I'd been so sure. Because I saw the Lady heal him, that's how. There's something else going on here. It has to be something else.*

He looked at Maldiriel, at the blood, Sekeu's blood, still wet on the fine elven blade. Peter's brow tightened. *Hadn't Leroy said Nick had a sword in the woods? Yes, he'd made a point of saying it.*

"Tanngnost."

"Yes."

"You saw Nick kill Sekeu?"

"Yes, well, no. I didn't actually *see* him do it. But I—"

"Did any of the kids? Did any of them see it?"

"Yes. Leroy did."

"Where's Leroy?"

"He went with the others."

Peter thought of the odd way Leroy had acted. Nothing he could put his finger on, but definitely not right. "I need to talk to Nick," Peter said and before the troll could protest, Peter snatched up the spear and ran out the door.

✳

THEY COME, ULFGER thought. Twenty-three, maybe twenty-four little boys and girls, all spread out, hunting the rabbit. He opened his eyes. He could see the faintest glow pushing through the tree tops as dawn's first light touched the low clouds.

He closed his eyes again, because he could see so much more with them shut. It seemed the longer he wore the helmet the further he could see, as though his mind and the helmet were melding, fusing, becoming one.

Just ahead, the rabbit had stopped again. Ulfger could sense the boy's disorientation, his fear. Beyond the rabbit, *they* waited at the forest's edge, the *Flesh-eaters.* So many Ulfger couldn't count them all, but he could sense their hate, their need for murder.

He'd followed the rabbit all night, kept it on course. When the rabbit slowed down, or strayed, he merely made his presence known and the little rabbit got moving again.

Avallach had been kind, too kind, had made it all too easy. The rabbit would lead the child thief and his brats right to the Flesh-eaters, right into their trap. *And then—oh, and then.* Ulfger laughed, couldn't help himself; he felt like he would never stop laughing.

✦

A TWIG SNAPPED, and Nick's eyes flew open. Faint light pushed through the tangled limbs above him. How long had he been asleep? He glanced anxiously about. *Was it here?* How could he have allowed himself to fall asleep with that horrible creature hunting him? Every time he'd thought he'd lost it, every time he'd stopped to catch his breath, it had appeared, its red eyes glowering at him, clawing their way into his head.

Nick tried to get his bearings, but the fog was thick. He could barely see twenty paces in any direction—another snap, somewhere behind him. Nick slid his hand around the hilt of his knife, wishing he'd held on tighter to his sword. He stood and crept off, but the ground was soggy and the sticky mud pulled beneath his feet. Suddenly footsteps came rapidly toward him. He saw Dirk staring at him across a thicket of thorns, the boy's eyes as wide and frightened as his own.

Nick raised his hands. "Dirk, I didn't do it! You got to believe—"

Dirk leaped forward and threw his spear. Nick managed to duck the missile; the blade whisked past his head and stuck into a tree.

"HERE! HE'S HERE!" Dirk shouted, yanking out his sword and charging through the thorns for Nick.

Nick ran, dashed into the bushes, found a small trail, and sprinted down it as fast as he could go. Shouts came from all around him and he spied several figures in the fog, running parallel to him through the trees.

Nick broke into a large clearing of gray, knee-high grass, and another group of Devils shot out into the clearing ahead of him. Nick cut away and darted toward a thin line of trees. He could see the burning fields through their branches and it occurred to him if he could make it out there, then maybe, *maybe*, the Devils wouldn't follow.

A spear whisked past him, so close he actually felt its wake. The Devils howled like beasts, and Nick knew how a deer must feel when chased by wolves. A shrill cry escaped his own throat—eyes wide, heart pounding, as his legs whipped through the tall grass.

The Child Thief

Nick closed in on the line of trees, could smell the soggy burned wood beyond. A spear slapped off his thigh, the shaft tangled in his legs. Nick went sprawling into the grass.

✦

PETER HEARD SHOUTS in the distance. Sounds were tricky in the thick fog. He stopped and cocked his head from side to side as he tried to locate their direction.

He'd found what he thought were Nick's tracks just before dawn and followed them. But the tracks had run together with those of the Devils and since then he'd been racing along, hoping to catch Nick before the Devils did. He'd also found other tracks, large, deep imprints. It would take someone of substantial weight to make such tracks. *A lone Flesh-eater?* That didn't seem likely. There was only one other possibility, and he didn't want to think of it. Whoever it was, they were tracking the boy.

More shouts. *They're near the burning fields,* Peter thought. He heard yelling, the calls echoing up and down the valley in the early morning quiet. Peter was horrified. *Don't they know where they are?*

"Avallach be merciful," Peter pleaded, and took off at a hard run. *Had not enough gone wrong?*

✦

NICK SAT UP. They had him, fanning out, circling him. *Is this how I'm going to die?* he wondered. Not killed by monsters, not by some drug dealer, but at the hands of a bunch of kids, kids that had just yesterday called him their brother. Not even his fear of death was so terrible as the looks he saw on their faces, the feverish glee that ran beneath the bloodlust, a murderous joy only experienced by lynching mobs. *"I DIDN'T DO IT!"* Nick cried. But no one was listening, they all had murder—his murder—in their eyes.

Dirk leaped for him, his sword pulled back, his eyes on Nick's neck, his face no different than that of a boy about to score a touchdown. A spear—a thick, heavy spear—hit Dirk in the middle of his chest, driving deep into his ribs, knocking him off his feet.

A loud cry filled the air. Flesh-eaters, a long, ragged line of them, burst from the trees. Men in armor and heavy boots came screaming into the grassy glade, brandishing swords, spears, and pike axes.

Nick made for his feet, felt thick, powerful fingers grab his arm, yank him into the air, then slam him to the ground. All the breath left Nick's body. A Flesh-eater shoved his face into Nick's. The man's lips peeled back into a mockery of a grin, exposing white gums and black teeth. His eyes, little more than slits of red, glared at Nick. "Gonna be all right, lad. Aye, we're here to save you."

Nick tried to break away, then felt a jagged blade against his neck.

"There, now," the man chortled. "You should stay put if you be wanting to keep your ears attached to the sides of your head."

NICK SAW A spear hit Redbone. It went through the boy's side, the point protruding out of his back. Redbone grasped the spear in both hands, screamed through clenched teeth, and collapsed to his knees.

The Devils were spread out across the glade. They stopped in their tracks; their faces, which only seconds before were those of bloodthirsty predators, were now wild with shock and terror.

"NOW!" commanded a tall man wearing a wide-brimmed hat, and more heavily armed men, at least thirty or forty of them, came rushing into the glade down off the east slope.

"RUN!" screamed Redbone. *"GET OUT OF HERE!"*

The Devils broke and ran, scrambling in all directions. The men gave chase. Spears flew from both sides, men and Devils alike falling to the ground. Nick saw the big blond Bear take two spears in the back. Bear didn't fall, just kept stumbling away, weaving like a drunk, wheezing and coughing up blood until finally a man hit him in the back of the skull with an ax. Another kid, a black boy from Brooklyn whose name Nick couldn't remember, was hit in the leg, a spear going all the way through his thigh. The boy fell to the ground and began dragging himself forward, clawing at the soft earth. Five men set to him with ax and sword.

Another group of Flesh-eaters came running into the clearing from the west side. They slung nets weighted with rocks at the Devils, bringing many down in a tangle then stabbing them to death as they fought to free themselves.

Nick caught sight of Danny and Cricket, they stood at the farthest end of the glade, frozen in place, their eyes wide with horror. *Run! What are you waiting for?*

A Flesh-eater gave a shout, pointed at the pair, and over a dozen men started toward them. Danny turned and ran back into the trees, followed a second later by Cricket.

PETER RACED DOWN the path. The din of battle, the screams of pain echoed eerily up the foggy valley. *Those are* Devils *dying!* his mind screamed at him. Peter leaped recklessly across a wide, rushing creek, careened down a steep path, heedless to the danger as he half-fell and half-slid down the loose stones to its bottom. He landed in a roll and was up again, running onward, determined to get to the fight before all was lost.

Peter skidded around a clump of thick oaks, and there, down the ledge below him, were Cricket, Danny, and a Devil by the name of Trick. They were surrounded by a wide circle of Flesh-eaters. The Flesh-eaters moved in, tightening the ring. Trick was doing his best to hold them off, yelling and slashing the air with his spear. Cricket and Danny both clutched their spears, all but paralyzed with fear.

Four Flesh-eaters rushed in at once, knocking Trick's spear aside and running him through. Pain twisted the boy's face and blood spurted from his mouth as he slid to the ground.

Peter snarled, leaped forward, and launched his spear. The weapon flew true, finding its mark in the breastplate of the forward-most man, piercing the thin metal and knocking the man to the ground. Peter yanked both of his swords from their scabbards and ran all out, launching himself off the ledge and into the air from almost twenty feet above the fight. He howled and the men looked up, their eyes going wide with surprise as a screaming demon came hurtling onto them.

Peter crashed into them feet-first, the men collapsing like bowling pins. Peter bounded up off the first man, leaving him headless. He landed on the second man and thrust his sword into his face before the man could even push his helmet from his eyes. Then he was away, cutting one man's arm off at the elbow with one sword while thrusting the other sword into the throat of another. He leaped and spun, his twin blades weaving a dance of death and dismemberment, leaving severed arms, legs, and necks in their wake.

When there was no more flesh to cut in front of him, Peter whirled, eyes blazing, not even bothering to wipe away the splash of black blood that ran across his face. Six men lay dead or dying at his feet, their moans music to his ears.

Danny let out a cry as the Flesh-eaters grabbed him and closed ranks. Peter spotted Cricket halfway up the embankment. She stopped and looked back at him.

"GET OUT OF HERE!" Peter cried.

Cricket hesitated, then scrambled to the top of the ledge and disappeared.

Peter glared at the eight remaining men, grinning as black blood dripped from his blades.

The men watched him as though he was possessed. But these were seasoned fighters, not new recruits, and they spread out into a defensive formation. One man drifted too far, and Peter was on him in a heartbeat. There came a quick clang of steel as Peter knocked aside the spear point, rolled, and cut the man down at the ankle. The man collapsed, screaming and clutching his spurting stump. Peter was up and away before the next man in line could come near.

Peter circled and they followed him with their swords and spears.

Shouts came from down the trail. More men were coming, a lot more men. Now it was the Flesh-eaters that grinned. Peter knew he had to end this fast. He took a step forward, and when he did, the man holding Danny thrust his sword under the boy's throat. "You move again and the boy dies."

Danny whimpered as blood trickled from the edge of the sword at his neck.

"I'll cut him. Cut him wide open, I will."

But there was more going on here than the men realized. Peter meant to save Danny if he could, but the darker truth was that Peter couldn't let the men take Danny, not *alive*. Not under any circumstances. Danny knew where the Lady was.

"Danny, say your prayers," Peter said, his voice like cold steel.

The men exchanged a nervous glance.

Peter came at them, running all out. The men tightened their ranks and leveled their spears. But this was what Peter had wanted. At the last second, he faked left, drawing their weapons to bear, then leaped right, launching himself from a large root, bounding up, and cartwheeling over the men. He struck out with both swords, the blades scissoring into the face of the man holding Danny, cutting the entire front of the man's face off, exposing his eye sockets, nasal cavities, and an open hole where his mouth had been. There came a horrible gargling cry; the man's tongue flapped like a windsock. He fell away from Danny, clutching what was left of his face.

Peter landed behind them. The men all tried to spin at once, but in different directions, crashing into one another and getting tangled in each other's weapons. Peter shoved his swords into the backs of the men on either side of Danny and snatched the boy free. Hauling him away, pushing him up the trail. *"RUN!"* he screamed. "Run, for the Lady's sake!"

Danny took off with Peter right behind him, and made it about four paces, then tripped, taking Peter down with him. Peter got one foot back under him when something hit him on the back of the skull.

Peter was still lucid enough to feel his face slap the hard earth, to feel the air go out of him, to see the men with their wicked grins and deadly spears circle him. Then he saw something else. There, far up on the hill, looking down, stood a tall figure in a woolly cape; a helmet with great antlers sat on its head.

Peter smiled. The Horned One had come to guide him to Otherworld.

PART IV

The Captain

Chapter Twenty

Samuel Carver

Redbone slipped again, jerking the rope against Nick's neck. Nick winced as the prickly cords bit into his flesh. He fought to keep his footing and could only watch helplessly as Redbone struggled to regain his feet. There was a terrible gash in Redbone's side; blood oozed out and ran all the way down his leg. And even though Redbone had been trying to kill him only an hour before, Nick still hated to see him suffer like this.

Just ahead of Redbone, Danny was blubbering and wouldn't shut up. In front of Danny was Leroy. Nick wished Leroy was the one with the wound in his side; he'd have no problem watching Leroy choke. Peter was in the lead, plodding silently forward. Nick had no idea what was going to happen to them, but whatever it was, it wouldn't be good.

The men strung out in a long procession both in front and behind the boys, their dark, leathery flesh glistening beneath a coat of oily sweat. Directly ahead trudged a group of pike-men with the heads of the dead Devils sitting atop their pikes. Dirk's lifeless eyes stared at Nick as his tongue lolled back and forth to the rhythm of the march.

Now that they were out in the open landscape and well away from the forests, the men had dropped their guard, staring at the trail with empty, soulless eyes, and dragging their spears as they tromped down the long, gray road. Nick did his best to avoid looking at them, at the thick veins running beneath their skin like worms, the bumps, scales, and horns. Apparently, the magic had twisted each man differently, and Nick found himself confronted with an endless variety of tortured bodies and the faces of men weary to their very souls.

The air was warm and humid, especially compared to the forests. Sweat rolled down Nick's face and into his wounds, stinging the raw flesh where the ropes cut into his neck and wrists. Nick's tongue felt swollen. He couldn't remember ever being so thirsty. Down here, in the flatlands, the earth was dried out. They kicked up a cloud of dust as they marched along, and soon were covered in the claylike powder. Nick tried to spit to clear his mouth of the grime, but his mouth was too dry.

Their guard, a short, one-armed man with a sour face and a festering of warts along his brow, whacked Peter on the shin with the butt of his spear. Peter stumbled but somehow managed to keep from falling. "Stop dragging your feet, you ugly cunny. Move it."

The man caught Nick looking at him and shoved his face into Nick's; his breath smelled like rotten meat. "He be a demon, y'know. That one." He whacked Peter with the blunt end of his spear. "Tell me you can see it?"

Nick didn't answer.

"Little fool," the guard spat. "How can you be so blind? Do you not see his pointy ears? He be Lucifer's own son, that one."

Nick turned away from the man.

"You see this," the guard pressed his scarred stump right into Nick's cheek. "It were him that done this." The guard took the blunt end of his spear and whacked Peter in the ribs. Peter let out a grunt and the guard laughed, then whacked Peter again.

"Beasley, enough," came a rough, weary voice. The voice came from the tall man with a thin mustache and goatee, wearing a wide-brimmed hat, what Nick thought of as a pirate's hat.

"Aye, Captain," the one-armed man sneered, then gave Peter a shove for good measure.

✦

CAPTAIN SAMUEL CARVER pulled at his goatee and scanned the line of captives. They'd captured five boys alive and had the heads of close to a dozen more to decorate the fort walls with. Though they looked like children, the Captain knew better and had made doubly sure their hands were tightly bound and their necks strapped to the pole before beginning the long march back to the fort.

The Captain studied the red-headed boy in the lead, a clot of blood drying on his scalp. The Captain resented that this demon child should have red blood. It wasn't right, not when his own pure English blood had turned black. Of course, what *was* right anymore? *It's him—the pointy ears leave no doubt.* This had to be the one they called Peter, the leader of this pack of heathens. How many times had this demon taunted them? Now, they not only had him, they had him alive. The Captain still couldn't believe it, would never have guessed it could be so easy.

The demons had come early, right on the heels of yesterday's success. The Captain *had* guessed that one right and marshaled every able-bodied man in preparation, intending to catch the demons by surprise. His plan was to hide his main body among the trees and draw Peter into an ambush with a smaller force. But no such plan had been needed. The demon children came straight to them, as though God had handed them over. The Captain almost felt disappointed, cheated. He'd come to expect more from this devilish creature. He moved up alongside Peter. "Tell me something, boy," the Captain asked in a deep, rough voice. "Did you give up? Is that it? Just tired of the game? Tell me, son. So I can put my mind to rest."

The red-headed boy met his eyes and held them. Even beaten and tied, the creature managed a sneer.

Captain shook his head. "Well, it's over now, at least for you."

One of the boys stumbled. The kid had a wild mop of hair with a red bone tied into it, a long scar that ran across his eye, and a nasty-looking wound in his side. The rope strangled him as he struggled to regain his feet. The Captain knew he had a right to hate them all, but found it hard to feel anything other than pity. Beneath the scars, the paint, the savage sneers, they were just children, or at least had been once. He knew a bit about Peter, how he stole these poor lads from the outside, bewitched them to do his bidding, turned them into savages. But no matter how savage they appeared, they all cried for their mothers once the Reverend started in on them.

Three of them looked to be fresh recruits; they had no scars, none of the tattoos and other wicked markings. The Captain dared to hold out a little hope. With these, there might be a chance. Maybe he'd be able to win them over, get them to talk, to help.

He'd rescued children before, and they'd all died badly, with their secrets undivulged, all except Billy. Billy had been fresh, like these boys. A little kindness and putting the fear of the Reverend in him, and the boy had come around. It'd been from Billy that he'd learned about Peter, about the Lady and the legend of her precious apple tree. But Billy hadn't known where the Lady and her tree were hidden.

It pained the Captain to think of Billy—he had been a sweet-natured child. But then the change took Billy, and it had driven him mad. The Captain had had to cut the boy down and it still grieved his heart.

The wounded boy continued to struggle for his feet, continued to strangle. The Captain sighed and pulled the boy back up. The boy gasped for air, all but snarling as he glared at the Captain. The Captain shook his head and wondered why he even bothered, why they'd even brought this one along. There'd be no hope for the likes of him. It would be an act of mercy to kill him now and spare him the suffering to come.

✦

A BRISK WIND chased a devil duster through a field of beaten-down cornstalks. Just beyond the withered crop, the fort rose from the sooty earth. The tall, spiked timbers of the outer wall were the same dull gray as the land and leaned against each other as though in need of support.

The procession clomped across a dilapidated log bridge spanning a small brook. The sound of gurgling water tortured Nick. He tried to wet his lips but his tongue was still too dry. Crosses lined either side of the road, made from bleached wood and bones, some jutting out of the ground at odd angles, others had fallen over, lying broken and half-buried in the parched dirt. *Graves,* Nick realized, hundreds of them, all the way to the fort.

Nick heard a moan escape Peter. At first, he thought the guard had hit him again, but then he saw and gasped. Abraham's head sat atop the wall of the fort. Nick looked away, but not before seeing Abraham's dead eyes, not before seeing the other skulls, dozens of them lining the post. *How many?* he thought. *How many boys have died for this island?*

A shout came from a tower near the gate and the gates swung outward. They were led into the compound and Nick got his first look at the village. The cabins were little more than huts, composed of straw roofs and crumbling sod and log walls. There were a few gardens here and there, sparsely populated with withered vegetables. He saw dried fish hanging from a line, then looked again: there, hanging among the fish, were several pixies, gutted and splayed. Everywhere Nick looked, crosses: big, small, made of twigs, made of thorns, made of bones, painted white, red, or black, some with hair, lace, shells, skulls, tied or nailed to them. They stuck up from the ground, hung along the roofs, along the walls, and from every doorway.

Most of the men were dismissed and drifted away. A handful of guards remained and steered them toward the center of the compound.

A woman peered out at Nick from within a dusky doorway. When their eyes met, she raised her crucifix, crossed herself, and withdrew into the shadows. She waited until they'd passed, then followed. Soon there were several women following them, creeping along but keeping their distance. These shriveled black-skinned women all looked the same to Nick, wearing faded, tattered, long-sleeved, ankle-length dresses, their stringy hair stuffed under bonnets, their red eyes wide and ominous.

The Captain brought them to a halt in front of a building with a cross set atop a leaning steeple. This building had been whitewashed at one time but now the boards were faded and as gray and grimy as the rest of the fort. The Captain left them in the yard with the guards and entered the building.

As they waited, a crowd gathered, surrounding them, glaring, pointing, and murmuring among themselves. They kept their distance, their eyes full of hate and fear, until a woman pushed her way to the front. She wore about her neck dozens of small crosses made of twigs. Unlike the other women's, her hair was loose and hung down in her face. She pointed a long, bent finger at Peter. "It be he!" she cried, in a frayed voice. She walked up to Peter and spat in his face.

When this woman didn't spontaneously burst into flames, the crowd became bolder, and their taunts grew louder and more lively. Someone chucked a clump of dirt at Peter, hitting him in the face. Soon dirt flew at

them from all quarters. A woman pushed past the guards and managed to rake her nails across Peter's cheek before they could knock her away. Nick felt hard fingers bite into his arm and found himself looking into the single angry eye of a hunched man. "Demon!" he spat. "You all be demons." A guard no sooner knocked the man away than a woman pushed in and grabbed Peter by the hair, yanking his head back and forth. "You took me John! You shall pay! By the Lord's own hand, you shall pay!" It took two guards to pull her off.

The crowd surged forward and several scuffles broke out with the guards. The guards couldn't contain them and Nick realized he was about to be beaten to death.

A sharp voice, like the crack of a rifle, cut through the rumblings. "*ENOUGH!* All of you. *NOW!*"

Heads turned and the crowd wavered.

"Move aside," the voice commanded.

The crowd grumbled but fell back. Nick saw the tops of black hats pushing up. The crowd parted and three men followed by the Captain strode purposely forward and stood before them. Two of the men were dressed in capes and long coats. They wore tall, wide-brimmed felt hats, what Nick thought of as pilgrims' hats, and both wore black wooden crosses around their necks. The third towered at least a head above anyone, a giant, square-jawed, bald man. He wore an armored collar and steel armbands over a studded leather doublet.

One of the caped men stepped forward and looked Peter up and down. One side of his face was dead, like that of a victim of a stroke, the dead eye milky and unblinking, that side of his mouth turned down into a perpetual frown. He carried a black staff capped with a simple gold cross. "It is truly he," the man exclaimed and pointed the staff at Peter. "The son of Lucifer himself."

A low gasp escaped the crowd and as one they fell back.

The crooked-faced man cocked his head to glare at Peter with his good eye. "God has brought you here to be punished. Has set this task in my hands. I do not intend to let our Lord down."

The man then moved on to Danny, Leroy, and finally Nick. He spied the blue rabbit's foot around Nick's neck and snatched it away with a hard yank. "Satan's toys," he spat and threw it to the dirt, grinding it into the mud as though snuffing out a cigarette butt. He grasped Nick's jaw in his hard hands and held his face to his own. "Tell me child. Do you remember the name of your father?"

Nick didn't trust himself to speak; he just nodded.

"We'll see," the crooked-faced man said. "Take them to the Captain's quarters."

CAPTAIN SAMUEL CARVER picked up the pitcher. He held it high and poured the cool water into his cup. He watched them, four filthy, miserable children sitting on the dirt floor of the cabin. They stared at the cup. Nothing makes a man thirstier than the stress of combat, and these boys hadn't had a drink since this morning, probably before. He brought the cup slowly to his lips and drank deeply, loudly, letting the water dribble down his chin and puddle onto the table. He finished the cup, smacked his lips, then poured another one. He pushed the pitcher across the table in their direction.

"Would any of you lads care for a drink?" he asked. "Just pulled from the well. Cool and sweet. One thing you have to give this godforsaken island. The water's very sweet."

Of course, none of them answered, but their eyes spoke, saying, "Yes, yes we would. Why, we'd gladly trade our left legs for a cup thank you very much." The Captain didn't want their left legs, and—he glanced at the two Reverends seated beside him at the table—he sure as hell didn't care a damn about saving their souls. No, all Captain Carver wanted, wanted more than the whole world, was to know where the Lady and her god-damned apple tree were hidden so that they could get the hell off this accursed island.

The Captain stood, strolled in front of the table, and pulled at his chin hairs. He looked down at the boys. What were their stories? It'd been a long time since he'd managed to capture one of these wild children, and longer since he'd actually gotten one to talk. He'd not heard word of the outside world since Billy. How much time had passed since then? Billy had claimed that not only had the colonies broken away from England, had formed a country of their own called the United States, but that these so-called *united* states were now at war with each other—over slavery, of all

things. Were they still at war? The Captain didn't think so, but he wanted to know the answer to that and so much more. But there'd be time for that later, he consoled himself. For now, he had to convince at least one of them that it would be in their best interest to assist him.

"I'm sorry for what you've been through," he said and meant it. These boys, even the savage one with the wild hair and scars, had all been ordinary children before that demon got a hold of them. It was only bad luck that'd put them in the path of that golden-eyed spawn of Satan. The Captain took another sip from his cup and smacked his lips. "I'd like to share my water. But I only invite friends to my table. Who among you will be my friend? Will come have a drink with me?"

None of them moved nor spoke, but they all eyed the cup.

"Loyalty is an honorable trait. But loyalty based on lies is loyalty misplaced. You've heard only half a truth, I warrant, from this Peter. Would you be so inclined to allow me to fill you in on the whole truth?" The Captain raised his eyebrows and glanced from face to face. "No objections? Good, we're off to a fine start then.

"A long time ago, I agreed to bring these good people," the Captain swept his arm toward the two Reverends, "the Saints, to the New World. A group of pilgrims that wanted nothing more than to escape religious persecution and find a place of peace to practice their beliefs." The Captain made a slight bow to the two humorless, stoned-faced men, and for the millionth time wondered what brazen act of blasphemy, what horrendous carnal sin he'd committed that could possibly have been so bad as for God to condemn him to spend not one lifetime but several with these fanatics. Was it the time he hired those four wenches in Portugal to share their delights, three being sisters and the last their mother? Was it the time he stole a casket of communion wine from the monastery, or maybe taking the good Lord's name in vain as many times as there were stars in the sky? He couldn't figure it out, couldn't think of any sin so great as to merit being marooned with this lot. It must have been something he'd done in a past life. He pushed the thoughts aside and continued: "Two storms sent us far off course, our supplies were dangerously low. Sickness had already claimed the lives of many. We were sea-weary and down to the last rations of rainwater when these shores showed themselves. I got down on my hands and knees and kissed these beaches that day. Ne'er had I been so relieved to have land back beneath my feet.

"The Saints were intent on making Jamestown before the weather turned. So we set camp, planning to stay only long enough to gather fresh water and replenish our stocks. Then the demons came.

"Several women came running into camp, terror-stricken and screaming of demon men. I'd heard of the native peoples of the Americas and their wild ways and thought it was just the womanly hysteria, but what I saw chilled me to the bone—not Indian tribesmen but demons indeed. Abominations with horns and tails, pointed ears and golden eyes, half-beasts and half-men, creatures that could've only crawled from the pits of Hell itself and *they were coming* for us. We shouted at them to leave yet still they persisted. We'd no idea what manner of sorcery they possessed: hexes, poxes, plague? When they wouldn't turn I shot the lead creature and almost wept to see that they were indeed mortal. We drove them off that day.

"We realized that these lands were bewitched and we made to leave right away. But even as we were bringing down the tents, the fog came. Like nothing I'd ever seen in twenty years on the seas, fog so thick it felt palpable. And this fog was alive. It swam with the faces of the dead, with horrible things that I could never describe with mere words. It rolled out of the forest and surrounded the ships. You couldn't see from bow to stern. To have tried to sail in that soup, with all the rocks and reefs, would've been to throw your life to the sea. And it was then that I began to suspect that we might've sailed into purgatory itself.

"The drums started, day and night, relentless. I saw brave men, men who'd gone toe to toe with pirates without batting an eye, fall down to their knees and beg God to show us a way out. But there was *no* way out.

359

Not in that fog. So we hid the women and children aboard the vessels, dug trenches, prepared our defenses, and tried to make peace with our souls.

"They came for us in the earliest hours of dawn, a horde of demons. I fought to remain steady as they burst from the tree line, but in my heart I wanted to run into the sea, almost preferring to drown than face such monsters. The very ground trembled as they charged, filling the air with their awful screams and howls. I would stand against any man, but these weren't men. These were Satan's own children. My legs trembled so bad I could hardly keep my musket fixed. I saw many a man openly weeping. But God spared us that day. Why? I know not. I cannot say it were a mercy. All I know is we fought off the demon horde and that is all that matters."

The Captain cleared his throat and took a swig from the cup.

"Some would argue it would've been better to have died that day. I believe many would've laid down their muskets and surrendered if they'd any idea what horrors lay in store." The Captain paused to consider how many times he'd contemplated letting the blood out of his veins in those early days. It was only the fear for his immortal soul and the hope that he might see his sons at least one more time before he died that stayed his hand.

"Day after day we waited for the fog to lift. Women, children, and grown men even feared to leave the ships. Life on board became unbearable, so when the fog didn't lift, we were forced to try and live on the island.

"Captain Williams of the *Foresight* and most of his party decided they'd rather risk the fog than set foot back on that shore. They left the harbor and disappeared into that swirling wall of gray. We never knew their fate for certain, but shortly thereafter we heard their screams, horrible sounds, like people being eaten alive. Those screams eventually turned to wails, fading to plaintive pleas, then, after many a long hour, just drifted away altogether. But sometimes at night, when the mist comes in from the sea and crawls beneath our doors, we still hear them, along with all those that have fallen, wailing and begging us to come into the evil mist and save them.

"We began to clear the land and build the fort. We planted crops and bred our livestock. We did our best to survive, hoping that each new day would be the day we could leave. But the island vexed us at every turn, blighted our crops, plagued our livestock, and cast spells on us that covered our skin with scaly pox, twisting our bodies and turning us into monsters. The change drove many mad, corrupted them into villainous murderers, and many had to be killed.

"I'd not yet learned of the Lady and her black arts, but all knew there was a source of great evil out there, plaguing us with its sorcery. The forests teemed with wicked creatures, the very trees themselves were possessed by demons. We began to burn them down, to push the evil back. We were determined to raze the entire island if we had to, whatever it took to rid us of this deviltry. And it worked, the forest began to die, the wicked people began to disappear. We saw less and less of the evil ones. I began to have hope.

"Later, once I'd learned of the Lady from Billy, it made more sense. It became obvious that the forest and creatures were indeed all a part of her sorcery, that our efforts weren't in vain. We swore never to stop until either we found her or we erased all traces of her sorcery from this land.

"So there lies the truth. You can plainly see how we've been trapped, tortured, vexed, and plagued at every turn. And if that weren't suffering enough, on top of all that wickedness, the sorceress has summoned that demon, Peter, to trick and steal children. To bewitch children to do *murder*! To force us to *kill* children to protect ourselves!" The Captain took a deep breath. "See me for who I am. Beneath this horrible skin I am a man, father of two boys. Do you believe I should ever wish to harm a child? Have you any idea of the horror in this? Can you not see what Peter is? How he and the Lady are using you? How willing they are to sacrifice your lives? Surely you can see? Yes?"

The Captain gave them a moment to think, to let what he had said sink in.

"All we wish is to leave this Godforsaken island. Look into your hearts. Who among you will help me?" The Captain clasped his hands behind his back, strolled behind the table. He put two cups in front of himself, poured the water, taking his time, letting the water dribble into the cups. The Captain pushed one of the cups across the table. He looked from face to face. "Now who will come and share a cup of water with me?"

The boys remained silent.

The Captain hadn't expected any of them to accept. Not yet anyway, not until they understood just what was at stake. He glanced over at the two Reverends. Men who'd once challenged popes and kings in their pursuit of religious purity, now reduced to little more than superstitious fools.

"Reverend Senior," the Captain inclined his head toward the crooked-faced man, "believes each of you is possessed by a demonic spirit. As a man of God, it is his sworn duty to try and free your soul. Exorcism is a highly skilled undertaking. Your Grace, if it's not too much to ask, would you be willing to inform these boys of the more delicate nuances of your craft?"

The Reverend Senior nodded and stood. The boys eyed him warily.

"We've come to find," the Reverend stated clinically, "that in a case of demonic possession, the possessed must undergo a series of tortures in order to drive the demon out. The host body must become so inhospitable that the demon can no longer bear to stay within. We start with drowning, as this does the least damage to the possessed. Here you're merely held under water until you drown—several times if deemed necessary. If this, in our judgment, doesn't free the possessed, we move to branding, or burning of the extremities. If there is still no success, we try breaking bones, starting with smaller bones in your fingers and working up to the leg and arm bones. And in the end, if all else fails, we burn the possessed to death. As this is the one sure way to cleanse the soul."

The Captain was still amazed, even after all these years, that the Reverend could discuss torturing children with no more emotion than if he were describing the process of churning cream to butter. But that was what made his words so effective, and the Captain was pleased to see that the Reverend's words weren't lost on the boys. He caught their quick, furtive looks, could plainly see the fear in their eyes.

"There's another way," the Captain added. "A way in which you could avoid all of these unpleasantries. Some simple act to prove you're not Satan's pawn. Perhaps one of you could tell us the whereabouts of the Lady? Of the magical tree? This simple act would prove that you were indeed the master of your own soul and there'd be no need to go through the painful rigors of an exorcism."

The Captain waited, and when none of the boys spoke, he added, "Oh, you should be aware that once this exorcism starts, there's little chance it will stop. For the Reverends know well that demons are full of tricks and cunning. That a clever demon will pretend to talk as the child, will say anything to try and stop the tortures. So think hard, boys, once you leave my cabin, you're in God's hands. Now take a moment and consider. For this will be your last chance."

The Captain strolled over to the window and pulled aside the curtain. The sound of hammering came into the room. "Are they readying the drowning cage already?" the Captain asked, addressing the Reverends.

The Reverend Senior nodded. "The Lord's work should never wait."

The Captain sighed. "No. No indeed." He studied the boys. The wild-haired one, the boy with the scar on his face, he'd be lucky if he made it through the day, but there'd been no hope for that one anyway. The two in the middle looked scared, but stubborn. If only they could truly appreciate what was at stake. But the round-faced boy didn't look stubborn. His eyes danced back and forth from the Reverend to the cup to the other boys. That one seemed to understand.

The Captain walked over, picked up one of the cups, and stood before the boys. "So who will drink with me?" He spoke to all of them, but his eyes were only on the round-faced boy.

The boy's lips trembled as though he were trying to make himself speak. The Captain sat the cup down in front of him and untied his hands. The round-faced boy held his wrist to his chest and rubbed the rope burns as he stared at the water.

"Go on," the Captain said. "There's no harm in it."

The boy bit his lip, his face tight as though in pain, then, slowly, he extended a dirty, trembling hand.

"Danny, *no!*" the boy next to him hissed.

Danny jerked his hand back as though bitten.

But the Captain smiled. He had his boy and knew it. The Captain picked the cup up, pulled Danny to his feet, and led the boy to the table, pulling out a chair and seating him. He put a hand on his shoulder and handed him the cup. "It's all right," he said, his voice soft, comforting, like when he used to talk to his own children. "It's all over. The night-mare. The horrible things they made you do. All over."

Danny clasped the cup in both hands and put it to his lips. He took a

363

big gulp, then another, and another until he gasped and choked and finally broke down and began to sob. The Captain refilled the cup.

"*YOU LITTLE FUCK!*" screamed the boy with the red bone in his hair.

The Captain nodded and one of the guards took a quick step over and kicked the wild-haired boy hard in the stomach. The boy doubled over, groaning, but still managed to glower at Danny.

The other two boys looked on with a mixture of confusion and despair.

It's done, the Captain thought, and sighed. "I have my soldier." He bowed to the Reverend Senior. "I thank you, your Grace. I leave the rest of them in your fair and compassionate hands." As the two Reverends led the other three boys from the room, the Captain thought, *And may God be merciful, because these twisted men will not.*

Chapter Twenty-One

Drowning Cage

M ove along," the Reverend Senior spoke in his cold, detached tone as the guards herded the boys back toward the town square. The second Reverend, a short man with a pinched nose and a protrusive overbite of jagged teeth—which made him look like a mole to Nick—trailed along beside them, his hands clasped together as though in prayer, staring at them with wide, pitying eyes.

Nick heard the commotion of the crowd. He tried to swallow and winced from the sharp pain in his parched throat. He found himself wishing he'd taken the water. All this talk of torture, it was a bluff, surely? A ploy? Then why was he so scared? Was it too late to change his mind? To fall to his knees and beg a cup of water? He wanted to hate Danny, but he'd almost given in himself. Would have, if he'd thought for a minute he could actually trust the Captain or any of these men. Because this whole situation was beyond hopeless, it was *ridiculous*. If not so tragic, it would be laughable. Both sides so blinded by their fear and hate of each other that they couldn't see they were all fighting for the *same thing*—for the men to leave this island. *Insanity!*

Nick couldn't fathom how many had died on both sides because they couldn't do as simple a thing as talk to each other. *And if they had, would it have helped?* Nick didn't believe so. The Lady would never have lifted the Mist, because she would've never trusted the men to leave, would only have feared the coming of more men. Both sides had been doomed the moment the men had set foot on Avalon, and *that* was the simple, tragic truth of this whole nightmare.

Nick heard a cry ahead, followed by a cheer. *Oh, no. What now?*

The guards pushed them into the square. Nick was confronted by sullen-faced men and women gathered in front of the church, but none of them paid him any heed, all their attention fixed on the large cross set atop a platform. "Oh, God," Nick gasped. Strapped to the cross was Peter.

They'd crucified him, binding his hands, feet, and neck tightly to the post with rope. They'd stripped him down to his waist, and Nick saw several angry welts across Peter's arms and chest and a fresh gash across his brow. Blood ran down Peter's cheek and dripped onto his chest. The giant bald man stood beside him, a short lash in his hand. Peter's eyes were closed, his face tight, lips pursed.

Nick, Leroy, and Redbone were left with the guards as the Reverend Senior went forward and gained the stage. Low murmurs ran through the crowd. The Reverend Senior stepped up and raised his staff. The crowd quieted. There was an atmosphere of excitement in the air like before the main event at a carnival.

"We've been plagued for far longer than an age by this child of Lucifer." The Reverend swept a hand toward Peter. "But now we have him. Proof that God has not abandoned us. Proof that our sacrifices are not in vain. Proof that we are God's chosen warriors. Lucifer has sent his own son to harry us, to test our faith. Today we send his son back. Back into the fetid pits of Hell from whence he came!" The Reverend smacked his staff on the platform and the crowd erupted in a jovial cheer, with several shouts of "Praise God" and "Amen."

The Reverend looked over to the giant bald man. "Ox, we are ready?"

The giant man pulled on a thick leather glove, stepped over to a black pot, and plucked an iron brand from a bed of red coals. He held the end up, for the crowd to admire a glowing cross. The crowd murmured its approval. The Reverend Senior nodded, then left the platform. Ox moved toward Peter.

The mole-faced Reverend leaned over. "Pay close attention, children. Let the demons amongst you see this very well. Let them see what awaits and maybe they will run off and your souls will be saved."

The painful knot in Nick's stomach told him what was going to happen and begged him to turn away. But Nick couldn't, and when the giant pushed the brand into Peter's chest, Nick saw Peter's eyes flash open, saw him clench his teeth and struggle not to scream as his flesh sizzled beneath the brand.

The mole-faced Reverend grinned, and what Nick saw was not the face of the devout, but the simple lewdness of a sadist.

Peter writhed against his bounds, his breath racing in and out of his chest as fast as a bird beats its wings. And somehow, through it all, Peter didn't scream. When Ox finally pulled the brand away, Peter's eyes rolled up into his head.

It was then, as the smell of burned flesh took Nick back to Marko, to the kitchen, that Nick knew it was all real. Knew that before this day was over, he'd wish he was with Marko, wish he was anywhere but in this nightmare.

"No," Nick moaned and began to tremble all over. "No." His small voice was lost among the cheers and taunts of the crowd.

✦

THE CAPTAIN WATCHED but didn't watch. He'd come to the branding only because it was expected. But he was sick of this charade. Sick of watching people lose a little more of their humanity each day, and sick to death of seeing people tortured in the name of God. What had happened to these people? The Reverend Senior had once been an inspiring leader, a moral compass for his flock. Rarely had the Captain ever met such a fair-minded man. *This island has taken so much,* he thought. *Has stolen our very souls.*

Another cheer, and the Captain could stand it no longer. Demon or not, it didn't matter, suffering was everywhere he looked. He didn't care to witness more. He'd made his appearance, surely that was enough. The Captain turned and began to walk away.

"Captain," a thin, strained voice called. The Captain knew even before he turned who it was. The Reverend Senior stood with his arms crossed, scrutinizing him.

The three boys, held under guard, were just behind the Reverend. Witnessing the branding of the child demon had stripped them of any savageness; all that was left were the wide-eyed faces of terrified, confused children. Against his best efforts, the Captain still couldn't help but think of his own boys in such a situation, and the thought all but brought tears to his eyes. *Given time,* he thought, *I could bring a few of them around. There's no need to torture them.*

"You find this act distasteful?" asked the Reverend.

The Captain didn't miss the underlining tone of the question. *Always watching,* the Captain thought, *always vigilant for the stray sheep.* The Captain's keen survival instinct had been sharpened not only in the forest but, even more important, here, in the village, where these men of God had become more obsessed with finding demons than with getting off the island. *Men who fear demons see demons everywhere,* the Captain thought. "No, Your Grace," the Captain said, and forced his eyes back upon Peter. "If you're referring to branding that demon up upon the cross, then no, it matters not."

The Reverend's good eye bored into the Captain's own until the Captain feared he might be reading his thoughts. "But, Your Grace . . ." the Captain said and hesitated—one misstep and he could find himself branded a heretic. "I do wonder if there might not be a better way for the children?"

The Reverend's eye narrowed and he cocked his head. "Better way?"

The Captain realized he'd made a poor choice of words.

The Reverend took a step toward the Captain. "You believe you know a *better way* than the Council?"

Better than a group of men that flogged themselves, a group of men who raced to denounce their own neighbors, brothers, sisters, wives? Yes, I most certainly do. But the Captain also wished to stay alive, so on this, like so many matters, he kept his true thoughts to himself. "Your Grace. None know better than the Council on these matters. My concern is only about how these boys might best serve the Council. If I could but have some time with them?"

The Reverend eyed him contemptuously. The Captain worked to keep his true emotions veiled, well aware that one word from this man and he would be on the cross next to Peter.

"Captain, God has been most gracious to provide you with fruit for your labors. Do not ask for more than you need."

The Captain bowed slightly. "Of course, Your Grace. The Lord has been more than generous today," he said, knowing he'd already gone too far.

The Reverend addressed the guards, "Take them to the pond and prepare them."

The Captain saw the terror on the boys' faces. Knew he'd be seeing those faces again, at night, when the mist came to haunt him.

THE CAPTAIN PUSHED into his hut, pulling the heavy tapestry across the door behind him, hoping to block out as much of the sounds from the square as possible. He leaned against the door post and let out a long breath trying to clear his mind and heart.

Domitila, one of the few people he could trust—thankfully, not everyone had lost their minds—was combing the tangles out of the boy's hair. The Captain was surprised at what a difference simply washing the boy's face and combing his hair made. It was obvious from Domitila's eyes that she was deeply moved by the presence of this child, and he found himself moved as well. When was the last time any of them had a child near, or any person, for that matter, whose flesh was not twisted and blackened?

Danny had finished the last bit of potato and gravy. He drank the cup dry and set it down. A muffled cry of pain came through the curtain. Danny stopped eating and pushed the plate away as though he didn't want to see it, didn't want to be reminded of what he'd done. He put his face in his hands and began to weep again.

The Captain signaled Domitila to take the plate away and moved over next to the boy. He laid a hand on his shoulder. "I understand your name to be Daniel," the Captain said. "A good Christian name."

Danny didn't look up.

The Captain pulled up a chair next to the boy. "Daniel, you must not torture yourself over this. You need to understand right now . . . you had *no* choice. No one understands this better than me. We're very similar, you and I. We're both trapped by circumstance and we've both been forced to do things that we don't want to do. Things we'd never have done otherwise."

The Captain lowered his voice. "Daniel, we need each other to get out of here. I need to be able to confide in you, to be able to trust you."

Danny raised his head and looked at the Captain, confused but curious.

"There's information I'd like to share with you. Information I couldn't mention in front of the Reverend. Can I trust you, Daniel?"

A trace of hope crossed Danny's face; he nodded cautiously.

"There's insanity all around us. It's like this place breeds it, both with the Reverend and with the Lady. You're a smart boy, I know you see it. You hear what's going on out there. It's madness, but it's out of *your* control— out of *my* control. Nothing either of us can do to change it. All we can do at this point is try to *survive* it."

The Captain sighed. "The others are in the hands of the Reverends now, in the hands of fanatics. There's no hope for them. I wish it were otherwise, but you were there. I gave them their chance and they made their choice. You cannot blame yourself for that.

"All I want is to get off this island. We both know that this Lady holds the key. If we can put a stop to her sorcery, the mist will go away and we can finally escape this hell.

"I spoke earlier of my sons; the oldest, he was around your age when I left. I cannot help but think of him when I look upon you. It's beyond me to do anything but try and help you. Daniel, if you can help me, I promise that together we will get off this island." The Captain laid a hand on the boy's arm. "Will you help me find the Lady?"

Danny nodded his agreement, then thrust himself against the Captain, wrapped his arms tightly about his waist, pressed his face against his chest, and began to sob.

It had been decades since the Captain had been embraced by anyone; to now have this young boy cling to him exactly as his own sons had once done overwhelmed him with heartsickness. *The Reverend will not have this child*, he thought. *No, I'll kill every one of them first.*

NICK SAT IN the cage with Leroy and Redbone, next to a small, dark pond. The cage was more of a basket, woven together from large strips of bark, bamboo, and twine. The basket was suspended a few feet off the ground from a long pole with a ballast attached to the far end. The villagers still had not bothered to give them water, but they had unbound the boys' hands. Nick rubbed his raw wrist and pressed his face against the weave. He could see past the crowd into the square where Peter hung listlessly from the cross. They'd branded him until he'd stopped moving, which meant he was either unconscious or dead. Nick was unsure which to hope for.

The crowd had migrated over to the pond, their faces tight, tense, many looked hungry for more suffering, but others seemed troubled. Nick took in a deep, quivery breath, well aware that *he* was the show now. He realized his whole body was shivering, but not from any chill.

A weak moan escaped Redbone. Nick leaned over to him and said, "Hang in there, man."

One of Redbone's eyes flitted open. He managed a weak smile, a shadow of his former ferocious grin. Then his eyes fell shut. Nick would've thought him dead except for the faint rise and fall of his chest.

"What're they gonna do?" Leroy asked, his voice high and strained. It seemed less a question and more just words coming from a scared boy. Nick wanted to pretend he didn't know, but he did. The Reverend had said they would drown them. From there, it wasn't too hard to figure out. He tried not to think what it would be like to be trapped in this basket beneath the dark water of that scummy pond. Did it hurt to drown?

The Reverend Senior walked over to the basket. He held a tattered Bible in one hand and his staff in the other. He faced the crowd. "Let us pray," he pronounced, and the crowd fell silent. "Lord, we are grateful for the faith you have placed in our hands. Give us strength that we may do your bidding. And bless these children and make them strong for the trials ahead. Amen."

"Amen," the crowd murmured.

The Reverend laid the Bible on the cage and closed his good eye. The crowd fell silent. "Demon," the Reverend called in a low, stern voice. "Hear me for I call you out in the name of the Lord Almighty. Leave these children. Return to the pits of Hell from whence you came." Slowly, he raised his head, his eye opened, and he glared at the boys. *"DEMON!"* he shrieked, his voice filled with wrath. *"LEAVE THESE CHILDREN!"* Spittle flew from his lips. "I demand it in the name of the Heavenly Father!" To Nick, it seemed that the Reverend was the one possessed. The Reverend slapped the side of the cage with his staff and locked his wide, fanatical eye on Nick. "I see you, demon! I see you very well. Leave now, or face the pain of drowning!"

The Reverend leaned in close. "Boys," he whispered, his voice suddenly gentle, kind. "If you can hear me call on the Lord to give you strength. Let Him hear your voice." The Reverend looked deep into Nick's eyes, searching. Nick saw a different person then, a soul overcome with compassion and pity. Why, the man was near tears. The Reverend reached through the bars, grasped Nick by the shoulder. "Please boy, please hear me." And at that moment Nick saw that this man truly believed he was helping them, and somehow knowing this made the situation even more horrifying. "Children," the Reverend called. "For the love of God, find the strength, break free. Defeat these demons. Lift up your voices. Let Him hear you!"

This was followed by many in the crowd, shouts of "Let Him hear you!" and "Call to the Lord!"

The Reverend stepped away, watching, waiting.

Lift up my voice? Nick thought. *And say what?* What was he supposed to say? Nick tried to find some words, but all that came out was, "God help me."

The Reverend slowly shook his head, then nodded toward the two men at the ballast and they swung the cage out over the pond. Leroy let out a weak cry. Many among the crowd jockeyed for the best spots along the bank, their faces eager, like a crowd's before a prize fight. Nick stared into the dark water.

"Children," the Reverend called. "Raise your voices to *God*!"

"OH GOD!" Leroy screamed. "Jesus, God, Lord, help us for Christ's sake! Jesus Christ, Jesus Christ, Jesus Christ, help us!" Nick didn't think that was what they were looking for, but he joined in just the same. "Jesus, please help us."

Then a strange laugh cut the air, causing all of them to fall silent. It was Redbone, his laugh hearty and piercing.

The Reverend's good eye squinted down to a mere slit. The crowd took a step back.

"*TELL YOUR ANGELS TO GO FUCK THEMSELVES!*" Redbone cried, then laughed again, and for a brief moment, it was the old Redbone, his wild, crazy grin in place. "You can all go fuck yourselves," he yowled, followed again by that mad laugh, then he choked, and coughed. Nick saw several specks of blood spray from his mouth and land on his chest.

The Reverend's face clouded; he pursed his lips as he waved to the men beside the ballast. The cage began to drop.

Nick searched the crowd, found hate and fear, faces eager to see him drown, but he also found many that appeared mortified, their faces full of pain and sorrow—*pity*. Many who held their hands clasped tightly together in prayer. These Nick reached out to. "Stop," he begged them. "Please make them stop." But none stepped forward, their eyes fell away from his, down to their feet or to the heavens above.

The water was warm, slimy, and smelled like a clogged sink drain. It was to his waist, then his chest, then his neck. Redbone's head sank below the surface. Nick saw the boy's eyes flash open, scared and confused. Nick splashed over and lifted him in his arms, trying to get Redbone's head above the water, but it was too late—for all of them. Nick took in a deep lungful of air. He heard Leroy scream, "Oh God!"—then they sank below the water.

Stay calm, Nick thought; he knew there was no way out of the cage. If he could remain absolutely still and calm, he might survive. But a darker thought came to him: *survive for what?* Wouldn't it be better to drown now than to have to go through the torments ahead? What had the Reverend said: *breaking bones, branding, burning?* He felt Redbone's body convulse once, then go limp. Nick thought the boy must have finally died, actually hoped so, hoped Redbone at least was free from this nightmare.

As the pressure mounted in Nick's lungs, he watched the surface light filtered down through the murky green water, a world of air so close but impossible to reach. The pain increased and soon began to overwhelm him. He'd heard stories that drowning was almost peaceful. If that were so, then why was he in such agony? Why did his chest feel like it was about to burst? His pulse thundered in his ears. White spots began to bloom then explode across his vision until a bright spectral light filled his head. The last of the air escaped his lungs in a convulsive burst of bubbles. He tried to inhale, but when the water entered his mouth, his throat closed up, choking him, gagging him, causing him to swallow several mouthfuls of the stringy brackish water. He grasped the bamboo cage, squeezing so hard he felt the strips cutting into his hand. Then his head broke the surface, and he was trying to suck in air. He got one lungful, then the contents of his stomach came pouring out of his mouth and nose in a painful, convulsive wretch. He fought to suck in air between heaves, only to choke and gag. He heard a distant, watery wail, like a baby's first cry, and realized it was him. Finally, he began to breathe again, huge lungfuls of air—sweet, sweet air.

Nick wiped the slimy water from his eyes and found Redbone lying in the bottom of the basket, his eyes open, his face pale and peaceful. The wild boy was dead. Nick turned away and spat to clear his mouth of the taste of his own bile. He heard someone else gagging and saw Leroy clinging to the side of the cage, his chest rising and falling rapidly as he tried to suck in breath. And despite all that he'd gone through, Nick found he still had room to wish Leroy had drowned.

"Lord, deliver them from their demons," the Reverend called. "Speak, children. Call out His name. Now is the time to disavow your demons." And on and on the Reverend went. *Demons, and angels, and God, and the Holy who-gives-a-fuck*, Nick thought. Nick now understood what Redbone must have realized: that they were screwed, that the only demons were these men in their long, black capes, that there was nothing they could say or do that was going to keep these twisted, sadistic men from torturing them to death.

Someone grasped Nick's hand. It startled him. Leroy had moved over and was staring at him with wide, terrified eyes.

"N-n-nick," Leroy stuttered. "Dude, I . . . gotta tell you something."

Nick yanked his hand away.

"Hey Nick . . . please don't be like that," Leroy begged, his voice rising and breaking. "I'm sorry. I'm sorry I'm such a fuck. But I need you to listen . . . please. It's about my dad. Something that happened. I gotta tell someone. Nick, please you got to listen."

No I don't, Nick thought, because he had no intention of spending what might be his last moments alive hearing anything Leroy had to say. He turned away.

"Nick," Leroy sobbed. "Don't do this. Okay, okay, I lied. I lied about everything. There, now will you listen to me? Please?"

Nick said nothing.

"I know I'm always fucking up. Just like back home. Just like with my dad." Leroy was quiet a moment. "But that business with Sekeu though . . . that was different. Everything's just so weird here. Y'know?" Then low, barely a whisper. "It . . . that thing, was in my head. I was just so scared. So fucking scared."

And Leroy didn't have to say any more than that. Nick knew exactly what he was talking about.

"Those eyes, they burned into me. It made me do it. *Made* me. You saw it, right Nick? You were there, in the woods. I know you saw it." The terror still showed on Leroy's face. "Felt its eyes, those *burning* eyes."

And Nick knew then, without a doubt, that the horned monster had been in Leroy's head, just like it had been in his.

"Look," Leroy said. "I need to tell you something. Gotta tell someone. Please, man. Please just listen to me." Tears were running freely down his face. "Something I did, something bad. It's about my dad."

God, Nick thought, *he won't quit.*

"Remember when everyone was talking about why they'd run away?" Leroy went on. "Because their parents or stepparents treated them crappy. They ran off 'cause they didn't have anyone that loved them. Anyone who'd look out for 'em. And how I agreed with them and all. Well that wasn't the case. My parents, they *loved* me. They loved me more than anything. Did their damndest to keep me out of trouble. But I kept fucking up, lying to them, stealing from them, arguing, fighting. And every time, no matter what, my folks tried to work things out, tried to fix things, to give me one more chance." Leroy was bawling now. "One day, I just went crazy and . . . you know what I did?" Leroy couldn't seem to get the words out. "I killed him. My own dad. I killed my dad."

Nick stared at him, horrified. This was just too much.

Leroy grabbed Nick's hand. Nick tried to pull free, but this time Leroy held tight. "You want to know why? You want to know why I killed my own dad?"

Nick didn't. Nick didn't want to hear another word. He could still hear the Reverend ranting on, and on, and on about God and Satan, could see the crowd glaring at him and Leroy like they'd personally nailed Jesus to the cross. Nick had had enough of this nightmare. He just wanted this whole mess over with and done.

"Over a beer. I stabbed my own dad over a beer. A dumb-ass beer. I tried to take it out of the house and he wouldn't let me. I don't even like beer. Just wanted to impress some stupid dudes on my street. Can you believe it? We got in a fight and I stabbed him, shoved a kitchen knife into his chest. I didn't mean to. I swear to God I didn't. I don't even remember how it happened. But it did. He's on the floor then, blood everywhere. Is he cussing me, does he look like he wants to kill me? No, he's just shaking his head slowly back and forth and looking at me with the saddest eyes you ever saw. He was sad for me, Nick, not him. Him, lying there dying and all he's thinking about is me! God!" Leroy made a sound like someone had just stabbed him. "I can't get his eyes out of my head." Leroy let go of Nick's hand, rolled into a ball, hugging his own legs, and began to sob uncontrollably.

Nick turned away. Tried to go away, to withdraw within himself, and when he did, it was his mother's face, her smile he saw, her voice he heard.

The basket began to sink back into the water. Nick clutched the bamboo, clenched his eyes shut, gritted his teeth, and pressed his forehead against the weave. "Mom," he whispered as he sank beneath the water. "I'm so sorry I left you. Please forgive me, Mom. Please." And the dark waters swallowed him.

✦

NICK CAME OUT of the darkness. It was not like waking, more like coming back from nothing. He heard muffled voices. He blinked; blurry, dark shapes leaned over him. *Where am I?* he wondered. He was cold and wet. His chest hurt. His stomach felt bloated, his throat burned—he retched violently and someone rolled him over on his side. He pulled his knees up to his chest and retched again; what felt like bucketfuls of salty water erupted from his throat. He felt like he was heaving out his very guts. He kept retching until nothing would come up but thin strings of bile.

"Come forth, my child," came a man's voice. And when he heard that voice, everything came back to Nick. He let out a long moan. So he'd not died. He'd tried. This time, when the black waters came he'd welcomed them. But it had been for nothing, for he was still here.

Nick wiped the water from his eyes and saw he was on the bank of the pond, with Leroy sitting next to him. Leroy's eyes were red and his face deathly pale. Redbone's body was laid out on the ground before them, his hands folded across his chest. Two women were wrapping him in a dingy sack cloth.

"Show yourself," the Reverend Senior demanded. He glared into Nick's eyes as though trying to see into his soul. He turned to the crowd and waved a thin wisp of a woman forward. "Eva."

The woman approached Nick and Leroy cautiously, the way you would approach a pair of poisonous snakes. Nick recognized her instantly as the woman who had spat on Peter. She wore the same long, chaste dress of all the women, but her hair was wild and unkempt, hanging down across her face in long, greasy strands. She leaned over Nick and he got a closer look at the dozens of crosses hanging from her neck. He could see they were made of bones—they looked human in shape, only tiny, and Nick realized they must be from the small people, the pixies and faeries and such.

"Eva," the Reverend said. "Are they free? Are the demons gone from these children?"

Eva thrust out an open palm, letting it hover just in front of Nick and Leroy. She pressed her other hand against her cheek, her eyes rolled back into her head, and she started to moan. Her hand began to tremble, her tongue fluttered in and out of her mouth, and a clucking came from her lips.

The crowd fell silent, watching her every move.

Suddenly she clutched her throat. Her eyes went wide as though someone was strangling her. She managed a few faltering steps backward before collapsing.

Nick stared on in disbelief.

Two women rushed forward and lifted Eva to a sitting position. Eva stuck a long, ragged finger out at Nick and Leroy and spoke in a harsh rasp, "The demons burn me! They burn me throat!"

As though on cue, the two women supporting Eva both clutched their throats, wailed, and fell to their knees. An anxious murmur flowed through the crowd as other women glanced uneasily at each other, then another woman fell to her knees, also clutching her throat, then another, and another. Soon most of the women that Nick could see were clutching their own throats and moaning as though in great pain.

"*THAT'S BULLSHIT!*" Nick cried. "You people are insane!"

"Take them to the post," the Reverend commanded.

The post? Nick thought. *What now?* A moment later he found out, as three men dragged him over to a field on the far side of the pond. There stood several scorched posts with blackened logs and ash scattered around their bases. The men bound Nick's arms behind him and tied thick ropes around his neck, ankles, and midsection, then proceeded to do the same to Leroy. Leroy hardly seemed to notice or care, his eyes distant, confused, lost.

The crowd had followed them over and now made way for two men carrying an iron pot, the same one that had sat next to Peter. Nick could see the smoldering coals and brands.

Nick's legs began to tremble. *I can't take this,* he thought, *I have to get out of here. I have to get out of here now!* He fought his bonds, quick, frantic movements, hardly feeling the pain as the rough rope bit and tore into his skin, unaware of the small, whimpering sounds that escaped his lips or the spittle running down his chin.

The Reverend Senior grabbed Nick's jaw in a hard, vise-like grip, holding the boy's head still. He glared into Nick's eyes and hissed. "I see you, demon. I see you very well. I see your fear. Now leave this boy," he shouted. "Leave him and save yourself the pain of God's mark!"

"You're crazy," Nick shouted. "You're fucking insane! Can't you see there's no demons here but you?"

The good half of the Reverend's mouth turned up in a smile. He obviously took Nick's words as vindication. Nick couldn't help himself at this point and screamed, *"YOU FUCKING LUNATICS!"*

The Reverend spun away from Nick and raised his long arms skyward with a dramatic flourish. *"SEE THE DEMON!"* he shouted. "It can't hide. Not from us. Not from *GOD!*"

"We see," responded the crowd.

The Reverend nodded to the giant bald man holding the brand. "Place the mark of our Lord on these boys. Place it so the demons cannot hide from it."

"HOLD!" called a voice from the crowd.

The Reverend spun around as though he'd been stung. The Captain stepped forward. The man with the brand hesitated, looking toward the Reverend. The Reverend held up a hand, to indicate that he should wait, and glared at the Captain. Nick could see he was making an effort to control his anger.

"Captain," the Reverend said, then his lips moved but he said nothing. He seemed to be searching for the right words.

"My apologies, Your Grace, but I have urgent news I believe you wish to hear."

The Reverend clamped his jaws together and spoke through clenched teeth. "Speak."

"The boy has agreed to take us to the sorceress's hideaway."

No, thought Nick.

The Captain stepped aside and Nick saw that Danny was behind him. Nick hardly recognized him. They'd cut his hair, washed and dressed him in what Nick could only think of as pilgrim clothes. Danny kept his eyes firmly on the ground.

"Child," the Reverend said. "Is this true?"

Danny didn't look up, just nodded in agreement.

The Captain moved up and spoke low to the Reverend. "They're not so many as we'd feared, Your Grace. They're not organized, and more, they fight amongst themselves. If we gather every able-bodied man and make one hard push . . . we can *take* her."

"Can we trust him?" the Reverend asked.

"Yes, I am certain."

"You're risking a lot on this boy's word."

"As you well know our stores are at an end. What few crops the demon children didn't destroy have withered in the field. We're facing starvation. Now is the time to make a bold move while still we can."

"I see," the Reverend said and appeared to contemplate this.

"We would need to leave right away, before they have time to regroup. Your Grace, we could have her tonight . . . *tonight*."

The Reverend's head nodded slowly up and down. "Yes, I believe this is what the Lord wants. Yes, right away then."

"Good," the Captain said and turned to go.

"Captain," the Reverend called.

The Captain looked back. "Yes?"

"I am coming with you."

The Captain couldn't hide his surprise or, Nick thought, his displeasure. Apparently, the Reverend saw it too. "Is there a problem?"

The Captain shook his head. "No problem." But it looked to Nick like there was.

The Reverend pointed at Nick and Leroy and addressed the guards. "Put them in the hold. We will deal with them upon my return."

Chapter Twenty-Two

Old Scabby

The Captain raised his hand and the long line of men came to a halt before the trees. He removed his hat, beating the gray dust from its brim, then studied Danny, giving the boy a hard look. They'd never before dared such a venture, to drive into the very heart of this wicked forest and its dark secrets. Now here he was, putting his life and the lives of his men in the hands of this boy, trusting not only the truth of the boy but that the child knew of the things he spoke.

The Captain took in a deep breath. His ability to take the measure of a man had meant the difference between life and death more than once over his long years at sea. He trusted his instincts. There was no deceit in this child. He simply wanted this nightmare to end, same as the rest of them. *And should this day lead us to our deaths?* the Captain thought.

Then what of that? He'd grown weary of this game. Better a quick death in battle than to starve as the last of their potatoes rotted in the dead soil. But the Captain didn't believe the day would end in their deaths. He had over seventy well-armed men. Peter and his demons had been crushed, and now his brave men were ready to find the sorceress and finish this mess.

The Captain signaled the men to form up and they marched silently into the trees, two abreast, weapons at the ready. They worked their way up a steady incline until they found a spot of high ground in which they could survey the gray land around them.

The Captain saw two wide, muddy creeks snaking through the marshland below. He sat a hand on Danny's shoulder. "Which one, Daniel? The one just below?" The Captain pointed. "Or the wider one farther north?"

"Farther north," Danny said without hesitation.

The Captain was relieved that the boy was confident in the path, but it troubled him that the boy was so quiet, so withdrawn. The Captain understood why, he just wished there was a way he could make Danny see that he was doing the right thing. *Well,* he thought, *there'll be time for healing once we're off this island, once we've left all the evil behind.* Then maybe he could start to heal as well. A wry grin pushed at the Captain's mouth. *How long,* he wondered, *did it take a man to put centuries' worth of nightmares behind him?*

It wasn't long before they came upon the creek, and still no sign of resistance; in fact, they'd found no sign of life whatsoever. The woods were gray, seemed dead. The Captain signaled them onward and the company fell silent, listening and watching as they resumed their march along the muddy bank.

The Reverend slipped, the second time in less than a minute. His personal guard, the thick-necked brute Ox (whose true name was Oxenburg; he had been the gunnery sergeant on the *Creed* before finding God), tried to lend the Reverend a hand, only to cause both men to slide into the knee-deep creek. The Reverend, the live side of his face now a nasty snarl, slapped Ox's big hands away.

The Captain was very careful not to let any sign of his smile show. Even out here, even among his own troops, the Reverend's influence was strong enough to have him flogged or killed at a word.

The Captain couldn't remember the last time he'd seen the Reverend outside the compound, much less in the wilds. The Reverend's cape was flamboyant and dramatic when he strolled about the village, but out here, among the brambles and mud, it caused considerable annoyance, collecting mud along the hem and—much to the Captain's delight—the Reverend was reduced to hiking the cape up like a woman carrying her skirt as he tried to navigate the thorns and muck.

It was as the last light of the day began to fade that Danny halted. The shadows had grown deep and impenetrable, and the woods seemed to close in about them.

"There," Danny pointed.

The Captain peered ahead, tried to see what the boy was pointing at. "What is it?" he asked.

"The stones. That's where we cross. That's the Lady's Wood there."

"Oh," the Captain said. "And her tree? Is it much farther?"

"No, not really."

After all he'd been through this long day, the Captain knew he should be weary, but instead he felt wide awake; his heart raced. After untold decades, would all finally end? It was all he could do to keep from sprinting up the trail. "Move out," he ordered. The men crossed the stones and marched into the forest, toward the Lady and her tree.

✦

ULFGER HELD CALIBURN out before him, examined the runes running along the broken blade. The sword had drunk plenty of blood this day, yet no stains marred its dark steel. How many had he tracked down—ten, a dozen?

He looked at the charred remains on the ground before him. The sword had found the two elves guilty, had worked its vengeance. Ulfger inhaled deeply, enjoying the smell of Avallach's justice. He bent, picked up one of their fallen torches, then stepped toward the elven barracks. He rapped the hilt of Caliburn against the barred door.

"I give you one last chance," Ulfger shouted. "Come out and face Avallach's judgment honorably or burn alive as cowards."

He could sense them, five of them, they'd barred and barricaded the door and hid within. He knew they wouldn't come out, their fear was too strong.

Ulfger strolled to the corner of the entranceway and set the torch to the shingles over the archway. The ancient wood caught easily and it wasn't long before smoke began to billow out from the cracks of the walls and windows.

He drank in their desperation, their panic, closed his eyes and watched them move to the back of the structure. He strolled around the building and waited beneath an oval window. *Avallach*, he thought. *You make this too easy.*

Ulfger heard them choking and coughing. The shutters sprang open and smoke poured out. An elf leaped through the smoke, landed hard, wiping frantically at his eyes as he stumbled to his feet.

Ulfger brought Caliburn down upon the elf's neck, but he didn't cut the elf's head off as he so easily could have. He merely nicked the elf, just enough to break the skin. He'd learned it was far better to let the sword decide who lived or died, who was honorable and who was a traitor. So far, it had condemned all it had touched. The elf let out a wail as his skin blackened and sizzled away from the bone.

A sharp pain drove into Ulfger's side. He let out a cry, fell to one knee. He was shocked to find a spear hanging from his ribs.

The remaining four elves sprang from the window and raced past him.

Ulfger grabbed the shaft and yanked it free with a loud grunt. There was no blood, but the wound was deep and there was a moment when it was hard to breathe. Then the pain receded, his breath returned. Ulfger tossed the spear to the ground and followed the elves. They headed north, toward the mountains, toward the Hall of Kings.

"Run rabbits, run," Ulfger called and smiled. "You'll never escape Avallach."

NICK DRIFTED IN and out of sleep. The cell that he shared with Leroy was little more than a hole dug into the side of a hill, barely larger than the two of them. It smelled of sweat and urine. Leroy lay crumpled in a tight ball in the deepest shadow, and hadn't spoken a word. Nick pressed himself against the plank door of the cell as far away from Leroy as their small confines would allow.

The fading glow of the day shifted through the slats, letting in just enough light that Nick could make out fingernail scores on the inside of the door. He let his fingertips trace the jagged marks and wondered how many other damned souls had spent their last days cramped in this pit.

The cell was on a slight rise; Nick could see into the village about fifty yards below. Torches burned around the town square. He could see the back of the cross, could see one of Peter's hands hanging limp and lifeless. Small groups of women occasionally drifted by, shouting taunts or throwing clods of dirt at Peter. Two men stood guard in the square, but they did nothing to discourage the tormentors.

"What a pisser," growled the guard leaning in front of Nick's cell. He tugged his cloak tighter around him. "Damn fog be thick tonight," he groaned, his voice rough as driftwood. He limped about, getting a fire going. The guard was missing his right eye, an ear, his right arm near the shoulder, and had a peg leg starting just below the knee.

He set a torch to blaze and carried it over to the cells. He leered in at the boys with his good eye. "It makes me bones hurt. This fog. Chills me down to me gullet."

Nick leaned away. He could hardly stand the sight of the scarred eye socket.

"Not pretty, aye?" the guard said, grinning toothlessly. "It were your kind done this to me." He jabbed at the open socket. "First time they got me eye. Not so bad. God gave me a spare y'know. Second time they's got me arm. Still, I ain't the sort to let a measly maiming bugger me, nay. But I stepped in one of them little demon traps you boys is so good a-fixin' and it cut me leg off at the knee. Then well, then I started to slow down a wee bit." The old guard set his head back and *hee-honked* like a donkey. When Nick only stared at him, he finally stopped. "Err . . . have to excuse me carrying-ons. If you don't learn to laugh at life it'll surely kill you, that I know." He looked Nick up and down. "You're a pretty sour looker yer'self. Bet ya could use a drink, aye?" He hobbled over to the fire and poured water from a clay pitcher into a crumpled tin cup. He pulled a small slat across the planked door and handed the cup to Nick.

Nick hesitated.

"Go on now, take it. I ain't gonna bite you."

Nick took the water and drank it dry, wiped his arm across his lips, then handed the cup back. "Thanks."

The guard cupped his hand around what was left of his ear. "Eh?"

"Thanks," Nick repeated, louder.

"Aye. Not a big deal. Don't know why they gotta treat you boys so mean. I say just chop off your heads and be done with it, aye. But does anyone listen to Old Scabby? Nay. They all got their airs. Too busy calling each other sinners. Trying to out-God one another. Bunch of silly douches, the lot of 'em."

The guard pushed his hand through the open slat and ran his scaly fingers lightly along Nick's arm. Nick pulled away.

The guard looked up and frowned. "Eh, sorry. A mangy sod like meself shouldn't be putting his craggy mitts on a boy." He hesitated, looking suddenly embarrassed. "Weren't trying to be fresh with you. No. Me Jolly Rodger ain't been good for much more than a hot piss for a half hundred years now and even that's been giving me trouble of late, aye, it has. When you've been covered with scales as long as me, you just tend to forget what a person's skin s'pose to feel like. That's all."

The guard was quiet for a while as he stared up into the cloudy night sky. "Tell me, boy. What's it like out there now?"

At first Nick didn't understand, then he realized the guard meant in the world of men.

"Are there still stars in the sky?"

Nick nodded.

"I wish I could fly. I dream about it sometimes. If I could fly, why, I'd soar out of this damnable fog, right up through them clouds right now. I'd just float up there and stare at them stars all the night long. I used to be a sailor and I know them stars better than me own wife's breasts. Just to see them one more time . . . err, them stars, don't rightly know if I'd be wanting to see me wife's breasts these days, just to see them stars one more time would be enough for me. I could die a happy soul."

The guard slid the slat back in place. Double-checked the chain holding the door shut, then stood and wandered back over to the fire. He lay down next to the fire, propping his head up on a blanket roll, and stared up into the clouds. Nick guessed Old Scabby was searching the sky for a flicker, a glimmer, or any other trace of a star.

And with all Nick already had to feel so bitter and bad about, he still found room to pity this old man whose only wish was to see a star. But it was easier somehow to feel bad for this man than to think about his mother, about Abraham, Sekeu, Redbone, or himself. Those thoughts were too painful. Nick wanted to cry but found he didn't have the strength, and fell into the merciful bliss of a dreamless sleep.

NICK CAME OUT of sleep with a start. Something had flitted across his cheek—*a spider?* He sat up fast. A faint bluish light caught his eye and there, standing between the slats of the door, was a blue pixie—and not any blue pixie, but the girl from the privy, the one with the wispy white hair.

What's she doing here? Nick wondered, and rubbed his forehead, trying to massage his muddled gears back into action.

She fluttered her wings and blinked softly. She looked terrified, glancing around in every direction as though unseen hands might grab her at any second.

Nick was glad she was all right. He managed to smile at her and when he did, to his surprise, she cocked her head and smiled back.

Again he wondered what she was doing here. She fluttered just out of sight. Nick pressed his face against the wood and understood. A chain, hooked onto a long, bent nail, was all that held the slat across his door in place. It would've been impossible for Nick to reach it, but the pixie was trying her best to pull it loose. Nick suddenly dared to hope.

But the chain was heavy for such a small creature, and she could barely get it to budge. She planted her feet against the plank and yanked over and over again. The chain inched up the nail, but each time she tugged the chain, it clacked loudly against the slat.

Nick glanced over to where the crippled guard lay next to the fire. The embers had burned down, giving off an eerie glow in the heavy fog. The guard's chin rested against his chest; it was hard to tell if the man was awake or asleep.

The chain clanged again and the pixie hesitated, buzzing away then back, as though trying to build up her courage. Nick remembered the dead pixies he'd seen on the line with the fish. He wondered what sort of traps the men set for pixies.

She landed back on the chain and looked at Nick. Nick nodded up and down rapidly, trying to encourage her, pleading with his eyes for her not to give up. The chain was at the very top of the nail now. She bit her lip, planted both feet on the board, and gave a mighty tug. The chain popped free, sending the pixie tumbling backward through the air. The chain swung down, hitting the door with a loud smack.

Nick's eyes went to the old guard, sure he'd be up and all this would be for naught. But the guard didn't so much as stir. He just lay there, his chest steadily rising and falling. Nick thanked the stars the man was hard of hearing.

Now that the chain was off, Nick only had to work the slat over. He stuck his fingers through the planks and slid it across an inch at a time. It fell off the clasp, landing with a thud in the soft earth. Nick pushed the door slowly open and slid out of his cell. He sat crouched in the shadows with his heart thumping. *What now?*

The pixie fluttered over to him, hovered right in front of his face, gave him a long, wet raspberry, grinned as big as the moon, and flew up and away, a streak of blue light disappearing into the mist. Nick allowed himself a grin. From here on out, pixies could steal his food any time they wanted.

Nick watched the guard, ready to rush him if he woke. But the guard did nothing more than grunt and snore. Nick peered beyond the rise; the shadowy shape of the back fortifications looked to be less than twenty yards away. It would be easy, in this fog, to slip over unseen, scale the ramparts, and be away.

I'm done here, he thought and headed toward the wall. *Done with the madness, done with Flesh-eaters, Devils, the Lady, and most of all . . . Peter.* He stopped. The Mist was rising, its silvery luminance swirling beneath the fog, its ghostly tendrils creeping through the fortification. He could actually smell it, that dusty dankness. It brought the boy to mind, the one with the Nike high-tops, the horrible scream forever frozen on his face. Nick gritted his teeth. *Can I do this? Can I go in there alone?* Then he heard them, or thought he did: the faint voices of children. A chill crawled up his back. He looked toward the square, to where Peter hung from the cross, and realized he was down to two choices and he didn't like either one of them. He kicked the mud. "Fuck," he whispered, and started back. "Damn it, Peter. You better not let me down."

Nick slipped toward the guard, his footsteps silent in the soft, moist dirt. *This is stupid,* he thought. *I should leave while I still can.* He found the guard's spear leaning against a stump, picked it up, and leveled it at the man's chest. *Do it,* he told himself. *You have to. If he awakes he'll ruin any chance of escape. Now, one hard thrust.* Yet Nick hesitated. He knew this man would kill him in a heartbeat. *But,* Nick thought, *this man gave me water. And he's just an old man that got caught up in this nightmare, same as me.* Nick lowered the spear. *And, if I kill him, how will he ever be able to see the stars again?*

Nick felt eyes on him and looked up—Leroy was staring at him from the open cell. Leroy didn't move, didn't make a sound, just watched. Nick didn't know what Leroy would do and didn't care. Nick carefully slipped the guard's sword out of its scabbard and, carrying the sword in one hand and the spear in the other, moved silently away, toward the town square.

Nick crouched in the shadow of a woodpile and tried to figure out his next move. A light thud came from behind him; he started. Leroy was there, right beside him. Nick flashed the sword around and leveled it at the boy's throat.

Leroy flinched, but held his place.

Nick kept the sword on him. "What'd you want?" Nick hissed.

"Give me the spear. I'm coming with you."

"No," Nick whispered.

"Yes," Leroy said, raising his voice.

Nick pressed the sword to Leroy's throat. "Shut up."

Nick heard a woman's laughter coming from the town square. He could see a few shapes through the shifting fog; one of them threw something at Peter and cackled.

Nick looked into Leroy's eyes. "I'm going to get Peter."

Leroy nodded.

Nick cursed himself for being a fool, and handed Leroy the spear.

THE CAPTAIN STOOD before the wooden structure and watched the flames lick the sky. He looked at Danny. "Daniel, what do you know of this?"

The boy shrugged, he seemed as perplexed as the rest of them.

"We're on the righteous path," the Reverend pronounced loudly. "The Lord smites our foes. His great hand leads our way. Here, here is the proof!" He jabbed at the small, smoldering bodies lying about on the ground. "God has burned them with their own flame!"

Well, someone had, anyway, the Captain thought. He sure hoped it was God, but he had a bad feeling it was something else, something that they didn't want to run into.

He picked up one of the discarded swords and examined it. These were finely crafted blades, odd to have been left behind, but there was plenty of oddness here. He held his torch near the soft earth. Small footprints were scattered everywhere, those of the pointy-eared folk or maybe the demon children, but it was the large bootprints that made him uneasy. He set his foot in one. The prints were substantially larger than his own.

He leaned down to Danny. "Where to from here?"

Danny pointed past the burning hall, to a courtyard.

"Form ranks," the Captain shouted. "Let's keep moving."

NICK PRESSED AGAINST the side of the hut. Leroy was across the way, against another. Nick signaled for him to hold as he peered around the corner. He leaned out slowly, careful to make no sudden movements, the way Sekeu had taught him.

There were two guards, but they were hardly guarding anyone, too interested in entertaining the two women. Nick recognized one of the women—Eva, the one who'd accused him of being a demon. He gritted his teeth, almost growled.

Eva was pointing at Peter and whispering to the group as they huddled. Apparently, she said something humorous, for her friend let out a snort, then quickly covered her mouth. The guards were doing their best to stifle their mirth.

Eva's eyes widened, as though struck with divine inspiration. She plucked up one of the guards' spears, raised the blunt end up, and pointed it at Peter's crotch. She glanced back and forth between the guards and her friend. They all watched her, barely able to contain themselves. Eva jabbed Peter in the crotch. The group practically had a fit as they struggled not to laugh out loud.

Nick saw Peter's face tighten. *So, you're alive after all.*

Eva jabbed Peter in the crotch again, hard, and this time Peter moaned and the guards doubled over laughing.

Nick nodded to Leroy, then launched himself at the guards. And he was fast. Nick was stunned to feel the fleetness of his own feet. He was on the first guard before the man even saw him. Nick bounded off the platform, swinging his sword forward with the full weight of his momentum, slicing the man's head off at the base of the neck. The head careened through the air and hit Eva in the chest, knocking her to the ground. The spear she held clattered to the stones. Eva's eyes flashed wide as Nick came for her, as though this time she were truly seeing a demon. She opened her mouth to scream and Nick shoved the sword down her throat, feeling only pleasure as the blade tore out the back of her skull. He planted a foot against her chest and yanked his sword free, leaving her convulsing in the dirt.

A shrill wail filled the night. Eva's friend had no trouble finding her voice or her feet as she ran screaming from the square. Nick saw Leroy pull his spear out from the other guard's chest.

They both looked to Peter. "Hurry!" Nick cried and they jumped atop the platform.

Peter's eyes sprung open.

Nick held the sword above the ropes but didn't start cutting. "Peter, you promised to take me back. Remember? Swear to it. Swear to it again right now or I'll leave you here."

"I swear," Peter said hoarsely, then grinned. Nick didn't like that grin.

They had him down in a moment, propping him against the platform. "Water," Peter rasped, as he rubbed his wrists. Nick darted over and brought back a canteen from beside the guard's fire. Peter guzzled the water, pouring it over his face and on the blistering welts running across his chest. They'd set the brand to him five times.

Nick heard people shouting, could still hear Eva's friend wailing on and on about demons and devils to the whole world. Nick leaped up, began pulling torches from their stocks and slinging them onto rooftops. The thatched roofs began to smolder then burn.

Nick snatched up the guard's sword and tossed it to Peter. He put an arm around Peter and pulled him to his feet. "Peter, can you walk?"

"Let's see," Peter said, already sounding better.

Leroy got his other arm and together they hurried from the square. Peter stumbled at first, but had his feet under him in short order and soon was walking—albeit a bit unsteadily—on his own.

A woman came quickly around a corner, saw them, and froze. Peter hissed at her. She clutched spastically at her crosses, nearly tripping over her own feet as she clambered away.

They heard shouts and the clanging of arms from somewhere behind them. Suddenly a man in a long cape stepped out from a hut just ahead. He held a torch out, squinting into the dark. It was the mole-faced Reverend.

"Oh, joy," Peter said, pushing away from Nick and Leroy, standing on his own feet. "It's playtime."

"What nonsense is going on here?" the Reverend snarled. He held the torch up and, when he saw the boys, his expression changed from one of irritation to that of horror. "Devils!" he gasped.

A wicked smile slid across Peter's face. "Devils indeed."

The Reverend threw the torch at them and ran. Peter batted the flame harmlessly away and leaped forward. Even with a limp, Peter caught the Reverend in three strides, dropped the man to the ground with a two-handed slash across the back of his knees. The Reverend writhed in the dirt, clutching his legs and screeching. Peter picked up the torch and moved in.

Nick could see people gathering in the square. "There's no time to play around, Peter," Nick said.

"Oh, there's always time to play," Peter replied, his voice cold and hard. He planted a foot on the man's chest, holding him down while he jabbed the sword into the man's shoulder, twisting the blade. The Reverend screamed, and when he did, Peter shoved the burning torch into the man's mouth.

"THERE!" someone shouted from the square. Nick saw a handful of men hobbling toward them, and it struck him that they were all amputees. Then it dawned on him that all the able-bodied men had gone with the Captain to find the Lady. Amputees or not, if these men caught up with them it would be over. "Peter," Nick shouted. "The Lady, think of the Lady." This brought Peter back around. He left the Reverend rolling on the ground engulfed in flame and they raced away toward the gate.

Five men blocked their way. They were cripples as well, but they looked determined to stop the boys.

Peter let loose a howl and charged. Nick saw their faces in the torchlight, the same faces that had cheered and jeered as he was drowning in the cage. He let loose his own howl and raced Peter for them, surprised to find not fear in his gut but only a terrible lust to make these men pay.

Nick zeroed in on the outside Flesh-eater. The man had a peg leg and a hook for a hand. The man brought his pike to bear but was unprepared for the speed and recklessness of Nick's assault. Nick's movements were quick and liquid as he knocked the pike aside and slipped past the man. The man tried to turn, but before he could even get a foot around, Nick kicked the peg out from under him. The man tumbled backward and Nick felt nothing but satisfaction as he hacked into the man's neck.

Peter dropped one, then, together with Nick, they hit the man between them at the same time, leaving him flopping about in a pool of black blood.

There came a cry, and both Nick and Peter spun in time to see the last man drive his sword into Leroy's gut. Leroy stumbled back, clutching his stomach, his face twisted in agony, and fell to his knees.

Nick leaped forward and slashed the back of the man's neck. The man swung wildly at him, missed, and Peter dropped him from behind.

Peter and Nick shoved the slat free of the gate, pushed the door outward. Peter took an extra second to snatch up a knife and tuck it in his belt. They got Leroy's arms around their shoulders and fled into the night.

✦

THEIR TORCHLIGHT BOUNCED and glittered off the high shear walls of the box canyon, illuminating the twisting vines, making them seem to dance like a nest of snakes. The Captain cut his eyes to the man next to him. "What do you think, Beasley?"

"I don't rightly like it, sir."

"Aye, I don't either," the Captain agreed. "Not one bit." He pulled at his thin mustache. "Maybe we should backtrack a ways. Send a few men up along the ridge, there. We could—"

"What *is* the trouble now, Captain?" called an irritated voice from behind them. The Captain turned to see the Reverend and Ox shoving their way up through the ranks. "Why the delay?" the Reverend asked, stopped, and stared ahead into the narrow canyon. "Why, it's a dead end." He snatched Danny by the collar and jerked him around to face him. "This your idea of a joke, boy? Are you toying with us?"

"No!" Danny cried. "The door is right there. I swear. I swear."

The Captain set his hand on the Reverend's shoulder. "Reverend, please."

The Reverend glared at the Captain's hand and the Captain promptly removed it.

"Beg your pardon, Your Grace," the Captain said. "But the boy tells there's a doorway hidden beneath the vines."

The Reverend squinted at the wall. "Well, is there?"

"We don't know yet."

"And why not?" he snapped. "What are you waiting for? Go check."

"All in time, Your Grace. First we must make sure the way is safe. There's no need to senselessly risk the lives of the men."

"Nonsense. God watches our path."

"Perhaps then the Reverend would like to lead the way?"

The Reverend set hard eyes on him but made no move to walk into the canyon.

"You there." The Reverend pointed to Beasley. "And you. Go see what you can find."

"Reverend," the Captain said sharply. "I refuse to allow—"

"*Captain*," the Reverend hissed through tight lips. "You tread a dangerous line."

The Captain sucked in a deep breath, fought the urge to slap the Reverend's almighty sneer from his face. "My apologies, Your Grace. I simply meant to suggest that this is a dangerous path, and we should proceed cautiously."

The Reverend waved the Captain away. "You've made your concerns plain enough."

The men, Beasley and his shipmate John, hadn't moved; they looked to the Captain. *Good men*, the Captain thought. Two men he knew he could count on to stand with him against any foe, including the Reverends and their fanatics. Loyal men like Beasley and John were fewer and fewer these days, for too many had fallen under the Reverend's influence.

The Reverend glared at the men. "Did you not hear me? The Lord needs you to be brave. You *will* move. *Now!*"

The Captain read a silent curse in the men's eyes, but they moved, because they knew very well that the Reverend wouldn't hesitate to have them nailed to a tree if they didn't.

Beasley and John crept slowly into the canyon, scanning the cliffs, watching the rocks and foliage for booby traps. They looked relieved when they made it to the wall without mishap. They pushed the vines aside, uncovering what looked to be a circular incision into the stone.

"Aye, it be here, Cap," Beasley called back over his shoulder. "It looks to be a—"

Something grabbed Beasley, wrapped around his arm, and yanked him against the wall. At first the Captain thought it was a serpent hidden among the vines, then he realized it *was* the vines. The thorny vines grabbed both men—slithering around their arms, legs, torsos, and necks—twisting, squeezing like boa constrictors. The men cried out and the Captain started forward, then noticed the vines along both sides of the small canyon unfurling, reaching for him. He stopped.

Beasley's eyes bulged and he let out a shrill wail. There came the undeniable snapping of bones as the vines bent the men's arms and legs into impossible angles. The men screamed and screamed, their cries echoing up and down the stone walls. The vines twisted the men, ripping their bodies apart. Blood and gore squeezed from their gullets, spattering down the leaves and landing in sloppy puddles on the white stones.

Sorcery, the Captain thought. *The Lady's hand at work.*

A panicked rumbling spread through the men, they began to knock into one another as they tried to press back down the narrow trail.

"HOLD!" the Captain commanded. "Mark, Thomas, Anthony, all of you. *STAND FAST!"* The men continued to shift nervously, but held their ground.

The Captain glared at the Reverend. The Reverend caught the Captain's accusing stare and looked away. *Watch your back,* the Captain thought. *First chance I get I'm going to gut you like a fish.*

"The boy," the Reverend said bitterly. "He tricked us! Ox, take the boy, send him into the vines!"

"No," the Captain said, his eyes burning into the Reverend. "Don't you blame the boy."

"Captain, my patience with you is at an end! I will—"

The Captain spun away, grabbed an ax from one of the men, hefted his torch, and stomped toward the vines.

"Captain," the Reverend called. "You *will* stop."

The Captain ignored him; he reached the vines and shoved the flame into their leaves, driving the snapping, whipping plants away from him. He brought the ax down onto one of the thick stalks near the ground. The blade sliced deep into the vine, a spray of red liquid spurted out. *Blood,* the Captain thought, and was not the least surprised.

He ordered the men forward and they followed his lead, burning and hacking the deadly plants back. Soon the vines lay writhing in their death throes upon the canyon floor, and there, before them, the circular edge of the door was revealed.

Chapter Twenty-Three

Avallach's Tree

ere. Lay him here," Peter said and helped Nick lower Leroy to the ground.

Leroy wrapped both hands about his gut and let out a low moan, blood oozing from between his fingers. Nick wished they had some cloth, some water, anything to help.

Peter glanced ahead, north, toward the mountains. "We have to leave him," Peter said, his tone cold and detached.

"What do you mean?" Nick asked.

"He's slowing us down."

"*NO!*" Leroy cried. "Don't leave me. Please. I can walk. *Please. Please* don't leave me."

"We'll come back for you later," Peter said, but, Nick could tell by the way Peter said it, there'd be no later.

Peter pulled Nick aside. "He's dead anyway."

"What?"

"It's a gut wound. A bad one. There's nothing for it."

"You don't know," Nick said. "He might make it. Maybe we can take him to the Lady."

"Can't you see? He won't get halfway there."

Leroy moaned again, the glow from the burning huts glistening off his wet brow. He bent over almost double. Nick glanced back, could just make out a handful of armed men milling about near the gate.

"Jesus Christ, Peter. He just saved your life and you're going to leave him here . . . for *them*?"

"I'm not going to leave him for *them*," Peter said coldly.

Nick looked at Peter, tying to comprehend.

Peter slid out his knife, keeping it hidden from Leroy. "A gut wound is a slow, painful way to die," Peter whispered. "It's best if we end this quickly. Trust me, it's a kindness."

Nick couldn't believe what he was hearing. "No way. No, you can't."

Peter's face was set. "Don't make this any harder than it needs to be," he warned and pushed past Nick.

Leroy saw Peter's face and his eyes went wide. "Peter, please," he blubbered. "Please, I can walk."

Nick jumped in front of Peter, leveled his sword at Peter's chest. "*Stop it. Stop this right now!*"

"This the way you want to do it?" Peter snarled. "Just like with Sekeu?"

"What? No." Nick shook his head. "You don't know what—"

Before Nick could even blink, Peter shot forward and slapped his sword aside. He landed a solid blow to Nick's chin, knocking him to the ground. Peter was on top of him, a knee planted in his chest, the knife to his throat.

"Tell me, Nick. What happened? What happened with Sekeu? Tell me quick. Tell me the truth and I might spare you. Lie to me and I promise you a painful death."

Nick felt the blade press into his flesh, felt warm blood roll down his neck. Peter's eyes were wild, scary.

"You're about to die, Nick. *Talk!*"

"*I DIDN'T DO IT!*" Nick shouted.

"Then who?"

"Ask Leroy."

Peter set his eyes on Leroy.

Leroy looked like a trapped animal; he shook his head rapidly back and forth. "*NO!* Not me! I didn't do it! It was *him*. The horned man!" Leroy began to sob. "The horned man made me. Made me do it. He made me!" Leroy was bawling now. "Peter, you got to believe me."

Peter's eyes thinned to slits, his lips pressed together, forming a tight line. He shoved Nick away and went for Leroy.

"*NO!*" Leroy screamed and tried to get to his feet, let out a cry of pain, clutched his stomach, and fell. Blood gushed out from beneath his hand as he crawled away from Peter, kicking and clawing at the dusty dirt.

Peter snatched him by the arm and yanked him up to his knees. "*LIES!* I'm sick to death of your lies. Do you have any idea what you've done?"

Leroy brought his hands together as though praying. "I'm sorry. I'm so sorry—"

"*SHUT UP!*" Peter cried and struck him hard across the face. "The heads of all those boys are on your shoulders! You brought ruin to Deviltree!" Peter shoved the knife into Leroy's chest.

Leroy's eyes went wide, locked on Nick as though begging him to help, then rolled upward and glazed over.

"You don't deserve this mercy," Peter spat. He yanked the blade free and let Leroy drop to the dirt.

"Oh, God," Nick whispered as he watched the blood pool beneath the dead boy.

Peter walked past Nick. "Let's go."

"You're insane!" Nick yelled.

Peter kept walking.

"Madness," Nick called. "That's all I've found here. Does Avalon breed insanity? Is that the nature of magic, to drive everyone out of their minds?"

Peter stopped, turned, his eyes flared. "What would you have me do? You think I didn't know about Abraham? Leroy brought this upon himself with his treachery, his lies. Now he's destroyed *everything*!" Peter slammed his fist into his palm. "I'd kill him again if I could."

"You're blaming him?" Nick scoffed. "I saw the heads back there. How many boys have you brought here? How many have died trying to save your precious *Lady*?"

Peter's face clouded. "Everything comes at a price. Or have you not learned that yet?"

"How many lives is she worth?"

"I'd give a thousand lives to save her."

"You mean you'd give the lives of a thousand children to save her. Don't you?"

Peter leaped at Nick, grabbed him, and shoved his knife beneath his throat.

"*GO ON!*" Nick cried. "Fuck, what's one more to you? What's one more head sitting out there on those stakes? You're a monster, the worst kind of monster. You deceive these kids with your promises and lies, get them to believe in you, to love you—to fucking *worship* you. Then what? Then what do you do? You lead them to their *deaths*. How many, Peter? How many have died for your *goddamn* Lady?"

Peter's face twisted into a knot of pain. A low sound somewhere between a moan and a growl escaped his pierced lips. He pulled the knife back and shoved Nick away.

"She owns your soul," Nick said. "Can't you see? The Lady has bewitched you."

"And what is love if not bewitchment?" Peter cried. "Nick, I'd hoped her love would find you. Open your eyes to the magic around you. Hoped you'd learn that there are some things worth fighting for—worth *dying* for. I thought I saw something special in you. But what a fool I was to trust a boy who'd abandon his *own* mother. You're blind. Blind as any of those men—to magic, to love, to loyalty. Nick, will you always be a runaway?"

Nick shook his head. "You never stop, do you? You're still trying to play me, trying to manipulate me. It's all a big game to you. Well save your breath, Peter. Because I'm done playing." Nick pointed toward the coast. "The Mist is there. Take me back. Now."

Peter laughed. "You're the one that's lost his mind."

Nick glared at him.

"You're not serious?" Peter asked. "No, forget it. I have to get to the Lady. Everything is at stake."

"I don't want to die for *your* Lady. My mother needs me."

"Not now, Nick."

"If it weren't for me you'd still be hanging on that cross."

Peter shrugged.

"You swore to me. Does your word mean nothing?"

Peter smiled wickedly, like someone who has just called checkmate. "I had my fingers crossed."

"What? What the fuck are you talking about?"

"That's the rules. You forgot to check."

Nick realized that Peter was serious. "That's *bullshit*! This isn't a fucking game, *Peter*!"

Peter shrugged again and began walking away.

Nick watched Peter go, watched until he was almost out of sight. He looked at Leroy, at the boy's dead eyes staring up at him as though still begging him to help. He glanced back to the burning fort, to the Mist beyond, took a deep breath, and followed Peter.

SMOKE AND THE smell of burned leaves filled the canyon. Even cut from their stalks, the vines still twitched and coiled, but were capable of little more. The Captain stood in front of the circular mark in the stone. "Heave!" he called and the men pushed against the stone. There came a grinding and the boulder swung inward, revealing a dark passage.

The men stepped quickly back to avoid any traps, but also, the Captain knew, to avoid being chosen to enter first.

The Captain caught the Reverend still glaring at him. He feared today he might've overstepped, finally pressed his luck too far. He guessed there was a good chance the Reverend would have him flogged if they made it back to camp, but the Captain had no intention of allowing that to happen. *It'll all be over soon,* he thought. *And when it is, I intend to see you hung like a common criminal.*

The Captain held his torch before him and peered into the dark tunnel, then back at his men. "Any takers?" The men studied their feet and examined their belts and harnesses. The Captain let out a sigh and drew his sword. "Then follow me." He ducked into the dark passage and sprinted toward the dim light ahead. *This is where they will take us,* he thought and steeled himself for an attack. He found no ambush, no traps, only a soft, mossy trail leading up to a steep, rushing creek.

The men filed out behind him, their torchlight setting the thick mist aglow. They marched two abreast up the path, weapons drawn, ready for whatever might challenge their right of way. But the forest was quiet, the only life the Captain caught sight of were the tiny lights darting about in the greenery.

This is too easy, the Captain thought. He didn't like it. *Where's the resistance? What are they waiting for?*

Ahead, dozens of waterfalls cascaded down the sheer mountain face, the stones so white as to almost glow, bright enough that they hardly even needed their torches. He would've considered it beautiful if he'd not been so aware of its bewitchment.

"Daniel, we're here, aren't we? This is her place?"

Danny nodded.

"Which one? Where does she hide?"

The boy hesitated.

"Daniel," the Captain whispered. "It is the right thing to do. So many have died because of her. Free yourself of her bewitchment."

Daniel slowly raised a hand and pointed to the smaller falls, the one farthest in.

The Captain led the men up to the falls. He could see that there was indeed an opening behind the cascading water. He looked back into the faces of his men, men who had served him well, both at sea and here, among the horrors of this demon land, men that still held on to their sanity after being plagued, twisted, and tormented, and for no other crime than landing on the wrong shore. The Captain was ready to end this nightmare, hungry to finally be able to strike back at the demon that had plagued him for an age. He could see his men were hungry too.

The Captain mounted the steps. His heart drummed in his chest. He had no idea what sorcery awaited beyond these falls, only knew it didn't matter, because it was time for a reckoning. One way or another, they would end it here and now.

"Steady men," he called. "On my order."

PETER DRANK DEEP, then dunked his head in and out of the stream, letting the cool water revive him. He rolled onto his back upon the sandy bank, trying to catch his breath, trying not to feel the stinging welts on his chest, the hundred bruises and scrapes from the beatings.

How many Flesh-eaters were there? He'd tried to take count in the fort, but had only been able to see the ones that passed before him. *What, forty? No.* He knew that was wishful thinking. He'd grossly underestimated their number before and there were more now. *At least sixty, seventy, maybe even more.*

And where were they? How close to the Haven? Could Danny remember the way? The odds were good, Peter told himself, that they'd get lost. If that were so, he could gather the elves, the witch, any Devils that had survived the ambush, and together they could pick them off. It would be dangerous, but they might still have a chance to save the Lady.

He heard Nick's words, "You lead them to their *deaths*. . . . How many have died for your *goddamn* Lady?" Peter frowned. *Stupid kid. What did he know about any of it? Anyway, now's not the time to worry about it—first, we save the Lady.*

Nick came crashing into the clearing, red-faced and out of breath. He dropped to his knees before the stream, gasping as he drank.

Peter had to admit, the kid had kept up well. He'd hardly slowed for the boy. Nick saw him staring, and Peter looked away.

Peter gave the boy a minute to catch his breath. "Come on. Deviltree's not much farther."

THE ROUND DOOR to Deviltree was wedged open. Peter pushed it slowly inward and peered in, sword ready. Most of the torches had burned out, casting the hall into a sputtering gloom. Peter saw no signs of conflict. "Hello," he called, received no answer, and entered with Nick right behind him.

Peter ran to the weapons rack. "Quick," he said, "gather what you need and let's be off." He tossed aside the Flesh-eater's sword and grabbed two blades better suited for his hands, strapped them over his shoulder, so that the swords crossed behind his back, then headed to the store bins, near the fireplace, to round up some rations. He caught sight of Sekeu's body and stopped. She still lay beneath the blankets, just as when he had left. He stared at the twist of long black hair and felt his hands begin to tremble.

Nick came up behind him but didn't say a word.

Maldiriel lay on the floor near the fireplace, Sekeu's blood still on its blade. Peter picked it up and wiped away all traces of the blood. "Nick," Peter said, his voice tight. "Sekeu would've wanted you to keep this."

Nick's brow tightened. He looked at the blade as though it were evil.

"It's a good blade," Peter said. "Might make the difference to your getting home or not. It's what Sekeu would want. For doing your best for her." He paused. "Her blood's on this blade. Her spirit is forever part of it now. Take it."

Nick met Peter's eyes. Peter could see Nick blinking back the tears. The boy nodded and took the sword, started to say something, when a scraping sound, like metal on stone, came from the back side of the chamber. They exchanged looks. Peter pointed to the far wall and the two boys spread out, swords ready.

"Over here," Nick called.

Peter rushed around. It was Amos, the Amish kid, the one who'd been shunned by his own family. He lay on a cot with a blanket half-covering him. His leg and stomach were bandaged and he looked pale. He clutched a tin cup. It was empty, as was the pail next to him.

"Peter," the boy rasped in a weak but elated voice. "Peter, you crazy motherfucker, you're *alive*!"

Nick nabbed the pail and dashed away toward the privy.

"Amos," Peter said, and kneeled down next to the boy, trying not to look at the bloody bandages. There was no need to ask how bad. Peter could see the boy didn't have much time left. He heard Nick in his mind again, *how many have died for your Lady?*

"Amos, where's everyone?"

"Shit if I know. I mean it's been one thing after another. There's been nothing but confusion after that fucking ambush."

Nick returned with the pail, filled up Amos's cup. Amos drank it all and Nick poured him another. Amos gave Nick a queer look, then turned to Peter. "Hey Peter, aren't we supposed to kill this sucker?"

"No," Peter sighed. "I'll explain later. Just tell me what's going on."

"Wish I knew. We were so scattered, y'know, after the ambush. I bumped into Huck and Cutter and they carried me back here. One by one the Devils, the ones that could, drifted back. Tanngnost left, went searching for who the hell knows what. Then Drael and a handful of elves came by looking for you. Drael said that Ulfger was killing everyone he ran into. Said—"

"*Ulfger?*" Peter interrupted. "No, you're confused, that's not possible."

"No, I'm damn straight on that. Drael said Ulfger had the Horned One's helmet and sword. That he was unstoppable."

It came to Peter, the figure he'd seen on the hill. He'd thought it was the Horned One. Could that have been Ulfger? And Leroy? Could there have been some truth to what he'd said about a horned demon? He felt Nick's eyes on him. *No*, Peter thought. *No way.*

Amos coughed and his face tightened. He clutched his stomach. "Sorry, man. This thing hurts like a mother. Anyway, where was I? Oh yeah, the elves. I'm pretty sure some of them went to warn the witch. Then . . . then, shit. I don't know. It's all a big jumble after that. Seem to remember the troll coming back, ranting and raving. Y'know the way he does. But no one seemed to have a plan or know what the fuck to do.

"Oh, hell, I almost forgot the biggest shit-bang of all. One of them elves shows back up. Says an army of Flesh-eaters are headed toward the Lady. After that they *all* left—Devils, troll, elves, everyone."

"How many?" Nick asked.

"How many what?" Amos asked.

"How many Devils left?"

"Oh," the boy's face clouded. "If you count me, maybe nine or ten."

Peter's heart sank, his eyes dropped to the floor. Nick didn't have to say a word. Peter knew what he was thinking.

"How about Cricket?" Nick asked, but looked like he was scared to know.

"The new girl?" Amos asked.

Nick nodded.

"She's fine."

Nick exhaled softly.

"Amos," Peter said. "I'm sorry but we have to go too."

"Good," Amos said. "You're just stinking up the joint anyhow." He grinned at Peter.

Peter tried to grin back. "We'll be back as soon as we can," he said, and hated how hollow his own words sounded.

"Sure thing," Amos said. "I'll be here. Y'know . . . holding down the fort." He winked.

While Nick refilled the water pail, Peter scrounged up a bowl of nuts and dried berries, leaving them with the injured boy. As Peter pulled the heavy door shut behind them, he tried hard not to think about Amos dying, alone, tried not to hear Nick's accusing voice in his head. *How many have died for your Lady?*

"AT MY LEAD," the Captain shouted. The men pressed together behind him along the ledge, weapons drawn, faces set, ready to battle whatever demons lay in wait.

"Now we shall see," the Captain said, took a deep breath, and charged through the falls. A hard slap of water smacked across the back of his neck, knocking him into the wall, but he was through. His feet pounded down a short cavern and all at once he found himself in a green glowing world of lush flora, of leaning cliffs and golden glowing stones. He made it another dozen steps, then came to a stop on the bank of a small, placid pond. He lowered his sword and stared around the garden. The men spilled in, but they too fell silent, coming to a halt behind him.

No horde of demons awaited, only the winged folk in all their variety, hovering or perched upon delicate flowering vines and bushes, along with dozens of docile animals: rabbits, deer, squirrels, colorful monkeys, and birds of every species, all silently watching them. The serenity, the complete peace and tranquility, so far from the hellish, demonic den they'd all expected, seemed to make the men forget why they were here.

But the Captain *didn't* forget. There was no sign of the Lady, but he had no problem finding her apple tree. It was the centerpiece of the sanctuary, seeming to float in the middle of the pond.

"At last," the Captain said and took the ax from his sergeant. He waded out into the pond, swimming the last few yards, and forded the small island.

Here it is, he thought, *after all these years. Here it is.* He hefted the ax and it was then that he saw her, on the far bank, the Lady. She was seated upon a throne of white stones. He realized she'd been there the entire time, that he'd mistaken her for butterflies and flowers.

The Lady stood, and when she did, the Captain saw that indeed, she was composed of butterflies, thousands of tiny white butterflies. Her thin, graceful form drifted onto the pond and stood there atop its surface, leaving only the lightest ripples beneath her. He met her eyes, her deep, cerulean eyes, and realized his mistake as they pierced into his soul. Everything seemed to become far away, as though he were watching himself in a dream. *Captain,* she called, her voice a sweet chorus in his head. *Come with me. Let me take you home. A siren's song,* he thought. *A death song.* But it had him, and all he wanted to do was to follow her into the pond. *Yes. My home is at the bottom of the pond. My wife and children are all waiting for me there.* He felt the ax slipping from his grip.

From somewhere impossibly far away, he heard the Reverend ranting and screeching his scriptures to the heavens, commanding the men to burn the demon's den, to destroy all of Satan's children. The Lady's hold on him wavered. *"NO,"* she hissed, and turned onto the men. Her shape grew in stature until she towered before them at nearly twice their height. The multitude of butterflies making up her body turned from white to red to black. She spread her arms. The golden stones faded and the garden darkened. The pond itself began to glow, an eerie green mist rose from its waters. The Captain felt his skin prickle as wicked shapes boiled up along the surface and began to slither and crawl toward the men, things with thousands of teeth and long, bony fingers, things that wailed and moaned.

"Away," the Lady cried at the men, her voice booming off the towering cliffs. "Lest you wish my children take you into the Mist. Lest you wish to wander for an eternity with your lost brethren."

The men stopped, unsure, some looking to turn and run.

"Hold your place," the Reverend commanded. "It's not but smoke and bluster. She has no power over *God's* children!" And to prove this, he ran toward the Lady, through the mist, leaving its flailing tendrils swirling in his wake. He swung his staff and the Lady broke apart into a thousand black butterflies.

The Captain felt himself released. He swung the ax at the apple tree, a heavy, solid blow. The blade sank into the fleshy bark and a gush of blood spurted from the wound. The Lady screamed as though he'd cut into her own flesh. He swung the ax again, biting deep into the trunk. Again the Lady wailed, not a cry of pain but one of sorrow, and the black butterflies fell from the air, dropping dead upon the surface of the pond.

The men fanned out across the garden and began slaying the animals, crushing the little folk beneath their boots.

The water bubbled around the small island and the Captain caught sight of a silvery shape spiraling up from the depths. The Lady broke the surface—no spectral illusion this time—he could plainly see she was of flesh and blood, a fine-boned woman with ghostly white skin and deep animal eyes. She touched him with those eyes, those dazzlingly blue eyes, held him. She extended her arms and her voice crawled back into his head. *Captain, please come home with me. Your children call for you.* And suddenly he could hear them, *his boys,* calling his name, calling him home.

"No," the Captain whispered and tore his eyes from the Lady, set his foot against the tree, and tugged the ax free. He hefted it high and chopped, again, and then again. The white leaves falling down around him like snow. With each stroke the Lady's voice weakened, was reduced to little more than pleading. He felt a hand on his boot. She was there, clinging to the bank, clawing at his boot, but she was frail, too weak to do more than shake him.

The air filled with smoke and the crackling of fire as the men set the trellises to flame. The pond turned red as the life blood of the tree flowed into its waters. With a final blow, the tree surrendered to gravity, toppling into the pond as though in slow motion.

The pond lost its glow, the mist died away. The Lady floated to the tree, curled herself among its branches, clutching it like a mother would a baby.

"Her spell is broken!" the Reverend shouted triumphantly. "Bring her to me."

Four men swam out. They threw a net about her and pulled her from the pond, dragged her across the mud and before the Reverend.

The Reverend spied the small star hanging about her neck. He tore it away and stomped it into the mud. He ripped off the golden clasps that held her gown, dashed them against a stone. "See to it she hides no other witchery," he commanded.

The men stripped her of her gown, then kicked her into the mud.

The Lady raised her head, her wild animal eyes wide and haunted. She stared at the flame devouring the flowers and bushes, at the mutilated animals, sprites, pixies, and nymphs—and, finally, the *Tree*. A long, anguished howl escaped her throat. The men took a step back. She climbed to her feet, naked, covered in mud, soot, and blood. She raised her hands outward, threw back her head, and wailed, and wailed; the sound echoing off the ceiling and reverberating along every wall and ledge. The pond rippled. The ground trembled beneath the Captain's feet, several stones dislodged from the walls and tumbled down into the garden.

"DEMON!" the Reverend cried, and struck the Lady across her forehead with his staff. She collapsed to her knees, swaying drunkenly as blood streamed down her face. The men seized her. They lashed a rope around her neck and dragged her away, past the dead and burning carnage and out of the sanctuary.

It was only then that the screaming of the maimed and wounded truly reached the Captain, that he became acutely aware of the acrid smell of burning flesh. He coughed and looked again at the apple tree. "Done. It is *done!*" The leaves of the tree began to wilt and turn gray before his eyes, the grass too. Bushes, vines, flowers, fruit, everywhere he looked it was the same: the plants were shriveling and withering away.

As the leaves dried out, the fire spread, and the men rushed to escape. The ground rumbled again and the ledges began to crumble, a large boulder crashed down and tumbled into the pond, sending a red wave overflowing its banks. The Captain leaped off the small island and splashed his way to shore. A flaming tree crashed down beside him, showering him in a storm of fire and ash. He made the shore and clambered his way over the bludgeoned carcasses and through the sparks and smoke to the cavern. He took a last glance back at the garden, now truly a vision of Hell. *At last*, he thought as he pushed out through the falls. *It is done at last.*

Chapter Twenty-Four

Ferry

I have them, Ulfger thought.

The elves had climbed up past the Hall of Kings, to the very peak of the mountain, but now there was no place left for them to flee. He could see them—down on the side of the ledge where even a billy goat wouldn't dare venture—clinging to the rocks against the buffeting wind.

Ulfger couldn't get to them, not with his sword anyway, but he could feel their fear and locked on it, made them shake with it, made their teeth ache with it, could feel them weakening, slipping.

White-hot pain suddenly flashed in Ulfger's head. He let out a cry. It came again, like someone striking his helmet. *"STOP!"* he bawled and clutched the helmet. He fell to one knee. A tremor rumbled beneath his feet. He saw dark smoke rising from the valley. It appeared to be coming from the Haven. Ulfger reached out with his mind, searched, but he didn't need his helmet, he saw their torches far below—an army of Flesh-eaters marching away from the Haven. *"NO!"* he screamed. "No, this can't be! What are they doing here? They *can't* be here!" And all at once he understood what the pain was from. *They felled the Tree.* He let out a wail and began to shake. *They've cut down Avallach's Tree!*

The mountain rumbled again, shaking so hard that Ulfger had to reach out to brace himself. He saw boulders break away and tumble down the steep cliffs. Ulfger found his feet and scrambled back down the ledge. By the time he'd reached the Hall of Kings, the flames from the Haven lit up the entire valley.

He stumbled into the chamber and came face to face with the broken tombs. Scattered bones and busted skulls greeted him, their dark sockets accusing him.

"No— *NO!* This is not my doing!" He kicked the skulls, tripped, and fell against the boat. He saw his father lying twisted in the hull. His father's eyes bore into him, sad and pitying.

The mountain trembled again. Cracks appeared all along the chamber and one of the windows broke and fell away.

"See what they've done?" Ulfger sobbed. "See. You laughed at me, but now look for yourself. They brought ruin, Father. See?"

All at once he heard voices. A billion voices, the cries of all of those that had ever lived and died on Avalon. Their wails echoed inside the helmet until his head rung with it, pounding his skull until he thought his ears would bleed. Ulfger screamed, tore off his helmet, flung it at his father. *"I DON'T WANT IT! I DON'T WANT IT!"*

A section of the ceiling came crashing in, showering Ulfger with stone and glass, exposing the sky above. He climbed into the boat, falling atop the dried fleshy remains of his father. He crawled beneath the cadaver, curled up in the bottom of the boat, and began to claw at his own face. "Take me with you," Ulfger bawled. "Father, please, please take me with you."

A WAIL FILLED the night. It came from everywhere, from the very land itself. Nick caught up with Peter.

Another wail came, followed by a tremor beneath their feet.

"What is it?" Nick asked.

"The Lady," Peter whispered, his face stricken, and dashed up the trail.

Nick raced after him, but Peter was running all out and soon he lost sight of him. It wasn't hard to figure out where Peter was going, though. A red glow grew above the tree line and Nick raced toward it.

The grade steepened, Nick's lungs felt on fire, his heart thundered in his chest, the muscles in his legs burned, yet he pushed on, running as hard as he could. He saw the sky was dancing with fireflies, but when he caught the smell of burning leaves, felt hot ash on his face, he understood those were not fireflies but sparks. Nick passed the elven hall, now little more than charred ruins, went through the courtyards, the small canyon, and up the ridge, dashing around the small brush fires.

He found Peter up to his knees in a small pond. The murky water looked red. *Blood*, Nick thought. *It looks like blood.*

It wasn't until Nick saw the floating bodies piling up on one end of the pond like some macabre dam that he understood that the towering ledges and waterfalls were gone, had crumbled in on themselves, that he was standing where the Haven had been. Water now gushed from the rocks like geysers while the treetops burned. Then he saw it—Avallach's Tree, its limbs curling inward like rigor mortis setting into a corpse, the white bark peeling away exposing bone-colored wood and shriveled veins.

Peter splashed about between the boulders, frantically gathering something from the bloody water. Nick walked up to the bank. Apples bobbed about the pond. Peter's pockets and pouch were stuffed full of them. He carried as many as he could hold and still tried to gather more. They spilled from his arms every time he scooped another one up.

Peter glanced at Nick, his eyes wild, desperate. "Help me! We *have* to save them. Every one of them."

Nick watched the body of a nymph drift by, half her face hacked away, one eye staring at him. Another tremor rumbled beneath them and several large boulders came crashing down not a hundred yards away. "Peter, we need to go."

Peter seemed not to hear him.

A strong breeze whipped through the valley, blowing Nick's hair from

his eyes. Nick thought it carried an oddly familiar scent, something besides the smell of burning leaves. At first he couldn't place it, then his eyes
widened. It smelled like the *city*—*like New York*! He heard a gull cry and
glanced up. Was that a star, or just ash? Nick dashed a few yards back
down the trail for a better view. There, faintly—*a star*! The clouds drifted
and he saw more.

Something fluttered by Nick's ear. A blue glow zipped by. *The pixie,* he
thought. She sputtered right up to his nose and boinked it. "Oww," Nick
said.

She flew a short way down to the path and lit upon the ground. She
flickered on and off and waved him over. Nick followed her and bent
down. He spotted the men's boot prints, dozens of them in the soft gray
mud. Then he saw what she was pointing at: a set of hoof prints. It took
Nick a moment. "The troll!"

"*PETER!*" Nick called. Peter didn't look up. Nick rushed up the path.
"Peter!"

Peter was on his knees on the bank, holding something. Nick noticed
he'd dropped the apples, they lay scattered about in the mud.

Nick shook the boy's shoulder. "The troll and Cricket—the Devils.
They went that way." He pointed. "We might catch them if we hurry.
Let's go—*hurry*!"

Peter slowly looked up, his face confused. "What?"

"C'mon. We have to catch them!"

"Why?" Peter said, shaking his head, his voice flat and lifeless. "It's
over."

"What?"

Peter held up a golden eight-point star. "See?"

"Yeah, so?"

"Her light, it's gone out." He cradled the star to his chest. "The Lady . . .
she's dead."

Another tremor, and a cliff crumbled, sending a massive rock slide
crashing into the valley. The water was now bubbling up all around
them.

"We gotta get out of here!" Nick said.

Peter didn't move, just stared at the necklace.

"Peter, get up!" Nick tugged Peter's arm.

Peter jerked back. "It doesn't matter!" he cried, his voice breaking. "None of it matters now. The Lady *was* Avalon. Without her there can *never* be another Avalon." Then low, so Nick could barely hear, "I will never sit by her side . . . *never*." Peter suddenly grabbed Nick, clutched his arm so hard that Nick winced. Peter's eyes were wide, intense, crazy. "They died! All of them. Died for nothing!"

"Yep, I know," Nick said. "You're a real son of a bitch. Now that that's settled can we get the hell out of here?"

Peter let out a wail and doubled over like he'd been stabbed in the stomach.

"Ah shit, Peter. Goddamn it, cut it out. C'mon now, get up!" Nick gave him a tug. Peter put up a weak struggle, then just quit, all the fight gone.

"I can't even remember their names," Peter moaned.

Nick hefted Peter to his feet, half-carrying, half-dragging him down the path as the muddy water swept around their feet. Nick could no longer see the tracks, not with all the water, but he caught sight of a blue glimmer dancing just ahead, and followed. Nick realized he could see his shadow and was shocked to find a full moon shining down on them. "Peter, the moon."

"The Lady's dead, her Mist is dying," Peter said, his voice flat.

The earth turned spongy. Water bubbled up everywhere. Dozens of small streams formed and raced them down the trail. Nick saw a magnificent oak tilt slowly over and sink into the gray mud. Soon trees were rolling over all around them, either collapsing or simply swallowed by bubbling sinkholes.

The trail leveled out and the streams formed into creeks, the creeks into small rivers. Nick spotted higher ground ahead, but there was a wide, fast-moving creek in their way. Nick glanced behind; only the tree tops could still be seen and those were rapidly disappearing. They had to ford the creek.

Nick pulled Peter into the cold current. It was to their knees in no time and rising by the second. Nick fought for the shore, but the rushing water was eating away the bank as fast as they moved toward it. The water around them turned rapid as the current rushed over fallen trees and boulders, forming swirling pools of churning debris. The creek suddenly swelled, sweeping both of them from their feet. Nick struggled to keep his hold on Peter as the current took them, spun them, pulled them beneath

423

the foaming waves. Nick wasn't sure which way was up, yet still would not let go of Peter. His back slid across stones and his head broke the surface. A towering boulder was right before them. Nick snagged a hold, fighting to keep his grip as he held Peter's head above the water.

"*GRAB HOLD!*" Nick screamed. "*GRAB HOLD, PETER! OR YOU WILL DROWN!*"

Peter made no effort. His eyes seemed to be welcoming death.

"*GODDAMN IT, PETER!*" Nick shouted. "*DON'T QUIT! DON'T YOU DARE—*" Nick saw the tree—an entire tree tumbling right for them. "Oh shit!" he cried as the limbs smashed into the boulder, raking across the stone, tearing Peter from his grasp and pulling them under in a tangle of twisting branches. Then all was churning bubbles and tumbling darkness as sharp pebbles and twigs and leaves pelted his face and arms. Nick's chest began to tighten, white spots flashed across his vision, and he realized he was going to drown after all, after all the crap he'd made it through, and he managed to be mad.

Nick slammed into something solid, and thick fingers grabbed hold of his arm, yanking him from the current. He fell onto a rocky bank, coughing and spitting out water. He heard a tired sigh and wiped the water and mud from his eyes. There, towering above him, was Tanngnost. Behind the troll stood Drael and four elves; behind them, sitting on the ground, was Peter, looking like a drowned rat.

"Nicky?" came a cautious voice. Cricket came up to him. She looked torn between relief and horror.

"Get away from him," commanded a stern voice. A Devil Nick knew as Cutter glowered down at him. Nick had never heard more than two words from Cutter, had rarely seen him join in on the games or jokes. He was a serious, reserved kid with dark, severe eyes, and Nick was alarmed to find those eyes locked on him now. Behind Cutter stood the remaining Devils, seven of them, and every one of them looked ready to slit Nick's throat.

"He owes us blood," Cutter said and slid his knife from his belt.

"Oh looky, the children are going to play," came a little girl's voice.

Nick spun around to see the three sisters, a handful of barghest, and the witch.

The Devils surrounded Nick.

Nick looked for Peter, but Peter lay crumpled in a ball, his hands wrapped around his head, lost to the world around him.

"You can't do that!" Cricket said. "You can't just kill him. Tanngnost, make them stop!"

The troll's eyes were filled with resigned sadness, but he made no move to stop them.

"Avallach demands your life," Cutter said, and the Devils nodded in agreement.

Nick looked from face to face and what he saw chilled him. Their faces—so like the Flesh-eaters in the village—filled with the same fanaticism, the same need to spill blood to appease their god.

"Leave him alone," came a low, flat voice. Peter.

The Devils exchanged confused looks.

"But Peter," Cutter said. "He killed Sekeu. He—"

"No," Peter said. "It wasn't him."

The Devils actually looked disappointed.

"Then who?" Cutter asked.

Peter didn't answer. He just held his head in his hands.

"We'll sort this out later," Tanngnost said. "For now we have to keep moving. The Lady can't be far."

Peter's head jerked up. "What? What did you say?"

"The Lady, Peter. The Flesh-eaters have her."

"She's alive?"

"Yes. Didn't you know?"

Peter was on his feet, he grabbed the troll's arm. "You saw her? You're sure?"

"Yes," the troll said. "I thought you knew."

Peter's eyes lit up, suddenly alert and eager. "Let's go!"

✦

THE CAPTAIN STOOD on the bank of the dark, rising water and watched the body drift past. A woman from the fort, floating facedown, her long hair reaching out like tentacles in the swirling current. A moment later, a portion of a roof drifted by, then two more bodies, a man and a woman, then a pig.

He looked to the heavens; for the first time in so many centuries they had the stars and moon—like the face of an old and dear friend—to light their way. *God, what a welcome sight.* But it did them little good when the very land was collapsing beneath their feet. The ships had succumbed to the sea ages ago. They'd stored the boats upstream from the fort. But if the fort itself was gone, how could they ever find the boats?

He glanced at the sorceress, or demon, or whatever she be. She stood nude, muddy, with dried blood streaking down her face and breasts. They'd strapped a rope around her neck and pulled her along, kicking and beating her when she'd fallen. But she didn't seem to feel any of it, only stared ahead, eyes focused on nothing. The Captain was disgusted by this senseless torment. Her spell was broken. They should kill her and be done. But the Reverend demanded they bring her back to the church, to burn her upon holy ground, to burn her before God. Only there was no more holy ground. So what would these madmen do now?

The wall of mist was sliding down from the sky, pulling away from the shore, evaporating even as he watched. Soon the sky and the sea would be clear. How many untold days and nights had he prayed for this? And now their prayers were answered. Now what? What good did it do them if they had no boats? They were still just as trapped—proof that God was merely playing with them.

Most of the men paced in tight circles or shifted aimlessly from foot to foot, staring slack-jawed up at the stars or down at the rising water. The others kneeled around the Reverend and lent their voices to his prayer as he paced rapidly to and fro, face to the heavens, begging God for a miracle.

The Captain kept Danny close. He saw the fear on the boy's face. The Captain scanned the horizon. There was no more high ground. Water bubbled up everywhere, streams, creeks, and rivulets were converging, rapidly covering all the remaining land. Soon they'd all be in the sea. Another bit of thatched rooftop slipped past. They might not have any boats, but if he could rope together some of this debris, Daniel and he might be able to drift to shore. Only he didn't believe the Reverend would allow it. No, if a miracle didn't present itself, he was sure the Reverend intended for them all to go down together. *Now,* he thought, *while the Reverend's distracted, it's a good time for us to slip away.*

The Captain spied a clump of boulders and bushes banking the water not thirty feet away. If they could get past that unseen, they'd be free. He grabbed the boy's hand and headed away. They'd barely made ten strides when a fervent voice called out. "Where are you going?"

The Captain knew that the Reverend was addressing him, but he kept walking.

"Captain."

The Captain cursed under his breath and turned.

"Captain, where are you going?"

"Trying to find higher ground," he lied.

"There is no high ground."

"We shall see."

"Bring me the demon child," the Reverend said coolly.

The Captain felt Danny press against him, the boy's hand tighten in his grip.

"Demon child?" the Captain said, and, realizing he was almost shouting, forced himself to lower his voice. "Daniel has led us to the sorceress. Has proven himself free of any demons." The Captain let his hand drop to the hilt of his sword. He continued to withdraw, one step, then another.

The Reverend's eye blazed. "We'll let God be the judge of that. Now bring me the boy."

When the Captain didn't comply, the Reverend nodded to Ox. The giant and a dozen men fanned out, surrounding the Captain.

The Captain looked from man to man, searching for a loyal face. He found none. These men were scared, fearing for their immortal souls— they'd do whatever the Reverend asked. *There's nothing for it*, the Captain thought. If he drew his sword, both Daniel and he would be dead in an instant. He whispered to the boy, "I'll not leave you. I promise."

The men approached warily, keeping a keen eye on the Captain. Ox pointed his sword at the Captain's throat while a guard pulled Danny away. "And his weapons," Ox said. The Captain eyed him sharply as he was stripped of his sword and knife. Once the Captain was disarmed, Ox grinned and smacked the Captain twice lightly on the cheek. "Good man."

Ox yanked the boy over to the Lady. He snatched the loose end of the rope tied about the Lady and looped it around the boy's neck, binding them together. Danny let out a strangled cry as the giant jerked it tight. Ox slapped Danny on the side of the head. "Stop your whining, brat."

The Captain clenched his hands into fists, fought to hold himself in check. He felt sure they'd all be dead soon. None of this should matter, but it did.

"ANGELS!" a man cried, his voice breaking with emotion. He pointed out across the water. "A city of angels."

As the fog swirled away, towers of glittering, spiraling lights materialized out of the night.

"The Kingdom of Heaven," the Reverend called, raising his arms out before him. He fell down to his knees, tears falling from his eyes. "God's Kingdom has come for us at last!"

The Captain found himself questioning his own senses. Could this be Heaven? He saw lights in the sky, some hovering, some blinking, others shooting along. Were those indeed angels? He heard a horn blaring somewhere in the distance. The breeze picked up, and he caught strange, unfamiliar smells, similar to oil and turpentine mayhap, and familiar smells as well, of fish, garbage, and sewage, like the canals of Venice. Did Heaven smell of sewage? The Captain didn't think so.

The horn again, louder, closer, but not like any horn he had ever heard before. Again, a long, continuous burst, this time much closer, much louder. Whatever it was, it was heading their way. The Captain searched through the last traces of the mist. There, a great glow coming toward them out of the night!

"A vessel," someone shouted.

Yes, thought the Captain, he could hear the water plowing against its bow, could see two levels of lanterns along its port side; this was a vessel, a magnificent vessel.

The Reverend got up off his knees and walked toward the approaching vessel, his arms outstretched. "The Lord has come for us."

NICK SAW THE Manhattan skyline break through the Mist, close enough he could just make out a few figures milling about the docks. The sight caused them to stop in their tracks, but only for a moment, as the land was disappearing beneath their feet. At this point, they were barely staying ahead of the tide.

"There they are!" Peter hissed, and pointed. And so they were. At least seventy Flesh-eaters clumped together on a spot of high ground.

Nick had no idea what the plan was. There was nothing they could do against that many men, and they'd all be in the harbor soon anyway. But this didn't seem to slow Peter down; he sprinted headlong after them, leaving the rest of them racing to catch up and Tanngnost huffing and puffing not to be left behind.

A horn blast broke the silence. *A ferry!* Nick thought. It sounded nearby. *There!* He could see its lights and . . . *oh no,* it looked like it was going to crash right into the Flesh-eaters! Nick recognized it at once as one of the Staten Island ferries. The ferry appeared to be trying to turn, trying to avoid a landmass that shouldn't even be there. The men leaped back, scrambling out of the way as the ferry slid to ground. A moment later, they were climbing up the front deck and boarding the ferry. *This should prove interesting,* Nick thought.

The barghest raced past, followed by the Devils and elves, all heading for the ferry. Nick realized that if he didn't get onboard he'd be going for a late-night swim, and took off after them.

The ferry reversed its engines and the water began to boil. The stern swung about, broadsiding the bank. Peter leaped onto the railing at the rear of the boat; the rest of the Devils and elves followed suit, then the barghest. Cricket splashed through the knee-high water until Peter pulled her up. Nick got a leg on deck, heard girlish giggles, and watched the witch and her daughters crawl up the sideboard like spiders.

Tanngnost brought up the rear, his long, galloping lope splashing through the swirling tide. The troll got a hand on deck and Peter, Cutter, and Huck helped haul him onboard just as the ferry pulled away into open water.

Now what? Nick wondered, and watched the last of the island disappearing into the bay. It wasn't sinking, but crumbling and dissolving, like stirring cocoa powder into milk. Sparkling phosphorescent vapors bubbled to the surface and evaporated into the air.

Nick thought he would've been glad to see the last of Avalon, but now, as an unexpected forlornness clutched him, he realized he didn't, at least not like this. He felt he was watching the very heart of the world dying, disappearing, and sinking away forever.

PART V

Ulfger

Chapter Twenty-Five

God's House

The Captain ran his hand along a girder. *A ship of floating steel,* he marveled. He glanced from light fixture to light fixture. *Light without flame.* These things were indeed miraculous, but they were not miracles. There was an explanation. These men and women were just people, not lost souls on their way to salvation, nor were they angels, despite the miraculous city or marvelous ship. He watched a balding man with sagging jowls and blotchy skin backing away, falling over his own feet as he stumbled up the narrow stairs to the second level. *No, most certainly not angels.*

The fore cabin had been full when they'd boarded. But once the passengers had gotten a good look at the bedraggled crew of castaways, they'd quickly scrambled to the back of the ship or upper decks. Even now the

Captain could see a few horrified but curious faces peeking at them from around walls and down the stairwells. He noticed there was one passenger who had not given up her seat, an elderly woman wrapped in a fuzzy yellow afghan. She didn't look so much horrified as simply perturbed.

The Captain walked over to the old woman. "Madam, may I?" He indicated the vacant seat next to her. She didn't answer, just gave him a sour look. The Captain decided it best to stand. After all, it was good to have the feel of the sea under his feet once more.

"Pardon me, madam," he began. "Do—"

"You think you could tell those damn fools to shut the door?" she said gruffly and tugged her afghan tighter around her.

The Captain followed her glare to where the Reverend and most of the men stood crammed out on the front deck, crowded so tight that they'd wedged the wide double doors open, allowing a strong, biting wind to blow through the cabin.

"You'd think they'd never been on a boat before," the woman huffed. She leaned forward, squinting through her tortoiseshell glasses, the thick lenses distorting her eyes, swallowing up her whole face, making her look to the Captain like some dour insect. "Sure are a *peculiar* lot."

The Captain had to agree, they were indeed a peculiar lot, pointing and cooing at the city like a bunch of pigeons, or wandering about gawking at the lights, prodding and caressing the seats, windows, and every shiny surface.

"Madam, if you don't mind, would you enlighten me as to the year?"

The woman sniffed loudly, then wrinkled her nose. "Good Lord, is that you?" She leaned away from the Captain. "You smell worse than a sack of sardines."

This brought a smile to the Captain. "The year, madam?"

"Are you asking me what year it is? Good gracious, have you been living in a hole or something?"

"Of sorts."

"It's 2005. No wait, 2006. It's 2006."

The Captain winced. "Of the year of the Lord?"

"Why yes, I'm certain. And you know how old that makes me? Ninety-two. You'd never guess by looking at me, would you? You wanna know how I stay so sharp, keep my figure? I walk every goddamn day. While those other old biddies are sitting around on their fat tushes, I'm putting in my two miles. Rain or shine. I've already outlived two husbands. You want to know what else?"

The old woman prattled on, but the Captain was no longer hearing her. *Over three hundred years.* He needed to sit down after all. How had three centuries slipped away? He'd often considered that time moved differently there in purgatory, but had clung to the belief that out here, in the real world, time was on hold. But time had not waited. His children, his grandchildren, even their children's children's children would be long in the grave. There was no one to return to. No home for him anywhere. What was left for him?

Someone was nudging him.

"What the hell's he carrying on about so?" the woman in the afghan asked.

The Captain blinked, he'd been so lost in thought that it took a moment to understand she meant the Reverend.

The Reverend stood on the bow, arms spread wide as though ready to embrace the city, his long, black cape fluttering dramatically in the wind. He was shouting to be heard over the ferry's engine, ranting on and on about God welcoming His children home.

"I wish I knew," the Captain answered.

"Well, if you ask me, the cuckoo bird has done eaten every one of that man's crackers."

The Captain's face hardened. "Yes," he said absently. "Something certainly has." And he thought of Danny—this child that he barely even knew—and realized the boy was all he had left that mattered and that the boy was at this very moment at the mercy of a murderous madman.

He stood and walked rapidly to the doors, needing to see the boy. Danny stood in front of the Reverend. The Captain attempted to make eye contact, to give the boy some reassurance, but Danny only stared down at the deck.

The Captain looked out past the Reverend. He could see they would be docking soon. Danny was running out of time.

435

✦

NICK GRIPPED THE railing and held tight. They were coming upon the ferry terminal fast, too fast.

Peter, the Devils, the elves, the witch and her brood had all climbed up onto the roof of the ferry and were now peering down over the front railing. There were two decks below them. Most of the ship's passengers were crowded on the deck directly below, the Reverend and Flesh-eaters on the deck below that, the very bottom deck.

Nick glanced over his shoulder at the pilot house. The pilot had one hand wrapped tight around the wheel as though for dear life, and the radio pressed to his lips with the other. He was jabbering away, not once taking his eyes off the group of barghest hanging from the rail just outside his window. Nick wished he'd pay a little more attention to where they were going, because it looked like they were heading straight for the pylons.

Peter sat perched on the lip of the overhang, sword in hand, poised to leap down upon the Reverend at any moment, his eyes restless and wild, like those of a bird of prey.

The Lady was tied to Danny, and both were held by the giant Flesh-eater, the one called Ox. Nick could see Peter struggling to hold back. But with that many Flesh-eaters around, even Peter seemed to understand that an ill-timed attack could cost the Lady her life.

The Devils watched Peter, ready to attack on his signal, every one of them prepared to throw their lives away, though not for the Lady, Nick knew, but for Peter, for their feral messiah himself. *How many more, Peter?* Nick wondered. *How many more is she going to cost?* Peter caught Nick staring at him and looked away.

"We're gonna hit!" Dirk cried.

Peter slid back next to Nick and gripped the rail. "Nick," he said. "She *is* Avalon. Do you not understand? If we can save her, then maybe it wasn't all for nothing. Maybe there's still a chance to begin anew."

Nick could plainly see that any remorse, any guilt Peter might have felt for all the dead was gone, forgotten. It was about the Lady, his precious Lady. *No cost is too high, is it, Peter?*

Too late the ferry's big engines switched into reverse. Nick braced himself. The ferry managed to miss the pylons—the first few, at least. There came a terrific jolt as the side of the ferry smashed against the remaining pylons, followed by a deep grinding and wrenching as the hull crashed into the dock. The ferry stopped with a final jolt, tossing most of the passengers to the deck. The passengers that could, were up and climbing over the gate before the dock workers even began to tie the boat down, heedless of the young, the old, or injured.

The ferry had two platforms to accommodate both decks of exiting passengers. Nick watched as passengers and crew exited from the upper decks, knocking and shoving each other in their panic. Meanwhile, the Flesh-eaters were leaving at a leisurely pace via the lower platform.

All at once it dawned on Nick that he was back in civilization, that he was free at last. The nightmare, for him at least, was over. *Oh my God, I'm here! I'm home!*

"Let's go," Peter called. He slid down the foot rungs on the outside of the ferry and leaped onto the upper docking level. The Devils and elves followed quickly behind. The witch and her brood scampered down to the platform, up the side of the building, and disappeared onto the roof. The troll began to ease his way down the rungs.

Cricket started after Peter when Nick grabbed her. "Wait," he said.

"What? No. We're going to lose them."

"Exactly."

"No, Nick. We have to save her."

"Are you mad? Cricket, look, we're here. We're back! We don't have to play Peter's game anymore. It's over."

"It's not over. Tanngnost said that if we can save her there's a chance she can rebuild Avalon. They plan to go into the wilderness and start over. All of us. You too, if you want."

Nick let out a mean laugh. "And after all their lies, you're going to believe that?"

Cricket jerked her arm away. "Yes. What else do I have to believe in? Where else do I have to go? The Devils *are* my family! Maybe one day you will learn what that means!" She spun away, slid down the railing to the platform, and pushed into the crowd.

Fine, Nick thought. *Fine. Go get killed. See if I give a fuck.* He watched her rush into the crowd. She looked so small now, here, back among adults. The crush of people knocked her about as they jostled forward, some businessman shoved her into the wall as he barreled past. Cricket stumbled but kept trying to press forward, then a large, red-faced woman crashed into her, knocking her to the walkway. "Goddamn it," Nick said and leaped down, rushing, shoving his way to her. He pushed a man aside, then grabbed Cricket by the arm, pulling her to her feet.

She shook him off. "I don't need your help."

"Like hell you don't."

Alarms were blaring everywhere. Nick searched for an exit, caught sight of Tanngnost up ahead. The troll wasn't having any trouble getting through the crowd—people were literally falling over themselves to get out of his way. Nick spotted several people pushing out an emergency exit off to the left. He grabbed Cricket's hand and pulled her through the door, down a short set of metal stairs, and into a dark parking lot. People scurried about in every direction, but they saw no sign of the Devils or the Flesh-eaters. They were deciding what to do next when several sharp reports came from somewhere back in the terminal; they sounded like gunshots.

A GARBLED SQUAWK blared through Officer Julio Sanchez's radio, followed by a snip of static. He hit the mic. "Come again?"

The voice repeated the message.

"Copy, we'll look into it." Julio spun to his partner—the bored-looking, paunchy officer leaning against the ferry turnstile. "Mac, holy shit, dispatch just got a frantic call from the ferry pilot. Something about a gang of black men terrorizing the passengers! Station thinks the pilot might be drinking though, he also said something about a large monster with horns."

Officer Mac suppressed a yawn. "Relax, rookie. The guy's overreacting. Just some kids screwing around."

Julio narrowed his eyes. How long had he shared this beat with Mac? At least three years. It seemed the man could call him something besides *rookie.*

"When you been at this job as long as I have, you've seen it all," Mac continued. "And believe me, *I've* seen it all. Just stay cool and everything will be peachy-keen. Got me?"

A sudden jolt shook the terminal.

"Whoa, what was that?" Julio said.

They could hear feet drumming along on the upper level, accompanied by shouts and yelling. Then alarms began going off. Four dock hands, a janitor, and some woman in a business suit came running down the corridor and leaped over the turnstile like they were in a steeple chase.

"I'm calling backup," Julio said.

Mac laughed. "Backup? For wh—" His face went pale and his eyes grew round.

Right about then, Julio was ready to bet that Officer "I've Seen It All" Mac had never seen a horde of black-skinned demons wearing rags and armor and carrying swords and spears, dragging a naked woman and a chubby boy by a rope. No, he was willing to bet his left nut that even Officer Mac had never ever seen such a thing.

The monsters filed down the wide walkway and into the turnstile. To Julio's surprise, they lined up in a rather orderly fashion and pushed through one at a time. Each of them appeared pretty taken with the apparatus.

His first thought was this was some sort of theater group, or maybe a bunch of hardcore Dungeons and Dragons players. He'd heard those gamers were into some pretty weird role-playing shit. He glanced again at the woman and the boy, saw the red welts on the woman's back, and ventured that this might be an S&M cult. But those weren't costumes. He could see their wiry muscles and veins working below their scaly skin, and on top of that, they smelled atrocious. *These people*, he thought, *whatever they are, they're real!*

Julio finally found his voice. "Hold up," he said as calmly as he could manage, wanting to keep things from getting out of hand.

"*STOP RIGHT THERE!*" Officer Mac cried, his voice high and shrill. Julio realized with horror that Mac had his gun out and was pointing it at the monsters. "Don't nobody fucking move!"

"Cool it, Mac," Julio whispered. "Would you please just cool it!"

A tall man in a black cape stepped forward. "Who are you?" he asked, looking Julio up and down. "Are you the Lord's men?"

"Just a sec, buddy," Julio said. "I'll ask the questions."

Another monster stepped up. "They're some sort of constables. Perhaps guards."

"A constable?" the caped man asked. "Where is your lord? We need to see the king."

The rest of the monsters had filed through the turnstile and were quietly surrounding the two officers. Julio found himself backing up, trying to keep them in front of him. He set his hand on the butt of his revolver and clicked off the safety.

"THAT'S FAR ENOUGH!" Officer Mac squealed. The gun was trembling in his hand.

Julio put in a quick call for backup and prayed Mac wouldn't do anything stupid in the meantime. Julio held up a hand diplomatically. "If I can just get you to—"

BLAM! Officer Mac shot one of the monsters.

The bullet punched a hole in the monster's stomach. It looked at the bullet hole and furrowed its brows, then stuck a finger in the wound and brought it back out covered in black blood. Its eyes flared and it grabbed Mac by the wrist.

The gun fired five more sharp reports. Some of the monsters stepped back, but the one that had hold of Mac, the one who now had six bullets in its gullet, groaned and fell over.

In a blink, one of the monsters drew a short sword and shoved the blade, to the hilt, right in Officer Mac's eye. The blade punched out the back of Mac's head, sending his hat flying off his comb-over.

Julio made a play for his gun, managed to get it clear of his holster, but that was as far as he got. Hard hands seized him and he felt something long and cold sink into his stomach over and over until everything went black.

THE CAPTAIN STOOD over the two dead men. Killing them hadn't been a very smart thing to do. Those men had been constables or guards, and he was sure that killing them wouldn't sit well with whatever powers lorded over this kingdom.

The Captain waited for the others to move on, then bent down and re-trieved the weapon from the guard. It was obviously a pistol, but of a sort he'd never seen—so small, and with no powder or fuses. Such a weapon could come in handy. He stuck it in his belt and caught up with the men.

What is this place? the Captain wondered. He caught sight of two filthy men sleeping next to a rifled garbage can. *Not Heaven,* he thought. *This is now, that's all. What the world has turned into while we were gone.* He studied the spiraling pillars of poured masonry, ran his hand along the gleaming metal and glass. *And it is both ugly and beautiful.*

441

The Captain suspected there'd be more guards coming soon. *Will they kill us?* he wondered. *Or worse, send us to their dungeons to rot? Have I merely traded one hellhole for another?* Now was the time to free Daniel and get out of here—escape these madmen before they got them both killed.

The men had stopped, bunched up around the bottom of a long flight of silver stairs. The stairs led to the next level. The Captain's eyes grew wide. The stairs were *moving*!

"Just jump on," Sid, the gangly midshipman, grumbled, and gave Robertson a bump.

Robertson shoved Sid backward and growled, "You just jump on."

Ox pushed them both. The two men tumbled onto the escalator and were slowly drawn up the moving stairs, soliciting a cheer from the rest of the men, who then began to push and shove one another to be next.

By the time the Captain had gotten on, he saw that many of the men were actually riding back down on the other side, grinning like children as they gripped the black handrail. Halfway down, Sid turned around and tried to walk back up the moving stairs only to bump into Robertson, causing both men to tumble down the steps and spill out onto the shiny floor.

"Enough," the Reverend cried.

The men frowned. But they rushed back on, laughing like loons as they jostled to be the first to the top.

They continued down a short corridor and found themselves in an immense chamber of glass and masonry. Light was everywhere. The very ceiling glowed.

People in strange garments were rushing through the chamber from all directions, mostly pouring down from the upper levels, all intent on one thing: exiting the building. When the Reverend and his men moved into their midst, the people didn't know which way to go, and in the ensuing chaos his men became separated into smaller and smaller groups.

There were two sets of glass doors ahead, leading out onto different sides of the building. In the wave of confusion, about half of the men headed out what appeared to be the front of the structure, while the rest followed the Reverend out the side. The Captain followed the Reverend, sticking as close to Danny as he could.

They pushed through the great glass doors and came out into the night lit with a million dazzling lights. Immense buildings of glass and steel towered above them, seeming to disappear into the very heavens. Several broad roads, not of stone but of some foreign dark masonry, lay before them. The Captain stopped. *What manner of sorcery is this?* Dozens of yellow carriages with blinding lamps rolled by at incredible speeds, and . . . there were *no* horses attached. *No, not sorcery. I know sorcery,* he thought. *This is something else. There's an explanation.*

The lights, the noise, the smells, the strange people, their dress, their oddness, all threatened to overwhelm him. He found himself wanting to look everywhere at once and at the same time wishing to close his eyes and not open them again. *Hold steady,* he commanded himself. *Now is not the time to lose one's mind.* He locked eyes on the boy. *My duty is to the boy. All this other—the whats and hows. It can wait.*

The Captain heard a strange, wailing noise, like hundreds of screaming demons, far away at first, but coming closer.

The men looked dazed, some stumbled forward in wonderment, while others were overwhelmed, choosing to keep their backs against the building, refusing to venture any farther.

"*THERE!*" the Reverend yelled triumphantly. "God's house."

The Captain followed the Reverend's gesture and was amazed to find that there, indeed, was God's house. A church with a towering white steeple sat just down the avenue. Atop the steeple, a gleaming cross was lit up by piercing beams of white light. The cross stood out against the looming towers like a divine beacon. Below the cross, a statue of some angelic saint looked down upon them with sad, forgiving eyes. Her arms were open, as though welcoming them home.

The Reverend pointed at the Lady and Danny. "Bring the demons," the Reverend cried. "Time we finish God's work." He raised his hands, clutching spastically at the sky as his eye flared with righteousness. "Lord, we come home to you."

"GET DOWN," NICK hissed. "They're coming."

Nick and Cricket ducked behind a parked van and watched as a large group of Flesh-eaters began filtering across the parking lot, staring about with their mouths agape.

Nick heard sirens heading their way. He tried to guess what would happen when the police arrived, what they would do with the Lady, Tanngnost, Peter, the Flesh-eaters, any of them. *This isn't going to end well for someone,* Nick thought. *Crap, and if they catch me?* He knew what that would mean: they'd take him home to his mother, deliver him right into the hands of Marko. *Wouldn't that just be some shit, after everything I've been through. I gotta get out of here.*

"There's the Lady!" Cricket said.

Nick spied the Reverend, then the Lady, as Ox marched her into the parking lot. She was still tied to Danny. Danny looked terrified but the Lady's face showed no emotion, she plodded along with her head down, looking so out of place, so fragile and vulnerable among the noise, glass, steel, and endless concrete.

"We have to do something," Cricket said.

"Do what? Huh? There's nothing the two of us can do. Look, now's our chance to get out of here before the police have this place surrounded."

"Are you kidding? Are you really gonna just run away?"

"I'm not going to get killed for her. Not for that creature. Not for Peter. Not for any of them."

"So you're just gonna abandon her? Just like that? Just like you did with your mother?"

"Don't give me any more of that crap," Nick snapped. "She's not my mother. I don't owe her a thing." But he knew that wasn't entirely true. He'd be dead right now if not for the Lady, dead or some sort of a half-mad demon, like one of those Flesh-eaters. She'd saved him. She'd taken the darkness from him, regardless of how any of this came about.

With what seemed like an effort, the Lady lifted her head and Nick found her eyes directly on him; they were silver now, all their color drained. He sensed her deep within his core, believed he heard her speak his name, a sound as soft as an echo, as though they were still beneath the dark waters of her pond. For a moment Nick could actually see the magical aura that surrounded her, the way it bled from her—tiny sparkling tendrils that flowed and trailed about her—could see magic hiding here and there, peeping out from among the metal and concrete, the garbage and asphalt. The magic flourished as the Lady passed, blooming like a garden after the first spring rain. He felt the magic within him, around him, felt it stronger than ever, understood that even here, in the city, in the world of men, magic *did* exist, woven into the very fabric of the earth. That magic was a fragile and threatened element, and without shepherds like the Lady, it would fade and the earth would become a darker, colder place.

Ox yanked the Lady forward, knocking her to the sidewalk. "To your feet, demon!" Ox yelled, and kicked her, sending her sprawling across the concrete.

Nick winced.

Ox grabbed the Lady by her hair, snatched her to her feet, and gave her a hard shove forward. Nick could see fresh blood streaming down both of her knees.

"Okay," Nick said.

"What?"

"Okay, we'll follow them."

Cricket nodded.

"Just in case, though," Nick added. "In case there's a chance. Something we can do. But you have to promise me you won't do anything stupid."

Cricket grinned. "Me? Never."

They were interrupted by a blaring car horn. The Reverend, followed by his flock, crossed an intersection and headed up the avenue. Nick looked ahead and saw the church, knew that was where they were taking the Lady, had several guesses to why and not one of them was good.

Nick and Cricket sprinted across the lot, staying low behind the vehicles, trailing the Flesh-eaters.

Nick caught the flash of emergency vehicles coming from far down the street. *The Lady's running out of time. Where's Peter? Where the hell did he go?*

A heavily wooded park bordered the avenue; Nick and Cricket ducked into the trees. They crept along behind the bushes, keeping pace with the Flesh-eaters. Nick had no idea what they were going to do, could do, but figured they'd stay close and wait for some chance, some opportunity.

The Flesh-eaters began to drift apart as they marched up the sidewalk. Many appeared distracted, more interested in this strange new place than the Reverend and his tirades.

Nick and Cricket came upon a long, rectangular pond with a small fountain in the center. There was good cover among the hedges on the far end of the pond, up near the street. They dropped down behind the hedge and pressed up as close to the road as they dared.

The Reverend headed for the church steps, pushing right out into the street. Several men and Ox pulling Danny and the Lady followed close behind. Car horns blared. There came the screech of tires as a taxi swerved, just missing the Reverend, spun sideways, and slammed into another taxi. The Flesh-eaters were showered in glass and metal fragments. There came more squealing brakes and cars began backing up in both directions. Men got out of their vehicles, shouting and cursing. Horns began going off all up and down the avenue.

The Flesh-eaters stood staring bug-eyed at all the commotion. For the moment, the Lady and Danny were completely unattended. *Now,* thought Nick. *We could grab her now. Just—*

Then, an odd thing happened, making no sense to Nick. The Captain moved up behind Ox and slid out the giant's sword. Before Ox even knew his sword was gone, the Captain brought the hilt down on his head—striking three solid blows. The giant dropped the rope and tumbled over. The Captain pushed Danny and the Lady back behind him toward the park, toward Nick and Cricket.

The Reverend saw the Captain and his good eye filled with outrage. "Stop them," he called. The Flesh-eaters barely noticed, still entranced by the wreckage and mayhem. *"STOP THEM!"* the Reverend screeched. *"STOP THEM! STOP THEM NOW!"* This brought the Flesh-eaters around. They locked steely eyes on the Lady and the Captain. Several pulled out their swords and moved to block the Captain's escape.

HORNS WENT OFF all up and down the avenue, and sirens came from every direction.

Where is she? The question repeated itself over and over in Peter's mind until he wanted to scream. For the hundredth time he scanned the clusters of gawking Flesh-eaters wandering aimlessly up and down the sidewalk, but still, no sign of the Lady.

They'd caught sight of the Flesh-eaters from inside the terminal and followed them out onto the street, keeping low and out of sight. But now Peter believed that the Flesh-eaters had become separated beforehand, understood that the Reverend and the Lady must've ended up with another group somewhere else, possibly on the other side of the terminal altogether.

Peter, the elves, and the Devils all ducked down as four patrolmen tromped past. When the police saw the Flesh-eaters, they halted, radioing for backup. Peter could see a line of officers forming a perimeter farther down the street and several more running up the sidewalk toward the terminal. "We're out of time," Peter hissed between his teeth. They *had* to find the Lady, had to find her *now.*

Peter signaled the Devils and elves and they slipped back up the street, back toward the terminal, heading for the parking lot on the far side.

"CAPTAIN, YOU *WILL* bring me the demons at once," the Reverend shouted in a voice that expected only obedience. He took a step toward the Captain.

The Captain pointed his sword at the Reverend. "No, Your Grace. I will *not.*"

The Reverend halted, his mouth tightening into a small, thin line. His good eye seethed. "Captain, you're not thinking clearly. Hand them over. That is a command."

The Reverend nodded to the men. They moved in, trying to circle them. The Captain knew if he let that happen, they were done. Keeping his sword on guard, he back-stepped, pressing Danny and the Lady through the hedges and into the park. The hedges blocked the men, at least for the moment. *Time to run*, the Captain thought, and it was then he realized his oversight. They couldn't run. Not with Daniel tied to the Lady. She could barely walk, much less outrun anyone. He needed to cut them apart, leave the Lady, and then maybe they could escape. But the rope was as thick as his wrist, would take some effort to saw or hack through it. Yet if he dropped his guard, even for a second, they'd have him.

The Reverend, his face rigid, followed the Captain into the park, flanked by several men. "I am God's right hand," the Reverend called, his voice sounding strained. "It is unwise to challenge the Lord's will."

The Captain laughed. "You're nothing more than a sadistic ass."

The Reverend let out a sound somewhere between a choke and a bark, the good side of his face twisted into a snarl.

The men pushed through the hedges. The Captain knew it was only a matter of moments before they attacked. More men were coming into the park; they drew their swords and filled in the ranks.

The Captain cut the air with his sword. "I can't take all of you, but I'll certainly gut the first man that comes near. Who has come this far only to die now?"

The men hesitated. None seemed in a big hurry to move, all only too aware of the Captain's prowess with the blade.

Ox came barreling forward, wiping the blood from his face. He caught sight of the Captain and spat. He snatched a sword away from the nearest man and started forward.

The Reverend put a hand in front of Ox. The giant halted. "Captain," the Reverend said. "You've lost your way, that's all. Be sensible, hand them over, and I shall forgive your indiscretion."

The Captain bumped into Danny, and a quick glance around showed him they'd come to a long, rectangular pond. His heart sank as he realized they were trapped.

The Reverend saw it as well and grinned. "Captain, I will not ask you again."

It has all been for naught. We're going to die here, after all we've been through. This is so senseless. The Captain looked from man to man, his eyes appealed to them. "Are you all blind? It's over. We're off the island. Look." The Captain pointed at a trash can spilling over with garbage. "This is *not* Heaven. God is not here. There is—"

"*NO!*" the Reverend shouted, his face a knot of rage. "*NO, IT IS YOU THAT ARE BLIND!*" His voice quivered as spit flew from his lips. "We did *not* sit in purgatory for an eternity for *nothing*! Somewhere in this kingdom God awaits us even now." He pointed at Danny and the Lady. "These dark souls are our passage. Proof of our unwavering faith and diligence. It is our duty to bring these demons before the Lord and then . . . and then . . . to claim our place by His side." His voice cracked. "I *will* take my place by the Lord's side!"

His madness has him, the Captain thought, and sadly he could see that same madness in the eyes of the men as they nodded along. "God help us all," he said, and, with his free hand, drew the dead constable's gun from his belt and pointed it at the lead man. It took the men a moment to recognize the weapon, but when they did, they looked unsure. The Captain aimed the revolver at the Reverend's face. The Reverend's good eye went wide. The Captain took a lifetime's pleasure in the Reverend's look of utter outrage.

"*YOU DARE NOT,*" the Reverend shrieked. "*I AM GOD'S SOLDIER. I MARCH BESIDE THE LORD!*"

"You march with the damned," the Captain said and squeezed the trigger four times. There came four deafening reports. The first shot missed completely, the second punched a clean hole in the Reverend's cheek, the third took out his dead eye, the fourth hit above the brow, and the entire side of the Reverend's head exploded.

The Reverend stood a second longer, his one good eye continuing to glare, then he crumpled to the ground. The Captain could see the back side of the Reverend's head was gone. There was a prolonged moment when they all just stared at the dead man's black brains.

ULFGER HEARD THE distant sirens and thought of demons, heard the lapping of waves beating against the hull, and finally dared raise his head. He pushed his father's corpse aside and gazed upon the towers of lights. *So many lights*, he thought. *What could it mean?* The wind took the longboat, pushed it directly toward the rocky sea wall.

Ulfger stared into the hollows of his father's eyes. "Enough!" he whimpered. "Enough! I beg you. Leave me be. Enough! Enough! *ENOUGH!*" Ulfger seized the carcass by the neck, twisting the leathery flesh until the head tore loose from the shoulders. He lifted the head by its long, braided beard and slammed it against the hull over and over, the sound like a war drum, grunting and spitting with the effort until he held nothing but a piece of shredded flesh. "There, now what do you have to say? What?" He laughed, close to shrieking, and threw the rag of flesh into the waves. "And when I find your sister, I'll send her to you. Send them all to you. And when I find the child thief, him I will feed to Caliburn." He patted the black sword.

Ulfger picked up the corpse and shoved it overboard, watched it drift slowly away into the darkness.

The boat ran aground against a large piling of stones. Ulfger heard commotion, loud popping sounds, four of them. Shouting, cries. He hefted Caliburn, crawled out of the boat, and climbed up the rocks.

He found well-lit pathways of poured masonry edged by trimmed hedges leading in all directions. He headed into the trees, toward the shouts, looking for her, for the runt, any of them would do, for he planned to kill them all . . . *every one.*

NICK JUMPED AT the sound of the gun, watched the Reverend topple. Both he and Cricket hunkered down, pressed themselves deeper into the wide hedge. They had the pond at their backs and the Captain stood just a few yards in front. Danny and the Lady were now so close they could almost touch them. Flesh-eaters were everywhere, leaving them no place to run. *Shit. How the fuck did this happen?*

The Captain turned the revolver on the Flesh-eaters. Not one of them moved.

"Just let me and the boy pass. That's all I ask," the Captain said calmly. "You can have the woman."

"*NO!*" Ox roared. "We do not bargain with demons and murderers. God's justice will be done."

Some of the Flesh-eaters looked as though they were waking up from a nightmare, like they'd had enough of the insanity, and began to fall back, but most stayed. Nick could see that these *believed*. It burned in their eyes, the same fervent faces that had condemned him back at the fort. And here, in this world, their mania seemed stronger than ever.

"The pond," Cricket whispered. "Get the Lady into the pond."

"What?" Nick said, then understood she meant for them to snatch the Lady and flee across the pond. "No," he hissed, grabbing her arm. "That won't work. We have to——" His mouth clamped shut. The Flesh-eaters were pressing in. They'd be discovered any second now. Did he really want to die in this bush, like a quivering rabbit? They had to do something, *anything*.

"Fuck. Fuck," he said, still trying to figure out how he'd gotten himself right smack in the middle of this nightmare. "Fuck," he said again, gritted his teeth, and stood up, just stood up like a jack-in-the-box—leaves and limbs fluttering off him, having no idea what he was going to do next.

Cricket popped up next to him.

The Flesh-eaters halted; all eyes fell on them—hard, murderous eyes, and Nick immediately regretted his rashness. "Ah fuck."

The Captain glanced over at them and blinked, cocked his head sideways, as though trying to make sense of what he was seeing.

"*DEMONS!*" shouted one of the Flesh-eaters, pointing at them with a wavering hand. "Demons," several of them echoed, glaring at them, their faces twisted with hatred and alarm, clearly vexed by how they could be here in this place.

Nick felt his heart would explode, felt if he didn't act, and act swiftly, his legs would buckle beneath him. He yanked out his sword, bared his teeth. "*THIS IS OUR CITY! DEMON CITY!*" he screamed, and screamed it so loud and forceful that even he believed it. "*WE'RE EVERYWHERE! A MILLION HUNGRY DEMONS AND WE'RE GOING TO EAT YOUR MOTHERFUCKING SOULS!*"

That rattled them. Fear flashed across their faces as they jerked about nervously, searching the trees, the bushes, behind them, above them. Even Ox appeared spooked, his eyes flickering back and forth in their deep sockets.

"Hurry," Cricket said and dashed over to the Lady. Nick jumped over, and together they hefted the Lady to her feet. The Lady looked at them with dazed, faraway eyes.

"C'mon, Danny," Cricket said harshly. "Help us!" But Danny just stood there, seemed incapable of doing anything but staring on in wide-eyed terror.

Nick gave the rope a hard yank, pulling Danny toward them. "Danny, move your ass!"

"This is her sorcery!" Ox said, then bellowed: *"WE MUST KILL HER. KILL HER HERE AND NOW. KILL HER BEFORE SHE BE-WITCHES US ALL!"* He raised his sword and charged the Lady.

The Captain fired, managed to hit Ox twice before his revolver clicked on a spent round. The shots barely even slowed the giant. The Captain made to intercept Ox, when two men rushed him. The night erupted with the shouts of men and the clang of steel on steel.

Cricket tugged both the Lady and Danny toward the pond. The Lady saw the water and her eyes came alive. The three of them stumbled down the bank.

Ox came for them, eyes blazing. He brought his sword about in a terrific arch, aimed at the Lady's neck. There was no time for Nick to do anything but act. He lunged forward, swinging Maldiriel upward with all he had. The blades clashed. The crushing jolt almost knocked Nick's sword from his hand, but he managed to smack the giant's blow aside. The blade missed its mark, slicing deep into the Lady's collar instead.

Ox roared, yanked his sword free, and turned on Nick.

Nick had an instant to realize this hulking monster was about to kill him, an instant to scream to himself to run. But he didn't run. A snarl escaped his throat and he attacked, striking for the giant's neck. Ox brought his sword to bear, and when he did, Nick feinted, sliding down low and fast, slicing the giant just beneath the kneecap. Ox let out a howl and swung for Nick's head. Nick ducked the blow and became aware that it didn't matter that this giant was massive and powerful, because he, Nick, was fast, impossibly fast, just like a certain golden-eyed boy he'd met in a

451

park a lifetime ago. He hacked into the giant's ankle, relishing in the feel of Maldiriel biting deep into the man's tendons. "Down, you bastard!" Nick cried. "Go down!"

Surprise and shock showed on the giant's face. He howled and collapsed to one knee. Cricket came at him from behind and thrust her sword into the back of his neck, her blade punching out the front of his throat. Ox's eyes went wide. He let out a loud gurgle and toppled over. Nick had seen far too many horror movies, where tenacious monsters get up time after time, to be satisfied with that. He let out a howl—a wild animal sound— and brought Maldiriel down with all his weight behind it, chopping the giant's head from his shoulders.

Nick looked for the Lady, saw her clutching her collar. Blood poured through her fingers. She collapsed to her knees, then slid into the pond, pulling Danny in with her. *She's done,* Nick thought. *There's nothing more we can do for her. Time to get out of here.*

A sharp cry, and another man fell before the Captain. Four men lay moaning at his feet. The Flesh-eaters fell back. Nick hoped that was it, that they'd had enough, when a dozen more men came running up, climbing over the hedges, filling in the ranks. There were too many now, just too many. He considered making a mad dash into the pond to take his chances there, but there were Flesh-eaters along both banks now, a few wading into the water, intent on seeing to it that the Lady never came out. But they needn't bother. Nick saw her eyes roll up in her head and she sank below the dark water while Danny just stood there, knee-deep in the pond, staring numbly at her.

This is it, he thought. *I'm not going home. I'm not going anywhere.* Nick ground his teeth together. *Shit. This wasn't supposed to happen. So stupid. Why had I been so stupid?*

"Shore up," the Captain called to Nick and Cricket.

Nick met the Captain's eyes, saw the will and spirit of a man who intended to live.

The Captain grinned at them. "I say if they want us, then we make them pay a heavy toll. What say you?"

Nick found the Captain's spirit infectious. He nodded back and closed ranks with the man. The Captain clutched Nick's shoulder, gave him a hearty shake. "Good to have such a sure hand at my side." Cricket followed suit, and the three of them stood back to back, swords out, daring the Flesh-eaters to come within reach. *"COME,"* the Captain yelled and waved the Flesh-eaters on. *"WHO'S NEXT TO DIE?"*

The Flesh-eaters pulled together and began to press in.

Nick's pulse thundered in his ears. His breath came hard and fast.

"Steady," the Captain said.

Nick clutched his sword in both hands, squeezing the hilt so hard his fingers hurt. "Mom," he whispered. "I love you Mom."

There came a bellow, followed by a loud snort, like a bull's. Everyone stopped. There, behind the Flesh-eaters, stood Tanngnost, carrying a thick branch. Gone was any trace of the fretting old meddler; what stood before them was a ferocious wild beast. Tanngnost peeled back his lips, exposing his tusks and giant canines. A long, deep growl rumbled up from his throat.

The Flesh-eaters shifted ranks, bringing their weapons to bear on the tall beast, when a howl cut through the night—a long, wailing cry. And there, out of the shadows, came the golden-eyed boy, racing for them, teeth bared, clanking his swords together, flanked on either side by Devils and elves.

"PETER!" Cricket cried.

Nick's heart swelled at the sight of the wild boy and he let loose a howl of his own.

Peter screamed and launched himself into the nearest Flesh-eater, slicing completely through the man's neck. The severed head flipped back and smacked the next man. Peter thrust his blade into that man, the next, then the next, eyes mad with bloodlust, weaving, ducking, kicking, slashing, dodging, cutting a path of death and dismemberment. The Devils and elves charged in right behind him, their screams and cries filling the park like a battalion of insane cats.

Nick heard girlish laughter, caught sight of the three girls as they skipped across the pond, only they were girls no longer, their hands twisted into claws and their mouths into fanged snouts. They fell upon the two Flesh-eaters nearest where the Lady had been. On the far side of the bank, the witch appeared, flanked by four barghest, her single emerald eye glowing. She walked casually across the pond toward the fighting as though on her way to a picnic.

The Flesh-eaters didn't know which way to turn, which flank to defend, and fell back in a confused tangle. The Captain did his best to further their confusion, leaping forward, striking down the nearest Flesh-eater from behind. Nick and Cricket followed his lead, and the three of them pressed into the Flesh-eaters.

The Flesh-eaters lost their spirit, lost any coordinated defense, stumbling into each other as they retreated. Nick hacked and slashed, Maldiriel biting and cutting through limbs. Nick saw their fear and realized with horror that he was smiling. Their screams and cries punctuated his howls, and at that moment he wanted nothing more than to kill every one of them, to cut them open and crush their beating hearts in his bare hands.

His eyes gleamed as he stepped over the dead and dying to get at the next soul.

The static of a bullhorn, then a deep, booming voice cut through the night. *"DROP YOUR WEAPONS AND PUT YOUR HANDS IN THE AIR!"*

"DROP YOUR WEAPONS NOW!" Sergeant Wilson shouted again and fired his revolver twice in the air. The crowd stopped then, breaking apart, clumping largely into two main groups. All eyes, all those strange eyes, fell on him and the half-dozen officers around him. In the sudden pause, the wails, screams, and groans of the wounded, the maimed, and the dying filled the air.

"What the good goddamn is going on?" the sergeant said as he surveyed the blood and gore, the severed limbs, the dozens of bodies writhing about on the ground. *Men? No,* he realized. *Look at their skin, their horns. Monsters?* The sergeant decided that was the best description: monsters decked out in armor and rags, carrying swords, axes, and spears. They were backing away from the small people. *Wait. Are those—? No, they can't be. Yes, kids! Those are kids. Wild kids wielding swords and spears of their own, and—* he lost his train of thought. "What the hell is that?" He pointed at some sort of huge, goat-headed beast. It had actual horns curving out of the side of its skull and was carrying a tree limb as though it weighed no more than a baseball bat. Blood and what looked like part of someone's scalp hung from the end of the limb.

A white flash caught the sergeant's attention and there, on the far bank, three little girls knelt over a prone body, their hands and mouths drenched in black gore. "Holy fucking shit!" And, just as the sergeant was ready to call it a night, he saw a green woman standing, yes, standing on the water and looking at him like she would eat his liver.

"Mother Mary Jesus all to fuck and back!" he cried. This didn't make any sense, none of it. Not a bit. *We're in some deep shit here,* the sergeant thought and shared a quick, fretful look with the other officers, then glanced back toward the ferry terminal. *Where was backup? Where the fuck were the ESU team, the special response guys, the dudes with the heavy calibers?* He hit his mic. "Need backup now!" he called, trying to keep the nerves out of his voice. "East side of Battery Park. Men down. Multiple armed suspects! Need backup right now! *Right fucking now!*"

All at once, several of the monster men began to walk away, rather casually even, like they'd just decided they didn't want to play anymore. *"HOLD UP!"* the sergeant yelled, pointing his gun from one creature to the next. *"EVERYONE JUST SIT TIGHT!"*

But no one was listening. The black-skinned men continued to withdraw, slipping away into the park in small groups and clusters.

"What d'we do, Sarge?" one of the officers asked while jabbing his gun at the monsters as though to ward them off.

The sarge didn't answer. He had no idea. This shit hadn't been in the manual. He only knew he couldn't let these guys get away. *Gonna have to shoot someone. Gonna have to start blasting these creeps away.* He squared his sights on a man wielding an ax, began to squeeze the trigger, when he noticed something weird, weirder even than all these monsters and little devils. The pond . . . it was *glowing*!

He lowered his gun for a better look. His brow furrowed. *What the hell?* Some sort of radiant mist was forming on the top of the pond.

Chemical agents? The sergeant's skin prickled. He'd slept through most of the lectures on bioterrorism, but had perked up once they'd started talking about the effects of chemical and biological attacks on the human organism. And the one thing he had learned was that he had no desire to spit up dissolving lung tissue or drown in his own body fluids.

The sergeant started backing away. Then something weirder happened (his definition of *weird* was expanding by the second) that made him forget all about chemical agents. There was something in this mist, lots of somethings. He heard sounds, strange, eerie echoes, like women weeping and children singing, caught sight of shadowy, eyeless children with pumpkin-size heads and deformed mouths that peeled back, exposing rows of prickly teeth, and crawling up behind them hunchbacked women with emaciated arms and legs, shriveled flesh and black holes for eyes, their distended abdomens swollen and pulsing, giant stingers dripping black, viscous goop protruding from the tips of their sagging breasts. They extended their arms to him, smiling sweetly, inviting him to dance.

The sergeant turned to run and ran right into a member of the special response unit. Behind the specialist was a squad of at least twenty well-armed ESU team members, hard, well-trained men who knew their business.

"What's going on—" the specialist started, but the sergeant didn't have time to answer questions. The sergeant had to go, had a doctor's appointment, needed to feed his goldfish, left his toaster oven on, *something*. The sergeant hauled ass out of there, leaving behind one very bewildered ESU squad.

A moment later, right about the time the swarm of disembodied heads flew screeching past, and the naked old women with the scabby raven heads started to dance merrily around the squad, to weave their cold fingers along their necks and scalps, the special response unit turned tail and followed the sergeant rapidly from the vicinity.

Chapter Twenty-Six

Horned One

✦

The Mist blanketed the park in a luminescent silvery glow, muting the shouting men, blaring horns, even the sirens. Peter felt as though he were in a dream; the whimpering and groaning of the wounded and dying echoing along with the sad song of the Mist.

The Mist? The Mist could mean only one thing. *The Lady's alive!* Peter thought. *There in the pond. She must be in the pond!*

The pond's glow faded, slowly returning to black. Peter jerked his swords free from the dead Flesh-eater at his feet, not even bothering to wipe the blood off, just shoving the blades back in their scabbards as he sprinted for the pond. He pushed past two wounded Flesh-eaters—supporting each other as they hobbled away—giving them not so much as a glance, focused only on the pond—on the *Lady*.

"Where is she?" Peter whispered, scanning the pool. He needed to find her, needed to see for himself that she was indeed alive. He saw Danny, standing knee-deep in the pond, the rope still tied around his middle. The rope was taut and sank below the water. Peter leaped into the pond, splashed out to Danny, and grabbed the rope, following hand over hand until he found the Lady. He gently pulled her to the surface, cradling her.

Peter saw her face, her half-open eyes—blank and lifeless, completely void of any color—then saw the angry gash in her collar. "Oh, no," he whispered. "No. No." He pulled her to shore and laid her on the bank.

She slowly opened her eyes and smiled at Peter. "Mabon, you found me." She touched his cheek.

The witch was there, beside them. "No Modron, you silly teat. It's just the boy. Your Mabon is dust and bones." She took the Lady's hand in hers. "Now, no more gibbering. Concentrate on your wound."

The Lady's eyes closed. She seemed to stop breathing altogether.

"Do something," Peter said to the witch. "Please, do something."

"Oh, stop your blubbering," the witch said. "There's little I can do. Avallach gave his healing touch to Modron, not me." She sneered. "Little bright and sparkly here was always his favorite. Look, she's stopped the bleeding at least."

"She'll be all right then," Peter insisted.

"Maybe. She's weak. She used herself up bringing on the Mist. She needs water. Pure, fresh water, not this stinking, stagnant pool. We have to get her out of here. Take her someplace where—"

"*PETER!*" Huck called. "Behind you!"

Peter whipped around, sword in hand in a mere blink. There, next to Danny, the *Captain*! He stood knee-deep in the pond, the rope in one hand, a long knife in the other.

Peter's lips peeled back. "*YOU!*" he snarled and pointed his sword at the man.

"Hold!" the Captain called, raising his hands, holding the knife up. "I just want the boy." He gestured to Danny. "Just want the boy, nothing more."

Peter couldn't believe his ears. This *demon*, this *monster*, dared ask to take a child—from *him*. After all the Devils that lay dead at this man's hands? "Never," Peter growled, and leaped into the pond, charging the Captain with a wide swing. The Captain parried the blow with his knife and fell away, causing Peter to barrel past. The Captain snatched out his own sword, readied himself.

"PETER, NO!" Nick cried, and jumped into the pond, splashing between them. *"STOP!"* Nick carried a spear, one of the large Flesh-eaters' spears. He brought the shaft up, blocking Peter.

Peter leveled his sword at Nick, placed the blade directly under his throat. "I'm warning you, Nick," Peter said coldly. "You've come before my sword too many times. Get out of my way. *Now!*"

"Just free Daniel," the Captain said calmly. "Send him with me and we'll go."

"WHAT?" Peter cried. "You will *never* take another child from me, not *ever.* All you will get from me is the edge of my sword."

The Devils splashed into the pond, spears and swords pointed at the Captain, holding him in check. The Captain didn't waver. He kept his guard steady.

"Peter, stop this!" Nick cried. "Look, open your eyes and look." He pointed at the bodies around the pool, to Ivy, her unblinking eyes staring up into the mist, to Carlos, lying on the bank, his throat open, a ribbon of blood feeding into the pond. "How much is enough? How many must die? You have your precious Lady, just let them go."

Peter tried not to look at the dead Devils. They'd died honorably, heroically. He wouldn't let Nick muddy their deaths, twist things around. Nick had it backward, that's all. "There's only one bastard to blame for their lives. One." Peter pointed at the Captain. *"Him."*

"No, Peter," Nick said. "The Captain fought with us. He saved your Lady. Does that mean nothing to you?"

Peter narrowed his eyes at Nick.

"It's true," Cricket called.

Peter let out a long breath, then set his glare on the Captain. "Leave now. Right now and I'll spare you. But the boy . . . that *traitor.* He stays. He owes me a debt."

The Captain shook his head slowly. "I will not leave the boy. Not with you."

The Devils tightened their grips on the spears, glanced to Peter.

Peter shrugged. "Then you will die, here and now."

Nick spun the point of his spear toward Peter. "No, not this time. I won't watch you murder this man. Not like Leroy. Never again."

Peter saw the conviction in Nick's eyes. *He's not bluffing. He means it. By all the gods, this stupid kid means it.* He glared at Nick. "Nick, you're going to get hurt, *bad.* This is your last—"

A scream cut through the Mist. Peter spun, ready for anything but what he saw. "Ulfger," Peter exhaled in a wounded breath.

Ulfger stood near the far end of the pond. His head cocked to one side as though hearing voices, his hair frayed, soot smeared across his face, his dark, brooding eyes haunted, crazed. The Mist swirled away from him and there at his feet lay—*Drael!*

"Oh, no!" Peter said and started forward, stopped. Something was wrong. Peter squinted, trying to make sense of what he was seeing. The old elf cradled his arm to his chest. It was turning black, the blackness crawling up his shoulder, then his neck, along his cheek. Drael's face cinched up in pain, and his skin began to smolder.

"What madness is this?" Peter hissed.

Drael let out another cry, a cry that made Peter's skin crawl. The elf rolled onto his back, began writhing in the grass, blood poured from his eyes, nose, mouth. His back arched, his fingers tore at his chest. He let out a final strangled cry, then lay still.

Peter stood frozen in place, could do nothing more than stare at the smoldering corpse of his old friend. "No," Peter murmured. "This isn't possible."

An elf darted forward, sent his spear shooting across the ground, catching Ulfger in the chest, punching through his chest-plate and deep into his heart. Ulfger stumbled back, looked at the spear like he was just—*curious.* He grabbed the spear, grunted, and yanked it out. No trace of blood touched the blade.

"What's going on?" Peter whispered.

"His blood is one with the sword," the witch said. "He cannot be stopped. Not by mortal sword and spear."

Ulfger's eyes fell on the Lady. He smiled at Peter. "I will have her head. Come, you runt. You little freak." He waved to Peter, as though inviting him to a hand of cards. "Come see if you can save your queen." He kicked Drael's smoldering corpse. "Come taste Avallach's judgment."

Peter snarled, sprang out of the pond, and charged Ulfger. He let out a howl and swung high with his left sword and low with the right. Ulfger smashed Caliburn against one sword, shattering the blade and knocking the weapon from Peter's grasp. But Peter's second blade sliced into Ulfger's thigh just above the knee. Ulfger stumbled and Peter slashed him across the back of the neck. A savage light flashed in Peter's eyes at the feel of steel biting flesh. *For Drael!* Peter spun around to finish Ulfger, but to his horror, to his total disbelief, he found Ulfger still on his feet. The giant seemed hardly affected by either strike. Peter fell back a step as the wounds healed right before his eyes. Ulfger pressed in, swinging for Peter's chest. Peter brought his sword to bear at the last second, but was off-balance and the blow knocked the sword from his hand and him to his knees.

Cutter rushed forward, jabbing his spear into Ulfger's stomach. Ulfger grunted, grabbed the hilt, and used it to knock Cutter into Peter, then stabbed the boy in the back.

Peter struggled to pull Cutter up when the boy screamed. Cutter's skin burned, actually sizzling and turning black right beneath Peter's hands. Peter let out a cry of horror; did not even see Ulfger swing at him. A huge gloved fist slammed into Peter's brow. Everything went very bright for an instant, then viselike fingers clamped around his throat, yanking him off his feet.

Peter struggled, kicked, and clawed at Ulfger's hand and arm, but Ulfger's grip was like steel.

The elves fell back, surrounding the Lady, leaving Peter to his fate, but not the Devils, they rushed in: Rex, Drake, Huck, Dash, and even Cricket came splashing out of the pond. They circled Ulfger, no clacking teeth, or wild war cries, only grim, resolute eyes.

Ulfger sneered at them, held Caliburn before Peter's face. "One touch," Ulfger shouted. "And your precious chief here is ash."

The Devils glanced at each other, unsure, their helplessness stripping them of their savagery.

Ulfger tightened his grip. Peter let out a strangled cry, felt the bones in his neck would snap at any moment. "Back," Ulfger said.

The Devils fell back.

"Ulfger," the witch called. "Heed me Ulfger. If you taste his blood you will not like what you find." The witch smiled and wet her green teeth with her tongue.

Ulfger dismissed her with a sneer. "Modron," Ulfger commanded. "Look at me. Look at me!"

The witch lifted the Lady into a sitting position. "Here now, dearie. Let's not disappoint Ulfger. Do take a look. You won't want to miss this. That I promise."

"Modron!" Ulfger called.

The Lady opened her eyes.

"Look what I've caught. Something dear to your heart." He shook Peter. "Does he remind you of your little Mabon? Watch, Modron. Watch your precious boy burn."

The Lady shook her head and raised a quivering hand.

Ulfger grinned, his eyes flashed. He took the black blade, set it against Peter's cheek, and slowly slid the edge down, cutting a long gash into the side of the boy's face.

Heat bloomed across Peter's cheek. He cried out and Ulfger tossed him to the ground.

Cricket screamed; the Devils, Tanngnost, the elves, all froze, all stared in wide-eyed dread.

Peter clutched his cheek, his heart thudding in his chest. He wanted to run, but there was nowhere to run, not from the poison. It was in his blood; he felt its heat course through his veins. He waited for the pain, for the burning, but the burning never came, only the warmth, spreading through his body. Peter pulled his hand from his face, found no blood. Touched the wound, felt it growing smaller, shrinking—*disappearing*.

Ulfger's smile faded; he looked on, confused.

A laugh, a cackling laugh came from the pond. It was the witch. "Oh, Ulfger, you big stupid ass, if you could see your face." She laughed again. "I tried to warn you. Don't you see? Don't you understand? This can mean only one thing."

Ulfger narrowed his eyes at her.

"Think about it, you big oaf. The wound does not bleed. The sword does not burn him? Why, Ulfger? What must that mean? Come now, you can do it."

Ulfger's eyes went wide. He shook his head.

"Yes," the witch said. "You see, don't you? Yes you do, my big stupid nephew. You see very well."

"No," he said. *"NO!"*

"Seems the Horned One had more than one little bastard running around," the witch laughed. "Oh this is truly delicious." She shook the Lady. "See, Modron. I told you you wouldn't want to miss it."

Ulfger glared at the witch, pointed Caliburn at her. "You lie, witch! You are full of lies!"

Peter made for his feet and Ulfger turned the black sword on him, held the jagged, broken point an inch from his heart. "Tricks. Lies. I will not—" Ulfger's eyes flared, he cocked his head sideways, again as though listening to some unseen phantom. His face twisted into a mask of despair and pain. "Why?" he mewled. "Why must you forever torment me? Why do you *hate* me so? I have been the good son—ever the *good* son." Peter tried to ease away and Ulfger's eyes came into sharp focus, blazed with unfathomable hate. "You!" His face pinched into a knot. "You are an *abomination!*" he screeched, and shoved Caliburn into Peter's chest, drove the blade all the way through Peter's ribs and out his back.

Blinding pain—Peter tried to scream, managed only a strangled gasp. Ulfger twisted the blade sharply left, right, then yanked the weapon free. Peter dropped, rolled in the dirt, clutching, clawing at the deep wound, his mouth working, trying to breathe. He felt air escape between his fingers, heard—felt—a horrible sucking come from the wound as the air left his punctured lung.

Ulfger laughed, a high, strained sound almost like wailing. He reared back for a second thrust when the Devils rushed in.

Rex dove in low, recklessly, going for Ulfger's knee, forcing Ulfger to switch his thrust from Peter to him. Ulfger missed, the blade driving into the dirt. The boy slashed Ulfger's leg. Dash drove his spear into Ulfger's stomach, the spear punched through the mail, sunk deep into Ulfger's gut. Ulfger let out a loud grunt, stumbled back. Drake and Huck were there, attacking from behind, Huck hacking low while Drake cut high.

Even through his pain, Peter admired their bravery, cunning, and coordination. For a moment it looked good for the Devils, looked to Peter like they might stand a chance, might be able to stop this monster, or at least drive him back. Then Ulfger yanked Caliburn from the ground, spun around—the sword seemed to weigh nothing in his hand—and his speed caught them all by surprise. He struck Rex in the side of the head, cleaving the boy's skull open; blood and brains followed the sword's wake as it cleaved through Huck's arm, then neck. Both boys collapsed into lifeless heaps. Drake ducked back, the sword missed his head but nicked his shoulder, the slightest scratch, yet his face showed he knew his fate, knew what that one scratch meant. An instant later, a dark patch bloomed, crawled up his neck, across his chest. Drake screamed, but did not stop fighting; even as his skin smoldered and peeled away from the bone, he rushed Ulfger. Ulfger knocked the boy away with his fist, leaving him to burn.

"No," Peter said in a strained rasp, almost out of his mind with pain, anger, and frustration. Ulfger was killing the Devils, *his* Devils, murdering every one of them while he lay in the dirt. "Fuck," he spat. Tears squeezed from his eyes as he forced himself to his hands and knees. He clutched his chest—there was no blood. The pain turned slowly to warmth, and he realized he could breathe again, that the wound was healing. *The sword. That cursed sword.*

Only Dash and Cricket were left. Dash jumped between Peter and Ulfger. Cricket slid over next to him. She looked so small before Ulfger's towering mass. Peter could see her fear, the utter terror in her face, yet still she stood, spear ready just as Sekeu had shown her.

Peter pushed slowly to his feet.

Ulfger laughed and came for them.

"DEVILS, DEVILS, DEVILS FOREVER!" Dash screamed and charged Ulfger, swinging with all his strength and speed. Ulfger met the attack with a crushing blow, cutting through Dash's sword and forearm, catching the boy in the stomach, almost slicing him in two. Dash flew back into Cricket and Peter, knocking them over. Ulfger raised Caliburn above his head. *"JUDGMENT COMES!"* he screamed.

A spear tore through the side of Ulfger's neck. His eyes went wide with surprise.

Peter blinked—there was Nick, his face hard, focused, no trace of the confused, scared boy he'd found in the park such a short time ago. This boy was lean and dangerous, his cold, piercing eyes the eyes of a killer.

Nick shoved the spear deeper into Ulfger's neck and shouted, *"GET AWAY FROM HER!"*

Ulfger dropped Caliburn, clutched the spear in both hands, gagging and strangling as he tried to wrestle it from Nick's grasp. Nick gave the spear a final, hard thrust and leaped over to Cricket. He grabbed her by the arm, pulled her to her feet, and cried, *"CRICKET, RUN!"*

Ulfger pulled the spear from his neck and fixed on Nick. Peter tried to shout, tried to get up in time. Ulfger threw the spear, catching Nick in the back, just below his shoulder blade. The spearhead sprung out from the front of Nick's chest. Nick looked at it for a moment, then collapsed to his knees.

"NICK!" Cricket screamed.

"Run," Nick said weakly, and fell over.

Ulfger and Peter locked eyes across the bodies of the dead and dying, the heat of their hate boring into each other. Peter's chest heaved, his lips peeled back, his golden eyes flared, his fingers ached to rip away Ulfger's flesh, to tear his eyes from their sockets. Caliburn, the deadly, black blade, lay in the dirt between them. The two half-brothers stared at it as one. Peter was quicker. He dove for the sword, snatching up the blade and coming up in a roll. He swung for Ulfger—the sword weighed nothing in his hands—it sliced through the giant's armor like paper, cutting deep into Ulfger's thigh. Ulfger stumbled back, fear in his eyes.

Peter felt the bite of the sword's spiked hilt, felt its heat, felt its pulse within him, felt its power. He heard the Horned One then—calling his name. Peter could see that Ulfger heard it too.

"No," Ulfger cried. "I am the *one*. Me, Father. *Me!*"

Peter hefted the blade and moved in, circling, stalking the giant.

Ulfger backed away, his haunted eyes rolling wildly in their sockets, frantically searching for some escape. His heel caught on Huck's body and he tumbled over backward.

Peter was at him.

"*NO!*" Ulfger cried.

Peter brought the black sword high over his head and down with all his strength. Ulfger put up his hands, tried to block the strike, but Caliburn sliced through his wrists, leaving two steaming stumps. Ulfger wailed with outrage and pain. Peter brought the sword down again. This time, the blade bit deep into Ulfger's neck. Ulfger's face twisted in agony. An awful, strangling sound gurgled from the deep gash across his throat. Peter grinned, letting the sword take him, reveled in its song as he brought the blade down over and over. Ulfger's wounds tried to heal, but Peter kept hacking and hacking, chopping and re-chopping, until, at last, Ulfger's head rolled away and his body fell limp.

The Mist swirled and danced around Peter. He felt the Horned One's wild blood—awakened by the sword, by the death and carnage—pumping in his veins. Peter's golden eyes blazed. He set his foot atop Ulfger's chest, pointed Caliburn heavenward, threw back his head, and howled.

The call echoed across the park.

✦

PETER CLOSED HIS eyes, listening to his own heartbeat. He heard men shouting in the distance and the warbling sirens growing louder, and knew the Mist was thinning again. The Lady's voice came to him, softly, but pushing all other sounds into the background. "Peter."

Peter opened his eyes, saw the Lady. She appeared a little stronger now, and some of the color had returned to her eyes. She beamed at him. "Peter," she whispered. "You are my champion—forever."

Peter glanced from Ulfger's body to the bodies of the Flesh-eaters. He jabbed Ulfger's head with the tip of Caliburn. Ulfger's lips quivered and his eyes flickered. Peter wondered if the head was still alive somehow, if the sword's spell could do that. He hoped so as he kicked the head into the pond. He stared at the bubbles as it sunk below the water and disappeared from sight. Then Peter strolled toward the Lady, a triumphant smile spreading across his face as his heart swelled. *Yes, I am your champion.*

A ragged sob cut the silence. Cricket cradled Nick in her lap; there was blood trickling from his mouth, but the boy was still alive, his eyes were on Peter—watching him, judging him. Peter's smile faded.

Peter stuck the deadly sword into the earth, came and knelt beside them. He clasped Nick's shoulder. The boy's skin was clammy. "Nick, you fought bravely. You're a true *Devil*. You saved—"

"Cut the bullshit," Nick snapped.

Peter flinched.

Nick caught hold of his arm. "How can you continue to play this game?" he hissed through clenched teeth. "Are you truly that blind?" He pointed at the smoldering husks of Rex, Huck, Drake. "Look! Look at them! They're all dead, all your Devils. Don't you even care? Or do they no longer matter?"

Peter tried not to look, but there was no escaping the wide, staring eyes of the dead, the stink of guts, blood, and burned flesh hanging in the Mist. Nothing noble or romantic, just death. He tried to pull away, but Nick held him, his face tight with anger and pain. "Don't you dare look away from them. Not after they gave their lives for you, stood by you when no one else would."

"No," Peter said. "They died for the Lady. They died honorably, defending their queen."

"She's not their queen, you stupid fuck." Nick coughed and blood spattered his chin. "It was you they worshipped, you they followed, and look where you led them. Look! You traded their lives for the Lady, your goddamn precious Lady. Was it worth it? Was she worth all their lives?"

Peter knocked Nick's hand away. "No," Peter growled. "It's not like that. You're always twisting things around." But even as he shook his head, he saw their faces, not in death, but in life. Those vibrant children who had followed him through the Mist on a promise—had laughed, cried, played, fought, and died alongside of him.

Peter caught sight of Danny and the Captain climbing out from the far side of the pool. He leaped to his feet, reached for Caliburn, then stopped, glanced back at Nick—at Nick's hard, cold eyes.

"What are you waiting for?" Nick said. "Go on. Kill them too. More blood for your goddamn queen. Right?"

Peter let out a hard breath and just stood there, watching as the Captain and Danny disappeared into the trees.

"Peter," the Lady called. "Come to me." She sounded stronger. Tanngnost carried her in his arms. The elves, the witch, the three girls, and the barghest all surrounded her. She smiled at him. "It is time to go."

Nick coughed, spat up a mouthful of blood. Peter looked, as though for the first time, at the spear protruding from Nick's chest. The boy was so pale; pain creased his eyes.

"Hold on, Nick," Peter said. "You're going to be all right." He dashed over to the Lady. "Modron," Peter called. "Hurry, help him before it's too late."

The Lady reached for Peter, took his hand, and smiled sadly at him. "I'm sorry, but there's nothing I can do for him."

"Of course there is. You can heal him. You can try."

"Peter," she said sternly. "We've no time for their kind, not now."

Their kind? Peter stared at her.

"Peter, please don't look at me that way. I know the human children are dear to you. But they are back in their place now. It is up to *their* gods to help them. We have to look after our own."

"Nick is *our* own. He's earned his place a thousand times over. You *owe* it to him."

The Lady's eyes flared. "Enough of this," she said sharply. "Would you have me risk everything for him? I must conserve my strength; there are many trials ahead."

Peter grabbed the Lady's hand. "Please," he said. "Just do what you can. Anything. Please, I'm begging you."

Her face softened. "Peter, don't fret so. You need to let go, put their kind behind you. You are my warlord now. Your place awaits. Now, I will hear no more of this. Tanngnost, we need to leave before all is lost."

Peter looked from face to face: the witch's smirk, the girls' wicked smiles, the cold eyes of the elves. Only Tanngnost seemed genuinely saddened by the dying boy. "I'm sorry, Peter," the old troll said. "I wish there was something I could do."

"Now come, Peter," the Lady said. "We must make haste."

They all turned away, leaving Peter standing there, the slain bodies of his Devils scattered around him.

NICK FELT A chill, a numbing coldness crawling toward his heart. *I'm not going to make it,* he thought. *I'm never going to see my mother again.* Tears rolled down his cheeks. *I have to tell her I'm sorry. Tell her how much I love her. Have to.*

"Peter," Nick called weakly. Peter didn't hear him.

"Peter," Cricket called. "Peter."

Peter slowly pulled his eyes away from the Lady, walked over, and knelt down next to them.

"I need you to do something for me," Nick said.

Peter nodded, distractedly.

"You have to find my mother." Nick coughed, it was getting hard to speak. "Tell her I love her. Tell her I'm sorry. And Peter." Nick clutched Peter's arm, pulled him close. "Kill them. *Kill* Marko and his friends. Will you do that?"

Peter didn't answer, he glanced to the Lady—Tanngnost was carrying her away, the refugees of Avalon following them toward the harbor.

"Peter, look at me. You made me a promise. You swore. No games this time. You *have* to do this for me. Okay?"

"I'll do what I can, Nick."

"No, swear it! *Fucking* swear it. Put your fingers out where I can see them and swear."

Peter's eyes dropped. "Nick, I can't. Not now. There are still things left to do."

"Goddamn you," Nick cried. "Listen to me. She lives near the park, where you found me. It's on Carroll Street, just off Fourth Avenue. The blue house. The only blue house on the street. Did you get that? Carroll Street. The blue house. You can't miss it." Nick coughed, spat out a mouthful of blood. "Go there, *kill* Marko. You *owe* me. You fucking owe me."

Peter nodded, but said nothing more.

Cricket was sobbing.

Nick's hands went numb; Peter's arm slid from his grasp. He wanted to say more, wanted to *make* Peter swear. To see in his eyes that he would indeed kill Marko. But it was too hard to speak. He smiled weakly at the golden-eyed boy. "The Lady," Nick whispered. "She has stolen your soul."

Nick's vision blurred. *So cold,* he thought and wished his mother was here. Wished he could see her one more time, feel her warm arms around him. That would be so nice, so good. He closed his eyes.

PETER WATCHED NICK'S hand drop lifelessly to the dirt.

Cricket stared at Nick. She was no longer crying, just staring. Her eyes were distant—lost.

The Lady's voice drifted to Peter across the last remnants of the Mist. "Peter, come to me." The troop waited for him in the shadowy trees.

"Cricket," Peter said. "Let's go."

472

Cricket looked at Peter as though he were a stranger, then into the shadows, to where the Lady waited. Cricket shook her head. "No, I'm not going."

"So much awaits, we must—" Peter stopped, let out a weary sigh. He touched Cricket's shoulder. "Good-bye, Cricket." She didn't look up.

Peter stood, pulled Caliburn from the dirt, studied the black broken blade. *I was there*, he thought. *When this blade was broken. I stood by his side, the Horned One—my* father, *when he carried it into battle.*

He tugged Ulfger's cape from his stiff body, used it to wrap the deadly blade. He took a last long look at the dead, a hard look into each of their faces, then into Nick's face. "I won't forget." He turned and followed the Lady.

PETER CAUGHT UP with her at the Battery. The Mist had drifted away and he could see the Statue of Liberty glowing green in the harbor. One of the elves leaped up onto the sea wall, pointed down the way. "There, a vessel." The elf squinted his narrow eyes and said with surprise, "It's the longboat."

Peter helped Tanngnost carry the Lady down the rocks to the blackened hull of the great boat. One by one, the last refugees of Avalon boarded: the witch, her daughters, Tanngnost and the Lady, the elves, finally the barghest, scampering up the bow and perching like gargoyles along the magnificent dragonhead. When it came Peter's turn, he hesitated.

"Hurry, Peter," the Lady said.

Peter set a hand on the rail, started to pull himself aboard, then stopped.

"Peter?"

He clenched his jaw and slowly shook his head.

The Lady gave him a stern look.

"I can't."

"Don't jest," the Lady said.

"There's something I have to do first."

"You don't mean the silly promise you made that boy?"

Peter nodded.

"Come aboard, Peter," the Lady commanded. "This is no time for games."

Peter opened his pouch and pulled out three apples.

The Lady's eyes grew round. "Avallach's seed," she said in awe. *"How?"*

Peter handed her the apples. She cradled them to her breast like newborns.

"Peter, do you know what this means? Why, Avalon can truly be reborn!"

Peter nodded again.

"Peter," her voice dropped low, seductive. "Everything you ever desired awaits." Her piercing, cerulean eyes glowed. "A new world, my champion. And you will sit by my side, sharing all the magical delights." Her voice deepened. "See it, Peter. See your rightful place. See your destiny fulfilled."

Peter saw her vision: he, the wild warlord of the Sidhe, romping through the magical forest with the beasts and wild faeries at his side, lord of all he sees. And it was indeed everything he had ever desired.

"Your heart is heavy for the children," she continued in that low, deep, lulling tone. "Peter, that is understandable. But that will fall behind you in the new day. Once you are by my side. Once all of Faerie dances about your feet, you will forget them and the pain will fade."

"Forget them?" Peter said, shaking away the vision. "No." His voice was strong and resolute. "I will not *forget* them. I will never *forget* them." He took a step back.

"Peter, you *will* come. You *must* come. A new world is a fragile thing. It's your place to carry Caliburn, to defend Avalon. You cannot deny your birthright. It is your *duty.* Now come aboard, I command it."

Peter held her eyes and shook his head. "I made a promise." He dropped the bundled sword in the boat next to the Lady. "Good-bye, Modron."

The Lady's eyes flared, and she bared her teeth, snarling.

"Modron," the witch laughed. "His father's blood has been awakened within him. Seems your charms no longer rule his heart."

The Lady glared at her sister, then it was as though all the air left her, and she sagged against Tanngnost. "Peterbird," she said, sounding weak,

tired, defeated. "My little Mabon. Don't leave me. I need you."

Peter pulled the star necklace from around his neck, took the Lady's hand, and laid it in her palm. "I'm not Mabon," he said softly.

The Lady stared at the lifeless star. She looked impossibly sad. Then her face grew grim and for a moment Peter saw the Lady he'd met all those summers ago, not the fragile woman but the goddess, the proud daughter of Avallach, the queen of Avalon. She pulled herself up straight, held out Mabon's star. "Do this for me. Keep it safe." Peter saw that its golden glow had returned. "When you're done playing games, bring it home to me."

Peter accepted the star but slipped it into his pocket rather than around his neck. He looked to Tanngnost. "Good-bye, old friend."

Tanngnost let out a deep, heavy sigh, shook his head sadly from side to side, but clasped Peter's hand firmly in his. "May Avallach go with you."

The last tendrils of the Mist swirled away. Peter heard men shouting far back in the park.

"We must go," Tanngnost said and let go of Peter.

"Peter," the Lady said. "Come home to me. Make it soon."

"Yes," agreed the witch. "And take good care of your eyes. One of them belongs to me." She grinned, showing him her long, green teeth.

The Lady set her hand in the bay; a swell of water gently rose beneath the boat, and they drifted from the rocks. The swell built behind the boat and pushed it rapidly away.

Peter stood there until he could no longer see them, until he heard the squawk of a radio and heavy footsteps coming down the walkway. Then he slipped away, disappearing into the shadows.

✦

THE SIRENS FADED as Peter put the park farther and farther behind him. He no longer crept through alleyways, walking instead along the main streets. He ignored the hard stares and wary looks, not caring who might notice him, hardly watching where he was going. *So much lost,* he thought, his heart so heavy he felt he might suffocate. *What have I done?* Again he saw the disappointment on the Lady's face, the look in Nick's eyes as he died. Peter set his jaw and pushed them from his mind, plodding onward into the night, concentrated solely on putting one foot in front of the other, as though he could truly leave all the pain behind.

He left Manhattan, scarcely noticing as he crossed the Brooklyn Bridge. Before long, the high-rises gave way to warehouses, then apartments and detached houses. He entered Prospect Park and soon found himself face to face with the green climbing turtle.

"Nick," Peter whispered. "I'm so sorry."

The turtle stared back with its ridiculous grin.

Tears bit at Peter's eyes. He wiped at them and gritted his teeth. "So damn sorry." The tears kept coming until a harsh sob shook his frame. He slumped against the turtle as tears for Sekeu, Abraham, Goll, his mother, Nick, and all the Devils that had died for him poured freely down his cheeks. He slid to the grass. The list was long, but Peter sat there, eyes clenched, arms tight about his knees, until he could name every one— every single one.

Eventually, a brisk wind blew. Peter opened his eyes, inhaled deeply— warmth, a trace of spring. His skin prickled, the night suddenly felt alive, as though the trees, birds, and bugs were watching him. He caught sight of a sparkle, then another and another. They raced to him, zipping along just above the dewy grass, circling him, spiraling round and round. *"Faerie folk,"* he said in wonder. Something blue shot past Peter's head, whirled about, and hovered right before him. It was one of the pixies, a girl with white, wispy hair. She hissed at him, then rejoined the flock as they frolicked about the trees.

Peter heard a whispering in the leaves, a voice calling for him to come dance with the night—it was his father. Peter recalled how the Horned

One had danced with him and the Devils around the great fire, granted them a place in Avalon. *You chose me, Father, to stand beside you at Merrow Cove, to fight by your side. Honored me, not Ulfger, but me.*

Understanding dawned on Peter and he began to grin. His father had indeed left him a gift, a great gift, and not the deadly sword. His father had claimed him when no other would, because the Horned One's spirit lorded over all wild things, whether pagan or Sidhe, of this world or faerie. And now his father had passed that spirit on to him.

Peter jumped to his feet, laughed long and loud, as though he owned the park, daring any to challenge him. He set back his head and howled—a primeval call not heard by men for a thousand years, one that made them remember why they are afraid of the deep dark forest.

I've no need of banners, titles, crowns, magic swords, or gilded courts. I'll never be confined to any realm. My domain is wherever the wild wind blows.

"I am the Horned One," Peter called. "The forest spirit, the lord of all wild things."

He dug in his pouch, pulled out one of Avallach's apples, and admired it. It was a sacred thing of remarkable beauty—the revered symbol of Avalon. Peter took a bite. "Yum." Smacking loudly, he headed off to find a house, not just any house, but a blue house on Carroll Street. His golden eyes sparkled and he touched the hilt of his knife. He looked forward to meeting Marko and his pals. He intended to have some fun with them—a really good time, because it had been *so* long since he'd had a really good time.

He felt his step lighten. The Sunbird came to mind, how wild and free it had been, free to fly wherever it fancied, whenever it pleased. Peter felt like that now, as though he could go anywhere, do anything, almost as though he could fly.

He glanced up at the stars and a wicked smile lit his face. "Time to play," he whispered to them and winked.

And the stars winked back, for Peter's smile is a most contagious thing.

Author's Note or
An Ode to Peter Pan

Like so many before me, I am fascinated by the tale of Peter Pan, the romantic idea of an endless childhood amongst the magical playground of Neverland. But, like so many, my mind's image of Peter Pan had always been that of an endearing, puckish prankster, the undue influence of too many Disney films and peanut-butter commercials.

That is, until I read the original *Peter Pan*, not the watered-down version you'll find in the children's bookshops these days, but James Barrie's original—and politically uncorrected—version, and then I began to see the dark undertones and to appreciate just what a wonderfully bloodthirsty, dangerous, and at times cruel character Peter Pan truly is.

Foremost, the idea of an immortal boy hanging about nursery windows and seducing children away from their families for the sake of his ego and to fight his enemies is at the very least disturbing. Though this is fairly understandable when you read in "The Little White Bird" (Peter Pan's first appearance) that as an infant he left his own nursery to play with the fairies in the park, but upon his return found the windows barred and his mother nursing another little boy—just the sort of traumatic event to leave anyone a bit maladjusted. Rejected, Peter returned to the fairy world and apparently decided things would be a bit more fun if he had a few companions. And, not being one to worry on niceties, he simply kidnapped them.

But what happens to these children after that? Here is a quote from the original *Peter Pan:* "The boys on the island vary, of course, in numbers, according as they get killed and so on; and when they seem to be growing up, which is against the rules, Peter thins them out; but at this time there were six of them, counting the twins as two."

Thins them out? Huh? What does that mean? Does Peter kill them, like culling a herd? Does he send them away somewhere? If so, where? Or does Peter just put them in such peril that the crop is in need of constant replenishing?

That one paragraph forever changed my perception of Peter Pan from that of a high-spirited rascal to something far more sinister. *"Thins them out"*—the words kept repeating in my head. How many children had Peter stolen, how many had died, how many had been *thinned out?* Peter himself said, *"To die will be an awfully big adventure."*

There is certainly no lack of bloodletting in *Peter Pan:* pirates massacring Indians and so forth, but those are adults killing each other—nothing new there. Much more intriguing to me is that murderous group of children—the Lost Boys. With them, Peter Pan has turned bloodletting into a sport, has taught them not only to kill without conscience or remorse but also to have a damn good time doing it. At one point the boys proudly debate the number of pirates they'd just slaughtered: "Was it fifteen or seventeen?" And how can any child not enjoy such lines as "They fell easy prey to the reeking swords of the boys." Or "He lifted up one boy with his hook, and was using him as a buckler, when another, who had just passed his sword through Mullins, sprang into the fray." Nothing like a good spilling of entrails to liven things up. And more chilling is Peter's ability to do all these things—the kidnapping, the murder—all without a trace of conscience: *"'I forget them after I kill them,' he (Peter) replied carelessly."*

Once I pondered these unsettling elements I began to wonder what this children's book would be like if the veil of Barrie's lyrical prose were peeled back, if the violence and savagery were presented in stark, grim reality. How would children really react to being kidnapped and thrust into such a situation? How hard would it be for them to fall under the spell of a charismatic sociopath, to shuck off the morality of civilization and become cold-blooded killers? Judging from what goes on in modern gang culture, and seeing how quick teens can be to define their own morals, to justify any action no matter how horrific, I believe it wouldn't be that hard.

And these thoughts were the seeds for *The Child Thief.*

✦

KNOWING THAT I didn't want to simply retell Barrie's *Peter Pan*, but instead create my own Peter, my own world, and the darker story behind the fairytales, I began to dig into the same Scottish fairy stories, myths, and legends that originally inspired James Barrie himself. And I was delighted to find a treasure trove of folktales from which to pull together the mythology for *The Child Thief.* Since these legends helped steer and form this novel, I thought some of you might find them interesting and have listed them below.

I found the details to these myths varied to some degree from source to source, from region to region, and I took liberal use of many of them for *The Child Thief.* But following here are the most common threads and elements I have drawn upon:

Avalon: Avalon, or "Ynys Afallach" in Welsh, is one of the Otherworld islands. It was originally ruled by Avallach with his daughter, Modron. It is where Caliburn (Excalibur) was forged and where King Arthur was taken by Morgan le Fay (Modron) to be healed of his wounds after the battle of Camlann. Like the name of Avalon (from afal, or "apple"), the apple is one of the most recognized symbols of Avalon, with counterparts in the Greek Hesperides, the Norse Apples of Youth, and the Judeo-Christian Fruit of the Tree of Life.

Avalon is closely associated with a similar Otherworld island, Tír na nÓg, called in English *the Land of Eternal Youth* or *the Land of the Ever-Young,* and thus I combined both mystical islands to some degree. Tír na nÓg is perhaps best known from the myth of Oisin, one of the few mortals who lived there, and Niamh of the Golden Hair. It was where the Tuatha Dé Danann, or Sidhe, settled when they left Ireland's surface. Tír na nÓg was considered a place beyond the edges of the map, located far to the west. It could be reached by either an arduous voyage or an invitation from one of its fairy inhabitants. The isle is visited by various Irish heroes in the *echtrae* and *immram* tales popular during the Middle Ages. Tír na nÓg is a place where sickness and death do not exist. It is a place of eternal youth and beauty.

Avallach: Avallach (also Afallach and Avalloc) was the son of Nodens, God of Healing. He was one of the Celtic gods of the Underworld. He ruled Avalon where he lived with his daughter, Modron, and her sisters.

Modron: In Welsh mythology, Modron (divine mother) was a daughter of Avalloc, derived from the Gaulish goddess Matrona. She is regarded as the prototype of the Lady of the Lake, Morgan le Fay, from Arthurian legend. She was the mother of Mabon, who bears her name as "Mabon ap Modron" (Mabon, Son of Modron).

Mabon: In Welsh mythology, Mabon (divine son) was the son of Modron. He is synonymous with the ancient British god, Maponos, and probably equivalent to the Irish god, Aengus Mac Og. Mabon was stolen from his mother three days after his birth. He then lived in Annwn until he was rescued by Culhwch. Because of his time in Annwn, Mabon stayed a young adult forever.

The Horned One: The Horned One I based in part on *The Great Horned God*, a modern syncretic term used amongst Wiccan-influenced Neopagans, which unites numerous male nature gods out of such widely dispersed mythologies as the Celtic Cernunnos, Herne the Hunter (English legend), Pashupati in Hindu, and the Greek Pan. A number of figures from British folklore, though normally depicted without horns, are nonetheless considered related, namely Puck, Robin Goodfellow, and the Green Man. To the Christians the horned god is the devil.

Other Influences

The names *Tanngnost* (meaning "tooth-gnasher") and his brother *Tanngrisnir* (meaning "tooth-grinder") are the names of the two billy goats that pull Thor's chariot.

Ginny Greenteeth (or Jenny Greenteeth) from English folklore is a river hag, similar to a Peg Powler; she would pull children or the elderly into the water and drown them. She was often described as green-skinned, with long hair and sharp teeth.

Famous in northern England, a *Barghest* is a form of black ghost dog or goblin dog.

A *Hissi* is a mischievous spirit or god from Finnish folklore.

In Irish and Scottish folklore the *Sluagh* were the spirits of the restless dead. Some consider them to carry with them the souls of innocent people that they have captured.

I've taken many liberties with the locations in and around New York, but there really is an old church topped with a white cross set amongst the skyscrapers of lower Manhattan. It is located just across the street from Battery Park and the Staten Island Ferry Terminal. Standing within the arch of the steeple is an angelic statue of Saint Elizabeth Ann Seton, her arms open, welcoming home any wayward pilgrim.

Fairytales of old were cautionary tales full of ghastly endings, serving as hard lessons for young and old alike. I for one believe that all myths and legends are sparked by some real event, person, or . . . *other*. So, should you find yourself alone in a dark corner of Prospect Park—or any other wild and untamed place—and the fireflies suddenly seem emboldened, the air alive with a silvery mist, listen closely and you just might catch the distant echo of a boy's laughter. And whatever you should decide to do then, just remember, you've been warned.

Brom

February 20, 2009

Acknowledgments

This book has been a long time coming. I've had a lot of encouragement, input, and help along the way and owe a lot of people booze and chocolate.

Foremost, Diana Gill, an extraordinarily gifted editor. I am in awe of her insight and intuitiveness for story and character. Time and time again she steered this novel out of the muck and took it much further than I ever thought possible. Thanks, Diana, for your voodoo.

To my manager, Julie Kane-Ritsch, for her friendship, enthusiasm, and diligence. There is no better feeling than knowing you're in good hands. Thank you, Julie.

To Emily Krump, Katherine Nintzel, Michael Barrs, and Olga Gardner Galvin for their invaluable input.

And a special thanks to the poor souls who read through my early drafts—a selfless act worthy of sainthood. There is a little of each of you in this novel: Luke Peterschmidt, Robert, Ivy, Killian, Devin, and Laurie Brom. And to Ben Reh for posing as Peter.